Human Croquet

Also by Kate Atkinson

BEHIND THE SCENES AT THE MUSEUM

Human Croquet

Kate Atkinson

Picador USA
New York

Picador® is a U.S. registered trademark and is used by
St. Martin's Press under license from Pan Books Limited.

The extract and illustration on pp 347-9 are taken from *The Home
Entertainer* edited by Sid Hedges, (Odhams Press). The publishers and
author have made every effort to trace the copyright owner and
would be pleased to hear from the author and/or artist or their
respective estates.

Library of Congress Cataloging-in-Publication Data

Atkinson, Kate.
    Human croquet : a novel / Kate Atkinson.
        p.   cm.
    ISBN 0-312-15550-6
    I. Title.
PR6051.T56H86   1997
823'.914—dc21   97-802
                                                                  CIP

First published in Great Britain by Doubleday, a division of
Transworld Publishers Ltd.

First Picador USA Edition: May 1997

10   9   8   7   6   5   4   3   2   1

For my mother,
Myra Christiana Keech

This green and laughing world he sees
Waters and plains, and waving trees,
The skim of birds and the blue-doming skies

'*Ode for the Spring of 1814*', *Leigh Hunt*

BEGINNING

STREETS OF TREES

CALL ME ISOBEL. (IT'S MY NAME.) THIS IS MY HISTORY. WHERE SHALL I begin?

Before the beginning is the void and the void belongs in neither time nor space and is therefore beyond our imagination.

Nothing will come of nothing, unless it's the beginning of the world. This is how it begins, with the word and the word is life. The void is transformed by a gigantic firecracker allowing time to dawn and imagination to begin.

The first nuclei arrive – hydrogen and helium – followed, a few million years later, by their atoms and eventually, millions more years later, the molecules form. Aeons pass. The clouds of gas in space begin to condense into galaxies and stars, including our own Sun. In 1650, Archbishop James Ussher, in his *Annals of the World*, calculates that God made Heaven and Earth on the evening of Saturday, October 22, 4004 BC. Other people are less specific and date it to some four and a half billion years ago.

Then the trees come. Forests of giant ferns wave in the warm damp swamps of the Carboniferous Era. The first conifers appear and the great coal fields are laid down. Everywhere you look, flies are being trapped in drops of amber – which are the tears of poor Phaeton's sisters, who were turned by grief into black poplars (*populus nigra*). The flowering and the broad-leaved trees make their first appearance and eventually the trees crawl out of the swamps onto the dry land.

Here, where this story takes place (in the grim north), here was once forest, oceans of forest, the great Forest of Lythe. Ancient forest, an impenetrable thicket of Scots pine, birch and aspen, of English elm and wych elm, common hazel, oak and holly, the forest which once covered England and to which, if left alone, it might one day return. The forest has the world to itself for a long time.

Chop. The stone and flint tools signalled the end of the beginning, the beginning of the end. The alchemy of copper and tin made new bronze axes that shaved more trees from the earth. Then came iron (the great destroyer) and the iron axes cut the forest down faster than it could grow back and the iron ploughshares dug up the land that was once forest.

The woodcutters coppiced and pollarded and chopped away at the ash and the beech, the oak, the hornbeam and the tangled thorns. The miners dug and smelted while the charcoal-burners piled their stacks high. Soon you could hardly move in the forest for bodgers and cloggers, hoop-makers and wattle-hurdlers. Wild boars rooted and domestic pigs snuffled, geese clacked and wolves howled and deer were startled at every turning in the path. *Chop!* Trees were transformed into other things – into clogs and wine-presses, carts and tools, houses and furniture. The English forests sailed the oceans of the world and found new lands full of wilderness and more forests waiting to be cut down.

But there was a secret mystery at the heart of the heart of the forest. When the forest was cut down, where did the mystery go? Some say there were fairies in the forest – angry, bad-tempered creatures (the unwashed children of Eve), ill-met by moonlight, who loitered with intent on banks of wild thyme listening furiously to the encroaching axes. Where did they go when the forest no longer existed? And what about the wolves? What happened to them? (Just because you can't see something doesn't mean it isn't there.)

The small village of Lythe emerged from the shrinking forest, a straggle of cottages and a church with a square clocktower. Its inhabitants tramped back and forward with their eggs and capons and occasionally their virtue to Glebelands, the nearest town, only two miles away – a thriving market-place and a hot-bed of glovers and butchers, blacksmiths and vintners, rogues and recusants.

In 1580, or thereabouts, a stranger rode into Lythe, one Francis Fairfax, as dark and swarthy of countenance as a Moor. Francis Fairfax, lately ennobled by the Queen, was in receipt, from the Queen's own hand, of a great swathe of land north of the village, on the edge of what remained of the forest. Here he built himself Fairfax Manor, a modern house of brick and plaster and timbers from his newly owned forest oaks.

13

This Francis was a soldier and an adventurer. He had even made the great grey ocean crossing and seen the newfoundlands and virgin territories with their three-headed monsters and feathered savages. Some said he was the Queen's own spy, crossing the Channel on her secret business as frequently as others crossed Glebelands Green Moor.

Some also said that he had a beautiful child wife, herself already with child, locked away in the attics of Fairfax Manor. Others said the woman in the attics was not his child wife but his mad wife. There was even a rumour that his attics were full of dead wives, all of them hanging from butcher's hooks. There were even those who said (this even more unlikely) that he was the Queen's lover and that the great Gloriana had borne him a clandestine child which was being raised in Fairfax Manor. In the attics, naturally.

It is fact, not rumour, that the Queen stayed at Fairfax Manor in the course of escaping an outbreak of plague in London, sometime in the summer of 1582, and was observed admiring the butter-yellow quince and flourishing medlar trees and dining on the results of a splendid early morning deer hunt.

Fairfax Manor was famous for the thrill of its deer chases, the softness of its goose-feather mattresses, the excellence of its kitchens, the ingenuity of its entertainments. Sir Francis became a famous patron of poets and aspiring playwrights. Some say that Shakespeare himself spent time at Fairfax Manor. Keen supporters of this explanation of Shakespeare's famous lost years − of which there are several, mostly mad − point to the evidence of the initials "WS" carved into the bark of the great Lady Oak and still visible to the keen eye to this day. Detractors of this theory point out that another member of the Fairfax household, his son's tutor, a Walter Stukesly, can claim the same initials.

Perhaps Master Stukesly was the author of the magnificent masque (*The Masque of Adonis*) which Sir Francis ordered up for the Queen's entertainment during her midsummer visit to Lythe. We can imagine the theatricals being performed, using the great forest as a backdrop, the lamps glimmering in the trees, the many mechanical devices used in the telling of the tragic tale, the youthful Adonis dying in the arms of a young boy Venus under the Lady Oak – a young, handsome oak much of an age with Francis Fairfax that once stood at the heart of the heart of the forest and now guarded its entrance.

It was not long after the Queen's departure from Lythe that Francis's wife first appeared, a real one made of flesh and blood and not kept in the attics, but none the less an enigmatic creature whose beginning and end were veiled in mystery. She arrived, they said, at the door of Fairfax Manor one wild, storm-driven night, dressed in neither shoes nor hose nor petticoat, dressed in nothing in fact but her silk-soft skin – yet with not a drop of rain on her, nor one red hair on her head blown out of its place.

She came, she said, from an even grimmer north and her name was Mary (like the dreaded Caledonian queen herself). She did not persist in her nakedness and allowed herself to be clothed in silks and furs and velvets and clasped in jewels by an eager Sir Francis. On her wedding-morning Sir Francis presented her with the famous Fairfax jewel – much sought after by metal-detectors and historians – well documented in Sir Thomas A'hearne's famous *Travels around England* but not seen for nearly four hundred years. (For the record, a gold lozenge locket, studded with emeralds and pearls and opening to reveal a miniature Dance of Death believed by some to have been painted by Nicholas Hilliard, in homage to his mentor, Holbein.)

The new Lady Fairfax favoured green – kirtle and petticoats and stomacher, as green as the vert that hides the deer from the hunter. Only her cambric shift was white – this piece of information being offered by the midwife brought in from Glebelands for the arrival of the Fairfax firstborn. Onlyborn. It was, she reported when she had been returned to town, a perfectly normal baby (a boy) but Sir Francis was a madman who insisted that the poor midwife had her eyes bound in every room but the birth-chamber and who swore her to secrecy about what she saw that night. Whatever it was that the poor woman did see was never broadcast for she was conveniently struck by lightning as she raised a tankard of ale to wet the baby's head.

Lady Fairfax, it was reported, was strangely fond of wandering into the forest dressed in her green damasks and silks, her hound Finn her only companion. Sometimes she could be found sitting under the green guardianship of the Lady Oak, singing an unbearably sweet song about her home, like a Ruth amid alien green. More than once, Sir Francis's game steward had frightened himself half to death by mistaking her for a timid hart, bolting away from him in a flash of green. What if one day he were to shoot off an arrow into her fair green breast?

Then she vanished – as instantly and mysteriously as she had once arrived. Sir Francis returned home from a day's hunting with a fine plump doe shot through the heart and found her gone. A kitchen maid, an ignorant girl, claimed she saw Lady Fairfax disappearing from underneath the Lady Oak, fading away until her green brocade dress was indistinguishable from the surrounding trees. As Lady Fairfax had grown dimmer, the girl reported, she had placed a dreadful curse on the Fairfaxes, past and future, and her monstrous shrieks had echoed in the air long after she herself was invisible. The cook clattered the girl about her head with a porringer for her fanciful notions.

Francis Fairfax fulfilled the requirements of a cursed man – burning to death in his own bed in 1605 along with most of his household. William, his son, was rescued by servants and grew up to be a sickly kind of boy, hanging onto life just long enough to father his likeness.

The Fairfaxes abandoned the charred remains of Fairfax Manor and moved to Glebelands where their fortunes declined. Fairfax Manor crumbled to dust in the air, the fine parkland reverted to nature and within a handful of years you would never have known it had ever been there.

Over the next hundred years the land was parcelled up and sold at auction. An eighteenth-century Fairfax, Thomas, lost the last of the land in the South Sea Bubble and the Fairfaxes were all but forgotten − except for Lady Mary who was occasionally sighted, dressed all in green, disconsolate and gloomy, and occasionally with her head under her arm for good effect.

The forest itself was gradually removed, the last of it taken during the Napoleonic War for fighting ships. By the time the nineteenth century really got going, all that remained of the once great Forest of Lythe was a large wood known as Boscrambe Woods, thirty miles to the north of Glebelands and − just beyond the boundaries of Lythe − the Lady Oak itself.

By 1840 Glebelands was a great manufacturing town whose engines thrummed and throbbed and whose chimneys smoked dark clouds of uncertain chemicals into the sky over its crowded slum streets. The owner of one of these factories, Samuel Fairfax, philanthropist and manufacturer of Argand gas burners, briefly revived the family fortunes with his mission to illuminate the entire town with gas lamps.

The Fairfaxes were able to buy a large town house with all the trimmings − servants and a coach and accounts in every shop. The Fairfax women wore dresses of French velvet and Nottingham lace and talked nonsense all day long while Samuel Fairfax dreamed of buying back the tract of land where Fairfax Manor once stood and making a country park where the people of Glebelands could clean their sooty lungs and exercise their rickety limbs. He was hoping that this would be his living memorial − *Fairfax Park*, he murmured happily as he looked over possible designs for the massive wrought-iron entrance gates and just as he pointed to a particularly rococo pattern ('Restoration') his heart stopped beating and he fell face first onto the pattern book. The park was never built.

Gas lamps were overtaken by electric ones, the Fairfaxes failed to see the new technology coming and grew slowly poorer until, in 1880, one Joseph Fairfax, grandson to Samuel, realized where the future lay and put the remaining family money into retail − a small grocery shop in a side street. The business gradually prospered, and ten years later 'Fairfax and Son – Licensed Grocers' moved into the High Street.

Joseph Fairfax had one son and no daughters. The son, Leonard, wooed and won a girl called Charlotte Tait, the daughter of the owner of a small enamelware factory. The Taits were of stern Nonconformist stock and Charlotte was not above lending a hand in the shop when required, although she soon fell pregnant with her eldest child, an ugly girl named Madge.

The villagers of Lythe meanwhile waited for Glebelands to crawl across the remaining few fields towards them and swallow them up. While they were waiting a war happened and took three-quarters of the young men of Lythe (three to be precise) and as the war drew to a close no-one cared very much when most of the village, along with the land where Fairfax Manor had stood, was sold to a local builder.

The builder, a man called Maurice Smith, had a vision, the dream of a master-builder – a garden suburb, an estate of modern, comfortable housing for the post-war, post-servant world of small families. Streets of detached and semi-detached houses with neat front gardens and large back gardens where children could play, Father could grow vegetables and roses and Mother could park Baby in his pram and take afternoon tea on the lawn with her genteel friends. On the land that once housed Sir Francis and his household, Maurice Smith built his streets of houses. Houses in mock-Tudor and pebble-dash stucco, houses with casement windows and porches and tiled vestibules. Houses with three and four bedrooms and the most up-to-date plumbing, porcelain sinks and efficient back boilers; cool, airy larders, and enamelled gas cookers.

Streets with broad pavements and trees, lots of trees – a canopy of trees over the tarmac, a mantle of green around the houses and their happy occupants. Trees that would give pleasure, that could be observed in bud and new leaf, unfurling their green fingers on the streets of houses, raising their sheltering leafy arms over the dwellers within. Different trees for every street – Ash Street, Chestnut Avenue, Holly Tree Lane, Hawthorn Close, Oak Road, Laurel Bank, Rowan Street, Sycamore Street, Willow Road. The forest of trees had become a wilderness of streets.

But at night, in the quiet of the dead time, if you listened carefully, you could imagine the wolves howling.

The Lady Oak grew on, solitary and ancient, in the field behind the dog-leg of Hawthorn Close and Chestnut Avenue. Points of weakness in the tree had been plugged with cement and old iron crutches propped up its weary limbs but in summer its leafy crown was still green and thick enough for a rookery and at dusk the birds flew *caw cawing* into its welcoming branches.

At the end of Hawthorn Close was the master-builder's first house – Arden – the one he built as his showpiece, on the long-lost foundations of Fairfax Manor. Arden had fine parquet floors and light-oak panelling. It had a craftsman-built oak staircase with acorn finials and its turret follies were capped with round blue Welsh slates, overlapping like a dragon's scales.

The master-builder had intended the house for himself but Leonard Fairfax offered him such a good price that he couldn't bring himself to refuse. And so the Fairfax family returned, unwittingly, to its ancestral abode.

Charlotte Fairfax had given birth (difficult though it was to imagine this) to two more children after Madge, in order – Vinny (Lavinia) and Gordon ('my baby!'). Gordon was much younger, an afterthought ('my surprise!'). When they moved into Arden, Madge had already left to marry an adulterous bank clerk and move to Mirfield and Vinny was a grown woman of twenty, but Gordon was still a little boy. Gordon had introduced Charlotte to a new emotion. At night she would creep into his new little room under the eaves and gaze at his sleeping face in the soft halo of the nightlight and surprise herself with the overwhelming love she felt for him.

But time has already begun to fly, soon Eliza will come and ruin everything. Eliza will be my mother. I am Isobel Fairfax, I am the alpha and omega of narrators (I am omniscient) and I know the beginning and the end. The beginning is the word and the end is silence. And in between are all the stories. This is one of mine.

PRESENT

SOMETHING WEIRD

IS-O-BEL. A PEAL OF BELLS. ISABELLA TARANTELLA — A MAD DANCE. I am mad, therefore I am. Mad. Am I? Belle, Bella, Best, never let it rest. Bella Belle, doubly foreign for beautiful, but I'm not foreign. Am I beautiful? No, apparently not.

My human geography is extraordinary. I'm as large as England. My hands are as big as the Lakes, my belly the size of Dartmoor and my breasts rise up like the Peaks. My spine is the Pennines, my mouth the Mallyan Spout. My hair flows into the Humber estuary and causes it to flood and my nose is a white cliff at Dover. I'm a big girl, in other words.

There's a strange feeling on the streets of trees, although what it is exactly I wouldn't like to say. I'm lying in my bed staring up at my attic window which is full of nothing but early morning sky, a blank blue page, an uncharted day waiting to be filled. It's the first day of April and it's my birthday, my sixteenth — the mythic one, the

23

legendary one. The traditional age for spindles to start pricking and suitors to come calling and a host of other symbolic sexual imagery to suddenly manifest itself, but I haven't even been kissed by a man yet, not unless you count my father, Gordon, who leaves his sad, paternal kisses on my cheek like unsettling little insects.

My birthday has been heralded by something weird – a kind of odoriferous spirit (dumb and invisible) that's attached itself to me like an aromatic shadow. At first I mistook it for nothing more than the scent of wet hawthorn. On its own this is a sad enough perfume, but the hawthorn has brought with it a strange musty smell that isn't confined to Hawthorn Close but follows me everywhere I go. It walks down the street with me and accompanies me into other people's houses (and then leaves again with me, there's no shaking it off). It floats along the school corridors with me and sits next to me on buses – and the seat remains empty no matter how crowded the bus gets.

It's the fragrance of last year's apples and the smell of the insides of very old books with a base note of dead, wet rose-petals. It's the distillation of loneliness, an incredibly sad smell, the essence of sorrowfulness and stoppered-up sighs. If it were a commercial perfume it would never sell. Imagine people being offered testers at brightly lit perfume counters, 'Have you tried Melancholy, madam?' and then spending the rest of the day with the uncomfortable feeling that someone has placed a cold pebble of misery in their stomachs.

'There, next to my left shoulder,' I tell Audrey (my friend), and Audrey breathes deeply, and says, 'No.'

'Nothing?'

'Nothing,' Audrey (also my next-door neighbour) shakes her head. Charles (my brother) makes a ridiculous snout and snuffs like a truffling pig. 'No, you're imagining it,' he says and turns away quickly to hide his suddenly sad-dog face.

Poor Charles, he is two years older than me but I'm already six inches taller than him. I am nearly two yards high in my bare feet.

A gigantic English oak (*quercus robustus*). My body a trunk, my feet taproots, my toes probing like pale little moles through the dark soil. My head a crown of leaves growing towards the light. What if this keeps up? I'll shoot up through the troposphere, the stratosphere and up into the vastness of space where I'll be able to wear a coronet made from the Pleiades, a shawl spun out of the Milky Way. Dearie, dearie me, as Mrs Baxter (Audrey's mother) would say.

I'm already five foot ten, growing at more than an inch a year – if this *does* keep up then by the time I'm twenty I'll be over six foot. 'By the time I'm forty,' I count on my fingers, 'I'll be nearly eight feet tall.'

'Dearie me,' Mrs Baxter says, frowning as she tries to imagine this.

'By the time I'm seventy,' I calculate darkly, 'I'll be over eleven feet high. I'll be a fairground attraction.' The Giant Girl of Glebelands. 'You're a real woman now,' Mrs Baxter says, surveying my skyscraper statistics. But as opposed to what? An unreal woman? My mother (Eliza) is an unreal woman, gone and almost forgotten, slipping the bonds of reality the day she walked off into a wood and never came back.

'You're a big girl,' Mr Rice (the lodger) ogles me nastily as we squeeze past each other in the dining-room door. Mr Rice is a travelling salesman and we must hope that some day soon he will wake up and find that he's been transformed into a giant insect.

It's a shame that Charles has stuck at such an unheroic height. He claims that he used to be five foot five but that the last time he measured himself, which he does frequently, he was only five foot four. 'I'm shrinking,' he reports miserably. Perhaps he *is* shrinking, while I keep on growing (there's no stopping me). Perhaps we're bound together by some weird law of sibling physics, the two ends of a linear elastic universe where one must shrink as the other expands. 'He's a real short arse,' Vinny (our aunt) says, more succinctly.

Charles is as ugly as a story-book dwarf. His arms are too long for his barrel-shaped body, his neck too short for his big head, an overgrown homunculus. Sadly, his (once lovely) copper curls have turned red and wiry and his freckled face is now as pocked and cratered as a lifeless planet, while his big Adam's apple bobs up and down like a Cox's Orange Pippin at Hallowe'en. It's a shame I can't transplant some of my inches, I have far more than I need, after all.

Girls are not attracted to Charles and so far he hasn't managed to persuade a single one to go out with him. 'I'll probably die a virgin,' he says mournfully. Poor Charles, he too has never been kissed. One solution, I suppose, would be for us to kiss each other, but the idea of incest – though quite attractive in Jacobean tragedy – is less so on the home front. 'I mean, incest,' I say to Audrey, 'it's hard to imagine, isn't it?'

'Is it?' she says, her sad doves' eyes staring at some point in space so that she looks like a saint about to be martyred. She is also one of the unkissed – her father, Mr Baxter (the local primary school headmaster), won't let a boy anywhere near Audrey. Mr Baxter, despite Mrs Baxter's protestations, has decided that Audrey isn't ever going to grow up. If Audrey does develop womanly curves and wiles then Mr Baxter will probably lock her at the top of a very high tower. And if boys ever start noticing those womanly curves and wiles then it's a fair bet that Mr Baxter will kill them, picking them off one by one as they attempt to scale the heights of Sithean's privet and shin up the long golden-red rope of Audrey's beautiful hair.

'Sithean' is the name of the Baxters' house. 'She-ann', Mrs Baxter explains in her lovely douce accent, is a Scottish word. Mrs Baxter was once the daughter of a Church of Scotland minister and was brought up in Perthshire ('Pairrrthshiyer') which accounts no doubt for her accent. Mrs Baxter is as nice as her accent and Mr Baxter is as nasty as the thin dark moustache which outlines his upper lip and as bad-tempered as the foul pipe he smokes, or 'a reeking lum' in Mrs Baxter's parlance.

Tall and gaunt, Mr Baxter is the son of a coal miner and still carries a seam of coal in his voice, despite his tortoiseshell glasses and his tweed jackets with leather-patched elbows. It's very difficult to say how old he is without knowing. Mrs Baxter knows how old he is though, she'd be hard put to forget as Mr Baxter makes a point of reminding her often ('Remember, Moira – *I am older than you* and I do know more'). Both Audrey and Mrs Baxter call Mr Baxter 'Daddy'. When she was a pupil in his class, Audrey had to call him 'Mr Baxter' and if she ever forgot and called him 'Daddy', he would make her stand at the front of the class for the rest of the lesson. Neither of them calls him 'Peter' which is his name.

Poor Charles. I'm convinced things would be better for him if he could be taller. 'Why – it isn't for you, is it?' he replies testily. Sometimes I catch myself thinking impossible things – like, if we still had our mother then Charles would be taller.

'Was our mother tall?' Charles asks Vinny. Vinny – as old as the century (sixty) but not as optimistic. Our Aunt Vinny is our father's sister, not our mother's. Our mother had no relatives apparently – although she must have had them once, unless she hatched from an egg like Helen of Troy, and even then, Leda must have sat on the nest, surely? Our father, Gordon, is tall, 'but Eliza?' Vinny screws up her face in a theatrical attempt to remember, but sees only a blur. The different features can be dredged up – the black hair, the tilted nose, the thin ankles – but the composite Eliza lacks all substance. 'Can't remember,' she says dismissively, as usual.

'I think she was very tall,' Charles says, forgetting perhaps how very small he was last time we saw her. 'Are you sure she wasn't red-headed?' he adds hopefully.

'Nobody was red-headed,' Vinny says decisively.

'Somebody must have been.'

Absence of Eliza has shaped our lives. She walked away, 'up sticks and left with her fancy man' as Vinny puts it, and for some reason forgot to take us with her. Perhaps it was a fit of absent-mindedness, perhaps she meant to come back but couldn't find the way. Stranger things have happened; our own father for example, himself went missing after our mother disappeared and when he came back seven years later claimed amnesia as his excuse. 'Time off for bad behaviour,' vinegary Vinny explains cryptically.

We have waited nearly all our lives for the sound of her foot on the path, her key in the door, waited for her walking back into our lives (*I'm home, darling!*) as if nothing has happened. It wouldn't be the first time. 'Anna Fellows from Cambridge, Massachusetts,' Charles reports (he is an expert on such things), 'left her house in 1879 and walked back in again twenty years later as if nothing had happened.'

If my mother was going to come back wouldn't she come back in time (as it were) for my sixteenth birthday?

It's as if Eliza never lived, there are no remnants of her life – no photographs, no letters, no keepsakes – the things that anchor people in reality are all missing. Memories of her are like the shadows of a dream, tantalizing and out of reach. With Gordon, 'our dad', the one person whom you might expect to remember Eliza best, there's no conversation to be had at all, the subject makes him mute.

'She must have been off her head (or 'aff her heid') to leave two such bonny children,' Mrs Baxter opines gently. (All children are bonny to Mrs Baxter.) Vinny verifies, frequently, that our mother was indeed 'off her head'. As opposed to 'on her head'? But then if she was on her head she would be upside down – and therefore also mad, surely? Perhaps 'off her head' as in no longer being attached to her head? Perhaps she is dead and wandering around on the astral plane with her head tucked underneath her arm like a music-hall ghost, exchanging pleasantries with the Green Lady.

If only we had some maternal souvenirs, some evidence to prove she once existed – a scrap of her handwriting, say. How we would pore over the dullest, most prosaic of messages – *See you at lunchtime!* or *Don't forget to buy bread* – trying to decipher her personality, her overwhelming love for her children, searching for the cryptically encoded message that would explain why she had to leave. But she's left behind not a single letter of the alphabet for us from which we can reconstruct her and we have to make her up from emptiness and airy spaces and wind on water.

'She wasn't a saint, your mum, you know,' Debbie says, reducing Eliza to her own pedestrian vocabulary. Eliza (or, at any rate, the *idea* of Eliza), isn't a cosy person, 'our mum'. Invisible, she has grown sublime – the Virgin Mary and the Queen of Sheba, the queen of heaven and the queen of night in one person, the sovereign of our unseen, imaginary universe (home). 'Well not from what your dad says,' Debbie says smugly. But what does 'our dad' say? Nothing to us, that's for sure.

Who is Debbie? She is the fat, wan substitute that four years ago 'our dad' chose to replace 'our mum' with. In his seven-year voyage on the waters of Lethe (the north island of New Zealand actually), Gordon forgot all about Eliza (not to mention us) and came back with a different wife altogether. The Debbie-wife with brown permed curls, little piggy eyelashes and stubby fingers that end in bitten-off nails. The doll wife, with her round face and eyes the colour of dirty dishwater and a voice that contains flat Essex marshes washed with a slight antipodean whine. The child wife, only a handful of years older than us. Snatched from her cradle by Gordon, according to Vinny, Vinny who is the Debbie-wife's arch-enemy. 'Think of me as your big sister,' Debbie said when she first arrived. She's changed her tune now, I think she would rather not be related to us at all.

How could Gordon have forgotten his own children? His own wife? In his lost years at the bottom of the world did he hear Abenazaar's wicked invitation ('New wives for old!') and trade in our mother for the Debbie-wife? Perhaps even now the treasure that was Eliza (greater than a king's ransom) is trapped in some dismal cave somewhere waiting for us to find her and release her.

It is hard to know what tales Gordon might have spun Debbie in the downunderworld but he didn't seem to have prepared her very well for the reality of his life back home. 'So these are your kiddies, Gordon?' she said with an air of incredulity when Gordon introduced her to us. She was probably expecting two charming

29

little moppets, delighted to be relieved of their motherless state. Gordon didn't seem to realize that in the seven intervening years we'd become underground children, living in a dark place where the sun never shone.

Heaven only knows what she was expecting of Arden – Mandelay, a nice suburban semi perhaps, maybe even a small castle where the air was sweet – but surely not this desolate mock-Tudor museum. And as for Vinny – 'Hello, Auntie V,' Debbie said, sticking out her hand and grabbing Vinny's claw, 'it's so lovely to meet you at last,' so that 'Auntie V's' face nearly cracked. 'Auntie V? Auntie V?' we heard her muttering later, 'I'm nobody's bloody auntie,' obviously forgetting that actually she was *our* bloody auntie.

My brother Charles left school with no talents discernible to his teachers. He works now in the electrical goods department of Temple's, Glebelands magnificent department store built to outdo the great London stores and once boasting a small Arcadian bower on its roof, complete with green sward, rippling brooks and a herd of grazing cattle. That was a long time ago, of course, almost in the time of myth (1902) and Charles must content himself with a more mundane environment amongst an assorted miscellanea of vacuum cleaners, hand whisks and radiograms. Charles seems neither particularly happy nor particularly unhappy with this life. I think that most of his time is taken up with daydreaming. He's the kind of boy – I can't imagine ever thinking of Charles as a man – who believes that *at any moment* something incredibly exciting might unexpectedly happen and change his life for ever. Much like everyone else in fact. 'Don't you think that something –' his eyes nearly pop out of his head as he searches for the words to articulate the feeling, 'that something's about to *happen*?'

'No,' I lie, for there's no point in encouraging him.

'I'm just marking time at Temple's,' Charles says, in explanation of his remarkably dull outer life. (Ah, but what does he give it? B–? C+? He should be careful, one day time might mark him. 'Och, without doubt,' Mrs Baxter says, 'that's the final reckoning.')

Charles also has his hobbies to occupy him – nothing so normal as stamp-collecting or bird-watching, the kind of pursuits that fulfil other suburban youth – but an obsession with the mysteries of the unexplained world – with aliens and flying saucers, with vanished civilizations and parallel worlds and time travel. He's preoccupied with life in other dimensions, yearning for the existence of a world other than this one. Perhaps because his life in this one is so unsatisfactory. 'They're out there somewhere,' he says, gazing longingly at the night sky. ('If they've got any sense they'll stay there,' snorts Vinny.)

Mysterious disappearances are his speciality – he documents them obsessively in lined notebooks, page after page, in his babyish round hand, cataloguing the vanished – from ships and lighthouse keepers, to whole colonies of New World Puritans. 'Roanoke,' he says, his eyes lighting up with excitement, 'a whole colony of Puritans in America disappeared in 1587, including the first white child ever born in America.'

'Yeah, well that would be because the Red Indians killed them all, wouldn't it?' Carmen (McDade, my friend) says, leafing through one of his notebooks – Carmen has no notion that private and property can co-exist in the same sentence.

Charles is looking for a pattern. The vast numbers of ships – the boats found crewless on the high seas and the Mississippi riverboats that have sailed off into nothingness – are not accountable to the perils of the sea but to alien kidnappings. The tendency ('Well, two anyway,' he admits reluctantly) of boys called Oliver to vanish on their way to the well for water, the number of farmers in the southern states of America observed disappearing in the act of crossing a field – the writer Ambrose Bierce who wrote an essay on one such disappearance entitled, 'The Difficulty of Crossing a Field' ('and then *disappeared himself*, Izzie!') are all part of some vast otherworld conspiracy.

The category that excites him most, unsurprisingly given our own parents' tendency to disappear, are the individuals – the society girl out for a downtown stroll, the man on the road from Leamington

Spa to Coventry – people who were going about their ordinary lives when they vanished into thin air.

'Benjamin Bathurst, Orion Williamson, Dorothy Arnold, James Worson' – a curious litany of human erasures – 'just like that!' Charles says, snapping his fingers like a bad conjuror, one red, red eyebrow cocked in the cartoon position of surprise (whether relevant or not) that he favours for most conversations. People plucked from their lives as if by an invisible hand, 'Dematerialization, Izzie – it could happen to anyone,' he says eagerly, 'at any moment.' Hardly a comforting thought. 'Your brother's a nutcake,' Carmen says, sucking a mis-shapen mint so hard that it looks as if her cheeks have just imploded, 'he should see a trick-cyclist.'

But the real question, surely, is – where do the people who vanish into thin air *go*? Do they all go to the same place? 'Thin air' must surely be a misnomer, for the air must be fairly choked with animals, children, people, ships, aeroplanes, Amys and Amelias.

'What if our mother didn't run off,' Charles muses, sitting on the end of my bed now and staring out at the blue square of window-sky. 'What if she had simply dematerialized?' I point out to him that 'simply' might be the wrong word here, but I know what he means – then she wouldn't have voluntarily abandoned her own children (us), leaving them to fend for themselves in a cold, cruel world. And so on.

'Shut up, Charles.' I put my head under the pillow. But I can still hear him.

'Aliens,' he says decisively, 'these people were all kidnapped by aliens. And our mother too,' he adds wistfully, 'that's what happened to her.'

'Kidnapped by aliens?'

'Well why not?' Charles says stoutly. 'Anything's possible.' But which is the most likely really – a mother kidnapped by aliens or a mother who ran off with a fancy man?

'Aliens, definitely,' Charles says.

I sit up and give him a good hard punch in the ribs to shut him up. It's such a long time ago now (eleven years) but Charles can't let Eliza go. 'Go away, Charles.'

'No, no, no,' he says, his eyes alight with a kind of madness. 'I've found something.'

'Found what?' It's still only eight o'clock in the morning and Charles is in his pyjamas – maroon-and-white striped flannel that say 'Age 12' on the label on the collar, but which he has never outgrown. If the aliens kidnap him will they believe what he tells them or what his label says? He seems to have forgotten that it's my birthday. 'It's my birthday, Charles.'

'Yeah, yeah, look—' From his striped breast-pocket he takes something wrapped in a large handkerchief. 'I found this,' he says in a church-whisper, 'at the back of a drawer.'

'The back of a drawer?' (Not my birthday present then.)

'In the sideboard, I was looking for Sellotape.' (For my present, I hope.) 'Look!' he urges excitedly.

'An old powder-compact?' I ask dubiously.

'*Hers!*' Charles says triumphantly. I don't need to ask the identity of 'Her' – Charles has a particular tone of voice, reverential and mystical, that he uses when speaking about Eliza.

'You don't know that.'

'It says so,' he says, thrusting it in front of my face. It's an expensive-looking compact, but old fashioned – thin and flat, like a heavy gold disc. The lid is a bright blue enamel, inlaid with mother-of-pearl palm trees. The clasp is still springy and snaps open. There's no powder-puff and the mirror is covered in a thin film of powder and the powder itself – a compacted pale pink – has been worn down in the middle to reveal a circle of silver metal.

'There's nothing at all to prove it's hers,' I tell him crossly and he snatches it back and turns it over so that an almost invisible shower of powder falls out onto my eiderdown. '*Look.*'

On its golden underside, striated in fine circles, there is an engraving. I hold it up to the square of blue and make out the stilted message:

33

To my darling wife, Eliza, on the occasion of your twenty-third birthday.
From your loving husband, Gordon. 15th March 1943.

I feel quite faint for a moment, even though I'm sitting up in my
bed. It's not so much the compact, nor even the words, it's the
pink face-powder – it smells sweet and old, it smells of grown-up
women and it is – without a shadow of a doubt – the evocative
topnote in the scent of sadness, *L'Eau de Melancholie*, that trails so
disconsolately at my heels.

'Well anyway,' Charles says, '*I* think it's hers,' and he pockets
it moodily and leaves without wishing me happy birthday.

A little later, Gordon pops his head round my bedroom door and
attempts a smile (even then my father manages to look sad), and
says, 'Good morning, birthday girl.' I don't say anything to him
about the powder-compact, it would only plunge him into greater
gloom and is unlikely to jog his memory about his first wife, for
nothing else seems to do. Perhaps in his seven absent years in
the downunderworld, Eliza was erased from his memory cells by
aliens? (This is Charles' theory, needless to say.) But then this is a
man who even forgot who he was himself, let alone his immediate
family. ('But isn't it wonderful that your daddy's alive and well?'
Mrs Baxter said. 'Why it's like – ' Mrs Baxter searched for the right
word, 'it's like a miracle!') Yet when he came back – walking in
the door as casually as Anna Fellows did in 1899, he remembered
who we all were perfectly. ('Isn't that a miracle,' Mrs Baxter said,
'suddenly remembering who he was after all that time?')

He hands me a cup of tea and says, 'I'll give you your present later,'
the words more cheerful than the tone in which he says them (it was
ever thus with my father). 'Have you seen Charles anywhere?' This
is another peculiar trait of my father's – he is constantly questioning
people about the whereabouts of other people – 'Have you seen
x?'; 'Do you know where y is?' – even though the person he is
looking for can easily be found in their usual habitat: Vinny in her
winged armchair, Debbie in the kitchen, Charles lost in a Bradbury

or a Philip K. Dick, Mr Rice doing heaven knows what in his room. Once, in her early days with us, Debbie knocked peremptorily on Mr Rice's door, duster and polish at the ready, and turned on her heel and came straight out again when she saw what he was doing. 'What?' Charles asked eagerly but Debbie refused to say. 'My lips are sealed.' If only her nose could be stopped up too.

I myself am usually to be found lying on my bed imitating the dead Chatterton, killing time by reading book after book (the only reliable otherworlds I've discovered so far).

'I expect Charles is in his room,' I tell Gordon and he makes a surprised face as if this is the last place he expected him to be.

Gordon would perhaps like Charles to make more of himself, but says nothing. After all, Gordon is a man who has succeeded in making less of himself. He was once a quite different person, heir to our own personal retailing fortune, the licensed grocery business of Fairfax and Son – an inheritance scuppered a long time ago by carelessness. Fairfax and Son, now called 'Maybury's', is at this very moment being converted into Glebelands' first supermarket and about to rake in profits for someone else, not us. And before that, before he was a grocer, Gordon was someone else again (also in the time of myth – 1941), a hero – a fighter pilot with medals and photographs to prove it. Once a bright, shining person, he came back from his seven-year sojourn a faded man, not really 'our dad' at all.

'Perhaps it's not really Daddy at all?' Charles conjectured quietly at the time. (For it's true neither the exterior nor the inward man resembled that it was.) But if it wasn't him then who was it? 'Somebody *pretending* to be Daddy – an impostor.' Charles explained, 'Or like in *Invaders from Mars* where the parents' bodies get taken over by aliens.' Or perhaps he was from the parallel world. A looking-glass kind of father.

Of course, he could just have been Gordon come home after seven years' absence with a new young wife and Eliza might never be coming back. But this version of reality was not to our taste.

'He's sad, your dad, isn't he?' Carmen says, unnaturally poetic. At least he's not mad or bad. But we'd prefer it if he was glad. 'Bit of a lad?' Carmen offers. But no, not really.

Malcolm Lovat. If I am to have a birthday wish it must be him. He is what I want for birthday and Christmas and best, what I want more than anything in the dark world and wide.

Even his name hints at romance and kindness (Lovat, not Malcolm). I have known him all my life, the Lovats live on Chestnut Avenue, and he has grown up handsome, tall and fit and with all his limbs in proportion – not as common as you might think amongst the boys of Glebelands Grammar.

Girls idolize him. He's the kind of boy you could take home to your mother (if you had one), the kind of boy you could take up to Lover's Leap and steam up the car – a boy for all seasons in fact. No-one ever mentions Malcolm Lovat without saying what a great future he's going to have, he's reading medicine at Guy's and is home for the Easter holidays at the moment. 'Following in my father's footsteps,' he says with a wry little smile. His father's a gynaecologist. 'Perverted' is Vinny's verdict on this particular speciality – she has had 'women's trouble' treated by Mr Lovat – 'what man wants to specialize in sticking his hands inside women? Perverts, that's what kind.' I wonder where Charles and I would get if we followed in our father's footsteps? Lost, presumably.

Malcolm wants to be a brain surgeon, which seems just as perverted to me; what person in their right minds would want to stick their hands inside other people's *heads*?

Poor Malcolm, his mother is an ogress. Both his parents are so intolerant and snobbish that it seems a wonder they have a son like Malcolm. Perhaps not such a wonder, for Malcolm is adopted. The Lovats were quite old when they adopted him, 'I don't think they knew what to do with me when they got me,' Malcolm says, 'I didn't drink gin and I didn't play bridge.' He has learnt to do both.

Unfortunately, he is a prince out of my star. 'I don't know

though, Iz,' he says, rather glumly, to me over a shared packet of crisps, 'Do I really want to be a doctor at all?' The dreadful thing is, he thinks of me as a *friend*. He runs a hand through his dark curls and brushes them away from his handsome forehead, 'You're a good pal, Iz,' he sighs. I am his friend, his 'pal', his 'chum' – more like a tin of dog food than a member of the female sex, certainly not the object of his desire. Too many years of wandering around the streets of trees after him like a large faithful pet have robbed me of female qualities in his eyes.

I fall back into a fitful morning doze, it's the weekend and even a birthday isn't enough to get me out of bed. The possibility of sleep is too precious. We are unquiet sleepers in Arden, we all of us hear the watches of the night being called by screeching owls and howling dogs. 'Not asleep yet?' a tousled Gordon enquires with a rueful smile as we encounter each other on the staircase in the middle of the night. 'Still up?' Vinny (irritable in hair-net and bed-jacket) asks.

When I wake up, the sky is no longer still, thin white clouds are racing each other across the window and the wind rattles the glass. Will anything happen to me on my birthday? (Apart from the pricking of the spindle.) I drag myself reluctantly out of bed.

Of course, I could have spent the weekend with Eunice. 'How would you like', she asked enthusiastically, 'to come caravanning with us in Cleethorpes? That would be a nice way to spend your birthday.'

Enthusiastic Eunice is the last person I would have ever *chosen* as a friend, but of course you don't chose your friends, they choose you. Eunice arrived in secondary school on the first day and attached herself to me like a mollusc and has stuck firmly on ever since, regardless of the fact that I've nothing in common with her and spend a considerable amount of time trying to prise her off. I think I was just the first person she happened to see when she walked through the school gates. ('Like she was under a spell or something?' Audrey muses.) But Eunice isn't

the kind of girl to fall under enchantments, she's far too sensible
for that.

She's very plain – white ankle socks, hair parted to one side and
fastened in a hair-slide, heavy black-rimmed glasses. She's looked
exactly the same for the last five years except that she's no longer
flat-chested and has black hairs on her calves as if someone's pulled
the legs off a web of spiders and stuck them on Eunice's legs. She's
a humourless girl who leads a very organized life – the sort who
lays out all her clothes for the next day before she goes to bed and
does her homework as soon as she gets in from school. My way
of being organized, on the other hand, is to go to bed *wearing* my
school uniform.

Eunice knows about *everything* and never lets you forget it, so
that you can't pass a post-box or a cat on the street without
Eunice expounding on the invention of the postage stamp or
the evolution of the sabre-toothed tiger into the cat. *Click, click,
click*, goes Eunice's brain. It's formed differently – where my brain,
for example, is a gallimaufry of art and poetry and overwhelming
emotions and you could dip into my mental hodgepodge and
come up randomly with *Idylls of the King*, the sinking of the
Titanic or the death of Old Yeller – Eunice's brain is modelled
on a reference library – holding an unnecessary amount of facts,
a clinical retrieval system and an advice desk that won't shut up.
Click, click, click.

She's a Guide leader, you can't see her uniform for badges,
teaches at Sunday School, sings in the school choir, plays in goal
in the school hockey team, is the school chess champion and likes
knitting. She intends to be a scientist and have two children, a boy
and a girl (she'll probably knit them), and a reliable husband with
a well-paid job.

Her mother, Mrs Primrose, always says, 'Oh you've brought your
friends home, Eunice!' – each time surprised anew that Eunice is
capable of making friends. The Primroses live in Laurel Bank, which
is too close for comfort.

'Primrose' we are all agreed, is a very pretty name and it's only a shame it's paired with 'Eunice' – she could surely have been called 'Lily or Rose or Jasmine or even . . . Primrose.'

This remark is addressed to Charles over my birthday lunch of macaroni cheese in an attempt to get him interested in Eunice as a girl instead of her previous incarnation as a crashing bore, on the principle that two misfits together might make a fit. 'Daisy,' Mr Rice adds, uninvited, 'Iris, Ivy, Cherry – I knew a girl called Cherry once,' he snorts. 'She was a bit of all right . . . Poppy, Marigold, Pansy . . . [Mr Rice is the most boring person alive] . . . Hyacinth, Heather—'

'Gorse, wort, bladderwrack,' Vinny interrupts him impatiently.

'Violet,' Charles says dreamily, 'that's a pretty name.'

Mr Primrose, Eunice's father, is an actuary by day, an actor by night (his joke). He runs a local amateur dramatic group – 'The Lythe Players' – and to illustrate his artistic tendencies wears a bow-tie to work and a cravat at home. I have resisted his blandishments to join 'The Players' as they're a ramshackle outfit that get laughed at even when playing tragedy. Especially when playing tragedy. Debbie has been recently persuaded to join but has so far not been allowed on stage. Even Mr Primrose, it seems, has his standards.

Mr Primrose has, in his time, made a rather effective Lady Bracknell. 'Oh, he's always practising stuff like that,' Eunice says. 'I found him with Mummy's négligé on the other day.'

Is this normal, I wonder? But then, what is normal? Not Carmen's family, surely – the McDades are liable to such casual violence that even the friendliest exchange with them is liable to result in injury – a box on the ear, a punch in the stomach. 'Yeah,' Carmen says, cracking gum like a whip, 'it's not nice, is it?'

Carmen's as thin as tapeworm and has waxy yellow skin that's nearly transparent so that all her blue veins show like a human biology diagram. Her feet are the worst thing about her – skinny and flat with splayed toes and far too big for the rest of her body, the veins on them like tangled railway junctions. If this is what her feet are like at sixteen, what will they be like when she's an old woman? But she's an old woman now really.

Carmen left school at the first opportunity and is already engaged to a square-set boy with the unlikely name of Bash, who could easily pass himself off as one of her brothers. She's got her future all mapped out – the wedding, the children, the house, the long path to old age. 'It's not very romantic, is it?' I venture, but she just looks at me as if I'm speaking a different language, one she doesn't know. Carmen's got a job on the cheese counter in British Home Stores, forcing me to spend quite a lot of time hanging around British Home Stores looking as if I need half a pound of coloured Cheddar.

It doesn't look such a bad job actually, I don't think I'd mind working on a cheese counter. It would leave my mind free to do whatever it wanted – which is nothing in particular, it's true, but I like being alone in my head, I'm used to it. But, of course, the very opposite would probably turn out to be the case and far from being free to roam around in its empty spaces, my mind would most likely be full of nothing but cheese. Carmen confirms this suspicion – 'Red Leicester' in particular, she offers, when I ask her to be more specific.

And poor Audrey, so quiet and self-effacing, so frightened of the blackhearted presence of Mr Baxter, that sometimes you have to look twice to make sure Audrey's still there. Perhaps that's how people disappear – not suddenly, as in Charles' unexplained world where people are mysteriously plucked from their lives, but by slowly, day by day, erasing themselves.

Elfin-bodied and angel-haired, Audrey is insubstantial, hardly part of the material world at all. 'Eat something, Audrey, please,' Mrs Baxter constantly urges, sometimes even following Audrey round the room with bowl and spoon as if waiting for her to inadvertently open her mouth so that she can take her unawares and pop food inside her. One day I half-expect to see Mrs Baxter regurgitating a little pellet of food and stuffing it down Audrey's beak. Audrey hasn't been well for weeks with some bug she can't shake off and mooches around Sithean bundled up in big cardigans and baggy jumpers looking miserable. 'What's wrong with Audrey?' Mr Baxter keeps snapping as if she's making herself ill just to annoy him.

We are all mis-shapen in some way, inside or out. Carmen's aunt, Wanda, works in a chocolate factory and supplies the McDades with endless bags of mis-shapes, rejected by quality control. After-dinner mints that have got their geometry all wrong – rhomboid instead of square; chocolate wafer biscuits that have been born as triplets instead of twins and mints that have lost their holes. Whenever I think of us – Carmen, Audrey, Eunice or myself – I think of Wanda's mis-shapes, girls' bodies that have been rejected by quality control.

Why don't I have friends of Nordic beauty – tall and golden and normal? Friends like Hilary Walsh. Hilary is the head girl at Glebelands Grammar, as was her sister, Dorothy, before her. Dorothy is now at Glebelands University (founded by Edward VI, one of the oldest in the country). Hilary and Dorothy are both big clever blondes who look as if they've just stepped out of a Swiss milking-parlour. No chance of them disappearing. The Walshes live in a vast Georgian house in town. Mr Walsh owns some kind of business and Mrs Walsh is a JP.

Hilary and Dorothy have an older brother, Graham, also a student at Glebelands University. Graham doesn't share his sisters' Aryan qualities – smaller, thinner, darker than his sisters, as if Mr and Mrs Walsh were just practising when they had him.

Good-looking boys, who are studying dentistry and law and look as if they're members of the Hitler Youth, hover around Hilary and Dorothy like wasps round a jam-jar, keen to study their biological perfection. My chances of ever being like them are zero. Next to them, I'm a chimney-sweep, a walnut-skinned beggar girl.

'What very *black* hair you have, don't you, Isobel?' Hilary remarks one day (it's unusual for Hilary to even talk to me), stroking a finger over her porcelain ('English Rose') cheek, 'And such *dark* eyes! Were your parents foreign?'

Hilary stables her white pony at the farm beyond Hawthorn Close and sometimes I see her riding round the Lady Oak field. In the early morning mist she could easily be mistaken for a centaur, half-horse, half-girl.

I can see her now riding in slow dressage circles around the Lady Oak. The branches of the tree are covered in tightly budded leaves, like little green jewels. To the Druids the tree was the link between heaven and earth. What would happen if I climbed the Lady Oak, would I reach heaven, or just some everyday giant shouting *Fee-fi-fo-fum* as he chased me down again?

'April Fool,' Debbie says (quite inappropriately) as she hands me a gift-wrapped parcel over the lunch table, and before I can have the surprise of opening it, says, 'A nice cardi from Marks and Sparks.' If I am the April Fool, then Charles, born the first of March, must be the mad March hare.

'Thank you,' I mutter rather ungraciously. I'd asked for a dog. 'But we've already got a dog,' Debbie bleats, indicating her own 'Gigi' – an apricot toy poodle that looks as if it's been lightly grilled around the edges and an animal that no wolf would own up to having helped evolve. Mr Rice has, helpful for once, tried to assassinate Gigi on several occasions, smothering, strangling, stretching, alas nothing has worked. (What does Mr Rice travel in? Shoes. Charles used to think this a great joke.)

'For God's sake,' Vinny says, as Debbie clears away the remains of the watery macaroni cheese from under her nose. Vinny snatches her plate back again. 'You're not even *eating* that,' Debbie protests.

'So?' Vinny sneers. (Vinny would make a good adolescent.) 'Even the dog wouldn't eat this stuff.' Debbie *is* a dreadful cook, it's hard to believe that she completed a year training to be a domestic science teacher in New Zealand. What would make a good birthday repast? Roasted swan and breast of lapwing, bud of asparagus, leaf of artichoke. And desserts, desserts moulded like castles and decorated like courtesans – studded with maraschino nipples and draped in piped swags of whipped cream. Not that I would ever eat a lapwing. Nor a swan, come to that.

Against all the odds, Debbie clings to the strict blueprint for family life that she came to us with four years ago, one which she herself received carved on tablets of stone from people called 'Mum and Dad'. 'Dad' was a school janitor and 'Mum' was a housewife and the whole family emigrated when Debbie was ten. This blueprint dictates that she must impose order on a disordered world, which she does by means of feverish housework. 'Someone take the key out of her back,' Vinny sighs wearily. Soon I expect we'll find Debbie in the hearth separating lentils from the ashes.

Arden has her in its thrall. 'This house,' she complains to Gordon, 'has a life of its own.' 'Possibly,' Gordon sighs. The house does seem to conspire against her – if she buys new curtains then a plague of moths will follow, if she puts down lino, the washing-machine will flood. Her kitchen tiles crack and fall off, the new central-heating pipes rattle and moan and bang in the night like banshees. If she polishes everything in a room then the minute she leaves, the particles of dust will come out of their hiding-places and regroup on every surface, sniggering behind their little hands. (We must imagine those things we cannot see.) The dust in Arden isn't really dust, of course, but the talcum of the dead, a frail composite waiting to be reconstituted.

She tries to grow vegetables in the garden and produces instead mandrake-rooted carrots and green potatoes. Greenfly and blackfly crowd the air like locusts, her runner beans are stunted, her cabbages are yellow, her pea-pods empty, her lawn as blighted as a blasted heath. Over the hedge, next door, Mrs Baxter's garden buzzes with honey-bees and is smothered in flowers – beanstalks that touch the clouds and each white curd on her cauliflowers as big as a tree.

Poor Debbie, lingering under the Fairfax curse that dictates nothing will ever go right or – to be more specific – everything will always go wrong just when it looks as if it might go right.

'Well, someone has to do it,' Debbie snaps at Vinny as Vinny queries the need to get up from the dining-room table to enable Debbie to polish it, 'and it's obviously not going to be you.'

'Certainly bloody isn't,' Vinny says, refusing to move so that Debbie has to polish around her while she chews on a cigarette, revealing her crocus-coloured teeth. Always an heroic *fumeuse* (Vinny's been kippered by nicotine), she's recently taken to smoking roll-ups, leaving shreds of Golden Virginia in her wake wherever she goes. 'This is disgusting!' Debbie proclaims every time she comes across one of Vinny's dog-ends with the life sucked out of them. 'This is disgusting!' Debbie proclaims as Vinny showers the macaroni cheese remains with a garnish of tobacco. 'Disgusting is as disgusting does,' Vinny murmurs enigmatically.

'Now, now,' Gordon says, forever trying to keep the peace. And failing. Poor Gordon. He has taken the loss of the family fortunes in his stride. 'I never wanted to be a grocer anyway,' he says, but did he want to be a lowly pen-pusher in Glebelands Corporation town-planning department? 'You can't go wrong in local government jobs,' Debbie encouraged approvingly, 'pension schemes and regular holidays and a chance of promotion. Like Dad.' ('What do janitors get promoted to?' Charles puzzled.) What did Gordon do when he was in New Zealand? He looks wistful and smiles sadly, 'Sheep farm.'

The only thing in the whole world that Debbie wants is the thing she cannot have. A baby. It appears that she is infertile ('Barren!' Vinny crows). 'Something wrong with my tubes,' Debbie explains (in less biblical terms) to all and sundry, 'women's trouble.' Tubes! I think of Debbie as a great Underground map – instead of nerves and veins and arteries perhaps she has the Metropolitan and the District and Circle.

'It's the curse of the Fairfaxes,' Charles tells her cheerfully.

To compensate for not being pregnant, Debbie seems to be growing fatter and fatter. She's like a big plumped-up cushion on legs. Her wedding ring is cutting into her finger and she's developed a cascade of little chins. Her inability to spawn is in stark contrast to the empire of cats in Arden (Vinny is their queen) which is expanding exponentially.

Elemanzer, one of Vinny's feline cohorts, entwines itself with playful malevolence around Mr Rice's ankles under the table. He gives her a swift kick and leers at me, 'Sweet sixteen, eh?', wiping macaroni cheese off his greasy lips. Mr Rice, the lodger who will not leave, has lately grown almost intimate with Vinny – sharing a glass of Madeira and a game of bezique every Friday evening. 'You don't think they have a *physical* relationship, do you?' Debbie whispers in horror to Gordon and Gordon snorts with laughter, 'When time goes backward.'

Mr Rice gives a little scream as the cat claws his leg in retaliation but must stifle it with his napkin or there will be trouble from Vinny.

'I'm making you a birthday cake,' Debbie says and from the oven comes the sound of something bubbling monstrously, beyond control. The kitchen is the most malign place in the house for Debbie, here is the cradle of chaos theory – a dropped teaspoon at one end of the kitchen can cause the oven to catch fire and everything to fall off the pantry shelves at the other end.

'Lovely,' I say and flee round to Sithean, the scent of sadness at my back. I pass Gordon in the back garden contemplating the big overgrown elder tree that is growing too close to the house. When you look out of the dining-room window nowadays all you can see is the tree and it taps and shakes its leaves against the window as if it would dearly like you to let it in. Gordon is leaning on a huge old axe like some philosopher-woodcutter. 'It's going to have to go,' he says sadly. He should be careful, witches have been known to disguise themselves as elders.

A more comforting smell than birthday cake greets me in Sithean. 'Marmalade,' Mrs Baxter says, scumming honey-coloured froth off the sugary mess bubbling in her big copper pan. The marmalade's the colour of tawny amber and melted lions. 'The very last of the

Sevilles,' she says sadly as if the Sevilles were some great aristocratic family whose fortunes had failed. 'Have a wee stir of the jeely-pan,' Mrs Baxter urges, handing me a long-handled wooden spoon, 'and make a wish. Go on wish, wish,' she says like a demented fairy godmother.

'For whatever I want?'

'Absolutely.' (I wish, naturally, for sex with Malcolm Lovat.)

'You could be having a party,' Mrs Baxter says, 'or playing a game.' Mrs Baxter would have us playing games all the time if she could. She has a book – *The Home Entertainer* (of which she's very fond) – a relic of the happy childhood she once had and a book that can provide a game for every occasion. 'Indoor pastimes,' she says, nodding happily as she stirs the marmalade, an 'April the First Party' maybe? 'An April the First Party,' she reads from the book, 'is often highly amusing, for all the world loves a fool. You must be careful, however, that the guests are congenial and chosen carefully.' This seems like sound advice to me.

Audrey is sitting hunched up at the kitchen table writing labels methodically in her neat handwriting – '*Marmalade – April '60*' – her golden-red hair escaping in a fine halo around her hairline. She looks up and gives me her lovely melon slice of a smile, always a surprise, like sunshine coming out from behind a sombre cloud.

Mrs Baxter pours the hot marmalade in one long shower of gold into gleaming glass jars. Mrs Baxter is a hedgecomber, her pantry's crammed full with jams and jellies and cheeses of every different kind – crabapple jelly and damson cheese, strawberry conserve and elderberry, rosehip syrup and sloe gin.

When the world has grown into eternal winter and the honeycombs are locked in ice and the sugar canes are withered, at least there will be Mrs Baxter's jam to cheer us up.

I set off back home again, carrying a jar of still-warm marmalade. ('Jam, jam, jam,' sour-toothed Vinny complains, 'can't she make anything else?'

'Does she think I'm not perfectly capable of making jam?' Debbie sniffs, on receipt of yet another jar, but nobody eats Debbie's accursed jam because as soon as she's made it, green spots, like lunar cheese, start dotting its surface.)

I turn round to close Mrs Baxter's gate and when I turn back round again – the most extraordinary thing imaginable – everything familiar has vanished – instead of standing on the pavement I'm standing in a field. The streets, the houses, the orderly lines of trees are all gone. Only the Lady Oak and the church – clustered around with a huddle of old cottages – remain. It's the same place and yet it isn't, how can that be?

I know from Charles' paranormal research that it's quite a common thing to suddenly disappear while crossing a field. Perhaps it's about to happen to me? I feel suddenly dizzy as if the planet's started to spin faster and I have an overwhelming desire to lie down on the earth and cling onto the grass to stop myself being flung off the planet. Or the other possibility, of course – that I'm going to be sucked down through the grass and into the soil and never be seen again for seven years.

I'm relieved to see a figure advancing towards me – a man in a long astrakhan-trimmed overcoat and derby hat. He looks odd but harmless, he certainly doesn't look like an alien about to abduct me, instead he tips his hat as he draws near and enquires politely after my well-being. In his hand he's carrying sheaves of paper – maps and plans – and he waves them at me enthusiastically. 'It's going to be a wonderful year,' he says. 'An *annus mirabilis* as these so-called educated folk say. Right here,' he booms, stamping his foot firmly on the muddy grass where Arden's big hawthorn hedge was growing a moment ago, 'right here I'm going to build an excellent house,' and he laughs uproariously as if this was a great joke.

I find my voice which has been lost for some minutes, 'And what year is this exactly, please?'

He looks startled. 'Year? Why 1918, of course. What year do you think it is? And soon,' he continues, 'there are going to be houses. Everywhere you look, there will be houses, young lady,' and he walks on, still laughing, marching on his way in the direction of Lythe Church, climbs over a wall and disappears.

Then I find my feet are back on the pavement and the trees and houses are all back in place.

I am mad, I think. I am mad therefore I think. I am mad therefore I think I am. Jings and help me Boab, as Mrs Baxter would say.

'Amazing,' Charles says enviously when I tell him, 'you must have been in a time warp.' He makes it sound like a normal occurrence, like a trip to the seaside. He proceeds to interrogate me for the rest of the evening about the minutiae of this otherworld. 'Did you smell anything? Rotten eggs? Static? Ozone?' None of these unpleasant things, I answer irritably, only the scent of green grass and the bittersweet smell of hawthorn.

Perhaps it was some kind of cosmic April Fool's joke? I'm only just sixteen and here I am already leaking madness like a sieve.

How am I to celebrate my birthday? In a perfect world (the imagination) I would be on the wild moors above Glebelands, the wind whipping at my skirts and hair, locked in passionate congress with Malcolm Lovat, but sadly he doesn't understand that we are destined for each other, that when the world was new we were one person, that now we are an apple cleft in two, that my sixteenth birthday would be the perfect occasion for us to reunite our flesh and indulge in violent delights. 'Well, they do a nice high tea at Ye Olde Sunne Inne,' Debbie suggests, 'and they do a lovely knickerbocker glory.' (*The Oldest Pub in Glebelands – Weddings and Funerals a speciality. Try our Ham Teas!*)

Still in a state of surreal shock from my encounter with the master-builder, I opt instead for The Five Pennies and sit-in fish and chips with Audrey and the inevitable Eunice who has not, unfortunately, gone to Cleethorpes after all. And not forgetting my invisible friend, the scent of sadness.

On the way home, even Eunice is silenced by the sight that greets us just as we turn into Hawthorn Close, for suddenly, without any pre-amble, the moon rises from behind the roof of Audrey's house.

Not any old moon, not the usual moon, but an enormous white disc like a big Pan Drop, a cartoon moon almost, its lunar geography – seas and mountains – a luminescent grey, its chaste rays illuminating the streets of trees with a much kinder light than the streetlamps. We're stopped in our tracks, half enchanted, half horrified by this magic moonrise.

What's happened to the moon? Has its orbit moved closer to the earth overnight? I can feel the moon's gravity pulling the tide of my blood. This must be a miracle of some kind, surely – a change in the very laws of physics? I'm relieved that someone else is sharing the lunacy with me – I can feel Audrey clinging onto my arm so hard that she's pinching my skin through the fabric of my coat.

A moment longer and we will be running for the woods, bows and arrows in our hands, hounds at our heels, converts to Diana, but then sensible Eunice pipes up, 'We're only experiencing the moon illusion – it's an illustration of the way the brain is capable of misinterpreting the phenomenal world.'

'*What*?'

'The moon illusion,' she repeats patiently. 'It's because you've got all these points of reference –' she waves her arms around like a mad scientist, 'aerials, chimney pots, rooftops, trees – they give us the wrong ideas of size and proportion. Look,' she says and turns round and suddenly bends over like a rag doll, 'look at it between your legs.'

'See!' Eunice says triumphantly when we finally obey her ridiculous command. 'It doesn't look big any more, does it?' No, we agree sadly, it doesn't.

'You lost those points of reference, you see,' she carries on pedantically, and Audrey surprises me by saying, 'Oh shut up,

Eunice,' and I point helpfully back down the street and say, 'You live back there in case you've forgotten, Eunice,' and we walk quickly on, leaving her to go home on her own. The moon carries on bowling up into the sky, growing smaller.

The moon makes no sense to me. Eunice can spout lunar data all day long and it would still mean nothing. I can see no order in the moon's journeys around the heavens – one day it's popping out of a pocket of sky behind Sithean, the next it's spinning above Boscrambe Woods, and the day after, there it is on my shoulder, following me down Hawthorn Close. It waxes and wanes with delirious abandon, one minute a thin paring of fingernail, the next a gibbous slice of lemon, the next a fat melon moon. So much for periodical regularity.

I lie in bed and look at my window full of moon. I see the moon and the moon sees me. It's high in the sky, shrunk back to its normal size, free and unfettered from the earth. A perfectly normal moon – not a blood moon, nor a blue moon – it isn't an old moon with a new one in its arms, just a normal April moon. God bless the moon. And God bless me. Faraway, in the distance somewhere, a dog howls.

WHAT'S WRONG?

SUMMER HAS BEGUN TO TAKE OVER THE STREETS OF TREES, CLOTHING everything in green again. 'Wouldn't it be funny,' Charles says dreamily, 'if one year the summer didn't come? A world of eternal winter?'

I awake from an unpleasant dream in which I found myself walking up a hill, a Jack-less Jill, to fill a bucket of water from a well at the top. As we know, trips to the well are fraught with the danger of alien kidnapping, so my dreaming self was quite relieved to find it still existed when it got to the top.

I lowered the bucket into the well, heard it splash in the water and hauled it back up. There was something at the bottom of the bucket, I'd fished something up in the water. I gaped in horror at its pale lifeless appearance – I'd caught a head.

The eyelids of the head were closed giving it a passing resemblance to Keats' death-mask, but then the lids suddenly flew open and the head began to speak, its nerveless lips moving slowly – and I recognized the Roman nose, the dark curls, the long lashes – it was the head of Malcolm Lovat. It was more like the toppled head of a statue than a real severed head – the break was clean and even, no blood vessels or frayed sinews floating like tentacles in the bucket.

The head emitted the most tremendous sigh and fixing me with its dead gaze beseeched, 'Help me.'

'Help you?' I said. 'How?' but the rope slipped out of my hand and the bucket clattered back down the well. I peered down, I could still see the pale face glimmering through the water, eyes closed once more and the words 'help me' echoing like ripples on the water before fading away.

What does the dream about Malcolm Lovat mean? And why his head only? Because he used to be head boy at Glebelands Grammar? (Are dreams that simple?) Because I was reading *Isabella, or the Pot of Basil* last night? It's hard enough trying to keep a geranium alive in Arden, I can't imagine trying to cultivate a head. Imagine the care and attention a head would need – warmth, light, conversation, combing and brushing – it would be an ideal hobby for Debbie. And basil would be even more difficult, given the malign environment of Arden.

I am, I know, a seething cauldron of adolescent hormones and Malcolm Lovat is the cipher of my lust, but decapitation? 'Freud would have a field-day with that stuff,' analytic Eunice says, 'heads, wells – all that suppressed lust and penis envy . . .' It's hard to believe that anyone could envy a *penis*. Not that I have seen many, in fact, apart from statues and an unfortunate glimpse of Mr Rice's addenda, I have only the evidence of Charles' anatomy to go on and it's a long time since I've seen any of that in the flesh, as it were. 'I'm speaking metaphorically,' Eunice points out. Aren't we all.

Carmen, the only one of us to have studied the subject in

any depth, reports that a plucked turkey and its giblets are the nearest she can get to describing it, but then Carmen's attitude to sex is surrounded with such an air of ennui that trainspotting seems positively dangerous in comparison. 'Well, it's one way of spending time,' she says indifferently. (If you spend time what do you buy? 'Less time,' Mrs Baxter says sadly.)

'Orite?' Debbie asks (her usual greeting) when I finally stumble down to the kitchen for a bowl of Frosties. She's meditating on a kitchen table of meat like a preoccupied butcheress – serried ranks of pork chops, anaemic sausages, big steaks sliced from the limbs of large warm-blooded mammals – a table full of dead flesh the colour of sweet peas. 'We're having a barbecue tonight,' she says by way of explanation.

'A barbecue?' It sounds like an invitation to disaster. Debbie's home entertaining is regularly doomed to end in disappointment and, not infrequently, ritual humiliation and social embarrassment. We have witnessed any number of 'little cocktail parties', 'wine and cheeses' and 'potluck suppers' turn into disasters. But Debbie is heedless, thrilled at the idea that she is about to re-introduce cooking alfresco to the streets of trees where no-one has charred a steak over a flame for at least a thousand years.

'For the neighbours,' she says optimistically as she scrutinizes a tray of pale bloodless sausages. 'I'm going to put them in buns with ketchup,' she adds. 'What do you think?' She could turn them back into a pig for all I care but I mutter something encouraging because she has a wild kind of look in her eye as if someone's overwound the key in her back and she's going too fast. She starts wiping steaks tenderly with a cloth as if they were the butchered bloody cheeks of small children and says, 'I think it'll be nice. It'll certainly be *something*.' (Although you could say that about a lot of things.)

She turns her attention back to the sausages and stares at them fixedly then looks at me and asks, in a suspicious voice, 'Do you think they've moved?'

'What?'

'Those sausages.'

'Moved?'

'Yes,' she says more doubtfully now, 'I thought they'd moved.'

'*Moved?*'

'It doesn't matter,' she says quickly. No wonder Gordon's worried about Debbie. He's said as much to me on several occasions, 'I'm a bit worried about Debs, she seems a bit . . . you know?'

I think he means mad.

I am saved from further discussion about the relocating sausages by a screech from the hallway that indicates Vinny wants attention.

Vinny's on her way out to the chiropodist. Vinny rarely leaves the house so when she does it's an occasion of some importance to her. She spends a lot of time looking forward to a glimpse of the outside world and then, when she returns, even more time complaining about the state of it.

'I'm a shadow of my former self,' she announces, peering through the misty patina of the rust-spotted hall mirror that Debbie has long ago given up trying to clean. Vinny was a shadow to begin with, now she's a shadow of a shadow. Her bones have turned to polished yellow ivory, her skin to shagreen. Shagreen enamelled with imperial-purple veins. Warts grow on the backs of her hands like lichen. Her breath is as full of sighs as a bagpipe.

She takes a compact out of her ancient mausoleum of a handbag and rubs her cheeks vigorously with face-powder that looks like flour and, scrutinizing the result intently, says, 'My chilblains are killing me,' as if they're to be found on her face rather than on her feet. She's dressed for the outside world – a brown gabardine coat and a grey felt hat that's a strange battered shape, like old dough that's been punched. Vinny's hat has an incongruous pheasant feather poking out of the top, expressing a jauntiness somehow at odds with the woman underneath. She takes her pearl-headed hatpin and sticks it into her hat, although from where I'm standing – loitering by the hallstand – it looks as if she's just stuck it through her head.

'Don't smirk,' Vinny says, catching sight of my face in the mirror.
'If the wind changes you'll stay like that.' I loll my head on one side
and make a face that Charles would be proud of. 'You look like the
Hunchback of Notre Dame,' Vinny says, 'only a lot taller,' and
deflates onto the hard little chair next to the telephone table. 'My
chilblains are killing me,' she adds with feeling.

'You said that already.'

'Well, I'm saying it again.' Vinny creaks forward and strokes
one of her shoes consolingly. They're new black lace-ups – witch's
shoes, that Mr Rice has presented to her with a flourish as a 'token
of his esteem'.

'I'll have to wear something more comfortable,' Vinny says.
'Go and get me my brown brogues, they're under my bed. Go
on – what are you waiting for?'

Here be dragons. Vinny's room smells of different things – school
canteens, small museums and old cold crypts. You would never
know that outside it's a warm day in June. Vinny's room has its
own micro-climate. A thin film of nicotine covers every surface. I
crunch my way through the crust of biscuit-crumbs and cigarette-ash
that coats the threadbare carpet. The old brass bedstead that once
housed my sleeping grandmother (Charlotte Fairfax, or the Widow,
as she grew to be known) is draped with Vinny's clothes – decaying
undergarments and thick darned stockings, as well as most of her
skirts and dresses – despite the fact that the room contains a cavernous
wardrobe big enough to house another country.

Gingerly, I lift the hem of the faded satin coverlet, heaven only
knows what has its home under Vinny's bed. A stoury fluff – the
slough of Vinny's bad dreams – rises up in the draught of air. On
the day of judgement, when the dead are resurrected, the dust
which is legion under Vinny's bed will rise up and reform into a
multitude. Plenty of dead skin, but no shoes, only Vinny's frayed
slippers standing, oddly, in neat fifth ballet position.

I poke around half-heartedly amongst the detritus and debris
that composes Vinny's soft furnishings. I swing open one of the

heavy doors of the wardrobe, taking extra caution in case the whole contraption topples over and crushes me. Vinny's wardrobe, once the Widow's, is a curious affair. 'A Compendium' it announces itself in a stylized script from sometime before the First World War. A 'Lady's Compendium' in fact, because there was once a matching 'Gentleman's Compendium' that belonged to my long-forgotten grandfather – 'my late father' as Vinny says, her intonation suggesting unpunctuality rather than deadness.

Vinny's wardrobe displays its sex boldly – shelves labelled *Lingerie, Scarves, Gloves, Sundries* and racks designated *Furs, Evening Wear, Day Dresses.*

Despite the amount of Vinny's clothing hanging on the bedstead (or, indeed, the amount hanging on the floor), the wardrobe itself contains a forest of clothes, clothes that I've never even seen Vinny wear. Until now I've only had the most cursory of glimpses into the reeking camphor insides of Vinny's wardrobe and I'm gripped by a strange fascination and can't help but finger the ancient crêpe day dresses, hanging limp and lifeless, and stroke the musty wool costumes and coatees that are evidence of a more stylish Vinny than the one that now snails around the house in dusty print overall and fur-lined, zippered slippers. Was Vinny young once? It's hard to imagine it.

A long fur coat of uncertain animal insists on being fondled and a tippet brushes itself eagerly against my fingertips. The tippet's made from a long-dead pair of foxes, unacquainted in life but now forever joined as intimately as Siamese twins. Their little triangular faces peer out from the dark depths of the wardrobe, their black bead eyes staring hopefully at me while their sharp little snouts sniff the fusty air. (How do they spend their time? Dreaming of unspoilt forests?) I rescue them and place them around my shoulders where they nestle gratefully, protecting me from the draughts that whirl around the room like major weather fronts.

Crammed into the bottom of the wardrobe is a stack of boxes – shoe-boxes like cat coffins, grey with dust, their ends labelled with black-and-white line drawings of shoes that have names (*Claribel,*

Dulcie, Sonia) and hat-boxes, some leather, some cardboard. In the shoe-boxes are many different kinds of footwear – a pair of cream sandals, stout enough for an English summer, a pair of patent black T-straps, itching to dance a Charleston. But no sign of the errant brown brogues.

A plaintive screeching from the foot of the stairs indicates that Vinny is growing impatient. Just then, I spy a stray shoe lurking at the very bottom of the wardrobe, a partnerless one – but definitely not Vinny's or the Widow's style. A high-heeled brown suede shoe with a strange piece of matted fur stuck to it, like a piece of dead cat. The inside of the shoe's spotted with mould and a rhinestone glistens from within the little nest of dead fur. The nap on it is dark and rough and the thin heel of the shoe is splayed at an angle like a tooth waiting to fall out.

The smell of sadness which has drifted at my back into Vinny's room, is suddenly overwhelming, enveloping me like a damp cloak and I feel quite queasy with misery.

Vinny's squawks are growing louder, is she going to have to go barefoot to the hospital? What am I *doing* up there? Have I climbed into the wardrobe and *disappeared*?

Hurriedly, I take the shoe and close the wardrobe door and, as I turn away, notice Vinny's brown brogues sitting amongst the clutter of her dressing-table, their tongues silent. Vinny, on the other hand, has reached a critical level and if she shrieks any louder will explode.

Charles sniffs at the inside of the shoe like a bloodhound, he lays the brown suede against his cheek and closes his eyes like a clairvoyant. '*Hers*,' he says decisively, 'definitely.'

Vinny is as unhelpful as ever. 'Never seen it before,' she says coldly, but when I first showed it to her she flinched away from it as if it was made of red-hot iron. 'Don't you dare go rooting around amongst my things again,' she warned and stomped away.

We know, in our bones and our blood, that the shoe has travelled through time and space to tell us something. But what? If we found its partner would it help us find the true bride ('it fits, it fits!') and bring her back from wherever she is now?

'She could be dead for all we know, Charles.' Charles looks as if he'd like to attack me with the shoe. 'Don't you ever think about her?' he says angrily.

But there isn't a day goes by when I don't think about her. I carry Eliza around inside me, like a bowl of emptiness. There is nothing to fill it, only unanswered questions. What was her favourite colour? Did she have a sweet-tooth? Was she a good dancer? Was she afraid of death? Do I have diseases I will inherit from her? Will I sew a straight seam or play a good hand at bridge because of her?

I have no pattern for womanhood – other than that provided by Vinny and Debbie and no-one could call them good models. There are things I don't know about – good skin care, how to write a thank-you letter – because she was never there to teach me. More important things – how to be a wife, how to be a mother. How to be a woman. If only I didn't have to keep on inventing Eliza (rook-hair, milk-skin, blood-lips). 'No, hardly ever,' I lie to Charles in an off-hand way, 'it was such a long time ago. We have to move on with our lives, you know.' (But where to?)

Perhaps she's coming back in bits – a drift of perfume, a powder-compact, a shoe. Perhaps soon there'll be fingernails and hair, and then whole limbs will start to appear and we can piece our jigsaw-mother together again.

'Whose shoe is this?' Charles asks a distracted Gordon, struggling to keep the barbecue charcoal alight. Gordon turns and sees the shoe and goes a strange colour, like raw pastry. 'Where did you get that?' he says in a hollow voice to Charles but then Debbie elbows us out of the way and says, 'Come on, Gordon, the guests'll be here soon and those coals need to be *glowing*. What's wrong? Dad never had any bother with it. What's that?' she adds, nodding her head in the direction of the shoe. 'Throw it away, Charles, it looks unsanitary.'

Mr Rice appears in the garden looking for something to eat

and when he finds only raw meat, disappears back inside. Mr and Mrs Baxter make a tentative appearance in the garden. Mr Baxter is rarely seen at any neighbourhood gathering. He casts a long shadow, even when he isn't standing in the sunlight.

Mr Baxter's hair has been newly cut in an army crop that bristles angrily from his scalp. Mrs Baxter's hair, on the other hand, is softly waved and the colour of small timid mammals. There's nothing harsh about Mrs Baxter. She favours neutral colours – oyster, taupe, biscuit and oatmeal – so that sometimes she just seems to fade right away into her pretty, chintzy living-room with its well-behaved curtain tie-backs and orderly teak display-unit. This is better than Vinny who wears funereal shades as if she's in permanent mourning for something. Her life, according to Debbie, who's more of a pastel person herself.

At the unexpected sight of Mr Baxter, Charles says, 'Right, I'm off then, I'm going to the cinema,' and before Debbie can say, 'Oh no you aren't!' he's gone. Poor Charles, he can never find anyone to go anywhere with him. 'He should get a dog,' Carmen suggests – the McDades have a pack of assorted dogs for every purpose – 'a dog would go anywhere with him.' But Charles wants someone who'll sit in the back row of the cinema with him, someone to rendezvous with in cafés and drink frothy coffee and eat toasted teacakes, and although a dog would probably be perfectly willing to undertake these duties I think it's a girl, not a canine, that Charles wants. ('Hmm,' Carmen says, frowning, 'that's a bit more difficult.') Why don't girls want to go out with Charles – because he looks so odd? Because he has strange beliefs and obsessions? Yes. In a word.

Mrs Baxter, unsure of the etiquette of something as novel as a barbecue, has brought a large Tupperware bowl with her which she proffers to Debbie. 'I just made a wee bitty coleslaw,' she says with a hopeful smile, 'thought you might be able to use it.'

'Or even eat it,' Mr Baxter says with a sarcastic smile so that Mrs Baxter grows flustered.

More neighbours begin to troop into the garden and Debbie grows increasingly edgy about her unglowing coals. The neighbours are

suitably impressed by Debbie's barbecue grill – 'very new-fangled'
– but less impressed by their uncooked food.

Mr and Mrs Primrose arrive with Eunice and Richard, Eunice's
unattractive brother. Mr Primrose and Debbie fall into an earnest
conversation about The Lythe Players' next production – *A
Midsummer Night's Dream*, which they're going to perform ('just
for the heck of it,' Mr Primrose laughs) on Midsummer's Eve
in the Lady Oak field. Why on Midsummer's Eve? Why not on
Midsummer's Night? 'As if it matters,' Debbie says dismissively.

Debbie has a speaking-part at last, playing Helena, and is constantly
complaining about the number of words she has to learn, not
to mention the awkwardness of those words, 'He [meaning
Shakespeare] could have made the whole thing a lot shorter in
my opinion, and he uses twenty words when one would do, it's
ridiculous. Words, words, words.'

I don't bother entering into an argument with her, or explaining
that Shakespeare is beyond all possible measure. ('Unusual,' Miss
Hallam the English teacher says, 'in a girl of your age to find such
enthusiasm for the Bard.') The 'Bard'! This is like calling Eliza
'our mum', bringing them down to the level of ordinary mortals.
'If anyone came from another planet,' I tell Charles, 'then it was
Shakespeare.' Imagine meeting Shakespeare! But then what would
you say to him? What would you *do* with him? You could hardly
take him around the shops. (Or maybe you could.) 'Have sex,'
Carmen says, sticking her tongue into a sherbet fountain in a vaguely
obscene way. 'Sex?' I query doubtfully.

'Well, you may as well,' she shrugs, 'if you're going to go to
all the bother of time-travel.'

Assorted hungry guests turn to Mrs Baxter's coleslaw and munch
their way through it stoically. Gordon delivers a plateful of
chops, black on the outside and a vivid Schiaperelli pink inside.
People gnaw politely at the edges and Mr Baxter discovers
a pressing engagement elsewhere. 'Is this horsemeat?' Vinny
asks loudly.

'I don't suppose you've invited the Lovats?' I ask Debbie
hopefully.

'The who?'

'The Lovats. On Laurel Bank. He's your gynaecologist.' Debbie
gives a little shudder of horror. 'Why on earth would I want to invite
him? He'd be standing there, eating a steak, and knowing what I
look like *inside*.' An unsettling thought. But he'd be exceptional
if he was eating a steak, no-one else is.

Faced, as he is, with so much 'women's trouble' (especially
such 'women' as Debbie and Vinny), one might feel almost sorry
for Mr Lovat – but he is not a particularly nice person – 'a cold
fish' in Debbie's estimation, a 'queer fish' in Vinny's – so an
unusual consensus there from the warring-parties, about the fish
part anyway.

Debbie has made dessert for the occasion – a sophisticated
moulded concoction, *Riz Imperial aux Peches*. 'Cold rice pudding?'
Mrs Primrose ventures doubtfully. 'With tinned peaches?'

Mr Rice reappears just in time for Richard Primrose to snig-
ger, a horrible kind of *snarf-snarf* noise, and say, 'Mr Tapioca!
Mr Semolina!'

I tell him this is an old joke, but Richard isn't interested in
anything a girl *says*. Mr Rice *is* beginning to look like a pudding,
now I think about it, a stodgy suet roly-poly one, with his pasty
skin and currant eyes. Richard himself would make a very poor
pudding. He's a bespectacled and bespotted youth the same age
as Charles and a first-year student of Civil Engineering at the
Glebelands Technical College. Richard and Charles have several
things in common – they are both equally pot-holed with acne
and subject to a similar red-raw shaving rash. They both also smell
faintly of old cheese rinds, although this is possibly true of all boys
(except Malcolm Lovat, of course), and they both have a geekish,
unsocialized quality which alienates them from both girls and their
male peers. Despite their similarities they detest each other.

There are some things they don't share, however. Charles, for
instance, is human (despite what he likes to think to the contrary)

but Richard is possibly not. Possibly an extra-terrestrial experiment gone wrong in fact — an alien's idea of what a human is like, put together from spare parts, the creation of a Martian Frankenstein.

He's the complete physical opposite of Charles, thin and lanky as a vine, his body dangling from his big coathanger-shoulders like an ill-fitting suit. Lantern-jawed, in profile his face is a concave new moon.

Richard keeps trying to make sly physical contact with me, shooting out a surreptitious hand or foot and trying to rub them against whatever bit of my body he can reach. 'Sod off, Richard,' I say nastily to him and stalk off.

'And this is?' Mrs Baxter says warily to me, holding up a collop of singed flesh.

'Poodle?' I offer hopefully.

'I think I might go home, dear,' Mrs Baxter says hastily. 'I should get back to Audrey.' Audrey is still harbouring 'Some kind of bug, summer flu,' Mrs Baxter says, 'probably.' Whenever she refers to Audrey's 'bug' I imagine poor Audrey playing host to some giant ladybird or shining iridescent beetle. 'What's *wrong* with Audrey?' Eunice asks, annoyed at a mystery that her *click-click-click* brain can't solve.

I wander disconsolately round the garden, the smell of sadness trailing at my heels — April's perfume hasn't been burnt up in the heat of June and lingers as a slight vibration in the air. Aren't ghosts supposed to squeak and gibber? What is it? Who is it? I can feel its invisible eyes on me, perhaps it's a manifestation of my adolescent energy, a mysterious poltergeist. If only Malcolm Lovat was here instead following me around. I wish to go by Carterhaugh, to kilt up my skirts, forfeit the fee of my maidenhead and walk on the wild shores of sexual passion.

'I saw you this morning,' Eunice says, appearing at my side, a bloody smear of tomato ketchup on her face. 'Pretty terrible barbecue,' she says cheerfully, 'I could have made a much better job of it.'

'Where?'

'Where what?'

'Where did you see me this morning?'

'In Woolworths, by the Pick 'n' Mix, you ignored me when I waved at you.'

But I wasn't in Woolworths, by the Pick 'n' Mix or anywhere else, I was in my bed, dreaming about Malcolm Lovat's head. 'Maybe it was your double then,' Eunice shrugs, 'your *doppelgänger*.' My self from the parallel world? Imagine if you were to come around a corner of the world and meet yourself – what questions you could ask! 'Do you have this odd feeling, Eunice?'

'Odd?'

'Yeah, as if something's not quite right . . .' But then the barbecue bursts into flames and the heavens open in an attempt to quench the fire and the social gathering comes to a wet and sooty halt.

I go round to see Audrey to tell her she hasn't missed much. Mrs Baxter's sitting at the kitchen table knitting something as delicate as a cobweb in a pattern of cockleshells and 'silver bells'?

'Hearts.'

'It's beautiful,' I say, fingering its snowy falls. 'A shawl, for my sister's first grandchild,' Mrs Baxter says. 'You remember, Rhona in South Africa.' Mrs Baxter always looks sad when babies are mentioned, perhaps because she's lost several babies herself. 'Never mind,' I try to comfort her, 'you'll be a grandmother one day, I expect,' and Audrey, who's standing at the cooker making unseasonable convalescent hot chocolate, accidentally knocks over the milk pan, sending it crashing to the floor.

When I come back from Sithean I find Charles has also returned and is sitting on a deck-chair amongst the ruins of the barbecue. The new-found shoe has disappeared back into obscurity. When closely questioned, Vinny – whose waste-disposal motto is, 'if it doesn't move, burn it' (and sometimes if it does move too) – admits to having barbecued it.

I pull out a deck-chair and join him in the twilight garden. The

rooks are coming home late, hurtling on their rag wings towards
the Lady Oak, racing the night, *caw-caw-caw*. Maybe they're afraid
of being transformed into something else if they don't get back to
the tree in time, before the sun dips below the horizon that saucers
blackly beyond the tree. Perhaps they're frightened of shifting into
human shape.

What's it like to be a *caw-cawing* crepuscular rook ripping through
the sables of night? A black bird flying high over the chimney-pots
and blue-slate roofs of the streets of trees? The last rook, a straggler,
dips its wing in salute as it flies overhead. What do we look like
from the air? A bird's-eye view? Pretty insignificant, I expect.

'Shape-shifting,' Charles says dreamily, 'that would be interesting,
wouldn't it?'

'Shape-shifting?'

'Into an animal or a bird or something?'

'What would you like to be, Charles?'

Charles, still wretched at having lost the shoe, shrugs his shoulders
indifferently and says, 'A dog, maybe,' and then adds hastily, 'a
proper dog,' as he catches sight of Gigi squatting indecorously in
the middle of the lawn.

'Maybe people can shape-shift into replicas of themselves,'
Charles says after a pause, 'and that's how you get *doppelgängers*?'

'Oh, do shut up, Charles, you're giving me a headache,' I say
irritably. Sometimes Charles' ideas are just too complicated to bear
thinking about.

'Do you think the aliens are already here?' he carries on
relentlessly.

'Here?' (On the streets of trees? For heaven's sake!)

'Living on the earth. Among us.'

Wouldn't we have noticed? Perhaps not. 'What do they look
like – little green people?'

'No – just like us.'

Just because you feel alienated, I explain to Charles, it doesn't
mean you're actually an *alien*, but he turns his face away, disappointed in me.

It's quite dark by now, the moon pale and distant, a white coin flipped up into a sky the colour of washable ink. The stars are all out, sending their indecipherable messages. Starlight, starbright. Debbie comes out into the garden and asks us what on earth we are doing out here in the dark and Charles says, 'Starbathing.' Really, the sooner he can hitch a ride back to his own planet the better.

I lie in bed for a long time trying to get to sleep even though I'm bone-weary. Wouldn't it be peculiar if Charles was right? If we came from somewhere else, far, far away and didn't know it? Perhaps on our own planet things are much better, like in the parallel world. The parallel planet.

I wait for the noise of gravel, like flaw-blown sleet, on my windowpane. I wish I may, I wish I might, have the wish I wish tonight – Malcolm Lovat shinning up the Virginia creeper that's slowly smothering Arden and entering my bedroom window so that our two bodies can melt into one. ('Melt?' Carmen says doubtfully – more of a beast-with-two-backs kind of girl herself.)

The Cats are murdering sleep, the walls rumbling with their engine purrs – *prut-prut-prut* as they snore their way to oblivion. The other occupants of Arden sleep less soundly. I can hear Charles' restless dreams – silver-suited spacemen wading through the nothingness of space and riveted tin rockets landing in the dusty craters of the moon, like something imagined by Méliès. Vinny's dreams are less audible, the noise of unoiled hinges, and Gordon isn't dreaming at all, but Debbie's baby dreams echo emptily around the house – fluffy, pink marshmallow dreams of stuffed rabbits and ducks, romper suits and pudgy putti bodies.

'Where's Charles?' Gordon asks, as he passes me on the stairs. 'He seems to have disappeared.' He's incongruously cheerful for having just made such a statement.

'Where's Charles?' Debbie shouts at me from the dining-room, where she's vacuuming the curtains with the nozzle attachment from the Hoover (she looks like an anteater). It's nine o'clock at night and sensible people are sprawled in front of their television sets. Like Vinny who's shouting abuse at Hughie Green from the comfort of her armchair.

'There's somebody at the back door,' Vinny says to me when I sit down. She leans forward and gives the fire a vicious poke. She's probably imagining sticking the poker into Mr Rice's head. Mr Rice has gone a-wooing and Vinny, who has got it in her head that there's some kind of 'understanding' between her and Mr Rice, is very, very annoyed. This understanding – or, more properly, misunderstanding – has arisen from a casual compliment from Mr Rice to the effect that Vinny would 'make someone a wonderful wife'. He might have meant the bride of Frankenstein's monster but he certainly didn't mean himself.

'There's someone at the back door,' the bride of Frankenstein's monster repeats irritably.

'I didn't hear anyone.'

'That doesn't mean there isn't somebody there.'

Reluctantly, I go and investigate. There *is* a strange scratching noise coming from the back door and when I open it, a hopeful whine directs my eyes downward to a large dog which is lying Sphinx-like on the threshold. As soon as I make eye contact with it, it leaps up and launches into its canine routine – head cocked to one side in a winning way, one paw raised in greeting.

It's a big ugly dog with fur the colour of a dirty beach. A dog of uncertain genetic origin, a touch of terrier, an ancient whisper of wolfhound, but more than anything it looks like an outsize version of the Tramp in *The Lady and the Tramp*. It has no collar, no name tag. It's the essence of all dog. It is Dog.

It keeps waving its huge heavy paw around in a determined effort to introduce itself so I bend down and take the proffered paw and look into its chocolate-brown eyes. There's something in its expression . . . the clumsy paws . . . the big ears . . . the bad haircut . . .

'Charles?' I whisper experimentally and the dog cocks one of its floppy ears and thumps its tail enthusiastically.

I suppose a better sister would have set about weaving him a shirt from nettles and throwing it over his furred-over body so that he could be released from his enchantment and resume his human form. I give him some cat food instead. He's absurdly grateful.

'Look,' I say to Gordon when he comes into the kitchen.

'Have you seen Debs anywhere?' he asks, scratching his head like Stan Laurel.

'No, but look – a dog, a poor, lost, homeless, hungry, lonely dog. Can we keep it?' and Gordon, who looks as if he might have been playing the game of Lost Identity from *The Home Entertainer* says vaguely, 'Mm, if you like.'

Of course, I know the Dog isn't really Charles under an enchantment and anyway he comes back from wherever he's been in time to drink Horlicks with Gordon. Neither Vinny nor Debbie are speaking to Gordon having simultaneously discovered the usurper dog finishing off the remains of supper in the kitchen. It will eat anything, it transpires, even Debbie's cooking.

With the arrival of the warm weather and the Dog, the flea population of Arden is on its way to achieving mastery of the planet, not to mention driving Debbie to the edge of it. 'Fairly louping with them,' Mrs Baxter laughs as one of them leaps off the Dog onto her nice white tablecloth.

'A lot of fuss about nothing,' Vinny says, catching one expertly and squashing its little jet-bead body between her thumbnails with a tiny explosive *crack*! (I imagine it's Richard Primrose's head.) Life at the level of the minutiae is fairly teeming in Arden – the fleas, the dust, the tiny fruit flies. And the invisible world, of course, is even more crowded than the visible one.

'Vitamins!' Vinny says. 'Who needs them?' 'Everyone?' I murmur. 'Molecules!' Charles says. 'Who understand them?' 'Scientists?' I venture. (Just because you can't see something doesn't mean it isn't important.)

Vinny is so scrawny, and probably cold-blooded, that no flea ever bothers biting her. Debbie, however – plump, warm-blooded and fine-skinned – is a banquet for them, a moveable feast.

Debbie blames the Cats (there's a musical waiting to be made), always a source of contention between the warring mistresses of Arden

(*A Word about the Cats*: There were no cats in Arden until the arrival of Vinny. Vinny used to have her own house, a dingy little terrace on Willow Road, but when our parents disappeared so thoughtlessly she had to give it up and come and live with us. She's never forgiven us. She brought the First Cat with her, the begetter of the Arden dynasty – Grimalkin, a bloodthirsty, belligerent grey female from whom we have bred many a fat fireside companion.)

Debbie is not the only person who dislikes the Cats. Mr Rice is not above administering the odd kick catwards when he thinks no-one is looking, unaware apparently that Vinny has radar in her ears and eyes on revolving stalks.

Sensing her unpopularity *à la* lodger, Elemanzer, Grimalkin's youngest and fiercest daughter, goes out of her way to annoy him, sleeping on his pillows when he's out and lying in wait on the stairs to trip him and even going to the length of getting pregnant and delivering her litter in Mr Rice's sock drawer.

For days after, we are entertained by the idea of Mr Rice delving into his drawer in the bleary light of dawn, expecting to come out with a blue and grey Argyle and screaming in horror as he discovered his socks have come to life – wriggling, damp and furry, in their little nest. And one very, very large, silver-grey tabby sock sinking its angry maternal teeth into his hand.

By the time summer comes one of those mewling socks, a handsome young kitten called Vinegar Tom, has gone missing and Vinny has become obsessed with the idea that Mr Rice had somehow had a hand in this disappearance.

Debbie and I are agreed on one thing (and one thing only), we loathe Mr Rice. We loathe the way he eats with his mouth half-open and the way he grinds his teeth when he's finished eating. We loathe the way he whistles tunelessly through those teeth when they aren't eating or grinding. We particularly loathe the way, at night, those same teeth grin out at us from a glass on the bathroom shelf.

I'm repelled at having to share a bathroom with him, not just because of the teeth but for the overwhelming smells he leaves behind — of shaving-foam and Brylcreem and the unmistakable (but not to be dwelt on) smell of male excrement. Once or twice I've encountered him coming out of the bathroom in the morning, with his dressing-gown hanging open and something slack, like a pale fungus, flopping out from its lair. 'Oops,' Mr Rice says with a leering grin. '*Death of a Salesman,*' I fantasize grimly to Charles.

'Men,' Vinny mutters with feeling. (Vinny was herself once married, but only briefly.) It seems men fall into one of several categories — there are the weak fathers, the ugly brothers, the evil villains, the heroic woodcutters and, of course, the handsome princes — none of which seems entirely satisfactory somehow.

'What's wrong?' Eunice asks impatiently as we walk home, Audrey-less, as usual, from school. I don't know, I have this peculiar feeling — both familiar and at the same time unknown, a dizzy, fizzy kind of feeling as if someone had dropped an Alka-Seltzer into my bloodstream. 'Bloodstream,' I say thickly to Eunice. We're taking a shortcut, to save time (but where will we put it? In the banks of wild thyme?) standing in the middle of a bridge over the canal and Eunice looks over the parapet in alarm at the murky wool-wasted water below.

'Maybe you've got a thing about bridges,' she says earnestly, more like Freud than Brunel. 'If you're frightened of crossing bridges it's called —'

Oh no, here we go again — Eunice has disappeared, the bridge itself has gone but — luckily — has been replaced by another one, little more than a series of wooden planks. The snicket, Green Man's Ginnel, that the bridge leads into is still there but the lamppost that overlooks its entrance has gone, as have the warehouses either side of it, replaced now by a couple of rough-looking wooden buildings.

I venture cautiously into the ginnel and emerge the other side into Glebelands market-place.

It still *is* the market-place, that much is clear – the market-cross stands where it always does, in the middle of the square and Ye Olde Sunne Inne is there on the other side, no words announcing its name any more, just the sign of the sun on a wooden board – not the present one, a garish yellow thing, but a muted, old-gold kind of sun. I expect it's not called Ye Olde Sunne Inne any more either, just the Sun Inn probably, because we're obviously back in the days when it was new, as it's just a hovel of its former self. Indeed, we seem to be back in Ye Olde Glebelands if the evidence of my eyes is to be believed.

Wooden carts barrel across the cobblestones, fishwives in sixteenth-century fustian are yelling their wares. A couple of dandies in velvet preen themselves on the street corner and when I approach them I catch a smell of something rank and unwashed. Will they look at me and scream? Can they see me? Can they hear me?

When I was in a time warp last time (not often we get to say things like that, thank goodness) the man I met in the field seemed to be able to communicate very well indeed, but this pair stare right through me and no matter how much I shout and jump up and down it seems I am invisible. Of course, if the laws of physics have been overturned there's no reason for things to remain constant from one experience to the next. Chaos could break out at any moment. Probably has.

I push open the door of The Sun, or Ye Sunne, I may as well see what it used to be like. This is, after all, the underage haunt of Carmen and myself (how confused my tenses feel), we have spent many a shadowy hour lurking in the Snug when we should have been in science class. If only I had paid more attention in Physics instead of dropping it for German. The front door in 1960 is a bright shiny red one, but in this unknown year of Our Lord it is a two-part wooden stable affair. Perhaps I should introduce myself with 'I come from the future'?

Maybe this is my own form of the moon illusion, maybe I've got the wrong set of references and am misinterpreting the phenomenal world?

There are only a couple of people inside, looking like extras from *The Private Lives of Elizabeth and Essex,* only a lot scruffier than is usual in Hollywood. They're all staring gloomily into their pewter tankards as if they don't know the Renaissance has ever happened.

In the shadows, in the corner of a high oak booth, there's a man with his eyes closed, he's quite young, in his twenties somewhere, and there's an odd familiar feel to him as if I've met him in the present – or what was the present in my immediate past but is now the future, if I ever go back there. Dearie, dearie me.

The man opens his eyes and looks at me. Not *through* me, like everyone else, but *at* me and he gives me a smile, sort of lop-sided and cynical, a smile of recognition, and he raises his tankard to me and I have an overwhelming desire to go over and talk to him because I think he knows me, not the everyday, exterior me, but the interior Isobel. The real me. The true self. But just as I take my first step towards him everything vanishes, just like before.

It isn't opening time yet and Ye Olde Sunne Inne seems to be deserted. It's definitely the present again – beer mats and beer towels and pineapple-shaped ice-buckets. I leave the Snug and wander through the Lounge and the Public Bar and finally find the back door of the kitchens open. I come down a passage full of dustbins and open a door and find myself on the market square again and see Eunice coming out of Green Man's Ginnel looking puzzled and I hail her from the other side of the square.

'Where did you go?' she asks crossly when she's negotiated the traffic. 'Gephyrophobia,' she says unexpectedly.

'Pardon?'

'Gephyrophobia – fear of bridges.'

'Right,' I say vaguely.

'Dromophobia – fear of crossing the street? Potamophobia – fear of rivers? Perhaps,' Eunice says airily, 'some deep-seated terror in your past is coming back to revisit you.'

What is she going on about? 'What are you going on about, Eunice?'

'You can have a phobia about anything, fire for example – pyrophobia – or insects – acaraphobia – or the sea – thalassophobia.'

Eunicephobia, that's what I have. I walk quickly across the road and jump on a bus without looking at the number of it and leave Eunice weaving in between cars, trying to follow me. I personally, for no discernible reason, have discovered a rip in the fabric of time, free-falling through its wormholes and snickets as easily as opening a door.

Are there other people who are dropping in and out of the past and not bothering to mention it in everyday conversation (as you wouldn't)? But let's face it, if it comes right down to it, which is more likely – a disruption in the space-time continuum or some form of madness?

What is the fabric of time like? Black silk? A smooth twill, a rough tweed? Or lacy and fragile like something Mrs Baxter would knit?

How can I trust reality when the phenomenal world appears to be playing tricks on me at every turn? Consider the dining-room, for example. I walk into it one day and find it has a quite different air, as if it's changed in some subtle and inexplicable way. It's as if someone's been playing What's Wrong? from *The Home Entertainer*, where one person leaves the room and the others move a chair or change a picture so that he (or more likely she, it seems) has to guess what's different when he comes back in. That's what it's like in the dining-room, only more so, as if, in fact, it isn't really our dining-room at all. As if the dining-room is a looking-glass room, a facsimile, a dining-room pretending to be the dining-room . . . no, no, no, this way utter madness lies.

Debbie comes in the room behind me. She's wearing a home-made version of a Tudor costume that unnerves me for a moment.

'Why are you dressed like that?' I've tried very hard to forget my trip down memory lane to Ye Olde Sunne and this is an unpleasant reminder.

She looks down at her dress as if she's never seen it before and then stares at me with her little eyes. 'Oh, dress rehearsal,' she says suddenly as if she's been translating what I said, 'Midsummer what'sit.'

I could tell her that she doesn't smell high enough to be authentic but I don't bother. 'Izzie?'

'Mm?'

'Do you think there's something missing from this room?'

'Missing?'

'Or something not quite right. It's like—'

'It's like it's the same room as before and yet it's not the same?'

She stares at me in astonishment, 'That's it exactly! Does that happen to you as well?'

'No.'

Perhaps there's a God (wouldn't *that* be amazing) who's playing some strange game with reality on the streets of trees. Or gods in the plural, more like.

'Anyway, I'm off,' Debbie says, gathering up her skirts.

'Your head perhaps?' I query.

'What?'

'Nothing?'

Will I ever escape the madness that is Arden?

Midsummer's Eve. The high-point of the year, more daylight than we know what to do with. In the Garden of Eden, every day was Midsummer's Eve. We should be jumping over bonfires or doing something magical. Instead Mrs Baxter and I are taking tea on the lawn, just as the master-builder intended. Audrey is languishing in her room. The Dog is sprawled on the grass, dreaming rabbits. Mrs Baxter's tortoiseshell cat is sleeping under a rhododendron. There's a fairy ring in the middle of the lawn, the grass flattened as if a miniature spaceship had landed there during the night.

Mrs Baxter's made a big glass jug of home-made lemonade and cuts slice after slice from a pink-coloured cake that looks like a bathroom sponge.

Mrs Baxter knows how to produce an amazing number of variations on a Victoria sponge, each embellished with a different decoration – chocolate cakes labelled with chocolate vermicelli, lemon cakes tagged with jellied lemon slices and coffee cakes signposted with walnut halves that resemble the brains of tiny rodents. Vinny has never even baked a cake, let alone been initiated into the protocol of decorating them.

Mrs Baxter also eats a lot of her cake of course and sometimes after she's eaten several slices back to back she'll put her hand over her mouth and laugh, 'Dearie me, I'll be *turning* into a cake soon!' What kind of cake would Mrs Baxter turn into? A vanilla sponge, soft and crumbly and full of buttercream.

'No wonder you're so bloody fat,' Mr Baxter says to her. Mr Baxter himself has never been seen to eat cake ('He's not a cake hand,' Mrs Baxter says sadly).

Mrs Baxter always gives me an extra slice of cake, wrapped in a paper napkin, to take home for Charles. Anyone watching me scurrying home from Sithean would think that there was some kind of endless birthday party taking place inside.

Today, in honour of the sun, Mrs Baxter has strayed from her usual beige spectrum and is wearing a sun-dress with brightly coloured red and white candy stripes, like an awning, or a deck-chair. It has thin red shoelace-straps and a lot of Mrs Baxter's flesh is on show – her fat arms and dimpled elbows and the voluptuously maternal cleft of her cleavage in which pink cake crumbs have lodged. Mrs Baxter's skin has turned to the colour of cinder toffee from working in the garden and she's covered in big freckles like conkers. She looks hot to the touch and I have to stifle a desire to jump down into the chasm of Mrs Baxter's bosom and get lost there for ever.

Mrs Baxter sighs happily, 'It's just right for playing Human Croquet,' but doesn't elaborate on whether she means the lawn or the weather or the mood. 'Of course,' she adds, 'we don't have enough people just now.'

Mr Baxter appears suddenly on the lawn, casting his menacing shadow over the tea-tray like an evil sundial and Mrs Baxter's cup trembles in its saucer. Mr Baxter gazes into the distance, far beyond the Albertine, towards the rise of green that is Boscrambe Woods.

'Cuppie, dear?' Mrs Baxter enquires, holding up a cup and saucer as if to make it clear what she means. Mr Baxter looks at her and seeing her sun-hat – a red plaited-straw coolie hat – frowns and says, 'Just come home from the paddy-fields, have you?' and Mrs Baxter knocks over the milk jug in her hurry to pour Mr Baxter's cuppie (they are an incredibly clumsy family). 'Silly me,' she says with a big smile that owes nothing to being happy. 'Nothing better to do?' he asks, raising an eyebrow at the bird-table. It is not the birds he is questioning though.

Mr Baxter doesn't like to see people idle. He's an auto-didact ('That's how I avoided the pit,' he explains darkly) and resents people who've been 'given things on a plate'. Maybe that's why he doesn't like cake.

'What are you doing?' he asks me gruffly.

'Just killing time until the play,' I mumble through a mouthful of cake. ('Oh dearie me, don't do that,' Mrs Baxter murmurs.)

Mr Baxter sits down, rather abruptly, on the grass next to where I'm sprawled in a deck-chair, exposing his thin, hairy legs above his grey socks. He's out of place in Arcadia, he prefers sitting on straight-backed chairs and watching parallel lines of desks stretching towards infinity. 'There's greenfly on the rose,' he says to Mrs Baxter in a tone that's suggestive of moral improbity rather than pest infestation. 'You're going to have to spray it.' Mrs Baxter hates spraying things. She never flattens spiders or bashes wasps or *cracks!* fleas, even house-flies are allowed to buzz freely around Sithean when Mr Baxter's back is turned. Mrs Baxter has an agreement with creeping and flying things, she doesn't kill them if they don't kill her.

Mr Baxter's smell rises up on a current of warm air towards me – shaving-cream and Old Holborn – and I try not to inhale.

'I spy with my little eye,' Mrs Baxter says hopefully, 'something beginning with "T",' and Mr Baxter shouts, 'For God's sake, Moira, can I get a bit of peace, please?' so that we don't find out what the 'T' is. Perhaps it's Theseus, even now striding across the field under the harsh suburban sunshine to exclaim that his nuptial hour is drawing on apace. 'Oh, they've started!' Mrs Baxter says excitedly, 'I must go and fetch Audrey.'

The play's the thing, but in this case a very bad thing and I shall draw a non-existent curtain over the Lythe Players' version of *A Midsummer Night's Dream*. It is comic where it should be lyrical, tedious where it should be comic and there is not even the slightest speck of magic in it. Mr Primrose, playing Bottom, could not be a rude mechanical if he rehearsed until the crack of doom and the girl pretending to be Titania, Janice Richardson who works in the Post Office on Ash Street, is fat with a squeaky voice. (But who knows, perhaps that's what fairies are like.)

Debbie comes home ashen-faced and at first I think this is on account of her dreadful performance – she may as well have handed the part over to the prompt – but she whispers to me over a mug of Bournvita, 'The wood.'

'The wood?'

'The wood, the wood,' she repeats, like Poe trying to write a poem, 'in the play,' she hisses, 'Midsummer what'sits?'

'Yes?' I say patiently.

'My thingie.'

'Character?'

'Yes, my character gets lost in the wood, doesn't she?' (The Lady Oak has heroically stood in for a thousand trees for the Players.)

'Yes?'

Debbie looks round the kitchen, a weird expression on her face, she seems to be having a lot of difficulty putting her thoughts into words.

'What's wrong?'

She drops her voice so low that I can hardly hear her, 'I was in a wood, for real, I was lost in a bloody great forest. For hours,' she adds and begins to cry. I think she's been too much in the sun. Shall I tell her about the ginnels and snickets and vennels of time? No, I don't think so. 'Perhaps you should see a psychiatrist?' I suggest gently and she runs out of the room in horror.

So there we have it. We are both as mad as tea-party hatters.

It's late, Midsummer's Eve has nearly given way to Midsummer's Day. Not a mouse stirs in the house. I draw a glass of water from the kitchen tap; tap water always tastes slightly brackish in Arden as if there's something slowly rotting in the cistern.

The kitchen feels as if someone's just walked out of it. I stand on the back doorstep and sip the water. My skin feels warm from the heat it's soaked up in Mrs Baxter's garden. I can smell the warmth still rising from the soil and the bitter-green scent of nettles. A thin paring of yellow moon has made a sickle-split in the sky and a star hangs on its bottom cusp, a rich jewel on the cheek of night.

I miss my mother. The ache that is Eliza comes out of nowhere, squeezing my heart and leaving me bereft. This is how she affects me – I'll be crossing the road, queuing for a bus, standing in a shop and suddenly, for no discernible reason, I want my mother so badly that I can't speak for tears. Where is she? Why doesn't she come?

The clock on the Lythe Church chimes the witching hour. *Caw.* A shuffling of feathers and leaves from the Lady Oak.

Under my feet moles mine and worms tunnel unseen. A bat flits through the ocean of darkness. Somewhere, far away, a dog howls and something moves, the black shape of a figure walking across the field. I could swear it has no head. But when I look again, it's disappeared.

PAST

HALF-DAY CLOSING

CHARLOTTE AND LEONARD FAIRFAX, PILLARS OF THE COMMUNITY, although Leonard soon a broken pillar, dead of a stroke in 1925 and robbed of the chance to enjoy his fine new house on the streets of trees.

Charlotte took over the business as if she had licensed grocery in her blood rather than enamelware. Charlotte, the Fairfax matriarch, embracing her widowhood with such Victorian vigour that she was known by all and sundry as the Widow Fairfax.

The Widow liked her fine house, the finest of them all on the streets of trees. It had five bedrooms, a downstairs cloakroom, a butler's pantry and airy attic rooms with fancy gables, in one of which the Widow kept Vera, her domestic drudge. Vera had an excellent view from her window of the Lady Oak, and beyond that to the haze of hills that looked like the work of a good watercolourist and, just visible in the distance, the dark green smudge that was Boscrambe Woods.

The Widow liked her big garden with its fruit trees and bushes, she liked the long drive at the front with its pink gravel chips and she liked the pretty wrought-iron and glass conservatory at the back which the master-builder had added as an afterthought and where the Widow kept her cacti.

The Widow had nice things. The Widow had things nice (people said). She had blue and white Delft bowls filled with hyacinths in the spring and poinsettias in her Satsuma ware at Christmas. She had good Indian carpets on her oak parquet and raw silk covers on cushions that were braided and tasselled like something from a sultan's divan. And in the living-room she had a chandelier, small, George the Third, with ropes of glass beads and big pear-drop crystals like a giant's tears.

Madge had escaped long ago by marrying an adulterous bank clerk in Mirfield and producing another three children.

Vinny looked as if she dined only on hard crusts and dry bones and was as sour as the malt vinegar that she dispensed by the pint from the stoneware flagon at the back. Vinegary Vinny, as old as the century but not quite as war-torn, born an old maid, but none the less married briefly after the First World War to a Mr Fitzgerald – a non-combatant chartered librarian with manic depressive tendencies – a man considerably older than his spinsterish wife. Vinny's feelings about Mr Fitzgerald's death (of pneumonia in 1926) were never entirely clear, although, as she confided to Madge, there was a certain relief in being released from the duties of married love. Vinny remained, however, in the small marital home which she had briefly shared with Mr Fitzgerald in Willow Road.

This at least, was her own domain, unlike the licensed grocery which her mother ran with a hand of iron and in which she was relegated to the role of mere shop assistant. 'I could be as good a businesswoman as Mother if she would let me,' she wrote to Madge-in-Mirfield, 'but she never gives me any responsibility.' The business was destined to be Gordon's and as soon as he finished school the Widow made him wrap himself up in a white grocer's apron and was very annoyed when he sneaked out of the house at night to go to classes at the technical institute in Glebelands. 'Everything he needs to know is right here,' the Widow said, pointing to the middle of her forehead as if it were a bull's-eye. Uncomfortable in his grocer's apron, Gordon stood behind the polished mahogany counter looking like he might be living a quite different life inside his head.

Then another war came and changed everything. Gordon became a hero, flying through the blue sky above England in his Spitfire. The Widow was excessively proud of her fighter-pilot son. 'Apple of her eye,' Vinny wrote to Madge-in-Mirfield. 'Blue-eyed boy,' Madge-in-Mirfield wrote back. Gordon was not blue-eyed. He was green-eyed and handsome.

Eliza was a mystery. Nobody knew where she came from, although she claimed it was Hampstead. She said *Hempstid* the way royalty might. She indicated, although not in a way you could pin down for certain, that there was blue blood, if not money, somewhere. 'The ruddy silver spoon's still in her mouth,' Madge said to Vinny when they first met Eliza. Her accent *was* odd, very out of place in Arden with its nicely buffed-up northern vowels. Eliza sounded stranded somewhere between a very expensive boarding-school and a brothel (or to put it another way, upper-class).

The first time that any of Gordon's family met the not-so-blushing bride was at the wedding. The Widow had been hoping for a nice quiet wife for her baby boy – drab with brown hair and an ability to budget. A girl who hadn't been too educated and with ambitions that stretched no further than a local public school for the clutch of Fairfax grandchildren that she would produce. Whereas Eliza was a – 'Vamp?' Madge supplied eagerly.

For her wedding, Eliza – as slender as a willow, as straight as a Douglas fir (*pseudotsuga menziesii*) – wore a navy-blue suit with a tiny pinched-in waist, with a white gardenia in her buttonhole and a little black hat made of feathers, like a ballerina's headband. The bad black swan. No bouquet, just crimson fingernails. The Widow gave a not-so-discreet little shudder of horror.

With her long steel-wool hair wired back in a bun, she looked like a Sicilian Widow rather than an English one. Her feelings about the wedding might be deduced from the fact that she had chosen to dress in black from top to toe. She watched intently as Gordon ('my baby!') slipped the wedding ring onto the finger of this peculiar creature. You would almost think she was trying to will Eliza's finger to drop off.

There was something odd about Eliza, they were all agreed, even Gordon, although what it was no-one could quite say. Standing behind her in the register office, Madge experienced a convulsion of envy as she noticed how thin Eliza's ankles were beneath her unpatriotically long skirt. Like bird-bones. Vinny wanted to snap them. And her neck like a stalk. Snap.

The Widow had insisted on paying for the reception at the Regency Hotel in case anyone thought that the Fairfaxes couldn't afford a proper wedding. It was clear that no-one on Eliza's side was going to turn up, let alone pay. Eliza, apparently, had nobody. *They're all dead, darling,* she murmured, her dark eyes tragic with unshed tears. The same tragedy seemed to have infected her voice, throaty with notes of whisky, nicotine, velvet. She was Gordon's treasure, found accidentally, Gordon plucking her from the wreckage of a bombed building in London when he was there on leave, even going back to retrieve her missing shoe (*they were* **so** *expensive, darling*).

My hero, she smiled as he placed her gently on the pavement. *My hero,* she said and Gordon was lost, drowning in her whisky eyes. *The age of chivalry,* bomb-dusted Eliza murmured, *is alive and well. And is called?*

'Gordon, Gordon Fairfax.'

Wonderful.

'Bit of a rush do, eh?' Madge's bank clerk husband winked, at no-one in particular, and Eliza swooped on him from nowhere and said, *Darling, are we really family now? So hard to believe,* and he retreated under a cascade of *Hempstid* vowels. 'Hoity-toity, that one,' Vinny said to Madge.

Eliza had dark, dark hair. Glossy and curly. Black as a crow, a rook, a raven. 'A bit of the tarbrush?' Vinny mouthed across the wedding cake to Madge. Madge semaphored amazement with her sherry glass and mouthed back, 'Wop?' Eliza, who could lip-read at a hundred paces, thought her new sisters-in-law looked like fish. Cod and Halibut. 'Plummy,' said Vinny dismissively to Madge over the sherry-toast to bride and bridegroom. 'Fruity,' said Madge's husband, raising a lecherous eyebrow.

Really, Eliza said to the bridegroom, *anyone would think I was a piece of wedding cake*, and Gordon thought that he'd like to eat her up. Every last crumb, so that no-one else could ever have her. What wedding cake? grumbled the Widow, for this was a wartime cake made with pre-war dates found at the back of the licensed grocery's store-room. A hasty affair, 'an expensive do,' the Widow said to her fish daughters, 'for a cheap you-know-what.' Why have they married so quickly? 'Something fishy,' said Vinny-the-Halibut. 'Suspicious,' said the Widow. 'Highly,' said Madge-the-Cod.

Do they **know** *Queen Victoria's dead?* Eliza asked her new husband. 'Probably not,' he laughed, but nervously. The Widow and Vinny lived in the Dark Ages. And they liked it there. Eliza said she couldn't decide which would be worse, to be Vinny in Willow Road or to be Madge-in-Mirfield. She laughed loudly when she said this and everyone turned to stare at her.

Charles was born on a train, an event due to the capriciousness of Eliza who decided she needed an outing to the Bradford Alhambra when any normal woman in her condition would be sitting at home with her feet up, resting her piles and her varicose veins.

'Premature,' the Widow said, warily cradling tiny Charles in her arms. 'But healthy, thank goodness.' Softened, momentarily, by grandmotherhood, she attempted a smile in the direction of Eliza. Vinny inspected Bradford from the ward window. She'd never been this far from home.

'And *big*,' the Widow added, admiring and sarcastic and moved – all at the same uncomfortable time. 'Just think,' she said to Eliza, her eyes narrowing as the sarcastic won the battle, 'what he would have been like if he'd gone the full nine months.'

Oh please – don't! Eliza said, shivering theatrically and lighting up a cigarette.

'A honeymoon baby,' the Widow said speculatively, as she stroked the baby's cheek. ('Whose honeymoon though? Eh?' Vinny wrote to Madge-in-Mirfield.) 'I wonder who he looks like?' Vinny wrote to Gordon. 'He certainly doesn't look like *you*, Gordon!' No-one had more artificial exclamation marks than Vinny! (No-one had written so many letters since the decline of the epistolary novel.)

He's an absolute cherub, Eliza said and, *Oh God, I'd give anything for a gin, darling.*

Charles' arrival even made the papers –

GLEBELANDS BABY BORN ON TRAIN

the *Glebelands Evening Gazette* wrote possessively. That was how the Widow found out about her grandson, Eliza having neglected to send a message from the hospital where she was taken when the train finally pulled into the station. 'Trust her to make the headlines,' snapdragon Vinny sniffed.

Born on a train. People falling over themselves to help, the guard upgrading her to First so she had more room to grunt and groan (which she did in a very ladylike way, everyone agreed), the guard thinking that the way she said *Darling, you're an angel* showed she was a First Class type anyway. It was difficult to know what to put on Charles' birth certificate. He was a philosophical conundrum, like Zeno's arrow, a paradox on the space-time continuum. 'Where would you say he was born?' Gordon asked, when he was next home on leave. *Why, First Class, darling*, Eliza replied.

★

86

Charles, sadly, was rather ugly. 'Handsome is as handsome does,' declared the Widow, the mistress of the baffling cliché.

Eliza, however (naturally, being his mother), declared that he was the most beautiful baby that ever existed. *Charlie is ma darlin*, she sang softly to a nursing Charles, who stopped the suck-and-tug at her breast long enough to smile a gummy smile up at her. 'What a smiley baby,' the Widow said, unsure whether this was a good or a bad thing. Eliza bounced Charles on her lap and kissed the back of his neck. Vinny unclamped her lips long enough to say, 'He'll be spoilt.' *How wonderful for him*, Eliza said.

Gordon came home on leave at last and met his son, by now freckled like a giraffe and with a carrot-coloured tuft of hair sprouting from the middle of his large, bald head. 'Red hair!' Vinny said gleefully to Gordon. 'I wonder where he got that from?'

'He's a sturdy little chap, isn't he?' Gordon said, ignoring his sister. He had already fallen in love with his red-haired son. 'He doesn't look a bit like you,' Vinny persisted, as Gordon carried Charles around the house on his shoulders. 'He doesn't look like Eliza either,' Gordon said and that much, certainly, was true.

Then Gordon had to go and fly through the greyer skies of Europe. 'You would think,' Vinny sneered, 'that he was fighting the *Luftwaffe* single-handed.' 'Nerves of steel,' the Widow said. A man of iron. *Heart of gold*, said Eliza and laughed her bubbling, rather frightening laugh. Before the end of his leave Gordon had managed to get another baby started (*an accident, darling!*).

'You'll keep an eye on Eliza, won't you?' Gordon said to his mother before he left. 'How can I not?' she said, her syntax as stiff as her back. 'She's under the same roof, after all.' In the bathroom, damp and steamy, the Widow had to brush through a forest of Eliza's stockings hanging everywhere and wondered how this could be part of her duty. And another thing, the Widow thought, how did she get these stockings? Eliza was never short of anything – stockings, perfume, chocolate – what was she doing to get them? That's what the Widow would like to know.

'At least this child won't be born on the move,' the Widow said to Eliza. The Widow was worried that Eliza might be thinking about the Turkish Baths in Harrogate or a day-trip to Leeds. Eliza smiled enigmatically. 'Bloody Mona Lisa,' Vinny said out loud to herself as she smoked cigarettes for her lunch at the back of the licensed grocery.

Eliza drifted into the shop, as pregnant as a full-blown sail. She sat on the bentwood chair reserved for weary customers next to the huge red, gold and black tea-caddies with their faded paintings of Japanese ladies, big enough to hide a small child in. Eliza pulled Charles on her knee and sucked his fingers, one by one. Vinny twitched with disgust. *He makes me laugh*, she said, and as if to prove it she laughed her ridiculous laugh. A lot of things made Eliza laugh and not many of them seemed very funny to the Widow and Vinny.

The Widow ran her dust-seeking fingers over the black bottles of amontillado, checked the moulded butter-pats (thistles and crowns), the bacon-slicer, the cheese-wires. She rang sales into the huge brass till, as big as a small pipe organ, with such ferocity that it flinched on the solid mahogany counter. Straight as an ironing-board and almost as thin. Her skin as pale as pale can be, like white paper that had been creased and pleated a hundred times. *The old hag.* The old hag with her wormwood tongue and her hag-hedge hair the colour of gunmetal and ashes. Eliza sang to cover her thoughts because no-one was going to hear what went on inside Eliza's head, not even Gordon. Especially not Gordon.

Eliza's belly was like a drum. She placed Charles down on the floor. The drum was beating from the inside. Vinny could see something pushing against the drumskin – a hand or a foot – and tried not to look, but her eyes kept being drawn back to this invisible baby. *It's trying to escape*, Eliza said and, from the handbag at her feet, she took out her powder-compact, the expensive one that Gordon had bought for her – blue enamel with mother-of-pearl palm trees – and put on more lipstick. She rubbed her red lips together, as red as fresh blood and poppies, and smacked them open again for

Vinny and the Widow's disapproval. She was wearing a funny hat, all sharp angles like a Cubist painting.

I'm going out, she said, standing up so quickly, so awkwardly, that the bentwood chair crashed onto the wooden floor of the shop. 'Where?' the Widow asked, counting money, making little piles of coins on the counter. *Just out*, Eliza said, lighting up a cigarette and dragging hard on it. To Charles, she said, *Darling, will you stay here with Auntie Vinny and Granny Fairfax?*, and 'Auntie Vinny' and 'Granny Fairfax' glared at this interloper in their lives and wished that the war would finish and Gordon come home and take Eliza away and set up house with her somewhere far, far away. Like the moon.

The baby arrived three weeks early and Eliza claimed to be as much surprised as anybody. The Widow, determined not to be caught unawares a second time, was already on a war-footing.

The fire had been laid in the hearth ready (these were drizzling spring days) and the Widow had the bed made up with sheets both boiled and bleached. A rubber sheet and a chamber pot were stowed discreetly under the bed and an army of washbasins and ewers had been marshalled for the natal conflict.

Widow's intuition made her come in from the conservatory where she was worshipping her cacti and she found Eliza on the stairs, clutching an acorn finial, doubled up in pain. Eliza was wearing her hat and coat and carrying her handbag and insisted that she was going out for a walk. 'Fiddlesticks,' said the Widow, who could recognize a madwoman when she saw one, not to mention a madwoman in an advanced state of labour, and she escorted Eliza firmly up the stairs to the second-best bedroom, Eliza struggling all the way. 'Hellcat,' the Widow hissed under her breath. She left Eliza sitting on the bed while she went off to boil important kettles. When she returned she found the bedroom door locked and no matter how much she rattled and shook, shouted and cajoled, the entrance to the delivery room remained barred. Vinny was summoned, as was the lumpen maid Vera and the man who helped the Widow with the garden. He eventually managed to kick the door in, but only after many encouraging shrieks from the Widow.

They found a tranquil scene in front of them. Eliza was lying on the bed, still with her outdoor clothes on, and was cradling something small and new and slightly bloody, wrapped in a pillowcase from the bed. She smiled triumphantly at the Widow and Vinny, *Your new granddaughter.* When the Widow finally managed to get her hands on the baby she found that the cord was already severed. A thrill of horror, like invisible electricity, jolted the Widow's flat body. '*Gnawed,*' she whispered to Vinny and Vinny had to run to the bathroom, hand clutched over her mouth.

And so Isobel was born on the streets of trees, near the muddled middle of the twentieth century, in a country at war, on the lumpy feather mattress in the second-best bedroom of Arden, her very first breath scented with the sour sappiness of new hawthorn.

The next morning the Widow went into the second-best bedroom, piously bearing a cup of tea for Eliza, and found Eliza, Charles and the baby all in a muddled heap together in the middle of the lumpy bed. The Widow put the cup and saucer down on the bedside table. The bedroom was awash with Eliza's expensive underwear, flimsy garments made from silk and lace that provoked the Widow's disgust. Charles was snoring gently, his forehead damp with sleep. Eliza rolled over exposing a naked arm, round and thin, but didn't wake. For a second, the Widow had a troublesome vision of her son in this bed, his clean, heroic limbs trammelled in semi-naked harlotry. She had a sudden desire to retrieve the chamber pot from under the bed and beat Eliza about the head with it. Or better still, she thought, looking at Eliza's white throat, strangle her with one of her own black-market stockings.

'Like animals,' the Widow said, slicing the cheese-wire fiercely through the centre of a big Cheddar, 'all in the same bed, and her with hardly anything on. What will they grow up like? She'll suffocate that baby. That isn't how we dealt with babies in my day.' Vinny imagined Eliza's milk-swollen breasts, smelt her scent – perfume and nicotine – and grimaced.

The Widow peered into the depths of the rosewood fretwork of the crib. 'There,' she said with unaccustomed affection, and Eliza tucked in the baby blanket with blue rabbits embroidered on it, blue for Charles. 'Gordon's daughter,' the Widow said, with more certainty than she'd ever said, 'Gordon's son.'

'She's got your eyes,' the Widow added generously. 'She's got your everything,' Vinny said, uncharmed. *I wish,* Eliza said softly, *that she will blossom and grow.* 'What a silly thing to wish for,' Vinny said.

Look, said Eliza softly, pulling back the shawl from the sooty head, *isn't she perfect?* Vinny made a face.

'What are you going to call her?' the Widow asked. Eliza ignored her. 'You could call her Charlotte,' the Widow pursued, 'it *is* a lovely name.'

Yes, but it's yours, Eliza purred and stroked the shell-whorl of the baby's ear. *Her ears are petals,* she said, *and her lips are little pink flowers, and her skin is made from lilies and carnations and her teeth—*

'She hasn't got any teeth, for Christ's sake!' Vinny snapped.

She's a little May bud. A new leaf. I might call her Mayblossom, Eliza laughed her gurgling laugh that set everyone's nerves on edge.

'No you bloody won't,' said the Widow.

Rock-a-bye-baby, Eliza sang, *on the tree-top,* and whispered the baby's name in its petal-ear. *Is-o-bel,* a peal of bells. *Isobel Fairfax.* Now the baby's life could begin. *When the bough breaks, the cradle will fall.*

'Isobel?' snorted the very unmerry Widow, and then was unable to think of anything else to say.

Darling, Eliza wrote to Gordon, *you'd better come home soon or I'm going to kill your bloody family.*

Life in the ever-after wasn't as happy as it should have been. Life, in fact, was *a bloody bore*, Eliza, hissing, *we have to get a place of our own*, at every opportunity. To Gordon. Gordon was no longer a hero, no longer flying in skies of any colour. He'd wrapped himself in his long white apron again and turned himself back into a grocer. Eliza was disappointed with this civilian transformation. The Widow, needless to say, was delighted.

A grocer, Eliza said as if the word itself was distasteful. 'Well, what did you expect him to do?' the Widow snapped. 'It's what he was born to,' she added grandly as if Gordon were the prince-in-waiting to some vast grocery empire.

Gordon was still a hero to Charles, especially when he did magic tricks for him, learned in the idle hours when he was waiting to scramble into the air. He knew how to take coins from Charles' fingers and make eggs appear from behind the Widow's ears. He was particularly good at disappearing tricks. When he worked his magic on the Widow she said, 'Oh Gordon,' in the same tone that Eliza said, *Oh Charles*, when Charles did something that amused her.

Eliza watched the Widow sweep up leaves on the back lawn. The Widow brushed furiously at birch and sycamore and apple, but the leaves were coming down like rain and every time she managed to make a pile the wind whisked them up in the air again. *She might as well try to sweep the stars from the sky.* 'I wish she'd just let us play in them,' Charles said glumly and Eliza laughed, *Play? The word's not even in the old hag's vocabulary.*

Charles and Isobel pasted dead leaves into a scrapbook, with glue that smelt of fish (*Vinny's blood*, Eliza informed them). Charles wrote the name of the tree beneath each leaf – sycamore and ash, oak and willow. The leaves had been salvaged from the Widow or scavenged off the pavements when Eliza and Isobel walked Charles home from school in the afternoons.

From the horse chestnuts on Chestnut Avenue they'd collected handfuls of the spiky green seed-pods that looked like medieval weapons and Eliza had shown them how to open them, splitting one with her sharp red fingernails, peeling back the soft white shawl around the brown chestnut inside, saying, *You're the first person in the world to see that.*

Gordon stood in the doorway and laughed, 'Not quite the same thing as discovering Niagara, Lizzy,' and then he offered to take Charles away for a manly tutorial on soaking conkers in vinegar, because it turned out that they really *were* medieval weapons, but before he could, Eliza threw a handful of unpeeled chestnuts at Gordon's head and he said, very coldly, to her, 'Let's have a bit of peace in this house for a change, shall we, Lizzy?'

Eliza made a face at his retreating back and when he'd gone said, *Peace, ha! There'll be no peace in this house until that old hag is dead and in her coffin and six feet under.* 'Six feet under what?' Charles asked. Charles had got glue all over him, a big leaf was stuck to his elbow. *Why, under the bed, of course,* Eliza said breezily as she glimpsed Vinny in the hall.

'There are leaves everywhere,' Vinny complained, coming into the room. 'It's worse in here than it is outside.' The leaves drove her out of the room again and she went to find out where Vera had got to with the tea-tray, oblivious to the rowan leaf, complete with its scarlet berries, that had attached itself to her salt-sprinkled grey hair like a strange botanical barrette.

'Moan, moan, moan,' Charles whispered. 'Why doesn't she like us?' Charles' mission in life was to make people laugh but he'd set himself a hard task with Vinny.

She doesn't like anyone, she doesn't even like herself, Eliza scoffed.

'She doesn't even *live* here,' Charles muttered, but was cheered by the sight of Vera slouching in with a tray piled high with tea and buttered toast, Eccles cakes and the Widow's apricot tea loaf. *God,* Eliza said, sucking hard on a cigarette, *cake, cake, bloody cake, that's all you get in this house.*

'Sounds all right to me,' Charles said.

★

93

After tea Eliza got out the fat wax crayons and colouring books for them on the dining-room table. Eliza was a generous art critic, everything her children did was *absolutely wonderful*. At the other end of the table, the Widow said something indistinct. She was sitting with her glasses perched on the end of her nose, turning collars and cuffs ('waste not want not'). Eliza told Isobel that she should be an artist when she grew up. 'That won't put food on the table,' the Widow said. 'And you be careful with those crayons, Charles.'

Eliza said nothing, but if you were close enough to her, you could hear the voodoo words she was incanting under her breath, like a swarm of bees. The Widow wiped the crumbs of cake from her fingerbones and left the table.

Charles bent over his drawing, frowning in concentration. He was drawing clumsy ideal homes – square houses with pitch roofs and window-eyes and mouth-doors. Isobel drew a tree with golden-red leaves and Gordon came in and said, 'Oh Margaret, are you grieving over goldengrove unleaving' and gave her his increasingly sad smile and without looking at him Eliza said, *She really is rather good, isn't she?* and gave Isobel a radiant, intimate smile that cut out Gordon.

Gordon laughed and said, 'We should have more, you never know what they might turn out to be – Shakespeares and Leonardo da Vincis.'

'More what?' Charles asked without taking his eyes off the sun he was drawing, a big golden-spoked eye.

More nothing, Eliza said dismissively.

'Babies,' Gordon said to Charles. 'We should have another baby.'

Eliza pushed a lock of hair out of Isobel's eyes and said, *Whatever for?* Gordon and Eliza had whole conversations now using intermediaries.

'Because that's what people do,' Gordon said, turning Charles' drawing round as if he was looking at it, although it was obvious he wasn't. 'People who love each other, anyway.' But then he must have come under the influence of Eliza's silent hoodoo because he suddenly left the room as well. It was all exits and entrances these days in Arden.

'Where do you get babies from?' Charles asked, after he'd finished his picture with two birds flying through the sky like dancing Vs.

Eliza flicked open her gold lighter and lit a cigarette. 'From the baby shop, of course.'

The origin of babies was a confusing issue in Arden. According to the Widow, they were delivered by storks, but Vinny's version had them being left under gooseberry bushes. Eliza's answer seemed much more reasonable. Especially as there was a whole row of gooseberry bushes in the back garden and no baby had ever appeared under any of them. And as for storks, they didn't even live in this country – according to Gordon – so it was hard to see how English children (let alone Welsh or Scottish) could ever get born at all.

The Widow came back into the room and gave a cursory glance at their drawings. 'Trees have green leaves,' she said to Isobel, 'not red,' as if she had never opened her Widowed window-eyes and looked at autumn.

Children, Eliza said irritably after the Widow left the room, *why would anyone want children? I wish I'd never had any of the damn things*, so annoyed that one of the wax crayons snapped in two in her hands.

'But you love *us*, don't you?' Charles asked, a worried look on his face. Eliza started to laugh, a weird swooping noise, and said, *Good God, of course I do. I wouldn't be* **here** *now if it wasn't for you.*

Eliza spent her autumn days lying on the wicker lounger in the conservatory, wearing her sunglasses as if she was on the beach, even though the skies were dull, reading library books and drinking whisky and smoking cigarette after cigarette until the conservatory was full of a hazy blue fug. The Widow's cacti looked unhappy. So did the Widow.

'Lizzy,' Gordon said, at his most reasonable, persuasive, cajoling. Helpless. 'Lizzy, don't you think you could help out around the house a bit more? Vera has all on looking after us all and Mother does nothing but cook.'

My hands are full with the children, Eliza said, without taking her eyes off her book. Although as far as Gordon could see her hands were full with a cigarette and a large whisky and the children were sliding noisily down the stairs on tea-trays.

In the autumnal evenings, when the children were in bed, Gordon and Eliza and the Widow sat round the coal fire in the front room listening to the wireless or playing cards. The Widow suspected Eliza of cheating but couldn't prove it. (Yet.) Sometimes Gordon just sat and stared at the fire while the Widow put her scratchy records on the old-fashioned wind-up gramophone.

The Widow made a fuss about giving Gordon supper. 'He needs looking after,' she said pointedly to Eliza, as she cut him a piece of last year's Christmas cake and put a windmill-sail of Wensleydale on the top. *Oh God*, Eliza muttered to the George the Third chandelier, *they even have the bloody stuff with cheese*. 'Oh, I *am* sorry,' the Widow said, in her grand Northern duchess voice, 'Did *you* want some, Eliza?'

While Gigli sang "Che Gelida Manina" on the old wind-up, the Widow poured tea into flower-sprigged cups. Eliza took her tea without milk or sugar and every time the Widow poured her a cup she said, 'Oh, I don't know how you can!' and crumpled up her white paper face.

Through a mouthful of cake, Gordon made the mistake of making a joke, for his mother's benefit, about how Eliza never made cakes and Eliza looked at him through half-closed eyes and said, *No, but then I do fuck you*, so that Gordon sloshed his tea into his saucer and started to choke on his old Christmas cake. The Widow smiled the bright, polite smile of the partially deaf and said, 'What was that? What did she say?'

By November, the trees on the streets were almost bare apart from, here and there, a stray leaf that lingered, flapping like a mournful flag and there were no more leaves to collect when Charles went to and from Rowan Street Primary School. Charles hated school. Charles hated school so much that he couldn't eat his breakfast in the morning.

The Widow's philosophy of child nutrition was simple – as much as possible at every opportunity. She paid particular attention to breakfast and insisted Charles and Isobel ate porridge, eggs, poached or boiled, toast and marmalade and drank half a pint of milk from big glass tumblers. *They'll blow up like balloons*, Eliza said, breakfasting on her usual cigarettes and black coffee. 'You'll waste away to nothing,' the Widow said accusingly to her and Charles looked up in alarm from his egg. Eliza did look thin, but surely she couldn't get so thin that she disappeared?

Charles was wiped clean of his marmalade (rather roughly by the Widow, with an old flannel) and hustled into his blazer and cap. His fat lower lip started to tremble and he said, very quietly, in Eliza's direction, 'I don't want to go to school, Mummy.'

'Don't be silly,' the Widow said sharply, 'everyone has to go to school.' Rowan Street Primary was a dark cramped place that smelt of wet gabardine and plimsoll rubber and was staffed by sour-faced spinsters who must all have been found under the same gooseberry bush as Vinny. An extraordinary amount of physical violence took place within its brick walls – Charles came home with reports of daily floggings, canings and whippings (thankfully on other boys so far) perpetrated by the headmaster, Mr Baxter. 'There's nothing wrong with him being a stern disciplinarian,' the Widow said, mercilessly strapping Charles' huge leather satchel onto his small shoulders. 'Little boys are naughty and they have to find out what's what.'

Oh, and big boys too, Eliza said in her affected drawl, dragging hard on her cigarette and staring through narrowed eyes at Gordon, eating the Widow's full cooked breakfast. *I often show Gordon what's what, don't I, darling?* Eliza smiled like a cat in the sun and the Widow turned the colour of her home-pickled red cabbage and looked as if she'd like to brain Eliza with the big chrome teapot that always formed the centrepiece of the table. Gordon stoically ignored all of this and, standing up, he took a triangle of fried bread from his unfinished plate and said, 'Come on, old chap,' (being an officer in the war had influenced his previously plebeian vocabulary) 'I'll give you a lift to school in the car.' Forced to accept the inevitable, a halo of doom hovered over poor Charles' striped cap. When he went over to Eliza to kiss her goodbye, she whispered fiercely in his ear, *You tell me if Mr Baxter ever lays a finger on you and I'll rip his head off and pull his lungs out through his neck.* If there was one person in the world more frightening than Mr Baxter it was Eliza.

Christmas afforded two weeks of respite for Charles and he spent many patiently maladroit hours making paper chains and fashioning decorations out of silver milk bottle tops. *Lovely, darling*, Eliza said, garlanding herself with a chain of milk bottle tops under the mistaken impression that Charles had made her a necklace.

Gordon drove into the country and came back with an enormous fir tree, stuffed into the boot of the big black car, its roots still clagged with soil. Eliza stroked its branches tenderly as if it were a wild animal and said, *Smell that*, and they breathed in the scent of coldness and pine resin and something even more mysterious. Gordon tamed it by putting it in an old barrel wrapped in Christmas paper and stringing it with tiny coloured lanterns.

Eliza made little dwarves from tissue and crêpe, their tissue-paper faces had crayon smiles drawn on hastily and match-heads for eyes. Their pipe-cleaner arms and legs clung for dear life onto the tree. *Sweet, aren't they?* Eliza said to everyone, delighted with her handiwork and no-one had the heart to tell her how dreadful they were.

For Christmas, Gordon gave Eliza a Victorian gypsy ring – gold with little emerald and diamond starbursts. Eliza held it against her pale cheek and said, *Does it suit me?* to Charles. The Widow viewed Eliza through hooded hawk eyes, angry at the thought of how much the ring had cost her baby boy. She handed over her own dull and dutiful mother-in-law present – a boxed set of monogrammed handkerchiefs.

Gordon had bought Charles a magic set which was far too old for him. 'You bought that for yourself really,' Vinny said, as prickly as pine needles. (Vinny had not been herself since peace was declared.) *Make her disappear, won't you, darling?* Eliza whispered (loudly) to Gordon.

The Widow carved the Christmas pork, a paper crown askew on her bun of grey hair and Gordon proposed a toast to the future, in French wine, and Eliza gave Charles and Isobel a glass of watered-down wine. The Widow sipped at her glass of blood-red wine and said, 'Liberty Hall here – we all know that, don't we?'

Summer came in and brought with it new next-door neighbours. The old people who'd lived in Sherwood since it was built died within a week of each other and the house was sold to a Mr Baxter. The very same Mr Baxter – to Charles' unending horror – who was the headmaster at Rowan Street Primary. It did seem particularly unfair that Charles, after dodging Mr Baxter all day at school, wasn't even safe in his own house and garden. Charles was fated – whenever he kicked a ball it had to end up on Mr Baxter's side of the fence, whenever he chose to shout at the top of his lungs, which with Charles was frequently, it was Mr Baxter who was snoozing in a deck-chair on the other side of the privet.

There was a shy Mrs Baxter too. Younger than her husband and built to motherly specifications – short and soft with no hard edges, unlike bony Mr Baxter. Mrs Baxter changed the name of her house, getting the man who did odd-jobs for the Widow to take down the brass plate on the gate that said 'Sherwood' and replace it with a wooden one with the word '*Sithean*' carved into it. 'Waste of good brass,' was the Widow's opinion, though whether she meant metal or money was unclear.

'She-ann', Mrs Baxter explained to the Widow, was a Scottish word. Mrs Baxter was Scottish too and had a lovely accent, peat and heather and soft sandstone houses.

The Baxters had a daughter – Audrey – the same age as Isobel. Audrey was 'a timid little thing' (according to the Widow) with

hair the colour of falling maple leaves and eyes the colour of doves'
wings. Mr Baxter was very strict with both Audrey and Mrs Baxter.
How awful other people's families are, yawned Eliza.

The Widow didn't respond enthusiastically to Mrs Baxter's
neighbourly overtures – she believed in keeping yourself to yourself.
Who else would want her? Eliza said, lying in her swimming-costume
on a rug on the grass, her long thin limbs looking incredibly pale
as if they'd never seen the light before.

There were very few people that the Widow wished for
neighbourhood intercourse with. The Lovats were one of the
few families she courted ('Invite that little Malcolm home,'
she said to Charles, bribing him with barley sugar). She had an
unnatural respect for the medical profession and no qualms about
gynaecologists, never having had women's trouble.

Gordon came home one day and said, 'How about a holiday then?'
and Eliza said, *Not with her*. And so just the four of them went to the
seaside and stayed in a boarding-house where they were summoned
down to the evening meal by the landlady beating a copper gong
in the hallway and Gordon made the same joke every time about
J. Arthur Rank until Eliza said, *For Christ's sake, Gordon, put a sock
in it, will you?* and then he didn't make the joke any more.

Gordon hired a beach hut from the line of primary colours that
stretched along the promenade and devoted his time to building
spectacular sandcastles. Charles had to wear a floppy cotton sun hat
like a baby because his redhead's skin burnt so easily. '*Was* there
anyone in your family with red hair then?' Gordon asked, unusually
snide, but Eliza just stared at him from behind her impenetrable
sunglassed eyes.

They buried Eliza in the sand. She sat unconcerned, reading a
book and occasionally looking at her children over the top of her
sunglasses and smiling. (*You've got me prisoner!*) She wore a glamorous
red halter-neck swimming-costume and the hot sunshine they had
all week turned her white skin a deep exotic colour.

In the evenings, Eliza and Gordon went walking along the prom, Eliza dressed in one of her expensive dresses. And when they came back to their room Gordon unzipped her out of her dress and undid her necklace and ran his fingers over her warm brown skin and buried his face in her dark, dark hair until she laughed and said, *Sorry, darling, the baby shop's closed,* and Gordon said how come she was a slut with everyone but him? And Eliza laughed.

I'm going for a walk, Eliza said, getting up suddenly from her deck-chair, *don't anybody follow me,* she said in a warning voice when Gordon started to get up. *I'm suffocating.*

She was wearing a red cotton skirt over her red swimming-costume and she'd hitched the skirt up high on one side so that men, sitting dutifully on the beach with their wives and children, turned their heads slyly to follow Eliza's lazy gypsy progress along the shoreline. At one point she bent down to pick something up and examine it before wandering on her way.

She walked a long way, until she was just a distant flame of red at the extremity of vision. By the time she wandered back the sun was no longer hot and the tide was lapping at sandcastles all along the beach.

'I thought you were never coming back,' Gordon said when Eliza finally returned. She ignored him and put her hand out to Charles, saying, *Look what I found,* handing him a big spiral shell, its outside a rough calciferous white but its inside a shiny satin-pink, *the colour of a baby's insides,* Eliza said, and Gordon said, 'For Christ's sake, Lizzy.'

Eliza lit a cigarette and watched as a wave crept up to her thin brown feet, with their toes painted the colour of holly berries.

'Come on then,' Gordon said to Charles and Isobel, 'J. Arthur Rank's going to be calling us any minute and we don't want to miss our tea, do we?'

They climbed the pebble-dash concrete steps up to the promenade but Eliza stayed where she was, the waves lapping her ankles by now. 'Bloody Queen Canute,' said Gordon, who didn't usually swear, 'let her bloody drown.' But Charles cried out at this idea and ran back to drag Eliza by the hand.

'You could make a friend of her,' Gordon said to Eliza as they looked down on Mrs Baxter in her garden, 'she's not that much older than you.' They were standing in the attic bedroom but Charles and Isobel weren't in it, they were in the bath being supervised by the Widow who was pretending to be a U-boat captain so that Charles' fleet of little boats could destroy her. Gordon stood behind Eliza, his arms round her waist and his head resting on her shoulder. Eliza was trying to ignore his head on her shoulder, trying not to flinch and push him off.

Mrs Baxter was attacking the long-neglected grass in Sithean's garden, leaning all her weight on the handle of the push-and-pull lawnmower and stopping every few minutes to untwine the long wet grass stalks from the roller. The smell of grass clippings invaded the hot attic room. 'She shouldn't be doing that in her condition,' Gordon said (Mrs Baxter was pregnant), a frown of concern on his face. Mr Baxter came out and said something to his wife. 'He's a funny so-and-so,' Gordon said. Eliza backed away from the window, backed into Gordon who encircled her waist with his arms and started walking her backwards, like a prisoner, to Charles' little bed until Eliza jabbed her elbow hard into his ribs and kicked him with her heel on his shin, so that he fell back on the bed in surprise and pain.

Gordon lay on the bed for a long time listening to the sound of the German fleet being destroyed ('Achtung! Achtung!' the drowning Widow screamed) and the noise of Mrs Baxter's lawnmower clattering in the evening air. He listened to the sound of the front door banging shut. Eliza went out all the time in these long summer evenings. Where to? *Just out.*

'An Indian summer,' the Widow announced. It was September and all the leaves on the trees were turning an old green colour. Charles and Isobel had both had the chickenpox and Charles hadn't started the new school year yet, Isobel wasn't due to start for another year. 'They're as fit as fiddles!' Vinny declared crossly whenever she encountered them.

Breakfast was always a difficult time of the day. The Widow was at her most officious, Eliza at her most indolent. '*You'll* be glad when Charles is back in school,' the Widow said over a particularly fraught breakfast-table. The September morning sun was spreading itself like butter on the Widow's white linen tablecloth. 'When they're *both* in school, come to that!' the Widow pursued, borrowing one of Vinny's exclamation marks. Gordon was still upstairs, shaving, scraping carefully at his handsome throat with an open razor.

Will I? Eliza said, carelessly flicking open her cigarette lighter. She inhaled deeply and said that if it was up to her she wouldn't bother sending her children to school at all. She hadn't put her make-up on yet and her face looked scrubbed and clean and with her hair scraped back in a ribbon, her Eskimo cheekbones were suddenly obvious.

'Well, it's a good job that it's not up to you then, isn't it?' the Widow snapped. Eliza didn't reply, except to raise one indolent eyebrow and butter a slice of toast — the kind of response that made the Widow's blood boil. ('She makes my blood boil,' she muttered to Vinny, pushing the old wooden Ewbank over the living-room carpet as if she was trying to mow it out of existence. Vinny, following her with duster and polish, had an unnerving vision of blood boiling up merrily in her mother's retort-body. The Widow didn't look as if her blood was boiling, she looked as if it was congealing with cold.)

'What would you *do* with them if they didn't go to school?' the Widow pursued, driven by curiosity to prolong this conversation, when on the whole she would rather she never had to speak to Eliza at all.

Oh, I don't know, Eliza said carelessly, blowing a small, perfect smoke ring for Charles' delight. She twisted a black ringlet, escaped from its ribbon fetter, around her finger and smiled at Charles. She was wearing an old paisley silk dressing-gown of Gordon's and a nightdress fancy enough to go dancing in – a long lace body and a bias-cut skirt in oyster satin – and she looked so slovenly beautiful that Gordon, standing unnoticed in the doorway of the dining-room, felt his heart clenching. *I'd set them loose in a big green field somewhere*, Eliza said finally, *and let them run around all day long.*

'What a lot of rot,' the Widow rat-a-tat-tatted back.

Isobel's porridge was a little island, grey and lumpy like melted brains, floating in a pond of milk. She dug her spoon into the middle of the oatmeal island and imagined being in Eliza's big green field. She could see herself, a tiny little figure in the middle of an ocean of green. 'Are you going to eat your food or play with it?' the Widow asked sternly.

Don't speak to my child like that, Eliza said, standing up and pushing her chair back as if she was about to attack the Widow with the butter knife. The shoulder of her dressing-gown had slipped down, exposing a naked shoulder and the northern hemisphere of one smooth round breast, rising out of the thicket of lace. Eliza's skin was flawless, it made Charles think of the creamy junket the Widow made but without the nutmeg freckles that he'd been sprinkled with. 'Look at you, you slut,' the Widow hissed at Eliza and Isobel curled her toes up tightly and ate her porridge as fast as she could.

'What's going on?' Gordon asked, walking into the middle of the room. Gordon's shirt (starched white by the Widow) and his newly shaved face seemed so fresh and unsullied that they shamed the breakfast table into a truce.

Gordon suddenly plucked Isobel out of her chair – spoon still in hand – and tossed her up so high that for a moment it looked as if she might not come down again. 'You'll hang her on the lampshade if you're not careful,' the Widow reproached. Vinny came in, hatted and handbagged ready for work, 'She'll wet herself,' she warned. *You wouldn't think she had a house of her own*, Eliza said loudly, *the amount of time she spends here.*

Gordon put Isobel back in her chair and said to the Widow, 'Wouldn't it be dreadful if anyone had any fun in this house?' and she said, 'There's no need to talk like that, Gordon.' Vinny couldn't resist chipping in with her two pennies' worth. 'Fun, Gordon,' she sneered, 'doesn't get the washing done.'

'What the bloody hell does that mean, Vinny?' Gordon said, turning on her aggressively, and because she couldn't think of a reply she sat down at the breakfast-table and poured herself a cup of tea.

Oh darling, Eliza cooed, walking over to Gordon and pressing the full length of her satin-and-lace body against him, so that Vinny put her hand over Charles' eyes. Eliza slipped her hands round Gordon's waist and, undercover of his jacket, tugged the shirt and vest out of his trousers and ran the flat of her hands over his bare back all the way up to his shoulder-blades so that he let out an involuntary, embarrassing moan. Vinny and the Widow were the mirrors of each other's disgust. Vinny's mouth puckered like a carp as she secretly mouthed the word 'whore' to the teapot.

Eliza stood on tiptoe and whispered in Gordon's ear, her curls tickling his cheek, her voice like burning sugar, *Darling, if we don't get a place of our own soon, then I'm going to leave you. Understand?*

Mrs Baxter lost her baby. ('How can you lose a baby?' Charles asked in horror. *Quite easily, if you try hard enough, darling,* Eliza laughed.) She went to the hospital suddenly one night. Mr Baxter came round to Arden, dragging Audrey by the hand and asked the Widow if she would look after her. The Widow could hardly refuse and Gordon brought Audrey upstairs and tucked her into bed next to Isobel. Audrey was very quiet and said nothing beyond, 'Hello' and 'Goodnight' but snored very gently, like a kitten.

Mrs Baxter's baby was early, too early, and died before it even saw daylight. 'Stillborn,' the Widow said over a breakfast of poached eggs and Gordon said, 'Ssh,' and gestured at Audrey. But Audrey was too concerned with trying to stop her poached egg slipping off the plate to notice.

Later, when Audrey had gone home, Charles asked what stillborn meant and Vinny said, 'Dead,' in her usual no-nonsense way. She was helping herself to toast while waiting for a lift to work. 'Where do dead babies go?' Charles asked. Vinny wasn't fazed for a second, 'In the ground,' and the Widow tut-tutted at the directness of this statement. 'Heaven, of course,' she placated, 'babies go to heaven, and become cherubs.' Charles looked at Eliza for confirmation. They never really believed anything anyone said if Eliza didn't verify it. *Back to the baby shop to be repaired*, she said, to annoy Vinny and the Widow.

'And if you don't get a move on for school, Charles,' the Widow crowed, 'you might find that you get sent back to the baby shop and get changed for another model!' Gloating at this finesse, the Widow gave Eliza a triumphant smile and swept out of the dining-room. Eliza narrowed her eyes and lit a cigarette. *One day*, she said, *one day I'm going to kill the old bitch.*

'We really will have to get a place of our own,' Gordon ventured to his mother. The Widow was in the kitchen making pastry for a Sunday plum pie with plums from her own Victorias, a great china bowl of them was sitting on the kitchen table. A wasp crawled slowly over the red fruit, dizzy with plum fumes. The Widow folded her arms, propping up her scrawny bosom and got flour on her blouse. Much as she would like to get rid of Eliza, when it came to it she couldn't bear the idea of Gordon ('my son') leaving home. 'It doesn't make sense,' she said, 'not when I've got so much room – and you wouldn't get looked after without me – and anyway this house is going to be yours one day, Gordon. One day very soon,' she added with a little catch in her voice. She lifted her apron to dab at her eyes and Gordon said, 'There, there,' and put his arms round her.

Eliza lay coldly in bed next to Gordon. The second-best bed. The sheets in Arden were as stiff as brown paper. She spoke over her icy shoulder at him, *Look at her – why doesn't she move out and live with Vinny and give us this house, or give us some money from the shop? The shop should be yours, she's an old woman, why is she hanging onto it? We could sell up and have some money, get away from this bloody hole. Do something with our lives.*

This was the most Eliza had said to Gordon in months. He stared through the dark at the wall opposite, if he stared hard enough at the wallpaper he could make out where the repeat began on the pattern of roses growing on a trellis. An owl hooted on Sycamore Street.

The Widow creaked stiffly into the front passenger seat of the big black car.

'It's half-day closing,' Gordon said to Charles, 'I'll be back at lunchtime.' Vinny climbed resentfully into the back – 'How is it that I always have to sit in the back? Why am I always second-best?' – and they all drove off to turn themselves into licensed grocers for the day, *prut-prut-prut*. Charles waved until the car was out of sight – and then a little bit longer because one of Gordon's tricks was to pretend to have disappeared round a corner and then just when you thought he'd gone he'd suddenly pop back. Not this time though.

A picnic, Eliza said, stubbing her cigarette out on one of the Widow's flower-sprigged plates, *it's half-term, after all, and we've done absolutely bloody nothing all week*, and she hauled the old wicker picnic basket out of its hiding-place in the understairs cupboard and said, *We'll take the bus into town and meet Daddy at lunchtime and give him a surprise.*

As a treat they sat on the top deck of the bus, on the front seats, and watched the streets of trees go sailing by below. The big branch of a sycamore snapped unexpectedly against the window in front of them, rattling its dead leaves that were like hands and Eliza said, *It's all right, it's just a tree,* and lit a cigarette. She waved the smoke away from their faces and crossed her legs and tapped one foot as if she was impatient about something. She was wearing Charles' favourite shoes, high-heeled brown suede with little furry pom-poms. *Mink* according to Eliza. Her fifteen-denier stockings were the same shade. *Mink*.

The bus trundled on, running along the street where Vinny's house was. Eliza stubbed out her cigarette under her shoe, twisting her foot hard, long after the cigarette was extinguished. Her bad mood radiated off her like the cold October sunshine. There was a bus-stop right outside Vinny's door and all three of them looked down into her tiny front garden and tried to peer through her lace-curtained windows, safe because they knew she was at work. Their faces were level with her bedroom window but its curtains were permanently shut against nosy top-deckers and it revealed no secrets to voyeurs. Vinny's house was a thin redbrick semi with a small, square bay and a mean porch, built when the master-builder's imagination had run out and his veins were flooded with alcohol (the master-builder's solid trunk was felled by a stroke in 1930).

Ugh, Eliza shivered, although whether at the house or its absent occupant wasn't clear. Both probably. Charles and Isobel didn't like visiting Vinny's house. It smelt of damp and Izal and boiled vegetables.

When they arrived at the shop they found the Widow standing by the scratched red-metal Hobart coffee-grinder dreaming about money and things coming off ration. Gordon lifted Isobel onto the polished mahogany of the counter so she could watch him weighing tea. The tea smelt dark and bitter like the Widow's hot chrome teapot with its knitted green and yellow cosy. Vinny was cutting a piece of Lancashire as white as the Widow's skin.

'Well, well, well,' Mrs Tyndale, a regular customer, said, bustling fatly into the shop, 'if it isn't Charles and Isobel.' She turned to the Widow, 'She's the image of her mother, isn't she?' and the Widow and Vinny raised their eyebrows in unison, communicating mutely with each other over the ramifications of this statement. 'It's lovely, isn't it,' Mrs Tyndale said, 'to see a happy young family!'

Eliza didn't respond in any way and disappeared into the back of the shop, followed by Gordon on an invisible lead. Mrs Tyndale leant conspiratorially over the counter and said to Vinny, 'Flighty thing, isn't she?' Vinny gave a funny squint smile and whispered, 'Flirty, too,' as if Eliza was some strange species of bird.

Eliza and Gordon reappeared, their faces tight and blank as if they'd been having an argument. *We're going for a picnic, we'll give you a lift home first*, Eliza said to the Widow. The Widow demurred. She was going to Temple's for lunch, she said, looking saintly, as if she was going to a church service, as if Temple's might really be a temple, not a department store restaurant. 'A picnic in *October*?' Mrs Tyndale enquired brightly and was ignored by everyone.

Eliza picked Isobel up from the counter and started nibbling her ear. Why, Vinny wondered, was Eliza always trying to eat bits of her children? *What a tasty little morsel*, Eliza murmured in Isobel's ear while Vinny patted butter aggressively, imagining it was Eliza's head. If Eliza wasn't careful, Vinny thought, she'd look around one day and discover that she'd eaten them all up.

The Widow, meanwhile, was wondering if this picnic was perhaps another of Eliza's impulsive outings. Perhaps she'd come back with another baby. Or perhaps, with any luck, she'd get lost and not come back at all. Vinny slapped a lump of butter down on the marble slab, they would never think of asking *her* on a picnic, would they? *Vinny*, Eliza's voice purred sweetly, *why don't you come with us?* and Vinny recoiled in horror – the last thing she wanted to do was go *anywhere* with them, she just wanted to be asked. 'Yes, do,' the Widow barked, 'some fresh air might put a bit of life in you.' *Poor Vinny*, Eliza said, fizzing with laughter.

It was quite a relief to see Eliza cheerful, even if it was only for a moment. She'd been bad-tempered for weeks. *I'm not myself*, she said and then laughed maniacally, *but God knows who I am*.

Gordon unwrapped himself from his grocer's bondage with a flourish and put his gabardine mac and trilby hat on so that he didn't look anything like a grocer. He could have been a film star with his thick, wavy hair. He stood at the door of the shop and raised his arms to play Oranges and Lemons and said, 'Off with her head!' and Isobel ran under the half-arch of his arms. Charles got excited and ran back three times to be executed. Gordon was just about to chop off Eliza's head as well when she said – very coldly, very Hempstid – *Stop it, Gordon,* and he gave her an odd look and then clicked his heels and said, *'Jawohl, meine dame,'* and Vinny snapped, 'That's not funny, Gordon – people died in the war, you know!' Eliza laughed and said, *No, really, Vinny?* and Gordon turned to her nastily and said, 'Shut up, why don't you, Eliza?'

I don't know what's the matter with you, Eliza said airily and Gordon stared at her very hard and said, 'Don't you?'

The shop bell clanged noisily on its springy strip of metal as Gordon pulled the door shut behind them. The Widow and Mrs Tyndale stood behind the glass in the upper half of the shop door and waved goodbye to the car, woodenly like Punch and Judy in their box. As soon as the engine started to *prut-prut-prut* they turned to each other, eager to comment on the behaviour of their not-so-happy young family.

'Where shall we go?' Gordon asked no-one in particular, tapping the steering-wheel with his leather-gloved hands as if it was a tambourine. *Anywhere,* Eliza said, lighting a cigarette. Gordon gave her an odd sideways look as if he'd only just met her and was wondering what kind of a person she was. 'How about Boscrambe Woods?' he asked, looking at Charles in the rear-view mirror. 'Yes!' Charles shouted enthusiastically. Eliza said something but Gordon accelerated noisily as he pulled away from the pavement and her words were drowned by the engine.

Vinny, relegated to the back seat as usual, was trying to shrink to protect herself from carelessly kicking feet and sticky hands. 'What do you think, Vin?' Gordon said and Vinny said, 'What – you mean someone's actually asking *my* opinion for once?' and lit a cigarette without giving an opinion any way and disappeared in a cloud of tobacco smoke.

Isobel closed her eyes almost as soon as the engine started. She loved the feeling of slipping down into sleep, breathing in the soporific drug of seat-leather, nicotine, petrol and Eliza's perfume.

They were still driving when she woke up. Eliza looked over her shoulder and said, *Nearly there*. Isobel's tongue felt like a pebble. Charles was picking a scab on his knee. His face was covered in freckles and the tiny elliptical craters of chickenpox scars. His snub nose twitched at the amount of cigarette smoke in the car. Gordon started to sing "Down by the Salley Gardens" in his nice light baritone. In profile his nose was straight and Roman and from low down on the leather of the back seat you could imagine him flying his plane through the clouds. Occasionally, he cast a glance in Eliza's direction as if he was checking to see if she was still there.

He braked suddenly as a thin stream of grey squirrel streaked across the road in front of the car and they all jerked forward. Vinny bounced her forehead off the back of the front seat with a little screech. 'God,' said Gordon, looking shaken, but Eliza just laughed her funny annoying laugh. Gordon stared at the windscreen for a while, a muscle in spasm in his cheek.

'And are *you* all right, Vinny?' Vinny asked herself, 'Oh yes, thank you, don't bother about me,' she answered and was jerked violently again as Gordon revved up the engine and accelerated off.

The cold was a surprise after being in the heat of the car for so long, the clear woodland air a shock after the tobacco smog. Eliza turned up the collar of her camel coat and pulled on her delicate leather gloves. *I should have worn a hat*, she said as she bent down to tie Isobel's scarf round her neck. Isobel could see a stray speck of mascara on Eliza's cheek, beneath her lashes. Eliza tied the scarf so tight that it choked Isobel and she had to put her hands up and tug it looser.

The scarf matched her Shetland tammy, both knitted for Christmas by the Widow. Charles was wearing his school blazer and cap while Vinny had on her belted navy-blue gabardine with matching sou'wester. Anyone looking at them at that moment would have seen a nice family – healthy, attractive, ordinary – the kind that graced the advertisements every week in *Picture Post*. A nice ordinary family going for a walk in the woods. They would never have been able to tell, just by looking at them, that their world was about to end.

Eliza licked the edge of her Christmas present handkerchief and bent down again to wipe the corners of Isobel's mouth. She rubbed so hard that Isobel was forced to take an involuntary step backwards. From somewhere above her head, Gordon's voice sounded hollow, 'Don't rub so hard, Lizzy, you'll rub her out,' and she could see Eliza's eyes narrowing and a thin blue vein on her forehead – the colour of hyacinths – grow visible through her fine skin and begin to throb. Eliza folded the handkerchief in a neat triangle and tucked it into the pocket of Isobel's plaid wool coat and said, *In case you need to blow your nose.*

The picnic wasn't a great success. Catering wasn't one of Eliza's skills. The cucumber in the fish-paste-and-cucumber sandwiches had made the bread soggy, the apples had rusting, mottled bruises under their skins and Eliza had neglected to pack anything to drink. By now they seemed to have walked a long way into the woods. 'When you're in a wood,' Gordon said to Charles, 'always follow the path, that way you won't get lost.' *What if there isn't a path?* Eliza asked, bad temper sharpening her voice. 'Then walk towards the light,' Gordon said without turning to look at her.

Eliza had carried the big tartan rug from the back seat and spread it on a carpet of beech leaves. *This is a lovely sunny patch*, she said with a febrile gaiety that convinced no-one. Charles dropped to his knees and rolled about on the rug. Gordon leant back on his elbows and Isobel snuggled into the crook of his elbow. Eliza sat like a well-behaved aristocrat, her long, thin legs in their mink-coloured stockings and elegant shoes looking out of place, stretched across the homely tartan rug, as if they'd wandered in from a mannequin parade. Vinny cast them envious glances, her own scrawny legs had all the shape of clothes-pegs. Vinny forced her poker body to bend into a kneeling position on the rug and pulled her skirt over her legs, she had the air of a refined Victorian traveller amongst primitive forest dwellers.

The novelty of rug-dwelling soon wore off. The children shivered disconsolately and ate jam sandwiches and Kit-Kats until they felt queasy. 'This isn't much fun,' Charles said and threw himself off the rug into a pile of leaves and started burying himself like a dog. Having fun was very important to Charles, having fun and making people laugh. 'He's just looking for attention,' Vinny said. *And he gets it – isn't that clever?* Eliza said. Charles' hair was almost the same colour as the dying forest – tawny oak and curly copper-beech. He could have got lost in the pile of leaves and never be found until the spring.

Vinny heaved herself up from the rug with a struggle and said, 'I have to go and you-know-what,' and vanished into the trees. Minutes passed and she didn't come back. Gordon laughed and said, 'She'll go for miles, to make sure nobody sees her bloomers,' and Eliza made a nauseated face at the idea of Vinny's underclothes and got up suddenly from the rug and said, *I'm going for a walk*, without looking at any of them and set off along the path, in the opposite direction to Vinny.

'We'll come with you!' Gordon shouted after her and she spun round very quickly so that her big camel coat swung round her legs, showing her dress underneath in a swirl of green, and shouted back, *Don't you dare!* She sounded furious. 'She has completely the wrong shoes on,' Gordon muttered angrily and bowled a rotten apple overarm into the trees behind them. Just before she disappeared round the turning in the path, Eliza stopped and shouted something, the words ringing clearly in the crisp air – *I'm going home, don't bother following me!*

'Home!' Gordon exploded. 'How does she think she's to get home?' and then he got up too and set off in pursuit of Eliza, shouting over his shoulder to Charles, 'I won't be a sec – stay here with your sister!' and with that he was gone as well.

The sun had disappeared from the trees, except for one little pool at the corner of the rug. Isobel lay with her face in the warm pool, drifting in and out of sleep, eventually woken by Charles leaping on top of her. She screamed and the scream echoed wildly in the silence. They sat on the rug together, holding hands, waiting for some other noise to take the place of the dying echo of the scream, waiting for the sound of Gordon's and Eliza's voices, of a bird singing, of Vinny complaining, of wind in the trees, of anything except the absolute stillness of the wood. Perhaps it was one of Gordon's disappearing tricks. One he was having difficulty with and any moment now he'd get it right and jump out from behind a tree and shout, 'Surprise!'

A leaf the colour of Charles' hair drifted down like a feather through the air and landed noiselessly. Isobel could feel fear, like hot liquid, in her stomach. Something was very, very wrong.

All sense of time had disappeared. It felt as if they'd been alone in the wood for hours. Where were Gordon and Eliza? Where was Vinny? Had she been eaten by a wild animal while doing you-know-what? Charles' broad, jolly face had grown pale and pinched with worry. Eliza always told them that if they got separated from her when they were out then *you must stay exactly where you are* – and she would come and find them. Charles' belief in this statement had waned considerably over the last hour or two.

Eventually he said, 'Come on, let's go and find everybody,' and dragged Isobel up from the rug by her hand. 'They're just playing Hide-and-Seek probably,' he said but his whey-face and the wobble in his voice betrayed his real feelings. Being the grown-up in charge was taking its toll on him. They set off in the same direction that Eliza and Gordon had followed, the path quite clear – hard, trodden-down earth, laddered occasionally with tree-roots.

It was growing dark by now. Isobel stumbled over a tree root snaking across the path and hurt her knees. Charles waited impatiently for her to catch up. He was holding something in his hand, squinting in the gloom. It was a shoe, a brown suede shoe, the heel bent at a strange angle and the little mink pom-pom dampened by something sticky so that it lay flat and limp like a wet kitten and the rhinestone was a dull gleam in the dying light.

Charles walked on more slowly now, carrying the shoe in his hand, then, without warning, he scuttled down into a dry ditch full of leaves, beside the path. The ditch was so full of leaves that they came up to Charles' play-scarred knees and made an attractive crispy-crunchy noise as he waded through them. For a moment Isobel thought this might be part of his endless quest for fun but almost as soon as he'd leapt in, he leapt out the other side. She followed him, scrambling down into the ditch and wading through the leaves. She would like to have lain down, sunk onto this comfortable leaf bed and gone to sleep for a while, but Charles was charging on so she clambered up the other side of the ditch and hurried after him.

He was brushing his way through a curtain of twigs that snapped back and hit her in the face like thin whips. When she finally caught up with him he was standing as rooted as a tree with his back to her, as if he was playing statues, his arms sticking out from his body. In one hand he was holding the shoe. The fingers of the other hand were stretched out wide and flat and Isobel took hold of Charles' sycamore leaf hand and together they stood and looked.

At Eliza. She was lolled against the trunk of a big oak tree, like a carelessly abandoned doll or a broken bird. Her head had flopped against her shoulder, stretching her thin white neck like a swan or a stalk about to snap. Her camel coat had fallen open and her woollen dress, the colour of bright spring leaves, was fanned out over her legs. She had one shoe off and one shoe on and the words to *Diddle-diddle dumpling* ran through Isobel's head.

It was hard to know what to do with this sleeping mother who refused to wake up. She looked very peaceful, her long lashes closed, the speck of mascara still visible. Only the dark red ribbons of blood in her black curls hinted at the way her skull might have been smashed against the trunk of the tree and broken open like a beech-nut or an acorn.

They pulled her coat close and Charles did his best to put the shoe back on her elegantly arched stocking-foot. It was as if her feet had grown while she slept. It was so difficult getting the shoe back on that Charles grew afraid that he would break the bones in Eliza's feet and eventually he gave up on the task and shoved the shoe into his blazer pocket.

They cuddled up to Eliza, trying to keep her warm, trying to keep themselves warm – one on each side of her like some sadly sentimental tableau ('*Won't you wake up, Mother dear?*'). Leaves drifted down occasionally. Three or four leaves were already snagged on Eliza's black curls. Charles stood up and, dog-like, shook leaves off his own head. It was really quite dark now, it was all very well saying follow the light but what if there was no light to follow? When Isobel tried to stand up her legs were so numb that she could hardly balance and fell down again. And she was so hungry that for a dizzy moment she wanted to bite into the bark of the tree. But she would never do that because Eliza used to tell them a story called 'The Oldest Tree In The Forest' so that Isobel knew the bark of a tree was really its skin and she knew how painful a bite on your skin could be because Eliza was always biting them. And sometimes it hurt.

Charles said, 'We have to find Daddy,' his voice shrill in the quiet, 'he'll come and get Mummy.' They looked doubtfully at Eliza, reluctant to leave her here all alone in the cold and the dark. Her cheeks were icy to the touch, they felt their own cheeks in comparison. If anything they were even colder. Charles started to gather up leaves and pile them over Eliza's legs. They remembered the summer at the seaside, burying Eliza's lower half in sand while she sat in her red halter-neck swimming-costume reading a book, wearing the sunglasses that made her look foreign and glamorous, and stubbing out her cigarettes in the sand turret they'd built around her (*You've got me prisoner!*). For a warm second Isobel could feel the sun on her shoulders and smell the sea. 'Help me,' Charles said and she shuffled leaves forward with her feet for Charles to scoop up in handfuls and throw on Eliza.

Then they kissed her, one on either cheek, in a strange reversal of the bedtime ritual. They left reluctantly, looking back at her several times. When they reached the ditch of leaves they turned round one last time but they couldn't see Eliza any more, only a pile of dead leaves against a tree.

To go back to the tartan rug and abandoned picnic and wait for rescue? Or onward to try and find a way out of the wood? Charles said he wished they'd brought the uneaten sandwiches with them. 'We could scatter the crumbs,' he said, 'and find our way back.' Their only blueprint for survival in these circumstances, it seemed, was fictional. They knew the plot, unfortunately, and any minute expected to find the gingerbread cottage – and then the nightmare would really begin.

Isobel was sorry now that she'd ever complained about Eliza's paste-and-cucumber, she wouldn't be scattering them, she'd be eating them. She was so hungry that she would have eaten a gingerbread tile or a piece of striped candy window-frame, even though she knew the consequences. They were both suddenly very sorry for all the food that they'd ever left on their plates. They would even have eaten the Widow's tapioca pudding. The big oval glass dish that the Widow made her milk-puddings in rose up before them like a mirage. They could feel the sliminess of the tapioca, taste the puddle of rosehip syrup that the Widow always poured in the middle, like a liquid jewel. Charles searched through his pockets and came up with a stringless conker, a farthing and a black-and-white striped humbug with a good deal of pocket-fluff attached. It was too hard to break so they took it in turns to suck it.

The wood was full of noises. Occasionally the darkness was shot through by strange sounds – screeches and whistles – that seemed to have no earthly origin. Twigs snapped and crackled and the undergrowth rustled malevolently as if something invisible was stalking them.

Every direction felt unsafe. An owl swept soundlessly on its flightpath, low over their heads, and Isobel was sure she could feel its claws touching her hair. She threw herself on the ground in a frenzy of panic that left Charles unmoved. 'It's just an owl, silly,' he said, yanking her back up onto her feet. Her heart was ticking very fast as if it was about to go off. 'It's not the owls we have to worry about,' Charles muttered grimly, 'it's the wolves,' and then, remembering that he was supposed to be the man in charge of this woeful expedition, added, 'Joke, Izzie – forget I said that.'

Moving on was slightly less terrifying than standing still waiting for something to pounce, so they soldiered on miserably. Isobel found some comfort in the warm grubbiness of Charles' hand clasped around hers. Charles remembered a snatch of verse, *It isn't very good in the middle of the wood.*

Tree after tree after tree, all the trees in the world were in Boscrambe Wood that night. *In the middle of the night when there isn't any light.* Perhaps instead of letting them loose in her *big green field*, Eliza has chosen to set them free in an endless wood instead. Isobel thought she would have preferred it if she'd just returned them to the baby shop.

The path turned a corner and forked suddenly. Charles took the farthing out of his pocket and said, 'Toss for it – heads right, tails left,' in the manliest way he could muster and Isobel said, 'Tails,' in a weak voice. The coin landed wren-side up and the little bird pointed its beak at the left-hand path. As if on cue, the moon – full to bursting – dodged out from behind her cloud cover and hung over the left-hand path for a few brief seconds like a neon sign. 'Follow the light,' Charles said decisively.

The path was becoming overgrown, brambles reached out and plucked at their clothes and tweaked their hair like bird's claws. It was so dark by now that it took them some time to realize they weren't really on a path at all any more. A few steps further on and their Start-rite shoes began to be sucked into the ground. Everywhere that they tentatively poked their toes proved wet and boggy. They had heard stories of people being drowned in quicksand, sinking into bogs and they plunged on quickly through thorns to a higher and dryer piece of ground.

'Things can't get any worse,' Charles said miserably, just before the fog started to advance, wraithlike, towards them. It curled around the trees and grew thicker, like opaque water, wave after wave, engulfing everything in a ghostly white sea of fog. Isobel started to wail, very loudly, and Charles said, 'Put a sock in it, Izzie. Please.'

Too weary to go any further, too confused by the fog, they curled up at the foot of a big tree, nestling in between its enormous roots, which arched over the ground like gnarled bony fingers. There were plenty of dead leaves here for a blanket but they remembered Eliza under her leaf cover and pulled their coats tighter. A cold counterpane of fog settled itself around them instead.

Isobel fell asleep immediately but Charles lay awake waiting for the wolves to start howling.

Isobel dreamt the strangest dream. She was in a great underground cavern, warm and full of people and noise. By the light of hundreds of candles she could see that the walls and the roof of the cavern were made of gold. At one end of this great hall a man sat on a throne. He was dressed all in green from head to foot and wore a golden band round his forehead. Someone handed her a silver plate piled high with the most delicious food, like nothing she'd ever tasted before. Someone else pressed a crystal goblet into her hand, full of a liquid that tasted of honey and raspberries, only nicer, and no matter how much she drank, the goblet was never empty. The people in the hall began to dance, sedately at first – but then the music grew more frantic and the dancing got wilder and wilder. The man with the golden band around his head appeared suddenly at her shoulder and shouted at her above the din, asking her what her name was and she shouted back, 'Isobel!' and immediately the hall – along with the lights and the music and the people – disappeared and she found herself alone in the wood, eating a rotting mushroom from a leaf and drinking ditchwater from an acorn cup.

She woke up with a jerk, her dream evaporating into the dawn – there was no sign of crystal goblet or silver plate, nor even of rotting mushroom and acorn cup – just the stillness of the forest. Charles was snoring, curled up tidily like a small hibernating animal. The fog had lifted, replaced by a watery dawnlight, nothing had changed, they were still alone in the heart of the wood.

PRESENT

LEAVES OF LIGHT

'ANCESTRAL LIFE – THE BACTERIA AND THE BLUE-GREEN ALGAE – CAME a billion years later. The blue-green algae were the first to know how to turn molecules of light into food. The oxygen released by this process changed the atmosphere of the Earth for ever, allowing the creation of life as we know it.

'After the blue-green algae came the mosses, the fungi and the ferns. By the end of the Devonian Era the first trees – *genus cordates* – were already extinct.

'In the Carboniferous Era there were forests of giant ferns, the first conifers appeared and the coal fields were laid down. 136 million years ago, the flowering and the broad-leaved trees made their first appearance. Most of the trees we know today were in existence by twelve million years ago,' Miss Thompsett's voice drones through the classroom. On my right-hand side, Eunice is as alert as a sheepdog as Miss Thompsett writes on the blackboard in her tidy writing –

$$CO_2 + 2H_2A + light\ energy - (CH_2) + H_2O + H_2A.$$

Miss Thompsett herself – dark green twin-set and box-pleated tartan skirt – is as tidy as her handwriting.

On my other side, Audrey is hunched up asleep, her arms pillowing her head on her desk. She has shadows as dark as bruises under her eyes and she is dreadfully pale. She's not really here at all, as if someone had made a really poor facsimile of her and sent it out into the world without telling it how to behave, an incompetent *doppelgänger*.

Miss Thompsett bores on . . . *outer layer of the epidermis and into the palisade cells* . . . she's giving us 'a brief history of photosynthesis', and the effect is like a sleeping draught. Her words pour into my ear and then curl around my brain like green fog . . . *chlorophyll, grana, photons* . . .

Eunice transcribes busily. Everything in Eunice's exercise book is neatly drawn, highlighted, coloured, labelled and underlined. Her diagrams are more exact than a textbook. On the board, Miss Thompsett is drawing molecules, the molecules are the size of ping-pong balls. The world Miss Thompsett inhabits must be gigantic, her primitive organisms the small size of small towns, her elephants the size of Sirius B.

My head nods and my brain grows cloudy and soon I've joined Audrey in sleep. 'Right,' Miss Thompsett says suddenly, so that I wake up with a jerk. 'Now draw me a cross-section of a leaf to explain photosynthesis.' I haven't the faintest idea what a leaf looks like in cross-section (well – green, thin, flat –

– but I don't think that was what she wants). I haven't even got the right textbook.

Apart from Audrey, everyone else is labouring over their leaves, and Miss Thompsett says, 'Problem, Isobel?' in a way that implies there'd better not be and I sigh and shake my head.

'Audrey Baxter!' Miss Thompsett says loudly and Audrey flinches awake looking like a startled cat. 'So good of you to join us,' Miss Thompsett says – but too soon, for Audrey is already out of her chair. 'I have to go,' she mumbles and disappears out of the door. 'What's wrong with Audrey, Isobel?' Miss Thompsett asks, a puzzled (though very tidy) frown on her face.

'She's not herself,' I say vaguely (but then who is?).

I bend over my biology textbook with my coloured Lakeland pencils and, to cheer myself up, draw a tree.

Not any old tree, but a wonderful, mystical tree that comes from somewhere deep inside my imagination. A tree with a gnarled and knotted trunk with bark, coloured in cinnamon and raw umber, and a huge head of leaves, parted down the middle. On the left hand side, I draw the leaves in every shade possible from the green spectrum – the colours of soft moss and trailing willows, of tangled timothy grass, of apple trees and primeval forests.

And on the other half of the tree – a bonfire of leaves, leaves flaming up in a conflagration of red-gold, ginger and bronze. Leaf skeletons toasted to the colour of fox-fur, leaves jaundiced to quince and sulphur, dropping like sickly jewels from the charred branches, leaves like topazes and lemons shooting up tongues of fire the colour of rosehips and blood. A leaf like the breast of a robin detaches itself and floats upward on a plume of wood-ash. And all the time that the right-hand side of the tree burns, the left half remains as green and whole as spring.

Perhaps this is the tree of life or Eve's knowledge tree? Zeus' own Dodona oak or the great oak sacred to Thor? Or maybe Ysggadril, the ash, the world tree, that in Norse mythology forms the whole round of the globe – its branches propping up the sky roof above our heads, full of cloud-leaves and star-fruits and its roots beneath the earth springing from the source of all matter. Trees of Life. It goes without saying that Miss Thompsett isn't impressed by my artwork.

'Finish these diagrams for homework,' Miss Thompsett orders pleasantly, 'and if you can find time, read ahead to the next chapter in your textbook.' Find time? Where might it be located? In space?

(But not in the great void, surely?) At the bottom of the deep blue sea? At the centre of the earth? At the end of the rainbow? If we found time would it solve all our problems? 'If only I had more time,' Debbie says, 'then I might get something done.' But *then* what would she do?

Eunice's cross-section of a leaf: Photons of light speed down sunbeam arrows for exactly 8.3 seconds and splash through the outer layer of the epidermis and into the heart of the palisade cells. The molecules of light race into the chloroplast, into the perfect little green discs of the grana. The light is drawn further and further in, helplessly attracted by the magnesium at the heart of the little chlorophyll molecules. Light and green embrace, dancing a wild jig of excitement for a tiny fraction of time while the little molecule of light gives up its energy. The chlorophyll molecule is so agitated by this encounter that it splits a water molecule into hydrogen and oxygen molecules. The plant releases the oxygen into the air for us to breathe. The hydrogen converts carbon dioxide into sugar which is used to build new plant tissue. 'Unlike the plant,' Eunice notes in bold fountain-pen, 'we cannot synthesize our own molecules of food from light so we must eat plants or animals that feed on plants and thus without photosynthesis we would not be able to exist.'

As the tide of summer wilderness has died down in the garden, several lost objects have been revealed – an old shoe (they're everywhere), a tennis ball, Vinny's second-best spectacles and poor Vinegar Tom, no longer a soft-sock kitten body, but a hard dried-out felt thing, flattened into the ground. It's not possible to say how he died but Vinny refuses to believe that Mr Rice is entirely innocent of felinicide.

Vinny is very upset by the young cat's death, normally she restricts herself to a narrow spectrum of emotions (irritable, irritated, irritating) so that it's quite disturbing to see her scarecrow shoulders vibrating with sobs and Charles and I try and placate her with a garden funeral. 'Cat that is born of cat has but a short time to live on this earth,' Charles says manfully as Vinny moans open-mouthed by the graveside. Richard Primrose intrudes, suddenly popping out from behind a rhododendron and sniggering, 'RIP – Rise If Possible, *snarf-snarf*,' and I have the satisfaction of seeing Vinny whack him with the spade.

Mr Rice falls from grace even further when Debbie discovers him on the living-room *chaise-longue* in a compromising position with a battleship-blonde called Shirley, the barmaid at the Tap and Spile on Lythe Road.

'Doggy position too,' Mr Rice confides smugly to Charles.

'Doggy?' Charles repeats, one baffled eyebrow cocked ready to go off. But now Mr Rice is lying doggo in his room waiting for Debbie to calm down. 'Sorry, old chap,' Gordon mumbles helplessly, ''fraid you're in the dog house.'

'Makes a change from you then,' Mr Rice sneers.

'Look,' Charles says, pressing something into my hand as I hurry out to school. A handkerchief, slightly grubby, folded in a limp triangle. '*Hers?*' I query, rather cynically. 'Yes,' Charles says, unfolding the triangle, 'definitely.' The handkerchief is monogrammed with an elaborate embroidered 'E' and as we cannot think of anyone else with that initial, I suppose it must be hers. A faint trace of memory, a barely decipherable twitch along the neurons (a faint *click*) reminds me of something. Charles presses it against his nose and inhales so hard that he snorts unattractively. 'Yes,' he says. I sniff the handkerchief less belligerently. I am expecting tobacco and French perfume (the scent of a grown-up woman) but all I can smell is mothballs. 'Found it in a drawer,' Charles says. I'm beginning to suspect that he's turning the house upside down, looking for Eliza, perhaps he's already pulling up floorboards and ripping down plaster.

But looking for Eliza is a heartbreaking and thankless task. We have done it all our lives, we should know.

None the less, I take the handkerchief and push it deep into my coat pocket before running the length of Chestnut Avenue to the bus-stop on Sycamore Street.

The bus makes its stately progression up the High Street while I try hard not to listen to Eunice, sitting next to me on the top deck, wittering on about adenosine triphosphate. Instead, I smoke a jewelled Sobranie pretending to be sophisticated and concentrate on imagining Malcolm Lovat without his clothes.

For a startled moment I think I must have conjured him into being, albeit fully clothed, for there he is – down on the pavement. The bus stops, ingesting passengers, giving me plenty of time to inspect his lovely dark curls, his smooth cheek and his slender surgeon's hands. What is he doing in Glebelands when he should be practising life and death at Guy's? But wait, who is this he is engrossed in conversation with? This person who is tossing her blond hair around like a horse advertising shampoo and simpering and smiling in a very girly way? 'Hilary!' I fume helplessly to Eunice. Eunice mimes being sick. 'What's he doing here?' I say, baffled.

'Oh, his mother's been taken ill,' Eunice says, without a trace of emotion. 'Cancer, or something.'

'And what's he doing with *her*?'

'Apparently they're going out together, have been for some time.' Is there nothing that Eunice doesn't know?

When she's talking to boys, Hilary has a way of holding her head on one side and half-closing her unnaturally blue eyes, a position that for some reason has the effect of raising testosterone levels in a radius of ten feet. She's undoubtedly pretty. 'Pretty awful,' Eunice says.

'That's it then, I'm going to have to kill her.'

'Good idea,' Eunice says reasonably.

Standing at the kitchen sink doing the washing-up in a half-hearted kind of way I glance out of the window and let out a scream of horror at the face looming fuzzily through the dark glass, a strange Quint-like figure trying to attract my attention. For a moment I think I've finally spotted my invisible ghost, but then understanding dawns – this is no ghost, it is Mr Rice standing in the garden, a halo of light from an electric torch illuminating a very unattractive sight. Mr Rice is giving a one-man show. His torchbeam is directed down at his other torchless hand, which is jerking up and down like a jackhammer around the toadstool of his penis. I recoil from the window in horror and when I next dare to look there's no sign of him.

When I can finally bring myself to go out and investigate, the garden appears to be devoid of human life, only the faint sound of someone whistling "On Top of Old Smokey" that quickly fades into nothing. The giant hogweed have probably got their hands on him.

Somewhere over on Sycamore Street an owl hoots softly, a ghostly *hoohoohoooo* that floats like a feather on the silent air, but Mr Rice has disappeared.

Mr Rice wakes up slowly from a bad dream in which he closed his eyes and embraced the barmaid Shirley only to open them and find he's holding the body of a decomposing Vinny, eyeballs hanging out and flesh liquefying. It leaves him feeling quite stupid.

None the less he chortles to himself at his ruse, he has put his suitcases of samples and a bag with his best clothes in the Left Luggage at Glebelands station, and is planning to walk out of Arden first thing after breakfast as if he was on his way to work and never come back! He owes nearly three months' rent and has no intention of paying it. Getting out of this dump will be a blessing, he thinks, if he can wake up, that is.

Mr Rice opens his eyes uneasily and sees double. His head feels thick and heavy, the result no doubt of too much brandy and Babysham in the Tap and Spile last night. He opens his eyes again. He isn't seeing double, his vision seems to have multiplied into a hundred honeycombed images. Mr Rice moves a leg and sees something thin and black and hairy waving in front of him. His legs were never very manly – but not that bad, surely? He tries the other leg, to the same effect. And then his four other legs.

Mr Rice screams, but it is a silent scream – all he can hear is an almighty buzzing in his head. He catches a hundred glimpses of himself in the mirror, oh no . . . it can't be . . . this is another nightmare from which he will wake very soon. Surely?

*He tries to move. His centre of gravity has shifted to somewhere else. It's impossible to co-ordinate so many arms and legs, or maybe they're just . . . **legs**. He decides to try and jump off the bed. He concentrates on all of his legs, one-two-three jump! and finds himself on the window-sill. The window is open, it is just possible, Mr Rice thinks, that he could squeeze through that space. The smell of Mrs Baxter's apple sauce cooking and a pile of dog excrement down in the garden are like a siren song to Mr Rice as buzzzbuzzzz-buzzzzzzzzzzz he pushes his big body through the gap and unfolds his iridescent wings . . .*

Next morning I get out of bed and draw the curtains, half-expecting to see Mr Rice still performing in the daylight. But he's not there, instead, in the morning mist, Mrs Baxter is in the field filling a basket with *trompettes de mort*. Bundled up in cardigans and wearing an old woollen hat like a tea-cosy she looks ancient, an old hen-wife gathering her potions. I suppose she'll cook the mushrooms for breakfast. How satisfying it would be if Mr Baxter's grilled mushrooms really did trumpet his death. Mrs Baxter and Audrey would be so much better off without him. Maybe then Audrey would cheer up and be herself again. Whoever that is.

I puzzle at what to say to Mr Rice over the breakfast bacon, but find I am saved from this nicety of etiquette as he doesn't appear at the breakfast table, never appears again in fact.

'Done a runner,' Vinny concludes, surveying the debris he's left behind. She brushes a bluebottle away. 'This stuff's breeding,' she says, finding pile after pile of magazines under the bed.

Vinny burns Mr Rice's magazines collection on a bonfire, holding each item with the wooden tongs that the Widow used to retrieve washing from the copper with. Mr Rice's magazines are an altogether more dirty kind of laundry than that which Vinny or Debbie are used to dealing with. We are baffled by Mr Rice's literary tastes. 'Why would anyone want to look at pictures of people in macs and gas-masks?' Debbie asks. I can't imagine. 'Poor old Auntie V,' Debbie laughs, not very nicely.

'Disappeared?' Charles asks eagerly, but Gordon assures him that Mr Rice has not vanished into the crowded air because he's had the foresight to take his suit and his suitcases of samples with him. Perhaps what I saw last night was some kind of valedictory salute.

'The bloody bastard bugger,' Vinny says, throwing his clothes on the bonfire. 'A real insect,' Debbie summarizes.

A plume of matching smoke curls up above the hedge next door, where I find Audrey tending a bonfire of leaves for Mrs Baxter. Her hair is loose and keeps lifting in the breeze and strands of the red-gold cover her face like a veil. 'We know nothing,' she says mysteriously, when she catches sight of me. Perhaps she's referring to the biology exam we've just failed.

The sadness of autumn is in the air, the smell of woodsmoke and earth and things long-forgotten. Over our heads the first skein of geese (the souls of the dead) scissor through the air, heading for their winter home, north of Boscrambe Woods, the creaking noise they make engenders a fit of melancholy in both of us. The Dog lifts its head, watching them make their black wingprints across the sky and gives a sad little whine. 'Here comes winter,' Audrey says. It was this time of year when my mother left and sometimes it seems to me that, in autumn, the whole world becomes an elegy for Eliza. Sometimes – like now – the loss of her swamps me, my heart turns hard like a stone and something drags my insides like the tug of a retreating tide. It's like being a child again, feeling her absence paralysing me until all emotion is reduced to one mantra, *I want my mother, I want my mother, I want my mother.*

Audrey sighs deeply as if in empathy. Despite being wrapped in a shapeless old coat of Mrs Baxter's, she seems to be losing her skinny child's frame and beginning to bloom, like a very late flower. This new womanhood doesn't seem to be a result of her eating any more though, in fact, if it's possible she eats even less, little-bird portions that she pecks dutifully at when someone's watching her.

In her kitchen, Mrs Baxter has a pot of mushroom soup on the stove ('Daddy's favourite') and is busy making a blackberry and apple pie with apples from her own tree and the very last of the year's blackberries from the church graveyard, unconcerned about what her blackberries might have been feeding on (flesh and blood). She presses a brown paper bag of apples on me to take home, 'For an Eve's pudding, or something.' But there is no Eve in our house to cook it.

Mrs Baxter rubs fat into flour, lifting it high in the air and then letting it fall again like fine, soft snow and says, 'Audrey's filling out at last, isn't she?' She cuts up the apples, slicing the full moons of cored apples into a dozen new moons.

Mrs Baxter's face has blossomed with an enormous bruise, like a gorgeous truncated rainbow – violet, indigo and blackberry-blue. 'Silly me,' Mrs Baxter says when she catches sight of me looking at it, 'I tripped over the cat and hit myself on the sideboard.' The Baxters' neat tortoiseshell tabby sits indifferently on the window-sill, gazing at the birds feeding at the bird-table in the garden. The kitchen door stands open to let in the bright blue October day outside. Sithean would be such a lovely place if it wasn't for Mr Baxter.

Mr Baxter is taking early retirement at the end of the Christmas term, although not through choice. There has been some heavily suppressed scandal at Rowan Street Primary to do with a small boy who had to be hospitalized after one of Mr Baxter's routine punishment sessions. Mr Baxter is like an overheated boiler that Mrs Baxter spends a lot of time trying to damp down.

On cue, he storms into the kitchen, destroying the peace, asking Mrs Baxter what the bloody hell she's done with his pipe and knocking the colander of blackberries all over the kitchen floor and I make a hasty exit in case he's about to blow up.

'There you are,' Debbie says when I come in, carrying the apples. 'Or are you?'

'Pardon?' We must be playing Lost Identity again.

Vinny sits at the kitchen table eating a biscuit at the same time as she smokes a cigarette, contemplating a huge, bloody ox heart sitting on a white enamel plate in the middle of the kitchen table like the results of an Aztec sacrifice (I could swear I can see it still pumping). I presume this is our tea for tonight and not the remains of Mr Rice. It doesn't seem to be Vinny's heart – it's too big and anyway her scrawny chest looks intact.

One of Vinny's subjects – Pyewacket, a gentlemanly black tom with white bib and tucker and spats – is delicately licking the heart in a way that looks oddly affectionate.

The cat does not attempt to drink from the saucer of milk which is also on the table, which is just as well as the milk is full of chopped-up fly agaric. 'Kills the bluebottles,' Vinny says by way of explanation and drags hard on a roll-up and lets smoke stream out through her nose, so that she looks like a dragon letting off a head of steam.

The Dog lays its head on Vinny's knee and starts to drool gently onto her skirt, its expression suggesting it's giving up its soul to Vinny (whereas in fact it's wondering if she'll drop any biscuit crumbs).

Debbie is too preoccupied to notice any of these assaults on kitchen hygiene. She's standing at the sink washing her hands over and over again as if she personally had just removed the heart. She is obviously mad. Yesterday I found her trapped in the living-room, watching the mantelpiece to see if anything had moved, quite unable to move herself. 'If I turn my back for one second they'll be off,' she said.

'They?'

'Those candlesticks.'

'Do you see that dog?' she says to me now and I follow her gaze to Gigi who is ripping an old slipper to shreds in a particularly psychopathic way.

'Yes, I see it.'

'It looks like Gigi, doesn't it?'

'Very like,' I agree. 'Identical, in fact.'

Debbie drops her voice to a whisper and looks around the room in a paranoid way. 'Well, it *isn't*.'

'No?'

'No,' she says, and gives my sleeve an urgent tug to move me out of Gigi's earshot. She moves her little piggy snout nearer my ear. 'It's a robot!'

Vinny snorts contemptuously and Gigi responds by snarling, retracting her upper lip to reveal a row of tiny discoloured shark teeth. Pyewacket looks up from his adoration of the ox heart and regards this stand-off with some interest. Chaos, I suspect, is about to break out in the kitchen again.

'A robot? Gigi's been replaced by a robot?'

'Yes.' What a bampot, as Mrs Baxter would say, but what can you expect from a woman sharing her one brain cell with a poodle on a turnabout basis. Whose turn it is today is anybody's guess. I take hold of the Dog's collar and present it to her like a dog show judge. 'And what about this Dog, is this the same Dog – or has it also been replaced by a robot?' To help her guess, the Dog runs through its limited range of facial expressions (sad, sadder, tragic) but she refuses to respond.

'Have you talked to Gordon about all this?'

'Gordon?' she repeats, giving me one of her mad looks. (Oh no, not him as well.) 'Yes, Gordon.' Debbie's eyes narrow (if that's possible) and she looks away, chewing her lip and finally says, 'The person pretending to be Gordon, you mean.'

★

'Look,' I say to Gordon when he trudges home from work, a suburban Atlas with the cares of Arden on his shoulders. 'Look, there really is something wrong with Debbie.'

'I know,' he says wearily, 'but I've taken her to the GP.'

'And?'

Gordon shrugs helplessly. 'He prescribed her some pills, said her nerves were frayed (frayed nerves, what an idea). Poor Debs,' he adds sadly, 'it would all be different if she had a baby.'

To make up for not having a baby, Gordon (the person pretending to be Gordon – who knows, she might be right, after all, Charles and I have had our doubts) does the best he can and takes her out for a meal to the Tap and Spile.

Charles has taken the Dog for a walk and Vinny and I are watching *Coronation Street* (Vinny's a member of the Ena Sharples fan club). She's preoccupied during the advertising break by the disintegration of her roll-up and keeps picking out shreds of tobacco from her mouth so that she looks like a tortoise trying to eat brown shredded lettuce. She's got a piece of cigarette paper stuck to her lip as well. She really ought to go back to smoking Woodbines.

'There's someone at the door,' Vinny says without taking her eyes off the television screen.

Vinny is covered in Cats, like someone in a surreal film – three on her lap, one draped around her shoulders, one at her feet. I half-expect to see one on her head in a minute. She could make a tippet out of the next two to die, that would be unusual. (Why do cats sleep so much? Perhaps they've been trusted with some major cosmic task, an essential law of physics – such as: if there are less than five million cats sleeping at any one time the world will stop spinning. So that when you look at them and think, *what a lazy, good-for-nothing animal*, they are, in fact, working very, very hard.)

Catskins Vinny picks up a toasting-fork and looks as if she's about to spear Gigi with it. 'There's someone at the door,' she repeats impatiently.

'I didn't hear anyone.'

'That doesn't mean there isn't somebody there,' she says. (Isn't this the way the Dog was introduced into the story? I must be having *déjà vu*, one more alarming little snag in the fabric of time, I suppose.)

'All right, I'm going, I'm going,' I say when she starts waving the toasting-fork at me.

I open the back door cautiously, you never know what might be walking abroad – it's nearly Hallowe'en and there is still the vivid memory of Mr Rice to contend with. I'm half-expecting there to be another dog on the doorstep, Arden is all exits and entrances, its thresholds the places where the interesting things happen. It isn't a dog, however, it's a cardboard box. Inside the cardboard box is a baby.

A BABY!

I close my eyes and count to ten and then open them again. It's still a baby. The baby is fast asleep. It's very small and apparently very new. There's a piece of ruled paper Sellotaped onto the box on which someone (not the baby, presumably) has printed in block capitals:

PLEASE LOOK AFTER ME

I doubt whether this exhortation is addressed to me personally, I am not particularly renowned for my nurturing skills, we don't have much direct experience of babies in Arden, I've never even seen one close-up.

My poor heart's turned into a little rib-caged bird, there's something exhilarating about finding the baby – like spotting fish in rivers (or foxes in fields or deer in woods) but at the same time finding the baby is terrifying (tigers in trees, snakes in the grass). And the baby isn't just a mysterious mis-delivery by the baby shop, it brings with it myth and legend – Moses and Oedipus and the fairy's changeling.

Gingerly, I pick up the whole box, I don't really want to handle the baby in case I damage it (or vice versa).

'Look,' I say to Vinny, holding out the cardboard box for her inspection.

'Whatever it is, we don't want any of it,' she says, pushing it away.

'No, *look*,' I insist. She lifts one of the flaps of the box and her mouth falls open in disbelief. 'What is it?'

'What does it look like?'

Vinny shrinks away from the cardboard box in the same way other people shrink from rodents. 'A baby?'

'Yes.'

She shakes her head in bafflement. 'But why?' But this is not the time for existential questions, the baby has opened its new eyes and started to bawl. 'Take it away,' Vinny says quickly. I place the box on the floor between us so that we can get used to it slowly.

Charles comes back with the Dog and we show him the baby, which has given up crying and gone back to sleep. The Dog sticks its head inside the box and wags its tail enthusiastically but then, unfortunately, starts to lick the baby and it wakes up and starts bawling again. Maybe the Dog can look after it, 'Like Romulus and Remus?' Charles says. 'Or Peter Pan.' (He knows, he is a Lost Boy himself.) The baby's crying has reached a critical level but unfortunately the Dog is the wrong sex to succour it.

Charles lifts the baby out of the box as if it's an unexploded bomb and holds it out from his body with his arms stiff so that the baby, thinking it's about to be dropped from a great height, starts to scream horribly. Vinny has a tentative go, jiggling it around in a self-conscious way, with a rictus of a smile on her face, but, as you might expect, this only makes matters worse. Luckily, just then Debbie and Gordon come home and although there are a few minutes of complete disbelief, followed by hysteria and ending in furious discussion, the end result is that Debbie 'will keep the kid'.

'You can't *keep* it,' Gordon says, horrified.

'Why not?'

'Because you just can't. It's not yours.' Debbie waves the ruled paper around under Gordon's nose. 'What does that *say*, Gordon?'

'I know what it says, Debs,' he says gently, 'but we have to take the baby to the police.'

'And what will they do with it? Put it in an orphanage that's what. Or,' she adds balefully, 'a prison cell. Nobody wants this baby, Gordon, and somebody has asked *us* to look after it. "Please look after me", it says so right here.'

'And what are you going to tell people?' Gordon asks incredulously.

'I'll just say it's mine.'

'Yours?' Gordon asks.

'Yes, I'll say it was a home delivery [which I suppose is true]. Nobody will know.' Debbie *is* fat enough to have had a baby without anybody knowing and you do hear about people giving birth without expecting to – standing at the cooker heating milk one minute, the next – a parent. 'People believe anything you tell them,' Debbie says. 'And we'll just say, "We've been so disappointed in the past that we didn't want to talk about it too much and spoil our luck." And look how lucky we are,' she adds, and starts to make baby talk to the baby that's such drivel that it drives Vinny from the room. The baby looks as though given half a chance it would be off as well. 'People don't *care*, Gordon,' Debbie says crossly when he starts objecting again, 'nobody cares what anybody does, not really. You can get away with murder and nobody would notice.' Gordon flinches and stares at the baby.

I suppose, in a way, it *is* like murder – for every one murder that's discovered there are probably twenty that pass unremarked. The same is probably true of babies, for every one you hear about that's been abandoned on a doorstep there are probably twenty taken in with the milk.

'He's hungry, poor chap,' Gordon says, visibly softening.

'It's a *her*, silly,' Debbie says (in her element now), unwrapping her baby gift to show Gordon, for the baby did not come naked to the doorstep of Arden, it came carefully gift-wrapped in a shawl as white as snow and as full of cockleshells as the sea.

There's more to photosynthesis than meets the eye really, isn't there? I'm thinking this as I walk along Chestnut Avenue on the way to the morning bus. It's the basic alchemy of all life – the gold of the sun transmuting into the green of life. And back again – for the trees on Chestnut Avenue have turned to autumn gold, a treasure of leaves drifting down on the pavements. Everything in the whole world seems capable of turning into something else.

And perhaps there's no such place as nowhere – even thin air is still *something*. (Composition of the atmosphere on the streets of trees: 78 per cent nitrogen, 21 per cent oxygen and 1 per cent the trace elements – the wail of the banshee, the howl of the wolf, the cries of the disappeared.)

Everything dies, but gets transformed into something else – dust, ash, humus, food for the worms. Nothing ever truly ceases to exist, it just becomes something else, so it can't be lost for ever. Everything that dies comes back one way or another. And maybe people just come back as new people – maybe the baby's the reincarnation of someone else?

The molecules of one thing split apart and team up with different molecules and become something else. There's no such thing as nothing, after all – unless it's the great void of space – and perhaps even there are more things than are dreamt of in our philosophy. (Just because you can't see something doesn't mean it doesn't exist.)

Perhaps there are molecules of time that we don't know about yet – invisible, rarefied molecules that look nothing like ping-pong balls – and perhaps the molecules of time can rearrange themselves and send you flying off in any direction, past, future, maybe even a parallel present.

Eunice is waiting for me at the corner of the street, looking pointedly at her watch – the usual dumbshow of punctual people who want to display their moral superiority to their unpunctual friends (how much easier if the punctual people just turned up late). The clocks have recently changed, a day late in our inefficient household where we never know whether time is going forwards or backwards. 'Spring forward, fall back,' Eunice chants. 'Daylight saving' – what an amazing idea. (If only you could, but where would you keep it? With the time that's found? Or the time that's kept? A treasure chest, or a hole in the ground?)

'You're late,' Eunice says.

'Better than never,' I reply irritably. Audrey's already waiting at the bus-stop. 'Look,' I say to her as I spot a red squirrel helter-skeltering around one of the solid sycamores and Eunice is prompted to explain to us in great detail why this is impossible as there are no red squirrels in Glebelands. (Perhaps it's Ratatosk who runs up and down the great ash Ysggadril?)

Eunice launches into a lecture about the differences between red and grey squirrels when Audrey absent-mindedly ventures, 'Not just the difference between red and grey then?'

I watch a red-gold leaf drift down and catch on Audrey's hair. It gives me a funny feeling in the pit of my stomach. I have to say something to Audrey. I have to say something about the baby, about the cockleshell shawl which Debbie handed swiftly over to our waste disposal unit (Vinny), to be burnt on a bonfire and which my memory now questions ever having seen. ('What happened to that lovely shawl you were knitting for your niece in South Africa?' I ask Mrs Baxter casually. 'Oh, I finished it,' she says, pleased at the memory, 'and sent it off in the post.' So there you go.)

'Here's the bus,' Eunice announces as if we can't see for ourselves the red double-decker steaming up Sycamore Street towards our bus-stop, its final outpost before it turns around and heads back into town.

And then I watch it disappear before my eyes.

'Hang on a minute,' I say, turning to Audrey in amazement to see if she's witnessed this extraordinary vanishing act but, lo and behold, she's gone too. And Eunice. And the bus-stop and the pavements, houses, trees, aerials, rooftops . . . the past has come crashing through into the present again without a by-your-leave.

I'm standing in the middle of an impenetrable thicket of Scotch pine, birch and aspen, of English elm and wych elm, common hazel, oak and holly, stranded in the middle of a great green ocean. It might not be the past, of course – instead of time-travelling I might simply have travelled – been picked up by some giant, invisible hand and deposited down again in the middle of a great wildwood. But it feels like the past, it feels as if the clocks have gone right back to the beginning of time, the time when there was still magic locked in the land. On the other hand, I can't have gone back much more than twelve million years, give or take a second or two, if Miss Thompsett's history of photosynthesis is correct. (*Most of the trees we know today were in existence by twelve million years ago.*)

I pick up a leaf skeleton. It is autumn in the past too. The mouldering mushroom smell of decay is in my nostrils. A dark blanket of green ivy covers the ground. It is incredibly quiet, the only sound is birdsong. Even the sweet birds singing hidden in the trees only contribute to the peace in their great forest cathedral. Perhaps I'm not at the beginning of time, but at the end, when all the people have gone and the forest has reclaimed the earth.

I like it here, it's more restful than the present, wherever that is. I shall gather nuts and berries and make myself a nest in the hollow of a tree and become as nimble as a squirrel in my great sylvan home. Does this forest have an end, does it have distinct boundaries where the trees stop, or does it go on forever, curling like a leafy shawl around the earth, making an infinity of the great globe?

But then, sadly, I am ripped out of my new Eden by the number 21 bus smashing through the wildwood in a great cracking and splintering of branches, sending leaves flying up in the air. The bus rolls towards me and stops. The ancient wood has vanished. I am back at the bus-stop.

'Izzie?' Audrey says, stepping onto the platform of the bus. 'Come on.' I climb on board and listen to the conductor ringing the bell and the engine revving noisily and proffer my fare with a sigh. How phlegmatic I am in the face of unravelling time.

I look at Audrey sitting next to me, reading over her French grammar, and say nothing. We all have our own secrets to keep, I suppose.

Why am I dropping into random pockets of time and then popping back out again? Am I really doing it or am I imagining I'm doing it? Is this some kind of epistemological ordeal I've been set? I should never have tried to kill time. I wasted it and now it's wasting me.

If I had more control it might be useful – I could go back and put all my money on the three o'clock winner at Sandown or patent the electric lightbulb, or any one of the usual fantasies of would-be time-travellers. Or – more thrilling – I could go back and meet my mother. ('You could meet her now if you had her address,' Debbie says, rather sarcastically.) I finger the leaf skeleton in my hand – it wouldn't really stand up as evidence in court, it looks exactly like one I could have picked up a minute ago on the streets of trees.

It's Hallowe'en and Carmen is sitting on my bed painting her toenails in a lurid shade called 'Frosted Grape' that make her feet look as if someone's pulled her toe-nails out with pliers. The Dog's sprawled on the floor trying to ignore Eunice who's explaining the evolution of the wolf into the domestic canine. 'See this tail,' she says, picking up the Dog's thin tail to demonstrate and which he immediately whips away from her in horror.

When she's finished martyring her toenails, Carmen does mine, a task made more difficult by the fact that the only light in the room is coming from the candlelit eyes and ghoulish grin of a turnip lantern that is sitting on the window-sill to light the way for the dead into the house.

Carmen is deep in preparation for her marriage to Bash. 'You don't think you should wait a bit?' I ask doubtfully.

'Oh come on – I'm sixteen, I'm not a *child*,' Carmen says, pushing a huge gobstopper from one side of her mouth to the other. When will I find someone who thinks enough about me to take me to the Gaumont on King Street, let alone marry me? 'Oh, it'll happen to you one day,' Carmen says airily. 'It happens to everyone – you fall in love, you get married, you have kids, that's what you do . . . someone will come along.'

('Oh, one day,' Mrs Baxter says, equally assured, 'your prince will come [she almost breaks into song] and you'll fall in love and be happy.' But what if the prince that came looked like Mr Baxter, all rusty armour and gimlet visor?)

But no-one will ever want me once they find out how mad I am. And anyway I don't want 'someone', I want Malcolm Lovat.

How shall I kill Hilary? Fly agaric? Aconite slipped from a ring on my finger? Bash her skull in like a boiled egg or a beechnut?

144

Or better still take her with me when I next fly through time and dump her in the pre-shampoo past, twelfth-century Mongolia say. That would teach her.

'What do boys see in Hilary?' Eunice says dismissively. 'So OK – she's got long blond hair and big blue eyes and a perfect figure – but what else has she got going for her?' (Eunice is annoyed with Hilary because she's beaten her in a chemistry test.)

'Hmm? What else?' Carmen explains patiently to her that that's enough for most boys. She fishes in her handbag for a packet of ten Player's No 6 and shakes out cigarettes on my bed. 'Go on,' she urges Eunice, 'it won't kill you.'

We suck on cigarettes. Carmen also manages to stuff in a mint, elliptical rather than round (perhaps if her mouth stopped working for more than a minute she would die). Audrey is, as usual, absent. 'What's wrong with Audrey?' Carmen asks.

'She's got flu again.'

'No, I mean what's *wrong* with her?' Somewhere in the depths of the house the baby cries. 'How's she getting on?' Carmen asks, cocking her head in the direction of what I suppose she intends to be Debbie.

'Well . . . it's hard to explain exactly. She's kind of loopy.'

'That happened to my mother after she had every one of us,' Carmen says, 'it goes away. Women's trouble,' she adds with a knowing sigh. I don't think Debbie's loopiness is going to go away, the baby is now the only person in her immediate family whom she doesn't think has been replaced by an accurate replica of themselves. The baby's squalls grow louder (in some ways it reminds me of Vinny) and all of a sudden the scent of sadness passes me by like a cold draught of air and I shiver.

'Someone walk over your grave?' Carmen says sympathetically.

'That's a ridiculous saying,' Eunice says (Eunice would be happier if words could be replaced by chemical formulas and algebraic equations). 'You'd have to be dead in order to be in your grave, but you're sitting here alive in the present.'

'The living dead,' Carmen says cheerfully, stuffing lemon

bon-bons into her mouth. Maybe we're all the living dead, reconstituted from the dust of the dead, like mud pies. The cries of the baby upsets my invisible ghost, making it waver and shimmer on the spiritual wavelength like an invisible aurora borealis. 'What's that funny smell?' (Spirit of health? Or goblin damned?) Carmen asks, sniffing the air suspiciously.

'Just my ghost.'

'Ghosts,' Eunice scoffs, 'there's no such thing, it's a completely irrational fear. Phasmophobia.'

But I'm not afraid of my ghost. He – or she – is like an old friend, a comfortable shoe. Phasmophilia.

'That sounds perfectly disgusting,' Eunice says, making a face which does nothing for her.

When they go, I put the light on and get down to my Latin homework. Lying on my bed, to the accompaniment of Radio Luxembourg on my little Phillips transistor, kindly bought for me by Charles for my birthday, on his staff discount.

Unfortunately, the message on the radio airwaves is as blue as blue can be – Ricky Valance telling Laura he loves her, Elvis Presley asking me if I'm lonesome tonight (yes, yes) and Roy Orbison declaring that only the lonely know how he feels (I do, I do). I roll over on my back and stare at the cracks on my ceiling. It seems I have been cast from a purely melancholic mould. I'm half sick of shadows, I really am.

I have to translate Ovid. In *Metamorphoses* you can't move for people turning into swans, heifers, bears, newts, spiders, bats, birds, stars, partridges and water, lots of water. That's the trouble with having god-like powers, it's too tempting to use them. If I had metamorphic powers I'd be employing them at every opportunity – Debbie would have been turned into an ass long ago, and Hilary would be hopping about as a frog.

And me, I am a daughter of the sun, turned by grief into something strange. For homework, I'm translating the story of Phaeton's sisters, a story of nature green in bud and leaf. Phaeton's sisters who mourned so much for their charred brother that they turned into trees – imagine their feelings as they found their feet were fast to the earth, turning, even as they looked, into roots. When they tore their hair they found their hands were full, not of hair, but of leaves. Their legs were trapped inside tree-trunks, their arms formed branches and they watched in horror as bark crept over their breasts and stomachs. Clymene, their poor mother, frantically trying to pull the bark off her daughters, instead snapped their fragile branches and her tree-daughters cried out to her in pain and terror, begging her not to hurt them any more.

Then slowly, slowly, the bark crept over their faces, until only their mouths remained and their mother rushed from one to another, kissing her daughters in a frenzy. Then, at last, they bid their mother one last terrible farewell before the bark closed over their lips for ever. They continued to weep even when turned into trees, their tears dropping into the river flowing at their feet and forming drops of sun-coloured amber.

('Rather an emotional translation, Isobel,' is my Latin teacher's usual verdict.) Only the lonely know how I feel.

Will I ever be happy? Probably not. Will I ever kiss Malcolm Lovat? Probably not. I know this catechism, it leads to the slough of despond and a sleepless night.

The dead, extinguished eyes of the turnip lantern stare at me through the dark as I try to get to sleep.

The dead will be walking abroad now, stepping through the veil from the other world for their annual visit. Perhaps the Widow will be found downstairs, reclaiming her bed from Vinny. Perhaps dead cats are already mewling and purring on the hearthrug and perhaps Lady Fairfax is even now gliding up and down the staircase with her head tucked underneath her arm like a music hall joke.

Where is Malcolm? Why isn't he knocking at my window instead of the cold, hard rain? Where is my mother?

I fall asleep with the smell of woodsmoke in my hair and the scent of sadness coiled around me like a vine, and dream that I'm lost in an endless dark wood, alone and with no rescuer, not even Virgil come to offer me a package holiday to hell as my forfeit.

BACKWARD PEOPLE

ISOBEL WAS SURE SOMEONE HAD JUST CALLED HER NAME, THE ECHO seemed to linger invisibly in the grey light and she pinched Charles' ear to wake him up. Someone *was* shouting their names, the voice sounded far away and hoarse. Charles stood upright and rammed his cap on his head. 'It's Daddy,' he said. Charles looked careworn, as if on the inside he'd aged several decades since yesterday. The voice drew closer, close enough for them to follow the direction from which it was coming. And then, suddenly, as if he'd just stepped out from a tree that he'd been hiding behind all along – there he was, there was Gordon.

He dropped to his knees, his body collapsing with relief, and Isobel stumbled into his arms and burst into tears, but Charles held back, looking on with empty eyes as if he suspected Gordon might be just another woodland mirage. An appearing trick.

'Come on, old chap,' Gordon coaxed softly and held out a hand towards Charles until finally Charles fell against the paternal gabardine breast and started to sob – deep, ugly sobs that racked his small body. Gordon laid his cheek against Isobel's curls, so that they formed another wretchedly sentimental tableau (*'Where have you been, Daddy dearest?'* perhaps). Gordon stared at a tree in front of him as if what he was seeing wasn't a tree but a gibbet.

'Time to go,' Gordon said eventually, reluctantly. Charles sniffed hard and wiped his nose on his sleeve. 'We have to help Mummy,' he said, the urgency of his message punctuated by woebegone hiccups.

Gordon hoisted Isobel up and carried her high on his chest, the other hand holding onto Charles. 'Mummy's all right,' he said and before Charles could protest they were brought up short at the sight of Vinny – Vinny whom both of them had completely forgotten about since she'd gone to do you-know-what. She was sitting on a moss-covered tree-stump with her head in her hands. She looked dark and gnarled like some ancient forest-dwelling creature. But when she stood up, with no word of greeting for Charles or Isobel, they could see that she was the same old Vinny and not some mythic creature. 'There you are,' Gordon said, as if he'd just encountered her in the back garden and – apparently sharing the same delusion – she replied, 'You took your time.' Her thick brown stockings were laddered and she had a scratch on her nose. Perhaps she'd been clawed by a wild animal.

The familiarity of the insides of the black car made them weak with happiness. They inhaled the seat-leather drug, Isobel thought she might die of hunger any minute, thought she might *eat* the seat-leather, perhaps Charles was thinking the same thing as he ran his hands over the leather of the back seat as if it was still attached to an animal. Their feet dangled above the floor of the car, their socks filthy, their legs latticed by scratches. 'Mummy,' Charles reminded Gordon, who gave him a stiff smile of reassurance in the rear-view mirror. 'Mummy's fine,' he said, pressing his foot down on the accelerator.

They didn't see how she could be fine, she didn't look fine the last time they saw her. Where was she now? 'Where is Mummy?' Charles asked plaintively. Gordon's eyelid tremored slightly and he stuck his indicator out and took a sudden right turn instead of answering. 'Hospital,' he said, after they'd been driving down this new road for a while. 'She's in hospital, they're going to make her better.'

Vinny, who was collapsed in the passenger seat, looking as if she needed a blood transfusion, came to life for a moment and said, rather groggily, 'Don't worry about her,' and gave a grim little laugh. 'At last, I get to sit in the front,' she added with a sigh and closed her eyes.

Charles took Eliza's shoe out of his pocket where it had been since last night and handed it silently to Gordon who dropped it and nearly lost control of the car. Vinny woke up, snatched the shoe and stuffed it in her bag. By now, the heel was hanging off like a tooth about to drop out.

'Are we going home?' Charles asked after a while.

'Home?' Gordon repeated doubtfully as if this was the last place he was thinking of going. He glanced at Vinny, as if to glean her opinion, but she'd dropped off to sleep and was snoring with relief, so with a heartfelt sigh, Gordon said, 'Yes, we have to go home.'

Back in Arden the Widow made them porridge and bacon and eggs before putting them to bed. 'The condemned man ate a hearty breakfast,' Gordon said, staring gloomily at his bacon and eggs. He cut his bacon up into small pieces and stared at it for a long time before placing a piece in his mouth as if it was a delicate thing that he might damage if he chewed it too hard. After a considerable effort he managed to swallow a piece and then put his knife and fork down as though he would never eat again. Vinny had no such problems and ate her way through breakfast as if a night in the woods was just the thing for giving an edge to your appetite.

The Widow woke them from their dreamless morning's sleep with lunch in bed as if they were invalids. They ate ham sandwiches, the last tomatoes from the greenhouse and lemon Madeira cake and fell asleep again and didn't see the Widow come in and clear away their trays.

At tea-time she roused them again, and they came downstairs for boiled eggs and soldiers of toast followed by leftover apple-pie. Perhaps this would be their lives from now on – eating, sleeping, eating, sleeping – it was certainly the kind of regime the Widow would approve of for children.

Gordon, Vinny and the Widow sat at the tea-table with them but ate nothing, though the Widow poured endless cups of tea – the colour of young copper-beech leaves – from the big chrome pot with its green and yellow knitted cosy. Their eggs waited for them in matching green-and-yellow jackets as if they'd just hatched from the teapot. Vinny sipped her tea daintily, her little finger crooked. The Widow observed Charles and Isobel very carefully, everything they did seemed to be of the greatest interest to her.

Charles took the cosy off his egg and hit its rounded skull gently with his teaspoon until it was crazed all over like old china. Gordon, watching intently, made a funny noise, as though his lungs were being squeezed and the Widow said, 'Stop doing that!' to Charles and leant over and sliced the top off his egg for him. She did the same to Isobel's egg and commanded, 'Eat!' and, obediently, Isobel poked a finger of toast into the orange-eyed egg.

The silence, for once, was astonishing – no head-nipping from Vinny, no lofty pronouncements from the Widow. Only Charles chewing his toast and the funny gulping noise Vinny made when she swallowed her tea. Gordon stared at the tablecloth, lost in some dark dungeon of thought. He looked up occasionally at the thick cotton nets at the bay window as though he was waiting for somebody to step from behind them. Eliza perhaps. But no – Eliza was in hospital, the Widow confirmed. Vinny's tongue flickered like a snake whenever Eliza's name was mentioned. Neither Gordon nor Vinny nor the Widow wanted to talk about Eliza. It seemed that nobody wanted to talk about anything.

But what *had* happened? Everything that had seemed so clear yesterday – the wood, the fear, the abandonment – today seemed elusive, as if the fog that enveloped them last night was still invisibly present. Charles was clinging to the one thing they were sure of – absence of Eliza. 'When can we see Mummy?' he asked insistently, his voice reedy with misery. 'Soon,' the Widow said, 'I expect.' Gordon put his hands over his eyes as if he couldn't bear to look at the tablecloth any more.

As if to help him, Vinny cleared away the dishes on a big wooden tray. Vera had been given 'a couple of days off' the Widow said and Vinny whined, 'Well, I hope you don't think I'm going to take her place,' and just to show what a bad servant she would make she managed to drop the entire tray of china before she got to the door. Gordon didn't even look up.

Before they went to bed for the third and last time that day, they came downstairs in their pyjamas to say goodnight. The Widow gave them milk and digestive biscuits to take upstairs and in exchange they gave goodnight kisses – depositing little bird-pecks on the cheeks of Vinny and the Widow, neither of whom could handle anything more affectionate. The Widow smelt of lavender water, Vinny of coal-tar soap and cabbage. Gordon hugged them one at a time, tight, too tight, so that they wanted to struggle, but didn't. He whispered, 'You'll never know how much I love you,' his moustache tickling their ears.

For a moment Isobel thought she was back in Boscrambe Woods. But then she realized that she'd woken up in her own bed and that the maniac making enormous gestures, like a mad mute, in the semi-darkness was in fact Charles, trying to get her to follow him down onto the first-floor landing.

A wand of light beamed through the gap in the curtains and they could hear the familiar *prut-prut-prut* of the black car's engine. They watched the scene down below from behind the curtains. Gordon (gabardine collar up and hat-brim down – like a villain), was standing by the open door of the car, saying something to the Widow that made her give out a little cry and hang onto his lapels, so that Vinny had to prise her off him. Then Gordon got in the car and slammed the door and without looking back drove away from Hawthorn Close.

The same fat lantern moon that had guided them in the wood only twenty-four hours ago, was hung now in the blackness over the streets of trees. At the top of Chestnut Avenue they could see the car pause as if it was deciding whether to go left up Holly Tree Lane or right along Sycamore Street. Then the black car made up its mind and turned left onto the road north, its rear lights disappearing suddenly into the night.

At breakfast next morning, Vinny was still there, cutting big doorsteps of bread and jam and saying, 'I'm going to come and live here for a while and help to look after you.' She waited for them to say something in response to this news but they said nothing because the Widow was always telling them, 'If you can't think of anything nice to say don't say anything at all.'

'Your daddy's had to go away on business,' Vinny continued, looking at them in turn, first one, then the other as if she was checking for signs of disbelief on their faces.

The Widow came into the dining-room and sat down at the breakfast-table. 'Your daddy's had to go away,' she announced hoarsely and started to dab at her eyes with a handkerchief which was monogrammed extravagantly (not with 'W' for Widow, but 'C' for Charlotte) and which suddenly reminded Isobel of something. She nearly fell off her chair in the hurry to scramble down from the table. She ran into the hallway, pushing a chair next to the hallstand so that she could reach the pegs, clambered up onto it and slipped her hand into the pocket of the plaid wool coat that had been hanging there ever since they came back from the wood, yesterday morning.

Eliza's handkerchief was still there, neatly folded in its white sandwich-triangle, still emblazoned with its initial, still bearing the traces of Eliza's perfume – tobacco and *Arpege* – and something darker, like rotting flower petals and leafmould. By the time Vinny hauled her down from the chair she was hysterical and pulled out a clump of Vinny's hair in the effort to escape her bony clutches. Vinny screamed (the sound of rusty hinges and coffin lids) and gave Isobel a sharp slap on the back of the knee.

'Lavinia!' the Widow rebuked sternly from the dining-room door and Vinny jumped at the tone of the Widow's voice. 'Remember what's just happened,' the Widow hissed in her unlovely daughter's ear. Vinny did an approximation of flouncing and muttered, 'She's better off without her anyway.' In the tussle Vinny managed to wrestle the handkerchief out of Isobel's hand and the Widow bent down and picked up the lace-edged, monogrammed trophy and swiftly tucked it into the stern bosom of her blouse.

In the days after Gordon drove into the night the Widow and Vinny were as nervous as cats. Every car engine, every footstep seemed to put them on the alert. They scoured the newspapers every day as if there might be secret messages hidden in the text. 'I'm a bag of nerves,' the Widow said, jumping and clutching her heart as Vera muttered her way into the dining-room with a tureen of soup.

The Widow tried to be nice to them, but the strain began to show after a while. 'You're such *naughty* children,' she sighed in exasperation. 'That's what happens to naughty children,' the Widow said, as she locked them in their attic bedroom in the middle of a Sunday afternoon as punishment for some transgression they'd committed. They didn't care, they didn't mind being locked up together. They almost liked it.

They were waiting for Gordon and Eliza to come back. They were waiting for the *prut-prut-prut* of the black car. They were waiting for Eliza to come home from the hospital. For Gordon to come back from his business trip. Their outer lives continued much as before – waking, eating, sleeping, starting school again after the half-term holiday – but they could have been robots for all this meant to them. Real time, the time they kept inside their heads, stopped while they waited for Eliza to come home.

Their sense of time grew distorted. The days crawled by at an unbearably slow pace, even going to school didn't seem to make much difference to the great stretches of empty time that yawned ahead of them. Mr Baxter allowed Isobel to start school early, 'to get her off your hands'. Mrs Baxter offered to walk them to school in the mornings and look after them until the Widow and Vinny came home at night. Mrs Baxter fed them milk and cake in her big warm kitchen, Charles pretending to be another little boy altogether in case Mr Baxter walked in.

Vinny, cross to begin with, was so much crosser at the turn that events had taken that she behaved as if she'd quite like to lock them up permanently. So she said anyway. Vinny's face had turned into an old crab-apple and the Widow had to keep her busy at the back of the shop, away from the customers, in case she curdled the cream or made the cheese grow mould. 'It's the change of life,' the Widow explained *sotto voce* to Mrs Tyndale over the broken biscuits (although not so *sotto* that Vinny couldn't hear).

It was the change of life for all of them, but it couldn't last, surely? Sooner or later Eliza would come out of hospital, Gordon would return from his business trip and everything would return to normal. Neither Charles nor Isobel ever thought for a moment that Gordon and Eliza had left them permanently in the clutches of Vinny and the Widow. The memory of a broken Eliza under a tree, her eggshell skull bashed and dented, her white throat, stretched (like time) beyond endurance, was something that they refused to think about. The Widow said that Eliza was getting better in hospital. 'Why can't we go and see her then?' Charles frowned.

'Soon, soon,' the Widow replied, her old milky-blue eyes clouding over.

Life without Gordon was marginally more boring, but without Eliza it was meaningless. She was everything – their safety (even when she was angry), their entertainment (even when she was bored), their bread and meat and milk. They carried her around like an ache inside, somewhere in the regions of the heart. 'Perhaps Mummy's not allowed to talk,' Charles speculated as they played Snakes and Ladders in their attic prison one gloomy Saturday. The cause of their imprisonment was unsure but might have had something to do with the large scratch on the Widow's dining-table and its relation to the penknife in Charles' pocket. 'Perhaps it's bad for her throat or something,' he pursued. Isobel was caught up in the coils of a particularly long snake and didn't notice that Charles had started to cry until it was brought to her attention by a big crystal tear – almost as big as the pear-drops on the Widow's chandelier – splashing onto the board between them.

They were used to each other crying, their waiting was seasoned and watered with tears. ('One or other of you always has the waterworks turned on,' Vinny chided raggedly one morning as Charles started hyperventilating on the way to school and had to be thumped hard by Vinny between the shoulderblades – a remedy on the kill rather than cure side of things.) 'Cheer up,' Isobel urged him now – but in such a melancholic tone that it only made him worse. She passed him the dice-shaker but it was a long time before either of them could make another move.

They were sitting by the fire, listening to *Children's Hour*, Vinny (in the armchair she'd claimed as hers) darning her thick stockings. Vinny was not a needlewoman – the darn she was labouring over looked like a piece of wattle fencing – and the Widow tut-tutted loudly at Vinny's botched handicraft.

Vera clattered in the background, setting the table in the dining-room. The Widow looked at Vinny and Vinny put her darning down. Then the Widow took a deep breath and leant over and turned the radio off. They looked at her expectantly. 'Children,' she said gravely, 'I'm afraid I have some very sad news for you. Your mummy isn't coming home. She's gone away.'

'Gone away? Where?' Charles shouted, leaping to his feet and adopting an aggressive, pugilistic stance.

'Calm down, Charles,' the Widow said. 'She was never what you'd call very *reliable*.' Unreliable? This hardly seemed an adequate explanation of Eliza's disappearance. 'I don't believe you, you're lying!' Charles yelled at her. 'She wouldn't leave us!'

'Well, she has, I'm afraid, Charles,' the Widow said dispassionately. Was she telling the truth? It didn't feel like it, but how could they tell when they were so helpless? The Widow signalled to Vera in the doorway and said, 'Come along now, dry those tears, Isobel – there's a nice cottage pie for tea. And a raspberry shape for pudding, Charles, you know how you like that,' and Charles looked at her with incredulous eyes. Could she possibly believe that a pink blancmange, no sooner seen than eaten, could possibly compensate for the loss of a mother?

It was already nearly two months since Gordon had driven away into the night with only the moon for company. One morning, the Widow received a letter in the post – a flimsy blue bit of paper with foreign stamps. She opened it and as she read it her eyes filled up with tears. 'Well, it's not as if he's dead,' Vinny muttered crossly to the teapot. 'Who?' Charles asked eagerly. 'Nobody you know!' Vinny snapped.

Before bedtime that same night, the Widow said she had some sad news to tell them. Charles' face was a picture of misery, 'Daddy's not left us as well?' he whispered to the Widow, who nodded sadly and said, 'Yes, I'm afraid so, Charles.'

'He'll come back,' Charles resisted stoutly. 'Daddy's going to come back.'

Vinny dipped a Rich Tea biscuit into her tea and nibbled it like a large rodent. The Widow's old liver-spotted hand trembled and her cup rattled on its saucer as she said, 'Daddy can't come back, Charles.'

'Why not?' Charles knocked his cup of cocoa over in his agitation. 'Cloth, Vinny,' the Widow said in a tone that suggested she was warning Vinny about the cloth rather than asking her to go and get one. They could hear Vinny saying, 'Clothvinnyclothvinny,' once she got into the hallway.

The Widow gathered herself together again. 'He can't come back because he's in heaven.'

'Heaven?' they both repeated in unison. The Widow forced them to Sunday School every week so they knew about 'Heaven' – it was blue and contained a lot of clouds and angels, but no-one in a trilby and a gabardine mac.

'Is he an angel?' Charles asked, puzzled.

'Yes,' the Widow said, after a moment's hesitation, 'Daddy's an angel now, looking after you from heaven.'

'He's not dead, is he?' Charles said bluntly and the Widow grew even paler, if that was possible, and said, 'Well, not dead exactly . . .' and put her hands over her face so they couldn't see it and sat like that for a long time saying nothing until they grew very uncomfortable and tip-toed out of the room and up the stairs. They went to bed not much the wiser, more confused, in fact, than before she imparted her 'sad news' to them.

It was ever-helpful Vinny who clarified the situation for them next morning at breakfast. The Widow was still in her room and Vera had slammed the big chrome teapot down and gone off to burn toast. Charles and Isobel were spooning in their porridge, keeping quiet because Vinny was never at her best in the morning. She lit up a cigarette and said, 'I hope you two don't think that things are going to be the same as they were before.' They greeted this remark with the silence it deserved. They were only too woefully aware that things were not as they were before.

'You're going to have to behave very well now that your daddy's dead.'

'Dead?' Charles repeated in horror. 'Dead?' And he turned as white as the Widow's suet pastry, as white as the Widow, and ran from the table. Later, he had to be dragged with some force from the understairs cupboard where he could be heard howling like a wolf-cub.

Gordon had died of a bronchial infection, in a London fog. 'Lots of people died,' Vinny said, as if that made it better. 'A real pea-souper,' she added, sounding quite proud of Gordon, for once. 'He was an asthmatic,' the Widow could be heard telling everyone, 'ever since he was a little boy,' and they could hear the murmurs of surprise and dismay from their sentry-post on the stairs. They had no idea what an asthmatic was, but it sounded serious.

There was a photograph of Gordon in an ornate silver frame on the sideboard. They'd never really noticed it while they had the real thing in front of them, but now it assumed a totemic kind of significance – how could Gordon be so visible and tangible (if only in two dimensions) – and yet be so beyond their reach? War-handsome in his RAF uniform, cap tilted rakishly, he was like a dashing stranger that they regretted not having paid more attention to.

Isobel lay in bed at night, imagining him walking off into a wall of white fog, fog like cotton wool wrapping his body, cotton-wool-fog filling his lungs and choking him. Sometimes in dreams he walked back out from the fog wall, walked towards her, lifting her up and tossing her towards the sky, but when she floated back down to earth Gordon had disappeared and she was alone in the middle of a vast dark wilderness of trees.

Where was Gordon buried? The Widow looked startled when they asked her. 'Buried?' She cranked up the gears in her brain, her eyes were full of little cog wheels – 'Down south, in London, where he died.'

'Why?' Charles persisted.

'Why what?' she responded tetchily.

'Why was he buried down there? Why didn't you bring him home?' But the Widow didn't seem to know the answer to this question.

Of Eliza, nothing remained. Except her children, of course. Charles asked to see photographs of her and the Widow said there weren't any, which seemed strange considering how many times Gordon had produced his old Kodak camera and said, 'Say cheese now, everybody!' Alarmingly, the picture they carried of her in their heads was beginning to fade a little more each day, like a photograph undeveloping, time unravelling – like the jumpers that Vinny laddered down to knit up afresh as something equally horrible. Perhaps Eliza would appear in a few years' time, knitted up as a quite new mother. 'Don't be ridiculous, Isobel,' the Widow said, her patience with them almost all used up. 'Maybe it's because you're such naughty children that she left you,' Vinny remarked one day when Charles had borrowed Vera's tin of Mansion polish to make the parquet of the dining-room into a skating-rink and Vinny had skidded its length on an Indian scatter rug.

To begin with, they haunted the second-best bedroom, trailing their fingers through Eliza's clothes hanging in the wardrobe, looking through the treasure trove of her jewellery box as if it was a reliquary. Charles found one of Eliza's red ribbons coiled up like a sleeping snake in a little Capodimonte pot with pink roses growing out of its lid. The Widow took it from him before he could hide it and said to Vinny, 'This has to stop, it's not healthy', and the next day when the rag-and-bone man came clopping down Hawthorn Close, Vinny was despatched to stop him and all of Eliza's things were hauled out of the second-best bedroom and into his cart. Vinny was dubious, 'This stuff's worth something – we could get some money for it.'

'I don't want money for it,' the Widow said coldly. 'I want rid of it.'

Mrs Baxter – bringing out an apple for the rag-and-bone man's horse – cried, 'Oh, all those lovely clothes, surely you're not giving them for rags?' She lifted the hem of a red wool dress and said sadly, 'Oh, I remember Mrs Fairfax wearing this, I thought she looked so lovely in it.' The Widow waited, tight-lipped, for Mrs Baxter to go away and when she was out of hearing said, 'I'm the only Mrs Fairfax around here!' which, sadly, was true. 'Nosy parker,' Vinny said and squealed as the rag-and-bone horse nudged her from behind.

People watched with interest from behind their curtains as the pile of Eliza's things made its slow progress around the streets of trees. The Widow had disseminated the facts of Eliza's disappearance ('run off with a fancy man') less discretely than you might have expected, usually tossing in some remark about 'poor' Gordon's hitherto unnoticed asthma.

Just after the most dismal Christmas imaginable the Widow succumbed to a bad attack of flu and Vinny was left to run the business alone. The first day, the delivery boy left, the second, Ivy, their recently acquired assistant. 'What are you doing with them?' the Widow croaked frustratedly at her from her sick-bed. 'Eating them?'

On a particularly grey and miserable January Saturday the Widow was still feeling too poorly to get up and Charles and Isobel were left to their own devices while she hacked and hawked in her bedroom. Mrs Baxter came knocking tentatively at the back door, offering her childsitting services but, regretfully, they had to refuse as they had firm instructions from the Widow to stay put because they were both harbouring thick colds themselves. Poor Mrs Baxter was forced to speak to them through the keyhole as Vinny had told them not to open the door to anyone.

They played on the first landing, Charles had his cars and trucks, Isobel had the farmyard animals. She placed her hen, with its brood of little yellow chickens, onto the back of a flat-bed lorry – red die-cast, Charles' favourite.

The Widow came out of her room and complained about the noise. She was wearing a thick plaid dressing-gown and a pair of old slippers, her hair was loose, hanging in a greasy grey hank down her back. She looked like an ancient savage queen. Her voice was hoarse but it didn't stop her from shouting at them, at the sight of so much mixed-up traffic and barnyard activity. 'What is this mess? Clear it up,' she said, towering over them where they were sprawled on the red and blue figured carpet runner.

She took hold of the banister-rail and said, 'I'm going to get an aspirin,' clutching her forehead as if she was trying to keep her head on. She had been so miserable the past few days that they couldn't help but feel sorry for her and Charles jumped up and said, 'I'll get one for you, Granny,' but Charles' reason for jumping up with such alacrity was two-fold: a) to get the aforesaid aspirin but b) because he had a dreadful case of pins and needles. The pins and needles had rendered his left leg so numb that when he put his weight on it, it gave way and he staggered into the Widow.

This alone would not have been enough to propel her down the stairs but the jolt of Charles' body made her put her foot out to maintain her balance and unfortunately the very spot on the carpet where she put the old-slippered foot was already occupied by the red die-cast lorry and its freight of yellow chicks. Her other foot kicked out, scattering cars and animals, while the lorry – recklessly parked at the edge of the top step – shot off the edge, taking its new cargo of slippered foot with it. Mother hen and yellow chicks were broadcast to the four winds and the Widow tumbled head over heels (or 'arse over tip' as Vinny would have had it) – grey hair-slippers-grey hair-slippers-grey hair – bumping off every step. Screaming. Screaming in a weird animal way, the way Mrs Baxter's old cat did when it ate rat poison. The screaming stopped when the Widow reached the foot of the stairs. She landed awkwardly on the back of her neck so that her vacant eyes seemed to be peering up at her splayed legs. It looked like a very uncomfortable position to be in.

Very, very quickly, they picked up the red lorry and the chickens at the bottom of the stairs. Then they scampered back up the stairs, retrieving as they went the carnage the Widow had left in her wake – cows and sheep, the brown carthorse, the fire engine, the black Rover, the milk float, the tiny milk bottles and the ducks and geese – throwing them in the toy box and carrying it up to their attic.

Then they went back downstairs again, trying not to look at the Widow as they skirted past her on the stairs. They threw on their wellingtons and coats, unlocked the back door and ran out into the rain in the back garden, ignoring all prohibitions not to do so.

The Widow's garden was always orderly and neat with

well-mannered flowers – snapdragons and stock and meticulous borders in patriotic white alyssum, blue lobelia and red salvia. The velvet green of the lawn could have graced a bowling-green and the trees – lilac, pear, hawthorn and apple – were never unruly. It was not an exciting garden to play in, but, as the Widow would have said if she could only have spoken – they'd had quite enough excitement for one day.

They played doggedly at the bottom of the garden where even a child with acute hearing, let alone one with their clogged-up, catarrh-fuelled ears, would have had difficulty hearing the screams of a falling woman. That was their alibi anyway.

They could hear Vinny's screams though as she came running out of the back door.

Weeks later, when they were playing marbles, Charles found a lone yellow chick beneath the hallstand where his marble had rolled and he held it up for his sister's inspection. Neither of them spoke. The little yellow chick also kept its secret. Thankfully.

And so they were left to the care of vinegary Vinny, the reluctant relative, the aunt from hell – as old as the century (forty-nine) but not as modern. Nowhere near. They'd never really given Vinny much thought before, beyond how best to stay out of her way, but now that everybody else had gone there was absolutely no avoiding her any more.

Vera handed in her notice as soon as the Widow died and went to live with her sister. The idea of Vinny as the mistress of the house was too much for her. Charles moved into Vera's room and Vinny into the Widow's room (the best bedroom) with her cat, Grimalkin, and complained that the mattress was killing her – which made them think of the Princess and the Pea (although Vinny would have been better cast as the pea rather than the princess) and Charles indulged himself in a series of fantasies about killer mattresses because there was many a time when they would have been more than happy to see Vinny swallowed up by horsehair and ticking.

Vinny was not the kind of person to be left in charge of children. She didn't like them for one thing, and took no pleasure in nurturing anything except her cat – a creature which provided a rare glimpse of Vinny's soft side. It was unnerving to come into a room sometimes and find her on her hands and knees peering under the sofa, cajoling 'Pussypussypussy' in a kindly voice, hoarse from lack of use.

'This is all your mother's fault,' Vinny fumed as she tugged at the knotted tangles in Isobel's hair. Neglected, Isobel's curls had grown haywire, and started to resemble a bush. 'I'm not a bloody hairdresser,' Vinny muttered, duelling with the Mason and Pearson hairbrush.

Charles sought refuge in bad behaviour. He got into fights at school, kicked and bit and got sent home in disgrace so that Vinny had to wallop him with the same Mason and Pearson. He raced around as if he was possessed, knocking things over, breaking things and then standing with a stupid grin on his face. He couldn't keep still. Perhaps it was because he was born on the move. When Vinny told him off he stood with his hands on his hips and laughed like a rocking automaton – *ha-ha-ha* – and Vinny had to slap his face to make him stop.

He wet the bed nearly every night – which had a particularly bad effect on Vinny, bundling his sheets into the copper boiler every morning with the kind of weepings and lamentations that usually accompanied biblical disasters. 'I don't know what's wrong with you!' she screeched, dragging him by one of his big ears up to his room.

One of the aspects of surrogate motherhood that never ceased to astound Vinny was the fact that children grew. If the Chinese could have developed a system of whole body binding, Vinny would have been their first customer. 'You can't have grown!' she screeched every time Isobel displayed stubbed toes from too tight shoes or

Charles' thin red-freckled wrists poked out from blazer cuffs. She would have had them, if she must have had them at all, as midgets. There was no right size for a child in Vinny's eyes, of course, apart from grown-up and gone.

Charles, undersized and long overtaken by his peers, was not so much a problem as Isobel. Vinny refused point-blank to buy another new school uniform when the old one was outgrown within six months.

'Mushrooming,' said Mrs Baxter kindly when she came round with a parcel for Vinny's inspection. 'Second-hand, but awfy good condition,' Mrs Baxter entreated.

Vinny declared that she wasn't aware that she was in need of charity, and Mrs Baxter said, 'Och no, no, no, *no* – not charity, it's just that Mr Baxter's school has a pool of uniforms – everyone agrees it's a sensible idea . . . and I thought that . . . they grow out of them so quickly . . . such a waste to buy new when . . . a good idea . . . lots of folk think so . . .' and eventually when it seemed that Vinny was doing Mrs Baxter a favour rather than the other way round, she accepted her parcel. Grudgingly and with bad grace. Could you drown in a pool of uniforms?

Charles' clown face mooned out from beneath his Billy Bunter cap – Charles had developed a huge stock of silly expressions through which he communicated with the world, as if perhaps it would love him more because he could cross his eyes and ping-pong-ball his cheeks at the same time. Sadly this was not the case.

The cold that Charles was suffering from the day the Widow died seemed never to have left him – his nose was permanently plugged with yellow-green snot and his ears bunged up with something similar. He inhabited the underwater world of the hard-of-hearing and it was only when the school nurse referred him to the hospital that anyone discovered the extent to which Charles was lip-reading his way through life, unscrambling words, like a dyslexia of the ears or aural Scrabble. 'You'd think he'd be able to hear,' Vinny said, disgruntled at having to sit in the hospital waiting-room for hours, 'when his ears are so big.'

Poor Charles, his pink Dumbo-flap ears stuck out from his head like his princely namesake's. 'Flying yet?' Trevor Randall – the arch-bully at school – asked him, and instead of being sensible and slinking away in cowardice, Charles punched him in the eye and had to be beaten into repentance by Mr Baxter.

Eventually, Charles was operated on and a kindly surgeon poked a hole through his eardrums and drained out all the yellow-green snot. Unfortunately, this didn't help him read any better and Mr Baxter still had to bounce wooden rulers off the palms of Charles' hands to help him make out the words on the page.

Charles refrained from telling Mr Baxter that when she came back, Eliza was going to rip Mr Baxter's head off and pull his lungs out through his neck. He was looking forward to savouring the look of astonishment on Mr Baxter's face. *Thwack! Thwack! Thwackkk!* went Mr Baxter's leather strap (or the 'tawse' in Mrs Baxter's quaint language).

Vinny's meagre nursing skills were tested to their limit by coughs and colds, viruses and infections, aches and pains, warts and verrucas – the parental loss documented by germs. Charles was hospitalized again, with a suspected appendicitis, and then discharged again, unable to explain the mysterious source of his pain.

Housekeeping of any kind was sadly wanting in Arden. Widowless, it had grown into a cold cheerless place. Vinny would only light the coal fire in the living-room when the thermometer dropped to Arctic depths. ('Watch out for that polar bear!' Charles said, russet eyes wide with horror and Vinny screeched and looked behind her. *Ha-ha-ha.*)

They wore gloves in the house and Charles sported a navy wool balaclava (knitted, very badly, for him by Vinny) that made him look like a goblin, all he needed were the two holes for his big pointed ears and the disguise would have been complete. Isobel had a pullover knitted by Mrs Baxter that had an intricate pattern of knots and ropes and cables all over it, like something a sailor might have knitted in a dream.

The house was unheated on the grounds of economy. Economy was pinchpenny Vinny's religion (yet she made a very poor economist). 'I'm trying to keep the wolf from the door,' she said, and narrowed her eyes (North Sea grey) and added, 'We're one step away from the poorhouse.' How could Vinny run the business and bring up children? What was she supposed to do? She brought in assistant after assistant to help in the grocery, all of whom seemed to have no purpose in life other than defrauding Vinny.

She spent long hours at night sitting at the dining-table cross-eyed over double-entry bookkeeping, unable to make sense of profit and loss. Not such a good businesswoman as Mother, it turned out.

Vinny scrimped but couldn't save. The Widow's huge meals were replaced by watery scrambled eggs, like lemon vomit, toast and dripping or Vinny's 'speciality' – steak-and-kidney pie, a glutinous grey substance sandwiched between cardboard crusts. They were always hungry, always trying to squirrel away food into their hollow insides. Sometimes Isobel felt so hungry that she wondered if there wasn't someone else inside her, an insatiably greedy person who had to be fed continually.

The Widow's white linen tablecloths and silver cutlery, her flower-sprigged crockery and ivory napkin rings had all been put away as being 'too much trouble to look after' for Vinny. Now they ate with Woolworths cutlery and old plaited raffia mats from Vinny's house. 'Serviettes,' said Vinny, 'are for people with servants,' and Vinny, God forbid, was no-one's servant. 'God gave us a tongue to lick our lips,' Vinny pronounced, 'he didn't create us with serviettes in our hands,' an argument full of logical holes – what about cigarettes? Teacups? Rich Tea biscuits? What indeed about 'God', who didn't get much of a look-in in Arden.

Mrs Baxter was quick to try and step into the mothering breach, clearly horrified by the sudden subtraction of family members – a grandmother, a father and a mother – within the space of such a short time. How? she frequently asked Mr Baxter. How could a mother leave her own children? Her ain weans? (Mrs Baxter was bilingual.) Especially such bonny ones? She must be off her head (or 'aff her heid').

Isobel watched for Mr Baxter marching off early for school and ran round to the back door of Sithean so that Mrs Baxter could dress her hair instead of Vinny, twirling it into neat plaits ('pleats') because the little girls under Mr Baxter's care weren't allowed to unleash their female tresses anywhere near the school building. Mrs Baxter also bought new navy blue hair-ribbons to tie up Isobel's plaits in big bows and said, 'There − don't you look pretty?' with a tremendous new-moon smile of encouragement that couldn't quite disguise the look of doubt on her face.

Audrey's lovely red-gold hair, hair that, let loose, flowed down her back like a rippling volcanic stream, a banner of flame, had to be roped into a big fat plait that hung almost to her waist. There was something about long untamed hair that induced Mr Baxter's bile. 'You should have all of that cut off,' he said, and it seemed a miracle that Audrey's long locks had lasted this long without being shorn.

Summer came. The back garden of Arden was taken over by weeds. Mr Baxter complained to Vinny about the state of the garden. 'I don't want your ruddy dandelions,' he shouted angrily over the beech hedge. Charles waited until he'd gone inside and then blew his dandelion clocks over the hedge while Vinny crowed her approval from the back doorstep. She just didn't understand neighbourliness.

It was Mrs Baxter who hefted out the dandelions though, Mrs Baxter who did all the gardening in Sithean. She grew raspberries and blackcurrants, potatoes, peas and runner-beans and tended the pretty Albertine rose that grew up the trellis which divided the lawn from the fruit bushes and vegetables. Bushes of rosemary, starred with tiny blue flowers, and dark spikes of lavender brushed against your legs as you walked along the garden path and the borders around the big semi-circular lawn were soft and ragged with Canterbury bells that chimed delicately and delphiniums that nodded in the breeze at a pale honeysuckle braiding itself in and out of the beech hedge.

There were new people – the McDades – on Willow Road. You could tell what Mr Baxter thought of Carmen McDade's name from the way his moustachioed top lip sneered whenever he had to pronounce it. The McDades had moved up from London and were such a big family that Mr McDade (a builder, of sorts) and Mrs McDade (a termagant) occasionally mislaid one of the smaller McDades without even noticing. 'Backward,' was Mr Baxter's professional judgement on most of the McDade clan, although Mr Baxter's definition of 'backward' was generous and had frequently included Charles. And even Mrs Baxter.

Carmen tucked her dress into her greying knickers and cart-wheeled across the green lawn of Sithean. 'A bit forward, that girl,' Mr Baxter said with a look of distaste on his face. But how could she be both backward and forward? There was no pleasing Mr Baxter. 'She's only a little girl,' Mrs Baxter protested.

'So?' Mr Baxter said darkly. 'They're all the same.'

Vinny couldn't cope, she was losing the family business. It was all the fault of Eliza. Mrs Baxter had a solution, hovering on the back doorstep with a plate of little pink cakes. Vinny picked one up suspiciously. 'Take them, take them, all of them,' Mrs Baxter urged.

The fairy cakes are not themselves the solution, but 'fostering?'

Vinny's eyes narrow suspiciously. 'Fostering?' Surely not, someone prepared to take the 'poor orphaned bairns' off her hands? Vinny contemplated. And then nearly choked on the little cake, 'Not orphans,' she said, somewhat inaudibly on account of the choking, 'they're not orphans, their mother's alive.'

'Yes, yes, of course,' Mrs Baxter said hastily. Mrs Baxter couldn't remember what Eliza looked like any more. When she thought about her she saw a figure in the distance – at the bottom of the garden, in the field – someone walking away. Vinny licked her fingers clean of icing and said, 'Why not?' But foolish Mrs Baxter hadn't discussed this proposition with 'Daddy' and he looked at her in complete disbelief. 'You're off your bloody head, Moira [so another one], I have to see that stupid boy all day long at school, I don't want him in my house as well. And that girl is *sullen*. Do you hear?' ('Charles can be rather silly sometimes,' Mr Baxter wrote in a restrained way on his Christmas report.)

Sometimes Mrs Baxter read to Isobel and she rested her head on the cushion of Mrs Baxter's pigeon-plump breast, balanced on the other side by Audrey, and for a brief moment she forgot about Eliza and Gordon and the Widow as she listened to Mrs Baxter's lilting peat and heather voice. Mrs Baxter was a surprisingly good storyteller, able to turn herself from a rampaging giant one minute into a tiny kitchen mouse the next.

Mrs Baxter knew the same stories as Eliza but when Eliza had told them they had frequently ended badly and contained a great deal of mutilation and torture, whereas in Mrs Baxter's versions, the stories all had happy endings. Mrs Baxter's Red Riding Hood, for example, was rescued by her woodcutter father who butchered the wolf and slit it open to reveal a grandmother as good as new and, needless to say, everyone lived happily ever after. In Eliza's version, on the other hand, everyone usually died, even Little Red Riding Hood.

Sometimes when they got to the end of a story, where everything had been put right and justice done, Mrs Baxter would sigh and say, 'What a shame that life's not really like that.' Mr Baxter didn't know about these reading sessions – Mr Baxter disapproved wholeheartedly of fairy stories ('stuff and nonsense') although whether he *had* a whole heart was debatable.

One day, Mr Baxter came home unexpectedly early from school and found the three of them in front of a blazing fire. Mrs Baxter was reading, her index finger following every line – because she couldn't find her reading-glasses — and at the point when Red Riding Hood was filling up her little basket with custards, they all suddenly became aware of Mr Baxter's presence in the doorway. Mrs Baxter's body gave a little spasm, like a frightened rabbit, and her reading-finger halted mysteriously on the word 'bobbin'.

Mr Baxter fixed them with his little pebble eyes behind his little pebble glasses for a long time before saying, 'Unlike her stupid brother, the girl can read perfectly well for herself, Moira — I should know, I taught her myself. And as for you, Audrey, you can go up to your room and do the extra arithmetic I set you.' Audrey scurried out of the room and Mrs Baxter said, 'Oh dear, Daddy, we were only reading. What harm is there in that?'

Next day, Mrs Baxter had one eye so swollen that she couldn't open it. 'Walked into a door,' she explained while brushing Isobel's hair, 'silly me.' Audrey was sitting at the breakfast-table with a bowl of cornflakes in front of her and kept lifting her spoon to her lips except it was the same spoonful of flakes over and over again. There were no more stories after that.

'Wait till our mother comes back!' Charles shouted at Vinny after a particularly vicious attack with the Mason and Pearson and Vinny snarled, 'I'd like to see that!' Vinny was doing her best to eradicate all traces of Eliza. The past wasn't a real place to Vinny. She never talked about it, she was a non-historian, the anti-archivist of all that had happened to them — retaining no souvenirs, no artefacts, no documents, no photographs, obliterating the evidence of their previous happy existence. Vinny made bonfires of the past, made bonfires of everything, nothing was safe from her flames.

Every week Vinny would stand in the back garden of Arden tending her bonfire, enveloped in a pall of smoke, ashes being tossed in the air around her like a medieval witch at the stake.

Eliza had been gone over a year. When was she coming back? Why was she taking so long? Sometimes it seemed as though the white fog that had enveloped them in Boscrambe Woods had got into their brains in some way. Perhaps that was how Gordon died too, not fog in his lungs, but fog clouding his brain, driving him mad. Perhaps the fog in the wood had driven Eliza mad, for she must have gone mad to leave them in the clutches of Vinny. She would never leave them, not voluntarily, not all the fancy men in the world could have persuaded her away from them. Surely?

Vinny's hair had gone completely grey, every time she passed the hall mirror, she stroked her convent coif and said, 'Look what you've done to me,' as if it was the mirror that had caused her problems.

Madge-in-Mirfield, now nursing an intimate and deadly cancer, couldn't help, her three grown-up girls didn't want to know. But Madge had a friend who knew someone who'd always wanted –

'Two little children?' Vinny asked hopefully, on a hospital visit.

'No,' Madge said, 'a little boy.'

'Well, that's better than nothing, I suppose.'

'It's all Eliza's fault,' Madge said.

Charles was very, very lucky, Vinny said. But he wouldn't stay lucky if he was a naughty boy. Mr and Mrs Crosland had a big car and expensive coats. Mr Crosland wore long camel and Mrs Crosland wore long beaver, even though it was a hot August day, and Isobel wanted to rub her face in the fur when Mrs Crosland sat in the living-room, drinking tea. 'Poor little thing,' Mrs Crosland said to Charles. Not-so-little Charles (a broad and stocky eight-year-old by now) stared rudely. Mrs Crosland didn't even glance at Isobel. Vinny pointed out Charles' good points like a pedigree breeder and Mrs Crosland murmured approvingly at her new pet.

Charles was in a cloud of misunderstanding – Vinny had not been entirely truthful, leading him to believe that Isobel was coming along as part of a package deal. They hadn't seen Vinny filling only the one suitcase. When the Croslands had finished their tea and used up their limited repertoire of small talk, Mrs Crosland said, 'Well thank you very much, Mrs Fitzgerald, I wish you all the best,' and climbed into the back of the big car. She patted the seat next to her and said, 'Come along, Charles,' and Charles reluctantly got in and was lapped in fur.

Vinny slammed the car door and Mr Crosland started the engine, lifting one hand in farewell without looking behind as he drove away in a crunching of gravel. Mrs Crosland waved a ringed hand and mouthed goodbye with her big crimson lips. Charles' pale face rose up behind the glass of the car window, his yelling silenced by the noise of the car engine. The car moved away slowly, down Chestnut Avenue and Charles' face reappeared in the back window. He seemed to be trying to claw his way through the glass.

His head disappeared suddenly as if someone had just yanked invisibly on his ankles and the car accelerated down the road and turned into Sycamore Street, performing exactly the same disappearing trick as Gordon had already performed, but going in the opposite direction. As with him, there was no reversing back round the corner, no cries of 'Surprise!' from the car's occupants.

Isobel ran after the car until she got a stitch and could run no more and then stood helplessly in the middle of the road so that the butcher's delivery boy, whizzing carelessly round the corner on his bike, had to swerve so wildly to avoid the little sobbing figure that he toppled over and the road was strewn with ration-sized parcels of meat and Vinny was able to secure a thin link of sausages in her apron pocket as she pulled Isobel to her feet and dragged her all the way home.

The dead of night, the world was dark and empty but nothing was frightening any more, not after the wood. Not so dark really, a full moon at the window gave everything a dull gleam, like pewter. This was the time to escape, to shin down the drainpipe, run across the wet grass of the lawn. The only noise in the house was the creak-creak sound of Mrs Crosland's snoring. Charles slid out of bed and felt the long carpet pile between his toes. His clothes were lying on a chair and he crept over to them. He seemed to have shrunk. His eyes were lower than the level of the top of the chair, his nose only reached the doorknob. His toenails click-clacked on the lino at the edge of the room.

Everything in the room was drained of colour, everything turned to shades of grey. When he listened, he could hear that the house wasn't silent at all – he could hear the mice eating in the pantry, the Croslands' old cat dreaming (about chasing the mice). Smells flooded his brain – the dust trapped in the rugs, the old gravy scents coming up from the kitchen, the carnation talcum powder Mrs Crosland had spilled in the bathroom. The smell of petrol seeping up from the garage made him heady, he prowled around the room trying to think, for once strangely comfortable inside his skin.

He loped over to the dressing-table in the corner of the room. The moon had turned the dressing-table mirror into steel. He could see the moon in the mirror, he could see his face in the mirror – no. No. It wasn't possible, it couldn't be. Charles raised his head and let out a tremendous howl of fear, running away from the mirror and leaping onto the bed and burying his head under the covers. In the morning it would all be different. Wouldn't it?

A week after he was kidnapped by the Croslands, Charles reappeared in a sudden unexpected rasping of gravel. The rear door of the car opened and – surprise! – Charles spilled out onto the ground so quickly that you would have almost thought he'd been pushed. The car door slammed again and the window was rolled down.

Mrs Crosland's face, powdered and lacquered like a Japanese geisha, appeared. 'He bites,' she announced, her voice resonating with disgust. 'He bites *ferociously*,' and Mr Crosland shouted over his shoulder, 'That child's *backward*, Mrs Fitzgerald!' Then the Croslands drove away in a bad-tempered wrenching of gears. Charles sat cross-legged on the gravel, swaying backwards and forwards like a rocking Buddha and laughing his clown laugh *ha-ha-ha, ha-ha-ha* at the sight of their car retreating down the drive.

The important thing about the disappearing trick – something that Eliza and Gordon seemed to have failed to grasp – is that the *real* skill was coming back again after you'd vanished. Unlike his parents, Charles had mastered both halves of the trick and to celebrate he executed a mad jigging polka of triumph up and down the drive – until he tripped and cut himself and Vinny said, 'I could have told you it would end in tears.'

Vinny was in the process of destroying Fairfax and Son, partly through alienating the customers ('Well, which do you want – Cheddar or Cheshire? Make up your mind, I haven't got all day!') and partly through appallingly bad management. Eventually she had to sell it at a knockdown price to a competitor and also sold her little terrace house on Willow Road, to a couple called Miller and every time she drove past her old house on the bus Vinny said, 'The Millers got a bargain there.' Vinny was Mrs Hard-Done-By, and nothing, but nothing, would ever be right in her world. Especially not her relatives.

'We'll be in the poorhouse soon,' she informed them. But she had an idea – they will take in lodgers, for what is the use of a house with five bedrooms if only three of them are occupied? Eh? They will give one of them over to a lodger.

Dimly, Vinny discerned that her poor housekeeping might not appeal to the paying-guest and she set about improving her housecraft. She studied the Widow's housekeeping books – an entire kitchen shelf of *aide-ménage* – *The Housewife's Handy Book, Aunt Kitty's Cookery Book, Everything Within, The Modern Housewife's Book* (for once upon a time the Widow was a very modern housewife). For a while, Vinny's enthusiasm even expanded to include the hobby section of *Everything Within* and she attempted, amongst other useful things, 'Sealing-Wax Craft' and 'A Dainty Craft with Cellophane and Silk Raffia.' It was very disturbing to come into the kitchen and find Vinny elbow-deep in papier mâché (the colour of her skin) or attempting to scale the artistic heights of 'Loofah Craft', clip-clipping away with scissors at the bathroom loofah to make a floral still life for the Unknown Lodger's room.

But infinitely worse was the *ancienne cuisine* which Vinny had suddenly become a disciple of, dishes dredged up from the cookery sections of the Widow's books that reeked of England between the wars. Dishes for which they must be guinea-pigs. 'Spaghetti Fritters', 'Rabbit Soup with Curry', 'Compote of Pigeons with Brain Sauce'. Vinny liked nothing better than recipes that began, 'Take a large Cod and boil whole . . .'

'This is disgusting,' Charles ventured over something called a 'Boiled Cow-Heel Pudding'.

'Disgusting is as disgusting does,' Vinny said unhelpfully. They never, ever, thought that they'd feel nostalgic for Vinny's old way of cooking.

Once Vinny considered she'd mastered landlady cuisine she turned her attention to the bedding, searching the depths of the Widow's linen cupboard and bringing out several pairs of Irish linen sheets which were only slightly mildewed. 'You wouldn't get anything better in a hotel,' she declared. Vinny had no idea what the quality of hotel bedding was, never having slept between any, but that didn't stop her fantasizing that Hotel Arden was about to give the Ritz a run for its money. Charles and Isobel couldn't imagine why anyone would want to lodge with them when the mattresses were so thin and the custard so lumpy.

Almost as soon as Vinny declared herself ready to take on all-comers, their first lodger appeared. Vinny was a little surprised because she hadn't even worked out how to advertise for one yet, but Mr Rice turned up on the doorstep ready with references and a proper-lodger kind of job – travelling salesman.

Mr Rice was aged somewhere between thirty-five and sixty-five and had an enormous handlebar moustache, possibly to compensate for the fact that most of his dark brown hair had been devoured by baldness so that the thing he most resembled was a boiled egg. Charles and Isobel exchanged dismal looks because they couldn't imagine anyone more boring. 'Don't worry,' Vinny said, 'there's plenty more where he came from.'

Mr Rice wore loud dogtooth-check jackets and mustard waist-coats and claimed he was a pilot during the war. 'Who's he kidding?' Vinny scoffed, but behind his back because she wanted his money.

'Here we are,' Vinny said, heading new lodgerwards, 'a nice plate of "Sweetbreads Royale".' Chatelaine Vinny – a bleak housekeeper in hard times. 'Well, Mr Rice,' Vinny said, shaving slices off an unidentified roasted mammal at the Sunday dinner table, 'how d'you like it here then?' Mr Rice is 'a gentleman' in Vinny's estimation and his arrival makes her quite skittish for a while.

At first she simpered, bowed and scraped to Mr Rice, wringing her hands in ever-so-humbleness and Mr Rice responded by praising her landladying skills to the skies when you might have expected him instead to puzzle over the 'Haddock Soufflé', and query the damp in his room and the disturbing character of some of his dinners ('Boiled Toad in the Hole,' Vinny announced, shy, yet proud, of her newfound talents).

At breakfast and tea, Mr Rice regaled them with tales from the road. 'A very funny thing happened to me in Birmingham this week, did I tell you?' he asked over a dish of 'Scotch Sheep's Pluck', that Vinny had laboured over all afternoon. Mr Rice had no sense of humour, in fact, if it was possible he had a negative sense of humour so that they knew that any story prefaced 'A funny thing happened' was inevitably going to be unbelievably tedious. What's more, funny things happened to Mr Rice *all the time* so that they rarely endured a mealtime without passing out from boredom.

'Mr Tapioca! Mr Sago!' Charles hooted, his forehead hitting the table as he doubled up in a maniacal *sotto voce* laugh. Isobel worried for Charles. He was nine years old now, yet half the time he behaved like his three-year-old self. Mr Rice appeared not to notice and helped himself to a spoonful of grey boiled potatoes and waxed lyrical about home comforts. 'Silly, silly boy!' Vinny hissed at Charles.

'Ah,' Mr Rice said, sniffing like a Bisto Kid as Vinnie handed over his slice of 'Sheep's Tongue Shape'.

Vinny took a cigarette packet from the pocket of her Empire overall and lit up. Her gnarled hands cupped around the cigarette would have looked better on a large bird of prey. She closed her eyes and sucked hard, with an expression that suggested pain rather than pleasure, and then blew the smoke out of her nostrils, while she dished up an exotic 'Railway Pudding'.

'Delicious,' proclaimed Mr Rice, a dribble of yellow custard creeping down his chin. Vinny batted her meagre eyelashes in a way that might have been interpreted as flirtatious. 'Something in your eye, Mrs Fitzgerald?' Mr Rice inquired through a mouthful of pudding.

'Parallel universes,' Charles said to Mr Rice, eager to expound his new theories to a listening ear, over a tea-table groaning with 'Croquettes of Liver'. 'What if there were other worlds where we had other selves – living out quite different lives, so say, Vinny was a film star [flattered, Vinny cast a rare smile of appreciation in Charles' direction] or Izzie here was the queen of an unknown country and I was –' Charles searched for a parallel life he would like – 'I was an Olympic athlete or a famous Shakespearian actor or a rocket scientist . . .' All this while, Mr Rice was staring at Charles as if he was a lunatic and when Charles' imagination finally ran down he fixed him with an unpoetic eye and said to him, 'You need to get a life, son,' and Charles blushed a colour that clashed horribly with his hair. But really there was only one parallel universe that they wanted to inhabit – the one where they had parents and, for preference, the same ones they had had before.

Another year passed. And then another. Eliza grew dark, stranded in the passage of time, growing into a memory. People were always telling Isobel that she looked foreign – Spanish or Italian – could Eliza have had Spanish blood? Vinny peered down the long dark tunnel to the past and saw something dimly, heard the vague word 'Celtic' and said, 'Not Spanish – Irish, I think.'

'Did she sound Irish?' Charles asked eagerly.

'Sound?' Vinny repeated helplessly. A whiff of *Hempstid* wafted down the tunnel. 'She sounded . . . ridiculous,' Vinny concluded. Eliza's faded and forgotten image plagued them. Where was she? Why didn't she come back? Why did no-one from her world come back? A sister or a brother? An aunt or a godmother? If Eliza couldn't come back then why not a childhood friend, someone knocking on the door saying, 'I knew your mother'? Someone who could tell them the little things – the books she liked to read, her favourite food, the season she liked best.

'Maybe somebody's kidnapped her,' Charles theorized, 'and held her captive against her will even though she pleaded with him to let her go so she could get back to her children?'

'Didn't she have a mother or a father?'

'Questions, questions, questions,' Vinny snapped irritably, 'can't you ask anything else?'

Isobel discovered the provenance of Audrey's hair (the genetic origins of Charles' remained mysterious however). Mrs Baxter's sister, Rhona, came to visit from South Africa and fingered Audrey's hair as if it was something precious and said, 'This is our mother's hair, Moira,' and Mrs Baxter said, 'I ken that, Rhona,' and their eyes filled up with tears.

Mr Baxter didn't approve of this sentimental hair, didn't really approve of Mrs Baxter's sister with her cheerful disposition and easy-going laughter. He looked put out when he came into the kitchen and found them all gathered round the Formica of the kitchen table, looking sad at the memory of maternal hair, and he rounded on Audrey, 'You know you'd be better employed learning your times-tables – you haven't even mastered the sixes yet,' before beating a hasty retreat in the face of so much hair-induced emotion.

'What a Gradgrind,' Mrs Baxter's sister laughed when he'd gone and Mrs Baxter smiled nervously and cut into a cherry and almond

Madeira which signalled itself boldly with a circle of glacé cherries like big drops of bright blood.

The advent of Mrs Baxter's sister brought much reminiscing with it. Until their mother died they'd had an idyllic childhood apparently. 'Full of fun and games, we were always up to high doh, weren't we, Moira?' Despite years under an African sun, Mrs Baxter's sister still had her lovely lilting accent, with its hints of heather and hills, and sang 'John Anderson, my jo' so beautifully that Mrs Baxter wept. 'Oh aye,' Mrs Baxter said with a faraway smile, 'they were grand days.' Whenever Mrs Baxter mentioned her life before Mr Baxter she became very wistful.

What happened in idyllic childhoods? 'We-el,' Rhona said, 'picnics, dressing up, putting on wee plays' – hoots of laughter from both of them at this particular memory – 'then we played a lot of games, our mother knew such good games –' At this point Mrs Baxter screamed and flapped her hands in the air and then ran from the room and reappeared, breathlessly, a few minutes later, thrusting a small red book into her sister's hands. At this, Rhona also lost the power of speech, dancing up and down on the spot and screeching. '*The Home Entertainer* – you've still got it!'

'I have,' Mrs Baxter beamed.

'Poison Spot,' Mrs Baxter laughed with tears welling in her eyes. 'Lemon Golf? Few things can roll more unexpectedly than a lemon!' she read out loud from the instructions.

'Human Croquet!' Mrs Baxter's sister said, in transports of delight. 'That was my favourite.' They played it, she explained, on the lawn of the manse. 'We had a lovely lawn. So green,' she added with an exile's sigh. 'Of course, you need a lot of people for Human Croquet.'

'And they all have to be in the spirit of the game,' Mrs Baxter added.

'Oh yes,' Mrs Baxter's sister agreed.

In the end they raided the fruit bowl, first for a game of Lemon Golf, played on the living-room carpet with an assortment of instruments – walking-sticks, an old hockey stick, a chair leg from the understairs cupboard and (as you would expect) lemons. This was followed by an energetic game of Orange Battle in which even Audrey became animated, and the untimely arrival of Mr Baxter – just as Mrs Baxter was flailing with her teaspoon at her sister's orange – couldn't quite dissipate the party atmosphere.

Mrs Baxter's sister returned to South Africa the next day and her departure left Mrs Baxter very sad. And very clumsy, it seemed, for she was black and blue all over, like a bad joke. 'I fell down the stairs,' she said, 'silly me.' Silly Mrs Baxter really ought to be more careful.

Time had flown. Seven years of it. Eliza was never coming back, she may as well be as dead as Gordon.

Arden was in decay, there was wet-rot in the floors and dry-rot in the stairs. The windows stuck, the doors jammed. The wallpaper peeled. The dusty drops of the Widow's chandelier were laced with gossamer cobwebs and chimed and tinkled in the fierce draughts that gusted through Arden, as if Boreas and Eurus were holding a competition somewhere in the vicinity of the front hall or the great eagle Hraesvelg was flying up and down just to annoy them.

While all the other houses on the streets of trees were being modernized and brought up to date, Arden had remained untouched since the master-builder nailed in the last slate himself.

The garden had become home to toad and frog, mouse and mole and a million garden birds. The nettles were waist-high, the soil latticed with ground-elder and a tangle of brambles was slowly clawing its way across the garden towards the back door. The Widow would have had a fit.

'There's somebody at the back door,' Vinny said, staring into the flames of the fire like an old sibylline cat. Vinny had a mouldering air about her too – dust caught in the cracks in her skin and her thin hair was turning to cobwebs. 'I didn't hear anyone,' replied Charles (now a deeply unattractive thirteen year old).

'That doesn't mean there isn't someone there,' Vinny said.

The glassy eye of the remains of a 'Baked Cod's Head' followed Charles as he walked through the kitchen to the back door. He opened the door and found Vinny was right. A man was standing on the doorstep. He took off his hat and, smiling sadly, said, 'Charles?' in a cracked voice. Charles took a step backwards.

'Remember me, old chap?' Charles couldn't have been more shocked if an alien spacecraft had just landed in the kitchen and a squad of Martians trooped out. 'Daddy?' he said in a small voice.

Vinny grumbled her way into the kitchen but when she saw Gordon the power of speech left her. She went quite green. 'Vin?'

'There you are,' Vinny said finally. Isobel came in to the kitchen and looked with interest at this stranger – there was something odd about him, something not quite right, but she didn't know what it was.

'Daddy?' Charles repeated. Daddy? How could this be possible? Gordon was dead, killed by the pea-souper, he'd been dead for over seven years. Was he a ghost? He had the eyes of a ghost, but not a ghost's pallor, he was lean and brown as if he'd been working in the sun. When they thought of Gordon they thought of the man in the silver-framed photograph – the RAF uniform, the cheerful smile, the wavy hair. This Gordon – ghost or impostor – had short cropped hair, lightened by the sun and what smile he could muster was far from cheerful.

'Daddy?' Charles repeated helplessly.

'Pleased to see me, old chap?' Gordon whispered, barely able to speak for emotion.

'But, Daddy – you're dead,' Isobel said.

'Dead?' Gordon said, looking inquisitively at Vinny who shrugged as if to say it was nothing to do with her. 'You told them I was *dead*?' Gordon persisted.

185

'Mother thought it was for the best,' Vinny replied testily. 'We thought you wouldn't be coming back.'

The story had suddenly changed. Gordon was alive not dead, perhaps the first known traveller to return from the undiscovered country. The world was no longer subject to the rules of logic where the dead were dead and the quick walked the earth. He'd never walked into the wall of fog, never drowned in the pea-soup. That was all a mistake. 'Somebody made a mistake?' Charles said incredulously. Yes, Gordon agreed, staring grimly at the wall behind them so that they both turned to see if there was someone there. There wasn't.

Someone (a dead person) had been wrongly identified as Gordon, the real Gordon had been suddenly struck by amnesia and gone abroad to live in New Zealand, not knowing he was the real Gordon, not knowing who he was. Not knowing anything. Perhaps Gordon had played too many games of Lost Identity and become confused? 'Amnesia,' they overheard him telling people later, in the same way that they had once heard the Widow saying 'Asthma' after he drove away from Arden a lifetime ago. The two words were very similar – perhaps the Widow and Gordon had got them muddled up somehow?

'I've got someone I want you to meet,' Gordon said, with a hopeful little smile. 'She's waiting in the car.'

Charles made a funny noise as if he was suffocating. 'Is it Mummy?' he asked, strung out somewhere between impossible hope and overwhelming despair. Gordon's features contracted in a grimace and Vinny said quickly, as if to explain, 'Ran off with a fancy man.' Gordon stared at her as if he was having trouble understanding and Vinny repeated impatiently, '*Eliza*, she ran off with a fancy man.' Gordon looked sick at the mention of Eliza's name.

'Is she?' Charles said urgently.

'Is who what, old chap?' Gordon looked dazed.

'Is Mummy in the car with you?'

Gordon seemed to contemplate the answer to this question for a long time but finally he shook his head slowly and said, 'No, no she isn't.'

'Hello there,' a bright little voice said suddenly and all four of them flinched and turned to stare at the person standing on the back doorstep. 'I'm your new mummy.'

The second coming of Eliza was no longer just around the corner, with its restoration of real right justice and suffering rewarded (the happy ending). And if the dead Gordon could become alive then perhaps the living Eliza could turn up dead. 'Wherever she is,' Charles said sadly, 'she's never coming back, let's face it, Izzie.'

PRESENT

EXPERIMENTS WITH ALIENS

DEBBIE IS HAVING TROUBLE GIVING THE BABY A NAME. I THINK THIS is because it is not her rightful property, the baby's identity is, after all, in question and to name it might be to somehow rob it of its true inheritance. (But does the baby know who it is?) 'Sharon?' Debbie tries out on Gordon. 'Or Cindy? Andrea? Jackie? Lindy? We don't want anything old-fashioned.' Like Isobel, presumably.

Debbie was right – the baby has been accepted on the streets of trees without a murmur and, as no-one has come forward to claim their mislaid infant, we appear to have it for life. Perhaps it really is a changeling, deposited by mistake, the fairies not realizing that we had no real baby in the house to exchange – for of course, the fairies' tithe to hell must be paid in human life every seven years.

The baby is the only person that Debbie thinks is still itself (perhaps because it has so little self) although she still communicates with the rest of us robotic doubles in much the same way as she's always done.

Debbie is now on an elephantine dose of tranquillizers which have no noticeable effect, certainly not on the strange, obsessive behaviour that she's in the grip of – the hand-washing, the wiping of door handles and taps, the hysteria if a vase is moved so much as an inch. Perhaps these are the rituals that ward off the madness rather than the symptoms of it. 'She should see a bloody psychiatrist,' Vinny says crossly, loudly, to Gordon. 'A trick-cyclist?' Debbie shrieks. 'Not bleeding likely!'

After a great deal of rummaging in the further corners of her brain, Eunice has come up (after a great deal of *click-clicking*) with her own diagnosis, 'Capgras's Syndrome.' ('Gey queer' is Mrs Baxter's diagnosis.)

'Capgras's Syndrome?'

'Where you believe that close family members have, in fact, been replaced by robots or replicas.'

'Gosh.' (Well, what else can you say?)

'Scientists believe (a contradiction in terms, surely?) that it's a condition related to the well-known phenomenon of *déjà vu*.'

(Now *that's* interesting.) 'It's to do with our sense of recognition and familiarity.' But then, what isn't?

'The first known case was cited in 1923 – a fifty-three-year-old Frenchwoman complained that her family had been replaced by identical doubles. After a while she began to complain that the same thing had happened to her friends and then her neighbours and then eventually everyone. In the end she thought her own double was following her everywhere.' (A-ha!)

Eunice rather spoils the scientific effect by dragging hard on a Senior Service, she has recently set foot on the primrose path (fittingly), where will it end? In sex and death I suppose.

What if these things are real though? What if, say, I really do have a double? Mrs Baxter, for instance, reports seeing me buying shampoo in Boots yesterday when I know for a certain fact I was in the middle of a double English lesson and, to be more precise ('about half-past-ten, maybe, dear?'), somewhere between

They flee from me that sometime did me seek

and

With naked foot stalking in my chamber.

Who did she see? My self from the parallel world or my *doppelgänger* in this world? ('A doubler?' Mrs Baxter puzzles.) A figment of my own Capgras's Syndrome? We know who we are, but not who we may be. Maybe. Maybe not.

'On another planet are you, Isobel?' Debbie asks sharply.

'Sorry,' I say absently. Debbie is still rattling off a list of names – 'Mandy, Crystal, Kirsty, Patty – oh God, I don't know, you have a go,' she says wearily. The baby (mute for once) gazes at me as if I am indeed a complete stranger, perhaps Capgras's Syndrome is infectious. I look deep into its vague eyes, cloudy with doubt, a little red-gold floss of hair has appeared on the top of its head.

'Fontanelle,' Debbie says. I've never heard that name before. 'It's not a name, silly,' Debbie says, smug in her knowledge of neo-natal anatomy, 'it's the name of that soft spot on the skull [beneath the red-gold floss] where the bones of the skull haven't closed up yet.' I think of boiled eggs with the tops scooped off.

'I suppose you have to be careful not to drop it on that bit then?'

'You have to be careful not to drop it, period,' Debbie says sternly.

I don't know – I can't imagine what to call it. Perdita perhaps.

'Do you want a lift?' Malcolm Lovat (home for the holidays) asks, encountering me walking home through town after school. Eunice has a chess match and absent Audrey supposedly has flu again. I have to speak to Audrey.

'A lift?' I repeat, feeling suddenly faint from hunger.

'In my car,' he says, waving his car keys in front of my face as if to prove it isn't a sedan chair or a donkey-cart that he's trying to inveigle me into.

'Your car?' I must stop repeating everything he says.

'My dad's just bought it,' he says in an inappropriately miserable way.

'Bought it?'

'I've been thinking of dropping out of medicine,' he says, opening the car door for me, 'the car's a bribe to keep me at Guy's.'

A pretty good bribe in my books. I'd stay at medical school if somebody bought me a car. Not that I'd ever get *in* to medical school. ('Do they have science or reason or logic,' Miss Thompsett asks sarcastically, 'where you come from, Isobel?' Where would that be? Illogical Illyria, the planet of unreason.)

'And might you? Drop out?'

Malcolm sighs and starts the car engine. 'Sometimes I think I'd like to – you know, just take off and disappear?' Why does everyone except Debbie want to disappear? Perhaps we should encourage Gordon to take up magic again – practise the vanishing trick on Debbie, or better still saw her in half.

'Everyone seems to have my life mapped out for me,' Malcolm says while I root around in the glove compartment for something to eat. Not even a mis-shapen mint. 'Do you want to go home?' he asks as we stop at a set of traffic lights.

'Not really,' I answer vaguely, in case he has something better to offer (East of the Sun, West of the Moon).

'You could come to the hospital with me, I'm going to visit my mother.'

'That would be lovely.' As far as I'm concerned, as long as I'm with Malcolm we could go and visit a morgue, or a crypt, or the pits of hell.

'Cancer,' Malcolm says as we drive into the hospital car-park. 'It's been incredibly rapid, it's eating her up.' I was just daydreaming about him flinging me onto a four-poster bed and telling me how beautiful I am compared with Hilary so the word *eating* suddenly jars horribly in my head.

'How awful.' I wonder if he's brought any chocolates or grapes.

In the absence of chairs, we stand like awkward bookends by Mrs Lovat's pillow. Her head's the only part of her visible, a bit like a character from Beckett and her hair looks like a collection of well-used Brillo pads. 'Hello,' Malcolm says, bending over and kissing her gently on the cheek. She bats him away with her hand as if he's a large fly. She seems to have swallowed a couple of the Brillo pads judging by the sound of her – more of a rasping kind of bark than a dulcet dying tone. But then she *is* an ogress, so what do you expect, and, after all, I remind myself, she is *dying*.

'Who's this?' she croaks. 'Come here, come closer, is this Hilary?' and she grabs my arms with her claw and yanks me nearer with a strength you wouldn't expect from someone at death's door.

She doesn't recognize me at all ('Well, of course not!' Mrs Baxter exclaims. 'You used to be an ugly duckling and now you're a—' She hesitates.

'A beautiful swan,' I prompt her. But we all know what ugly ducklings grow up into. Ugly ducks.) 'I thought you said she was pretty?' Mrs Lovat says accusingly to Malcolm and then sighs and says, 'I suppose she'll have to do.' For what? Some kind of maiden sacrifice to restore Mrs Lovat to health? But no, for she appears to be bequeathing me her son on her death-bed – 'Take him,' she says carelessly, from somewhere inside the crisp white sheets of the hospital-bed. 'Look after him for me, Hilary, someone has to.'

I laugh nervously and begin to explain that I am not Hilary – the cancer has obviously begun to nibble her brain by now – but then it strikes me that I quite like deputizing for Princess Hilary so I close my mouth and instead stare at the shape of Mrs Lovat's body under the pale-blue hospital counterpane. Perhaps she'll conjure up a priest from inside the bedclothes and marry us so that when Malcolm finally realizes I am not Hilary it will be too late.

Mrs Lovat seems quite big for someone who's being eaten up, although if you look closely you can see that there isn't actually a definite outline of legs. That would be a strange thing, wouldn't it, if diseases started at the feet and ate their way upward? I suppose the head would get pretty vociferous as time went on.

It seems churlish to upset a dying woman – none the less it *is* a little presumptuous of his mother (if not unnatural) to be handing him over so eagerly to the first person she sees. And although I want him, do I really want to look after him? Isn't it supposed to be the other way round? (The head suddenly floats before my eyes, *Help me* . . .) My stomach is rumbling embarrassingly loudly but there is nothing to eat, unless you count Mrs Lovat herself, of course.

Eventually, after an interminable amount of very poor small talk, Mrs Lovat bids us a rather unfond goodbye. At the hospital entrance we encounter Mr Lovat, walking around importantly with a stethoscope round his neck. 'What are you doing here?' he asks bullishly when he sees his son. 'You should be studying, just because it's the holidays doesn't mean you can become a layabout!' This seems a little harsh, your mother only dies once after all (unless you were unlucky and she took it into her head to defy the laws of physics).

Poor Malcolm, I suppose all unhappy families resemble one another (but all happy families are happy in their own way, of course). But then, do happy families exist, or happy endings come to that, outside of fiction? And how can there be an ending of any kind until you die? (And how can that be happy?) My own imminent death – of starvation – can hardly be happy, unless I kiss Malcolm Lovat first, of course.

'Have you got anything to eat, Malcolm?'

'There's an apple in my jacket pocket, I think.' How intimate a thing it is to place your hand inside someone else's pocket – and have the bonus of pulling out food as well, a lovely rosy-red apple the kind that in another plot would be smeared with poison. But not this one. 'Thanks.'

We stop at the fish and chip shop in Tait Street – this is more like it – and eat our pokes of chips parked up on Lover's Leap, a hill from which no Lover has ever Leapt, certainly not in living memory. In the memory of the dead it may be different, of course.

From Lover's Leap there is a panoramic view of Glebelands and the surrounding countryside – the great industrial valleys to the west, the wild moors to the south, the pastoral hills and woods to the north. In the daytime the sky is so big here that you can see the curve on the great ball of Earth. In the dark, at our feet Glebelands twinkles like an earthbound constellation.

'It's like –' Malcolm suddenly says, furrowing his handsome brow in the effort to find the right words for something, 'it's like you're just *pretending* to be yourself – and there's a completely different person inside you that you have to hide.'

'Really? Not a completely *similar* person dogging your footsteps then?'

He gives me an odd look, 'No – someone inside that you know people aren't going to like.'

'Like a fat person hiding inside a thin one? And anyway, everyone likes you,' I point out to him, 'even *Mr Baxter* likes you.'

'That's just the outside me,' he says, staring through the car windscreen. There is nothing (perhaps) between us and the Northern Star. He should count himself lucky that people like his outside person, people don't like Charles inside or out. He puts an arm round me (exquisite bliss) and says, 'You're a good friend, Iz,' and gives me the last chip.

'Well,' he says, 'best be getting back, I suppose.' There is to be no kiss then, let alone any Leaping. 'Right then,' I say disguising my disappointment. I am Patience on a monument. How long will I keep my passion silent? Until my tongue is cut out and my silver-scaled sardine tail is turned into awkward, unwieldy legs? Perhaps not quite that far.

★

As Malcolm drives me home along Chestnut Avenue I notice a woman, walking along the pavement ahead of us, caught in the headlamps of the car. She's wearing an elegant kind of sheath dress in printed silk with a matching bolero top and a hat, as if she's just been to a garden party, incongruous on a November night. The legs beneath the calf-length dress look incongruous as well – well-muscled, like a male ballet-dancer's.

There's something about her that doesn't seem quite right ('What's Wrong?') and when she turns into the drive of Avalon, the Primroses' house, I peer inquisitively through the windscreen at her as she stands underneath the porch-light. For a second I see her features quite clearly and despite the amount of make-up, not to mention the wig, those features are unmistakably the property of Mr Primrose. I suppose he could just be rehearsing for a play, improvising in character for a night out. On the other hand, perhaps not. How deceptive appearances can be.

When I walk into Arden I'm confronted with the sight of Vinny walking up and down the hall, cradling the baby, with a cigarette hanging out of the corner of her mouth in a futile attempt to prevent ash dropping on the baby. Why has Vinny been left holding the baby?

'Because there's no-one else to do it,' she says, keeping a wary eye on the baby, which is wailing its head off.

'Where's Debbie?'

Vinny snorts with malign laughter. 'Standing guard over the corner-cabinet probably.'

Vinny's right, Debbie is monitoring the contents of the china-cabinet in the dining-room. 'The second I turn my back,' she says resentfully, indicating a pair of Worcester plates and a Dresden shepherdess, 'they all move around.'

'Really?'

'But they're not stupid – the minute anyone else comes in the room they don't budge an inch.'

This surely isn't part of Capgras's Syndrome? 'You don't think they're close relatives or anything, do you?'

She gives me a look of profound disdain. 'I'm not a complete idiot, Isobel.' But can she tell a hawk from a handsaw? That's the question.

She stalks off, forgetful of the wailing baby, and takes a duster and polish from somewhere about her person (soon it will be white rabbits) and starts rubbing the doorknobs. Again and again. And then some more.

'So he took you to see his dying mother in hospital,' Audrey says dubiously, 'and you think that was a *date?*'

I am lolled on Audrey's bed. She's looking very soulful, like Lizzy Siddal in Rossetti's *Beata Beatrix*. *Beata Audrey*. I really have to say something to Audrey. But what can I say – 'By the way, Audrey, did you leave a baby on our doorstep?' Audrey is the only person I have told about the baby not being born in the normal way to Debbie, not being born at all to her, in the hope of her shedding some light on the mystery.

'Are you OK, Audrey?'

'Why shouldn't I be?'

'There's nothing you want to . . . well, tell me?'

'No,' she answers and turns her face away. ('That lovely shawl you knitted,' I say conversationally to Mrs Baxter, 'you know, the one for your niece in South Africa? Did she – er – like it?'

'Oh, I don't think she's got it yet,' Mrs Baxter says. 'I sent it surface mail because the baby isn't due until next month. It takes for ever,' she adds, although it's unclear whether she means the mail to South Africa or the gestation of a child.)

I return to Arden, carrying a newly knitted bonnet for the baby and a still-warm pot of lemon cheese which I leave on the kitchen table without saying anything to Debbie because she's deeply engrossed in re-ordering the cupboard under the sink in alphabetical order (Ajax to Windolene).

Vinny appears to have taken over the cooking again and is stirring a large pot (requisitioned once as a witches' cauldron for The Lythe Players' production of *Macbeth*) in which a calf's brain is simmering. 'Taste this,' she says to me, fishing something indescribable out of the pot. Hastily, I decline and go upstairs to my room.

Certain things dawn on me slowly. For one – the strange 'Autumn Leaves' patterned stair-carpet has been replaced with an older and old-fashioned one – red, figured with blue and green (much nicer) – and the stairs have suddenly sprouted brass stair-rods – 'sprouted' may not be the correct verb for the sudden appearance of stair-rods, but what is? Apart from 'rain', of course? I pause on the landing to try and work this one out. The new flock wallpaper has also disappeared and been replaced with a heavy anaglypta, painted magnolia above the dado – long gone under Debbie's regime – and dark green below.

I must be in the past. Just like that. But is it my own past? I cast around for clues, will I see my younger self coming out of a room? (Perhaps that's how we get doubles? Bring them back from the past?) A noise makes me look back down the stairs. A young woman (not me) has just entered the hallway and is now coming up the stairs. Judging by the way she looks – low-waisted dress with a handkerchief-point hem above her thin ankles – I must have pitched up around 1920.

She walks past me, quite oblivious to my presence (thank goodness she doesn't walk *through* me, that would be unnerving) and races up the stairs to the attic. Curious, I follow her into my own room – which is my room and yet not my room – where she sits at a heavy Victorian dressing-table and peers at her reflection in the mirror. She seems to be getting ready for a party, judging by the dress – a hand-made turquoise silk, scattered with big rosettes in the same material, astonishing in its ugliness – and the number of rejected outfits strewn around the untidy room.

She's rather plain to look at, but there's something attractive and open about her expression – the kind of youthful optimism that seems to have passed by me and Charles – and Audrey too, come to think of it. She sits looking at herself for quite a long time and then suddenly loosens the chignon of hair at the nape of her neck and picks up a big pair of dressmaking shears that are sitting on the dressing-table and with one awkward cut, relieves herself of her hair.

The result is a disaster but she tidies it up with the shears into a rough approximation of a flapper bob and ties on a squaw-type headband of sequins and looks at the result with some pleasure. An indistinct voice floats up the stairs with the message that Mr Fitzgerald is here for her and growing impatient.

When she leaves the room, I'm close on her heels. Down on the landing she almost trips over a little boy – seven or eight years old, cute in his little sailor suit – who gasps at the sight of the shorn locks. She ignores him. We reach the downstairs hallway, the girl is ahead of me, walking into the living-room, met by a scream from someone invisible. 'Your hair! What have you done to your hair, Lavinia?' and an uncertain male voice (Mr Fitzgerald, I suppose) saying, 'Good God, Vinny, what on earth have you done to yourself?'

Vinny! I would never have recognized our aunt in this young girl. It just goes to show. The Arden of Vinny's youth is much nicer than the one we inhabit today, it smells of lavender and roast beef and gleams with modest wealth. I'm about to slip into the living-room behind Vinny when an extraordinary thought strikes me – the little boy at the top of the stairs – the handsome, blond little sailor-boy – must be my father!

I turn round and run back up the stairs – but too late, the Autumn Leaves are already carpeting the stairs and the young sailor-boy is coming out of the second-best bedroom with tired eyes and thinning, greying hair and our ridiculous doorstep baby dribbling milky vomit onto his Shetland pullover. 'Hello, Izzie,' he says with his despondent smile, 'what are you up to?'

'Not a lot,' I say with enforced cheerfulness. If I told him the truth he would never believe me. Soon we will all be in the hands of the trick-cyclist.

'Look,' Charles says, reaching furtively into his pocket.

'What?' He holds aloft a lock of hair, a black curl, held together by a frayed strip of faded red ribbon. '*Hers!*' he says triumphantly. He looks completely mad.

'How can you possibly know that? Where did you find it?'

'On the first landing, in that dish on the window-sill.' I know the one he means, a little Spode box with a lid on, but I've looked in there many times and there's never been so much as an eyelash, let alone a lock of hair. 'Maybe it's materialized out of thin air,' Charles says eagerly. 'It's like finding clues, isn't it?'

'Clues to what exactly?'

'*Her,*' he whispers as if we might be overheard. 'Where she is.' A lock of hair, a powder-compact, a twice-lost shoe and a strange smell – not much of a map. In court this evidence wouldn't add up to a mother. It would add up to madness. I refuse to even touch the lock of hair. I don't want a black curl, I want the whole Eliza, quick and breathing, an entire person inside her skin, the hair growing from roots on her head, the veins throbbing with robin-red blood. Why can't I go back and find *her*?

The weather begins to grow colder and colder. And then colder. Perhaps this is the beginning of Charles' eternal winter, a glacial spell cast over the land? I'm used to the cold of Arden, I would be useful in polar experiments – how long can a five-foot-ten-inch, ten-and-a-half-stone girl last in the Antarctic without special thermal clothing? For ever if you were bred in Arden.

I'm trying to keep warm, sitting in my room, wearing gloves, scarf and hat and wrapped in my eiderdown like a Sioux Indian. The oil-fired central-heating, insisted on by Debbie at such great expense, only works sluggishly at ground level. I can feel my blood congealing and my marrow growing ice crystals, my bones preparing to shatter like icicles. It's an extreme test of my polar constitution, but I'm surviving, despite the fact that every time I exhale I almost disappear in a white cloud of frosted air. Why can't we just hibernate, like the squirrels and the hedgehogs? Wouldn't that make more sense? I could curl up under a great pile of quilts and eiderdowns and only poke my nose out when the air has begun to warm up again in spring.

I'm trying to write an essay on *Twelfth Night* – 'Appearances can be deceptive: discuss'. I like Shakespeare's masquerading heroines, his Violas and his Rosalinds, if it came down to it I'd rather be one of them than a Hilary. If I was a Viola I would have a Sebastian to twin me, one face, one voice, one habit, but two persons (an apple cleft in two). Perhaps incest wouldn't be so bad if it was with someone you were so close to. Malcolm Lovat, for example.

I'm reminded of Mr Primrose – Rosalind and Ganymede, Viola and Cesario – in the same body. I suppose it's all a matter of perception really – what you see depends on what you think you're seeing. And anyway, how can we tell if what we're seeing is real? Reality seems to go out the window when perception comes in the door. And, if it comes right down to it, how do we know there's such a thing as reality? Dearie, dearie me, soon I will be as solipsistic as Bishop Berkeley. Do *I* even know who I am? 'To thine own self be true,' Gordon says occasionally (although not lately). But to which one?

Twelfth Night, I write with a sigh, with some difficulty because of the gloves, is about darkness and death – the music and the comedy only serve to highlight what lies beyond the pools of golden light – the dark, the inevitability of death, the way time destroys everything. ('But, Isobel,' my English teacher, Miss Hallam, protests kindly, 'it's one of his *lyrical comedies*.')

If I could go back in time (which I can, of course, I know) and meet Shakespeare, I could ask him to verify my reading of the play. That would be a surprise for Miss Hallam – 'Yes, Miss Hallam, but

Shakespeare *himself* says that the *carpe diem* theme of *Twelfth Night* is, by definition, a morbid one . . .' Of course, Miss Hallam would just think that I'm off my head.

I look out of the window at the bare black branches of the Lady Oak, scrimshawed against the ivory of a tea-time sky. Troops of crows are racing the twilight to reach the shelter of its branches. The rooks settle themselves quickly into the branches of the tree and when the last wing has been rustled into position and the last *caw* has faded beyond an echo, you wouldn't know that the tree is full of birds unless you'd stood there yourself and watched them disguise themselves as black leaves.

Soon it will be the year's midnight and I can feel the solstice blues coming on me. And the rain it raineth every day. I should be out amongst the Christmas lights of Glebelands, sitting in the Three Js Coffee Bar – even a milky coffee and a Blue Riband with Eunice would be preferable to this melancholy. I am made of absence, darkness, death; things which are not.

I sink down on my back, cocooned in the eiderdown, drugged by boredom and cold, and comfort myself with imagining that this is St Agnes Eve – any minute my dream lover (Malcolm Lovat) will cross the threshold and ravish me and carry me away from this dreariness. On cue, there's a knock at my bedroom door.

'Come in,' I shout hopefully, but it's no dream lover, only Richard Primrose, standing in the doorway, shuffling his feet (a strange concept) nervously as if he needs to go to the toilet. 'How did you get in here?' I demand, startled by his extreme ugliness.

'Your mum let me in,' he says, aggrieved at being accused of breaking and entering.

'My mum?' I reply, startled for a moment until I realize he means the Debbie-mother.

'Congratulations,' Richard says awkwardly.

'On what?'

'The baby.'

'The baby?' I'm not at all sure we should be congratulated on the baby, its screams are even now bouncing off the flock wallpaper on the staircase below as if someone was about to cut it up and put it in a pie. 'Is that why you're here?'

'No,' he says gruffly and wrinkles his nose at the smell of sadness. 'I was wondering if you wanted to go out?'

'Go out?' I echo blankly. (It's pouring with rain, why would I want to go out?)

'Go out,' he repeats peevishly, enunciating the words loudly and clearly as if I might be a foreigner. Or an idiot. He's staring so intently at a point behind my left shoulder that I turn round to see what, or who, is there. Nothing and nobody, needless to say.

'Go out,' I repeat cautiously. 'Do you mean [surely not] on a date?'

'Well,' he says, looking sullen, 'we don't have to call it that if you don't want to.'

A wave of mild hysteria begins to roll over me. 'What shall we call it then? A fig? A prune?' Richard flushes in an unattractive way that highlights his rampant acne and unexpectedly lurches towards me and pushes me down on my bed. He's surprisingly heavy, he must be made of some dense alien material, I can feel the air being squeezed out of my lungs. He kisses me, if you can call it that, in a disgusting, slurpy, slippery kind of way, trying to push his tongue up against the portcullis of my teeth. Where's a time warp when you need one? Or the Dog? Or a woodcutter?

When Richard's tongue discovers my gums he starts getting very excited and he has to shift his position to accommodate a body part that's swelling faster than yeast, giving me an opportunity to free my knee and jerk it into his bulky groin. He rolls off the bed and onto the floor, clutching his detumescence, before scrambling up and, spitting, 'You bitch, I was going to invite you to a party, but I wouldn't now if you paid me,' and turns on his heel and stomps downstairs.

'Drop dead,' I shout after him. The unbelievable cheek of it – I would sooner have an amorous relationship with the Dog than Richard. Indeed, it makes you question why bestiality is so frowned upon and yet sexual intercourse with someone like Richard is considered perfectly *normal*.

Anyway, I don't need Richard and his parties, I have my own to go to. A party given by no less than Hilary. She hands me the invitation as I come out of English, hand-written on a little white card – *Dorothy, Hilary and Graham have pleasure in inviting you to their Christmas Party* – to be held on Christmas Eve. 'You don't have to bring a present or anything,' she says, looking less than enthusiastic about inviting me. I'm baffled. Why on earth *is* she inviting me? Is she confusing me with someone else? My *doppelgänger* (perhaps she's the kind of girl who gets invited to parties)?

Perhaps Hilary is planning some dreadful revenge on me for having inadvertently stepped into her dainty girlfriend shoes and being introduced to Malcolm's newly erased mother? (For she has died apparently. I have been round to offer my condolences but there was no-one home.)

'Oh,' says Mrs Baxter, thrilled at my good fortune, 'I'll make you a party dress, shall I?'

'Are you sure? So close to Christmas?'

'Och, don't worry ["dinnae fash yersel"], I'll make time.' What will she make it from – the fabric of time itself, or will she unravel it and knit it up anew?

The Dog has pushed its way restlessly into my room (sometimes it feels compelled to try all the beds in the house in one night) and lies like a dead weight across the bottom of my bed. In its sleep it emits radio signals, high-pitched little whimpers that mean it's dreaming about rabbits. The Dog and I (another musical waiting to be made) wake up with a simultaneous start.

I know we've just heard a very odd noise even though everything is deathly silent now. I creep downstairs, the Dog padding silently after me. The clock in the living-room strikes two and the chimes echo through the house. The Dog overtakes me and leads the way to the old conservatory. There is broken glass on the tiled floor from a pane where a bird crashed through once like a falling star. There is soil on the floor, spilt from broken clay pots. The smell of neglect is everywhere. Some few of the Widow's hardier cacti still survive, their prickled bodies grey and dusty.

Then suddenly the whole conservatory is filled with a weird green light, a fluorescent neon green, coming from above. The green light is moving, passing over the house, descending to hover over the garden. It's like a huge green jellyfish, pulsing with energy. White lights like arc lights seem to move around at random inside it, causing it to pulsate more. The Dog, ears flattened as if it's flying, crouches on the tiled floor and whines.

I can feel the green light flooding me, filling me with the warm static feeling that comes from thunder and sunlamps – not ultra violet, but ultra green. My mind begins to feel extremely agitated, as if it's full of large, angry wasps buzzing around in a frenzy trying to escape. The smell of rotten eggs invades the conservatory.

I feel dizzy, gravity isn't working properly for me, I'm going to become detached from the ground, rise up like a slow rocket, out of the hole in the conservatory roof. I forget to breathe. My whole body is being sucked up into the green jellyfish, I'm several feet off the floor.

Then, shockingly, it's gone, disappeared – absolutely and completely – as if it was never there. The night is black again, the conservatory dismal. I look down and one ancient cactus has turned green and quick and a scarlet flower like an angel's trumpet is slowly opening at the end of a spiny finger. I reach out to touch it and prick my own finger on a spine.

I leave the conservatory, it doesn't feel like a dream, the steps I take seem real, the air is cold and I'm very tired. What was that? The past? The future? My people from another planet come to take me home? Surely if an alien spaceship had just spent several minutes hovering over the house someone else would have noticed? I pass

Charles' room, I can hear him snoring soundly. Poor Charles, what he wouldn't give for these experiences. What I wouldn't give not to have them.

The next morning there are no traces of green jellyfish, no alien mementoes left behind, just a red swelling on my pricked finger and the scarlet flame of the cactus flower. 'That's a miracle,' Gordon says when he sees it.

This is ridiculous. There should be some rule about time warps (no more than one per chapter, for instance) and surely you should at least be able to tell what bit of the space-time continuum you're in.

If time isn't always going forward – which apparently it isn't in my case – then fundamental laws of physics are being broken. What about the Second Law of Thermodynamics? What about death, if it comes to that? Experimentally, I drop one of Arden's old flower-sprigged plates on the kitchen floor where it smashes nicely. 'What are you doing?' a harassed-looking Debbie asks, an even more harassed-looking baby slung over her shoulder.

'I'm just watching this plate.' (Debbie, of all people must surely understand this.) 'I'm conducting an experiment to see if time can move backwards – if it can, then the pieces of this plate will rise up and re-form.' But the Second Law of Thermodynamics holds good and the plate remains in pieces on the floor.

'You're mad, you are,' Debbie says, stuffing the rubber teat of a bottle into the baby's mouth.

'You're one to talk,' I say before having to rescue a choking baby. I haul it all the way up to my room and feed it lying on my bed while attempting a critical analysis on one of Shakespeare's sonnets. I don't suppose this is how he imagined his readers. If he imagined them at all.

The party dress Mrs Baxter is making for me is made from a peculiar synthetic material that crackles when it moves. It's pale pink, covered in darker pink roses and has cap sleeves and a sweetheart neckline and a big skirt that Mrs Baxter has made even bigger by lining it with a stiff pink net-petticoat so that it's begun to resemble a big pink puffball.

In the pattern-book it seemed like the dream-dress, the kind that's so sublimely gorgeous that the girl inside it is transfigured into a ravishing beauty – the focus of all the eyes in the room. (This is never true, as we know, but that doesn't stop people believing it.) I might have done better to go and wish under the Lady Oak for my three dresses (one is never enough) – the first as silver as the moon, the second as gold as the sun and the last one the colour of the heavens, sprinkled with silver-sequin stars.

Mrs Baxter has had to make several adjustments already to the pink dress, 'I swear if I watch you long enough I can *see* you grow,' she grumbles pleasantly, letting the hem down for the second time. The dress has just made the transition to my body from the tailor's dummy that stands guard in the corner of Mrs Baxter's bedroom. When it was worn by the dummy it looked reasonably presentable, but on me it doesn't look right at all somehow.

I look like a huge pink amoeba, grown to fill the whole of the cheval-mirror. Mrs Baxter, on her knees at my feet, says something unintelligible through a mouthful of pins and then starts to choke and spit all the pins out like a hail of Lilliputian arrows or a shower of elf-shot.

She cocks her head to one side like a deranged spaniel and says, 'I thought I heard Daddy's car.' She shakes her spaniel-head. 'But it's not. I'm as mad as a mushroom, I really am. I'm growing quite dottled, I'm such a bag of nerves.'

A bag of nerves. What a truly dreadful expression that is. And what kind of a bag? A handbag, such as Mr Primrose's Lady Bracknell might have carried? Or a soft sack (a bag of frayed nerves), like a dead cat's body?

Mr Baxter's baleful presence is watered down in the Baxters' bedroom – a cut-glass ash-tray and a copy of the *Reader's Digest* on his bedside-table and a pair of neatly folded blue-striped pyjamas on the left-hand pillow are the only indications of his presence. I can't imagine what it must be like lying so close to 'Daddy' every night. Mrs Baxter's own night attire – a pink brushed-nylon nightie – sits demurely on the right-hand pillow and a pair of pink furred slippers ('baffies') are parked by the side of the bed. The rest of the bedroom is sprigged and ruched in a very feminine way that must really get on Mr Baxter's own nerves.

Mrs Baxter pins up my hem. 'Look at me,' she says, catching sight of herself in the mirror, 'I look like a tattie bogle.' She does look a bit of a mess, her hair needs a shampoo and set and her make-up is patchy, as if she put it on in the dark. It's not helped much by the red marks on her cheekbones – like Iroquois war-paint – where Mr Baxter has punched her. 'Silly me, I walked into a door,' she adds, fingering her war-paint. 'I've really let myself go, haven't I?' she says, regarding her reflection sadly. (But where has she let herself go *to*?)

'There,' Mrs Baxter says, as she puts the last pin in place in the hem of the pink dress and I twirl round to view myself, filling the cheval-mirror with whirling pink roses (for an uncomfortable second I am reminded of the young Vinny's turquoise party dress). My mother should have been here, handing out fashion tips – telling me that pink isn't my colour, that the roses are too full-blown and that I need a tight belt at my waist to make me look shorter. 'Very nice, dear,' Mrs Baxter says instead.

When the fitting of the pink dress is over we go down to the kitchen to eat cakes that are appropriate to our madness. Mushroom cakes – little pastry cups filled with sponge and topped with coffee buttercream, the buttercream scored with a fork to look like gills and a marzipan stalk stuck in the middle. Mrs Baxter doesn't, thank goodness, attempt to model a cake on the Death Caps that have spawned beneath the Lady Oak.

I take a cake to Audrey who's sitting in the living-room, by the fire, with a listless look on her face. She looks at the little cake as if it was poisonous and whispers, 'No, thanks.' The baby's wailing

210

drifts on the cold wind from Arden and Audrey flinches. 'Audrey
. . . what's wrong?'

'Nothing,' she says miserably. ('And . . . um . . .' I say helplessly
to Mrs Baxter, 'how much does it cost to send a shawl surface mail
to South Africa?'

'Dearie me,' she says with a puzzled little frown, 'I'm not sure
– it was Audrey that took it to the post for me.') I suppose in the
hatch and brood of time it might all come right.

At the back door of Arden I bump into Gordon, coming home
from work. 'Hello, Izzie,' he says sadly. He's wearing a dull beige
overcoat and carrying a battered leather briefcase. The baby is parked
in the kitchen in its pram, sobbing quietly as if it's forgotten how to do
anything else. Debbie has moved on to trying to control the pantry,
reorganizing everything into alphabetical order. She's got as far as the
jam – of which, thanks to Mrs Baxter, we have a great deal – and has
just started a sub-classification for it – Apricot, Blackcurrant, Damson.
After every couple of jars she has to go over to the kitchen sink and
wash her hands like some strangely domesticated Lady Macbeth.

Gordon gives me a dismal look. I think of his sailor-suited former
self and feel very sorry that it should have come to this.

'I thought the baby would make everything all right,' he mutters
(I don't think that's how babies work), 'but it's just made it worse.'
Tenderly, Gordon lifts the baby from its pram and murmurs, 'Poor
thing,' into its red-gold floss. He carries the baby upstairs and the
next time I see it is through the half-open door of the second-best
bedroom where it's sleeping peacefully with the Dog lying guard
by its cot. (The Dog is very subdued since it time-travelled.) We
really should take it back to where it came from, or at least return
it to the baby shop and explain it's been sent to us by mistake.

I've been bullied by Eunice into attending the Lythe Players'
pantomime in the church hall on Poplar Road. Eunice is making

her acting début, playing the back end of the cow, and for some reason wants people to witness this public humiliation. I try to entice Charles to come with me, although I suppose the sight of Eunice as half a cow is hardly going to endear her to him sexually. But, sensibly, he's having a quiet night in with the Dog. Debbie is fully occupied with the baby and the world of moving objects and Gordon is fully occupied with Debbie. 'Go on,' I urge Vinny, 'you might enjoy yourself.' (Highly unlikely.) I must be desperate for company if I'm reduced to asking Vinny. But there you go. And anyway, since encountering her younger self I feel differently about her somehow.

'Oh, all right then,' she says sticking her hat on her head. 'I know I'll regret it but I can't listen to that little bastard [she means the baby] yelling a minute longer.'

As we walk along Chestnut Avenue, a very weird thing starts to happen. Every time we walk towards a lamppost, the light starts flashing on and off. When we've passed it, it stops flashing – and the next one ahead of us begins to flash instead. On-off-on-off.

We stop-start along Chestnut Avenue, testing each lamppost, trying to work out some pattern. Are they signalling something to us? Is my body interfering with the national grid in some way? (My body electric.) Or Vinny's? I explain to Vinny that the doors of perception are hanging crazily off their hinges these days.

I am at odds with the material world – every day confirms some new alienation. Perhaps I *am* from another planet, I think glumly, as we approach the church hall, and my alien compatriots are trying to send me morse code via the streetlamps.

The pantomime goes according to plan – Jack scatters his magic beans everywhere, Mr Primrose as the Dame (naturally), dressed in what look like kitchen curtains, makes many a *double entendre* and Eunice and her anonymous other half hoof clumsily to the music provided by a Boy's Brigade drummer and a couple of brass band rejects who play cheerful, tinny music at such a lick that even the village lads and lassies can't keep time, let alone the poor cow.

(Do you keep time in the same place that you save it? If so why is it so difficult to find? It must be in a very safe place. Gordon's always doing that, going around with a puzzled expression looking for something he can't find, saying, 'But I remember putting it in a safe place.')

Jack's beanstalk is pulled on a string up to the roof, its green-painted paper leaves growing and reproducing miraculously as it climbs towards the heavens where the moon and all her starry feys will be twinkling prettily in the dark to greet it.

'Look,' Charles says cautiously to Gordon who's in the middle of preparing a bottle for the baby which is propped up awkwardly in its pram uttering more variations on the basic cry than a song-thrush.

'What?' he says, looking over his shoulder. The feeding-bottle slips out of his hand when he sees the black curl, lying like a big inquisitive comma on the palm of Charles' hand. Gordon stands rigid and unmoving for several seconds and then snatches the curl from Charles and dashes from the room.

Wearily, I pick up the bottle and plug the baby with it.

I'm lying in bed, staring at the ceiling, in a bedroom flooded with blue moonlight, wondering why sleep doesn't come (perhaps the Cats have used it all up) when I hear a soft footfall coming up the stairs. The doorknob turns – gleaming in the moonlight thanks to Debbie's incessant polishing – and I await expectantly. Will it be my personal phantom or the Green Lady (perhaps they are the one and the same thing)? But no – the shade that stands on the darkened threshold is my father.

'Izzie?' he whispers through the dark. 'Are you awake?' He tiptoes over and sits on the end of my bed, staring at something in his hand. I struggle into a sitting position and he holds the thing in his hand up for my inspection. It's the lock of black hair, darker than black in the moonlight. '*Hers*,' he says in a wretched voice. A thrill goes through my whole body, at last he's going to tell me about Eliza. About how beautiful she was, how much he loved her, how happy they were, what a terrible mistake it was when she walked off, how she always meant to come back –

Instead I can feel his gaze through the gloom as he says in a flat voice, 'I killed your mother.'

'Pardon?'

PAST

THE FRUIT OF THIS COUNTRIE

UP IN THE THIN BLUE AIR GORDON WAS FREE, IT WAS ONLY WHEN he came down to earth that the problems began. Falling to earth in flames like some metal-bound Lucifer was easier than facing the narrow future that lay ahead of him if he survived the war. Gordon didn't care much either way for his sisters but he loved his mother and he didn't want to hurt her.

He wasn't thinking about these things when he met his fate. He was slightly drunk, he'd been at some club that he didn't know the name of, the kind of place where things got out of hand after midnight. He'd been with a group of Polish airmen and left because he knew he couldn't keep up with their drinking. And he was tired, he was so tired, he just wanted to get back and put his head down. 'Spot of shut-eye,' he said, making his excuses to the Polaks. He was staying with the sister of a friend and her husband – nice place, very smart in Knightsbridge, the kind the Widow would have pursed her lips at. The sister and her husband

217

too. Too modern. Too fast. He never got there. The clanging of bells and the air full of brick-dust stopped him.

The fire brigade were already there and a lot of people standing around. Somebody said, 'There's people inside, you know.' Gordon could smell the gas from the fractured pipes but he walked into the broken house, thinking that it must have had a grand entrance before it was bombed – columns lay broken across the vestibule and a length of intricate plaster cornice tripped him up. He started choking on the dust and suddenly felt very sober. She was standing there, veiled in dust so that you might have thought she was a life-sized statue fallen from a niche, but he could tell she wasn't a statue because she smiled at him and Gordon lifted her up in his arms and carried her out.

Outside he put her down very gently, as if she might break if he was too rough with her. When he asked her if she was all right, instead of answering, she put out a hand and fingered one of the lapels on his greatcoat and smiled again – a strange smile, very inward-seeming, as if she had an amusing secret that she wasn't about to tell him.

He took his coat off and wrapped her up in it and she looked up at him, straight in his eyes in a way that strangers never did, and whispered, *My hero.* And the rest of the world around them may as well have disappeared because the only thing Gordon could see were her tragic, exotic eyes and the only thing he could hear was the husky notes of her peculiar voice saying, *My shoe, I've lost my shoe,* and Gordon laughed and dashed back into the bombed-out building and actually found the shoe. He knew it was ridiculous but he didn't care. She put a hand on his shoulder to steady herself while she put the shoe on. Her grimy naked foot was slim with a ballerina's arch and blood-red toe-nails – erotic and incongruous amongst the broken limbs and wreckage that was accumulating around them. One poor chap was brought out on a stretcher past them as dead as a doornail. 'Did you know him?' Gordon asked her sympathetically but she just shook her head sadly, *Never seen him before.*

218

Gordon was afraid she was going to walk away now she had her shoe and he knew this was urgent. He knew this was an important moment in his life, perhaps the most important – full of meaning that he couldn't quite decipher. He was going to have to seize the moment, it would be the end of everything if he made a mess of it. He offered her his arm, 'Can I take you for a cup of tea? There's a café round the corner?'

The age of chivalry is alive and well, she laughed, and took his arm and he could feel how she was shaking all over, like a leaf.

Eliza was as mysterious as the moon, waxing and waning towards him, she had her own phases – sometimes generous, sometimes mean – and always her dark side, unreachable, secret, hidden.

He couldn't really believe her. Couldn't believe how easily she'd given herself to him, couldn't believe how she felt. Her silk-skin, smooth and cool, pressed against his hot body made him fear that he was going to die. The way she crept up from the foot of the bed, her tongue like a cat on him, but not rough like a cat. The smell of her – the strange scent that was partly perfume, partly her skin and partly something so mysterious that he'd never smelt it anywhere before.

The way she said, *Of course, darling,* when he asked her to marry him. Just like that, so that he was frightened because nothing this wonderful could ever last. It would drive you mad if it did. And it made him as free as being in the blue sky over this tiny green country, gave him power over his mother, over Arden, over the whole world. To begin with.

And he never did think it would last and he wasn't surprised when it didn't because someone like Eliza was never going to be happy with the meagre slice of life he ended up offering her and he hated her for that so much that his brain hurt with it sometimes. His failure with Eliza was his failure with life and her contempt and her scorn were what, in his heart, he knew he deserved. When he put his hands round her neck he felt how easy it was to stop her, to make her quiet – to have power over her. It was astonishing, he could squeeze the life out of her as easily as if she was some small animal – a hare or a dove – and he wanted to say to her, 'There, aren't you sorry now?' but she was gone and he'd destroyed the only thing that meant anything. That was the measure of what a failure he was.

She was enchanting, spellbinding. 'Oh she doth teach the torches to burn bright,' Gordon said with a self-conscious laugh to the Widow, when he first told her about the momentous thing that had happened to him (Eliza) and watched the Widow's lip curl ever so slightly at this fancy talk. Gordon couldn't help himself, it was like being possessed. It was all he wanted to talk about at dinner and supper, and while being paraded around the neighbourhood by the Widow when he was on leave. Words about Eliza fell unbidden from his mouth. 'She's just not like other people,' he said eagerly to his mother as she folded caraway seeds into dried-egg cake mixture. 'No?' the Widow said, raising a grey caterpillar eyebrow. 'And that's good, is it?'

Eliza stopped time. She took you into some bright circle with her where everything stopped, time and fear, even war. 'Cheap glamour,' Vinny muttered over the sacks of flour in the storeroom. 'Oh no,' the Widow said balefully, 'it comes very expensive, believe me.' It clutched at the Widow's strong heart to see her own perfect manly Gordon being fooled by something as tawdry as sex. How could he be so gullible? So stupid? It pained her that he couldn't look at his own mother and see the pattern of a good woman, but that instead he'd been seduced by all that knowingness.

Gordon had to feel sorry for his mother because it was obvious that she'd never experienced anything like this, not that he wanted for one minute to think of his mother like this and even if he wanted to think about it he would have been incapable of imagining it. His mother may have been young once (although he couldn't imagine that either) but she had surely never been like Eliza.

Eliza was a miracle, her human geography sublime – the long curve of body, the hills and vales, her face buried in the pillow so that all he could see was the forest of black curls on her head. The matching copse of hair between her thin legs, the extraordinary cupolas with their dark-brown aureoles – the kind of breasts that Englishwomen would have been embarrassed by, the kind of breasts that Gordon had only previously seen on foreign prostitutes.

The look of her – the seed-pearls of sweat that glistened on her pale apricot-fruit skin, the damp tendrils of hair sticking to the back of her long neck, the faint down on her thin, round arms, the perfect white half moons of her fingernails (rarely glimpsed except when she was removing her nail varnish), the lazy smile. The smell of her – perfume and tobacco and sex. The taste of her – perfume and tobacco and sex and salt-sweat.

Sometimes he lay awake half the night just watching her sleeping, pulling back the sheets and studying the different parts of her body, the neglected inner crease behind a knee, a perfect clavicle – thin like a hare-bone, the fragrant inside of her wrist with its vulnerable dark blue veins. Once he took her nail scissors and clipped a curl from her hair without her knowing and felt strangely guilty for days afterwards.

You wouldn't find her match anywhere in Glebelands, in the whole of the north ('Not outside of a brothel anyway,' Vinny wrote to Madge).

Even the crudest bodily functions took on a kind of sublime meaning. The Widow would have been disgusted. 'I worship you,' he whispered in her ear and she rolled over and gave her strange laugh, burying her head in the crook of his arm. Gordon wondered if he sounded ridiculous. She was sublime, transcendent, not an earthbound creature at all. 'You can't put your wife on a pedestal, Gordon,' the Widow warned, chopping cabbage with her enormous knife. 'There's more to marriage than the physical side,' and Gordon blushed at the idea that his mother could even begin to imagine the things he did with Eliza.

Mothers and their sons, Eliza laughed (rather spitefully), *how they want them.*
    'I don't know what you mean.'
    Don't you? No, I don't suppose you do.
    And in her room the Widow took off her layers of strict underwear and viewed her saggy, baggy wrinkled body with her ancient dugs and her chicken neck and cursed Eliza.

Eventually, inevitably everything that was once new and precious became everyday and familiar. 'No honey in that hive any more,' Vinny wrote, 'only a nest of hornets.' Why couldn't Eliza settle for the ordinary and the familiar, for the daily round of meals and work, the comfort of children? Gordon craved ordinariness now. He wanted her to be normal, like everyone else. He didn't want other men looking at her because he knew every man that looked at her was thinking about what she would be like in the bedroom and he knew what she was like and that made it worse.
    Not that she was like that any more, not with Gordon at any rate.

Gordon remembered some things – he remembered putting his hands round her thin neck, he remembered her ridiculous laugh, gurgling and bubbling in her throat, he remembered how he felt when he hit her head against the tree, shaking the life out of her – exultant, triumphant at his victory over her. He wanted to say, 'See? See – you can't win every fight, you can't always have your own way, you can't drive me to madness and get away with it.' But it was no good because she couldn't hear him. His triumph melted into nothingness, without her there was nothing. And then – nothing. He had no idea what he'd done all night, he must have wandered round the wood, everything forgotten, even his children. In the cold light of day it was beyond belief.

'I have to go to the police,' he said as soon as the Widow had given the children breakfast ('First things first') and got them to bed. 'Stuff and nonsense,' the Widow said. 'You're not going to hang over *her*.' But Gordon didn't care. They could have erected the gibbet right there in the kitchen of Arden and he would have mounted the scaffold. 'No, Gordon,' the Widow said grimly, 'absolutely, definitely not.'

'The best thing,' the Widow said (for she was completely in charge now), 'would be for you to go away for a bit. Maybe abroad.'

'Abroad?' said Vinny, who'd never been further than Bradford, of course.

'Abroad,' the Widow said firmly.

'My baby!' the Widow thought out loud. She always knew Eliza was trouble, would drag him down into the mire with her. She was better off dead. Poor Gordon, under the spell of a slut. Who was going to miss her? (*They're all dead, darling.*) Nobody, that was who. Gordon could go abroad and they would say he'd died – dreadful accident or something. Asthma. Something. And the Widow would never see him again, but at least he would be safe. Anything was better than the noose. 'My baby!'

Vinny was more annoyed than she'd ever been in her life. She'd spent most of the night wandering in the wood, having taken the wrong path after going off to do 'you-know-what' and, all in all, had probably had the worst time of her life, even counting her wedding-night.

The wood had been so much more than a wood for Vinny, it had been an ordeal by twig and bramble, spectre and will-o'-the-wisp and for this she entirely blamed Eliza. If she hadn't finally stumbled into Gordon after hours of wandering and weeping she would have undoubtedly gone mad. Although, of course, what happened then was almost as bad.

Vinny was glad she was dead. That's what she said to herself anyway, but she couldn't forget the sight of Eliza's rag-doll body under that tree. Vinny had touched the blood on her hair, felt the ice on her skin. Vinny had done something she never thought she would do – she'd felt sorry for Eliza.

Vinny would very much like to forget these things. She would like to forget Gordon clutching her arm as if she was a life-belt, dragging her over to the tree, tears streaming down his face and sobbing, 'What am I going to do, Vin? What am I going to do?' I never wanted to go on a bloody picnic anyway, Vinny thought crossly.

Eliza had been trouble, right from the beginning. Trouble with her big eyes and her thin ankles and her stupid voice, *Oh Vinny, darling, could you possibly* . . . always laughing at poor Vinny as if she was stupid. But that didn't matter now, they must all save themselves as best they could.

And Gordon went. Walked out, left everything behind, even the murder of his wife. And he put it all away in some dark place that he never threw light on and he'd gone on and worked hard and grown weather-beaten and become a different person, had met Debbie at a dance, courted her, quickly married her – she couldn't have been more willing even though 'Mum and Dad' didn't really approve – after all he was a divorced man. That's what he told them, that's what he told everyone, 'divorced' with such a sadness in his eyes that no-one wanted to probe further, except for Debbie, of course, for whom Eliza was a dark and unknown rival, the first Mrs Fairfax.

And then suddenly he had to go back. He had to see his children. His mother. He had to go back to England and find the old Gordon. He didn't realize that none of these things were the same any more.

He'd got what he'd so stupidly wished for. He'd got an ordinary life. He didn't need to go to prison for murder, didn't need to hang for killing Eliza, he had his punishment every day. He'd lost his treasure, greater than a king's ransom. He'd lost Eliza.

PRESENT

EXPERIMENTS WITH ALIENS (Contd.)

'YOU KILLED MY MOTHER?' I REPEAT IN DISBELIEF. THIS ISN'T HOW it's supposed to go at all.

Gordon sits slumped on my bed with his head in his hands.

'You killed my mother?' I prompt him. He looks up at me. In the dark his eyes are like black holes. When he opens his mouth – another black hole. He shakes himself like a dog, pulls himself together. 'Well, what I mean . . .' He stumbles then visibly pulls himself together. 'What I mean is I killed her spirit.' He shrugs. 'I wanted her for what she was, but when I got her I wanted her to change.'

That's an old familiar tale, but it's all I'm going to get. Gordon pats my leg under the eiderdown – 'Sorry if I woke you, old thing,' – and disappears back into the night. The Dog follows him as far as the doorway, and then flops down on the threshold with a sigh of exquisite misery.

THE ART OF SUCCESSFUL ENTERTAINING

ON CHRISTMAS EVE I WAKE UP SLOWLY FROM A BIZARRE OVIDIAN dream in which Eunice had been in the act of turning into a cow – a real one as opposed to a pantomime one, lowing mournfully at me for help. Her lower half (gymslip and white ankle socks) was still recognizably Eunice but her head was completely bovine. The metamorphosis had just reached her arms and she already had hooves where her hands had been, but (thankfully) no udders yet. I was just thinking that Eunice gave a whole new meaning to the word 'cowgirl' when I wake up.

It's a cold, sunny morning. I can hear the baby gurning and carols being sung on a radio somewhere in the house. Charles bursts into my room without knocking and asks irritably if I've got any wrapping-paper, 'I've only got one present left to wrap and I've run out.' I mutter something negative and put my head back under the covers. It's the middle of the afternoon when I wake up again and outside it's already growing dark. Blink

230

and you miss the daylight at this time of the year. So much for saving it.

I struggle out of bed, feeling exhausted, it's as if I haven't slept at all. My party dress is hanging on the wardrobe door but it's too early to put it on, that would be like asking an accident to happen. Despite what Hilary said about not bringing a present I have bought her a boxed set of Bronnley lemon soaps which are sitting gift-wrapped ready on my bedside table. I think it is best to smooth my passage into this sophisticated milieu of the Walshes. Although, of course, the only reason I want to be at this party is to steal away Malcolm Lovat from under Hilary's little nose.

I come downstairs still in my dressing-gown. Debbie and Gordon are both in the kitchen, Gordon at the sink wrestling with tomorrow's turkey, a small frozen butterball, lethal enough to fling from a catapult and destroy an entire castle and its occupants. The relation of dead poultry to male genitalia is still something of a puzzle to me but it's hardly something I can discuss with Gordon, heroically delivering the turkey of a bloody plastic bag of giblets. We would be better off with a roasted suckling baby at our festive table, at least then there might be enough white meat to go round.

Gordon sees me and smiles. He seems to be completely ignoring his mad wife who appears to have turned into a mince pie factory – there must be a hundred of them piled on the kitchen table. I hope she's not planning some kind of Christmas party. 'You're not planning a party, are you?'

'No. Should I be?' she asks, attacking a helpless rectangle of pastry with a fluted cutter like a little hollow crown. I decide to leave her to it.

In the hall Vinny is wheeling the baby up and down in its pram. The baby regards Vinny with a glum expression as if it had been expecting something better from life. Who can blame it? Vinny seems to be disappearing before my eyes, so thin and insubstantial that she's more like a cloud of dense ectoplasm than a human being. She's drying up, desiccating like a dead beetle and she's developing a strange aura, a cross-hatching of cobwebs around her outline as if she's fraying at the edges (it could be her nerves). Perhaps the baby's sucking the life out of her.

The baby has a name at last, I suppose if it had been left much longer Vinny, the Keeper of Cat Names, would have ended up christening it Tibbles or something. Although Tibbles might suit it better than the new-fashioned name it's been given – Jodi.

'I'll do that,' I offer reluctantly, taking over the pram handle from Vinny who staggers off gratefully to her room, followed by several Cats who have been prowling around jealously.

Perhaps we could take the baby and leave it on someone else's doorstep, they might be fooled into thinking it was an anonymous Christmas present. They might even think it's a manifestation of the second coming – Jesus come back to earth as a girl. (Now that would be something.) But the baby doesn't look like it wants to save the world, it looks as if it would settle for what we all crave in Arden – a good night's sleep.

It's quite a peaceful activity walking up and down the hall with the pram, rocking up and down on the handle occasionally. There's no hurry anyway – 'Don't go too early,' is Mrs Baxter's advice, 'there's nothing worse than being first at a party,' well, except perhaps for never being at parties at all.

'I thought you had a party to go to?' Debbie says, breaking into my reverie. I look at my watch in amazement – it's several hours later than I thought it was. How can that be? I must have completely lost track of time. Again.

'Time playing tricks, eh?' Gordon laughs (almost) as I pass him on the stairs.

So. I have the shoes (white stilettos that I can hardly walk in) and the frock, of course, but what about the rest of me? I need my mother, I need my mother to turn me into a real woman, but in her absence I do the best I can, damping down the frizzled snakes of my hair with Vitapointe so that I end up smelling well basted, like Christmas dinner. Not to mind, I think, putting on the fur tippet which curls comfortably round my neck.

I am going to walk into the party and Malcolm Lovat will catch a glimpse of me, walk towards me in a dream, we'll melt (yes, melt) into each other's arms, he'll peel the pink dress off me and inflamed by so much naked flesh we'll swoon into – why don't I have a mother advising me against such a rash course of action? (I'm sixteen, for heaven's sake, I'm a *child*.) Why isn't my father asking me where I'm going as I fly so eagerly down the stairs?

'Where are you going?' Gordon asks.

'Just out,' I say airily and a little frown pinches his brow. 'I'd give you a lift,' he says, 'but –' and he indicates the kitchen at his back, now so full of mince pies that they're rolling out of the door. 'It's OK, I'll get the bus,' I reassure him hastily.

He reaches out and straightens my coat collar. But I have no time now for such *tendresse*, I am away to forgo my virtue and the clock's upbraiding me with the waste of time. 'How are you going to get back?' Gordon shouts after me. 'There'll only be a skeleton bus service tonight.'

'It's OK. I'm getting a lift off Malcolm Lovat,' (there's nothing like being optimistic). Although the idea of a skeleton bus service has a certain novel – if somewhat ghoulish – attraction.

The Walshes' house turns out to be a gracious Georgian affair with pillars and a portico. My chest is tight with party anticipation. I pause for a second at the gate to savour the air of excitement, all the lights are on in the rooms and a tree in the garden has been strung, not with the garish coloured lights of the seaside prom, but with tasteful white globes like bright little moons. The wrought-iron gates at the foot of the driveway are wide open and on one of them is hung a large holly wreath, embellished with a red ribbon bow, a badge of cheer and festivity to welcome us partygoers. I walk up the path, dress rustling, take a deep breath, and ring the doorbell.

The door is flung open as soon as my finger touches the bell, as if someone has been standing behind it waiting for me. Taking the role of footman is a frog-faced boy I have never seen before who smiles breezily at me and says, 'Hello there – whoever you are.'

I certainly haven't arrived too early, the house is buzzing with chatter and excitement and svelte girls – all of them spilling over with self-confidence and spilling out of expensive dresses which are definitely not hand-made. 'Go in the living-room!' the boy at the door bellows cheerfully at me above the noise, pointing at a doorway on the left from which The Shadows are twanging loudly.

Inside the living-room Hilary's parents – 'John and Tessa' – stand smiling, as if they're part of a wedding reception party, only they have their outdoor clothes on. Dorothy, Hilary's older sister, is hovering around next to them, a vision in lemon tulle.

'We're going to leave it to you now,' Mrs Walsh laughs gaily, 'you young things all together, while we have to go to the boring old Taylor-Wests' do, I really rather envy you.' Who this statement is addressed to isn't entirely clear but as the nearest person I feel a duty to laugh and nod sociably as if I know *just* what she means. Mr Walsh gives me a funny look and, turning to Dorothy, says, 'Now, Dotty, you've got the Taylor-Wests' phone number if you need us. Just remember, don't turn the music up too loud and make sure you give all these poor fellows a Christmas kiss.'

'Dotty' laughs graciously and says, 'Don't you worry about us, Daddy, you get yourselves off – and have a wonderful time!'

So this is how normal families behave, I always knew it! (Why, they might even be happy.) Oh, how I love John and Tessa and Dotty and Hilary. Where is Hilary? Not that I'm really interested in Hilary, but she is the thread that will lead me to the object of my heart's desire (Prince Malcolm). 'Where's Hilary?' I ask in my politest voice and Dorothy turns to look at me and smiles indulgently as if I'm a quaint but backward relative. 'I think she's in the kitchen with the fruit punch,' she answers and then laughs uproariously at this 'joke'. 'That didn't sound right, did it?' and Mr and Mrs Walsh laugh as well, bright, tinny laughter that could set my teeth on edge if I wasn't in such a festive mood.

Mrs Walsh pulls her mink coat (the foxes at my neck flinch in distress) closer around her body and kisses Dorothy's cheek goodbye. I'm half-expecting her to do the same to me but her eyes gloss over me as she turns to Mr Walsh and trills, 'Come on then, Johnny, we'd better leave them to it.'

Hilary is indeed in the kitchen with the fruit punch, doling it out with a glass ladle in a very ladylike way, like an aristocratic WVS woman. 'There you are, Isobel,' she says, giving me a charitable kind of smile. The glass punch cups have tiny glass handles that are impossible to hold. I hand over the gift-wrapped soaps, 'I brought you a present,' which she takes cautiously, as if the box might contain something venomous. She puts it down without unwrapping it, turns her back and starts fiddling with a plate of Ritz crackers that have been given sophisticated party toppings that Debbie would envy – bits of Gouda and cocktail onions, stuffed green olives and tiny shiny black fish eggs like fleas.

I sip my fruit punch awkwardly, trying to stop the little cup slipping out of my big hand. It tastes, rather disgustingly, of orange squash and Ribena. Just then the captain of the football team, a loutishly handsome boy called Paul Jackson, comes into the kitchen, winks at me and pours an entire bottle of vodka into the fruit punch. When Hilary turns round he stuffs the bottle into his jacket pocket and smiles at her. She smiles back and says, 'Canapé, Paul?'

Hilary and Paul seem very interested in each other and not very interested in me and so I help myself to some of the newly fortified punch (which now tastes of orange squash and Ribena, with a hint of nail varnish remover – a slight improvement) and slope off to try and find somebody who might be interested in *me*, like Malcolm Lovat, for example.

Everyone at this party seems to know everyone else and yet I know nobody – I've certainly never seen any of these people in school, where have they all come from?

The Walshes' house has many mansions and I wander through the different rooms, each one alive with chattering party-goers, each one presenting a different tableau of conviviality. Trying to infiltrate these hard knots of people is like trying to get into a rugby scrum. Emboldened by anonymity, I try varying social tactics. 'Hello, I'm Isobel,' I say shyly on the outskirts of one group – and am completely ignored. Perhaps I've accidentally put on my cloak of invisibility.

'Hello, my name's Isobel, what's yours?' I try, more loudly, on the edge of another group and everyone turns round to look at me as if I'm an unwelcome imbecile. There's no sign of Malcolm Lovat anywhere.

I overhear someone say, 'God, have you seen that dress, what does she look like?' and the other person replies, 'A strawberry tart,' and hoots with laughter. Do they mean me? Surely not. I slink back to the kitchen. Hilary has disappeared (if only) and been replaced by her brother Graham who's grinning at me in an odd way. 'Hello, Is-o-bel,' he says in an affected kind of way.

Graham's with a group of his college friends, all dressed in sweaters and corduroy jackets and stripy scarves just in case anyone mistakes them for anything else. To my horror I suddenly realize that one of them is Richard Primrose.

'Surprise,' he says, *snarf-snarfing*.

'Why are *you* here?'

'Graham, my good friend here,' he says, draping his extra-long arm around Graham's shoulder in a drunken way, 'invited me, of course. And I told *him* to invite *you*,' he laughs, jabbing in my direction with his finger. He can hardly stand, he's so drunk. 'This,' he says, gesturing to the rest of the group, 'is my kid sister's friend,' his voice drops to an artificial whisper, 'the one I was telling you about.' They all look at me as if I'm an exhibit in the zoo and I feel myself blushing to a shade that probably accessorises quite well with my dress.

They crowd around me, one of them says, 'Hello, Is-o-bel, my name's Clive,' and another one says, 'Hi, I'm Geoff.' This is amazing, to be the focus of so much male attention and for a deluded second I imagine the dress must be weaving its magic and I've been transfigured into a magnetically attractive person.

They are so close that I can smell the alcohol fumes coming off them, more beerily pungent than just vodka-laced punch. One of them puts his arm round my waist and laughing and smirking, says, 'Well, Is-o-bel, we've all heard what a goer you are. How about giving me a try?'

'Goer?' I repeat, mystified, wriggling out of his unpleasant embrace. 'Goer? What do you mean?' In my mildly befuddled brain I wonder if a 'goer' isn't some kind of snake – or is it an island? 'Goer?' I puzzle to the nearest boy? (Clive, I think, but they're indistinguishable really with their little beards – you can just tell they're all jazz fans.)

'Yeah,' he says, fingering the edge of one of my cap sleeves, 'we've heard how accommodating you are, Is-o-bel. Izzie-Wizzie, let's get busy.'

'Old Dick here,' another one of them says, nodding his head in Richard's direction, Richard sniggers, 'has been telling us that you do anything, Is-o-bel.' He snorts with laughter. 'Things that *nice* girls don't do.' '*Nice* girls,' another one chuckles and mimes being sick.

'Not like Ding-Dong here,' another one, possibly Geoff, says (they're as numerous as mince pies). 'We've all heard what Dick gets up to with you, Ding-Dong.'

'Yeah, pussy's in the well,' another one of them leers. The foxes at my neck growl protectively.

I glare in disbelief at Richard. 'What on earth have you been *saying* about me?' He has the grace to look slightly shame-faced but at that moment Dorothy strides into the kitchen with a tray of dirty glasses and the pack of boys all wheel round to watch Dorothy's magnificent breasts and bottom. 'What an arse,' one of them sighs quietly and Dorothy says, 'I hope you know what you're doing, Isobel!' with a disgusted expression on her face, before sweeping out again.

Slightly chastened for only a moment by Dorothy's commanding presence, the baying pack now close in on me in a way that's really quite frightening. They're all built like half-backs and I don't think that the fox tippet's going to be an adequate champion if it comes to a contest between us. Richard's keeping his distance on the outside of the circle, reviewing my discomfort with a supercilious smile. I vow to kill him at the first opportunity.

One of them starts singing, *Ding-dong bell, pussy's in the well,* and Graham makes an amateur pass at my sweetheart neckline. Flight's the only solution here and I turn to one of them and give him a hefty kick on the shin before shouldering him out of the way and heading out of the back door and into the garden.

I'm expecting the Walshes' back garden to be as tamely suburban as the ones on the streets of trees, but it resembles a stately home in its landscaped vastness, it's like unexpectedly entering another dimension. (Appearances can be deceptive.)

I sprint across the grass as fast as I can but my movements are hampered by the heels on my shoes and the large volume of pink I'm wearing, and I haven't got very far when Graham does a rugby tackle on me, sending me crashing onto the frosted grass of the lawn. His hand slips down into the bodice of my dress, determined apparently on this particular goal, but I manage to jab him hard in the ribs with my left elbow and he rolls off me, yelping with pain. I have lost one of my shoes by now, and I hastily kick off the other one as I scramble to my feet.

Up and running again, I make for the far end of the garden, thinking there might be a gate out onto the street somewhere. Glancing behind, I see two of them racing across the grass after me. Why is this happening to me? I'm supposed to be waltzing rapturously in Malcolm Lovat's handsome arms not running for my virtue.

I'm running now over a smooth, flat piece of lawn and only realize that it's not an ordinary lawn when I trip over a croquet hoop and thud heavily to the ground. (Maybe this is what *The Home Entertainer* means by Human Croquet.) One of the boys is on me now, hanging on to me round the waist as I struggle to get up. I wrench myself free and hear something rip. Maybe it's his head coming off.

I set off again at a gallop, the two boys hallooing and tantivying behind me. I notice a big silver birch growing by a perimeter wall and veer over to it thinking that I might be able to scramble up it and onto the wall but when I get to it I discover that its branches are too high to reach. 'Gotcha, Ding-Dong!' one of the boys shouts.

I'm done for. All I can do is stand and try and get my breath back, I feel sick from exertion and can't raise a scream no matter how hard I try. It's like being trapped in a nightmare. I lean against the trunk of the silver birch gasping for air like a dying fish and send up a small silent plea for help. Why do I have no protector in this world, someone watching over me?

I can't even move, my legs feel as though they're full of lead shot and my feet are rooted to the ground. One of the boys, Geoff, I think, runs straight up to me and stops, the mad Dionysian light in his eyes turning to confusion. He seems to look right through me. The other one, Clive, runs up to join him, and then bends over double to get his breath. 'Where'd she go?' he asks, panting. 'This way, somewhere,' Clive says, looking around everywhere except at me. 'Fucking little prick-teaser,' he adds and puts his hand out onto my left shoulder and leans his weight against it as if I'm just part of the tree.

But when I glance down at his hand, I see that where my left shoulder should be, where my right shoulder should be – where my entire body should be, in fact – is the silvery, papery bark of the birch. My arms are stiff branches sticking out from my sides, my previously bifurcated legs have turned to one solid tree trunk. I would scream now, but my mouth won't open. Call me Daphne.

Everything begins to grow dim and blurred at the edges and the next thing I know I'm sitting on the cold ground, underneath the tree, with no sign of any of the boys, and Hilary marching across the lawn towards me. 'What on earth are you doing out here, Isobel? You haven't seen Malcolm, have you? I can't find him anywhere.'

I trail back into the house on Hilary's heels. There seems little point in telling her that I've just recently turned into a tree. I am not what I am. I am a tree therefore I am mad, a mad person subject to massive delusions and hallucinations. 'Having a nice time?' Hilary asks dutifully, her eyes already scanning the kitchen for someone else to talk to other than me. 'Oh yes, absolutely,' I reply, taking a cocktail sausage from a Prima cabbage that's stuck all over with sausages on sticks so that it looks like it's just come from outer space.

I go up to the first-floor bathroom to try and clean myself up a bit. There are twigs and dead leaves in my hair, my stockings are laddered to shreds and my stiff net petticoat is in tatters. This must be what ripped during my ordeal out in the back garden. The pink dress is no longer the colour of sugar and spice, it is now the pink of pigs and embarrassment and tinned salmon.

I remove the ragged petticoat from the dress with one final rip. A couple of dead leaves are caught in the holes of the net. I look around for a bin but there isn't one so in the end I stuff the petticoat behind the hot-water tank in the airing cupboard. The tank isn't lagged and is giving off an incredible amount of heat, bubbling away like a particularly perverted medieval torture instrument. It's huge, Hilary would fit inside exactly.

When I come out of the bathroom I almost trip over Hilary, who's now locked in a swooning embrace with Paul Jackson, the captain of the football team. She seems to move around the house at a rapid speed, perhaps she has a *doppelgänger*, a kind of body-double standing in for her during the more tedious moments. Not that her clinch with Paul Jackson looks exactly tedious – his hand's thrust up her skirt and his knee is pushing her legs apart. I wonder what Mr and Mrs Walsh would say if they could see her now. Had they any idea how much (if any) alcohol was going to be consumed on their premises? Or how much debauchery was going to be unleashed the minute their backs were turned? I doubt it very much somehow. Still, it's encouraging to see Hilary being unfaithful to Malcolm, she seems indeed to have forgotten all about him. She looks as though she's about to throw up and when she comes up for air reveals a vivid love-bite across her windpipe, I almost expect to see blood on Paul Jackson's teeth. 'Isobel,' she slurs, trying to focus on me and going cross-eyed with the effort. If only Malcolm could see us side by side now – it would be only too obvious who was the right girl for him. (*Me.*)

'Isobel,' she repeats with some effort, 'have you seen Graham?'

'Graham?'

'Graham, my brother,' her head lolls forward onto Paul Jackson's shoulder, 'insisted you were invited.'

'Did he? What as – the entertainment?' I ask her indignantly, there's only one reason he wanted me and that was because of the lies Richard has told to get his own back on me. I start explaining this to her but she's dropped off to sleep and is snoring pig-like and Paul Jackson is already twanging her suspenders again. He catches my eye and says, 'Sod off.' So I do.

I head down to the living-room again. Out in the hall, a big grandfather clock strikes the half-hour – half-past eleven – where has all the time gone? (Where *does* it go? Is there some great time sump at the bottom of the world?) My sojourn as a silver birch must have disposed of hours of it.

A lot of changes have taken place in the living-room since I was last in it. Gone are the innocent Shadows, the bright overhead lights, the junior cocktail party chit-chat. Now it resembles nothing so much as an inner circle of hell – the dark writhing shapes, the tortured moaning noises of people *in extremis* – and it takes several seconds for the dark shapes to resolve themselves into necking couples – standing, sitting, lying – all fumbling at each other with orgiastic enthusiasm.

In the hallway someone's being sick, and Dorothy, also ravaged by drink by now but still immensely practical, gets the vacuum cleaner out and starts hoovering up the vomit. I debate with myself whether I should tell her what a bad idea this is but decide to keep my meagre housekeeping tips to myself when she hoovers in my direction and snarls, 'You're really a bit of a tart, aren't you, Isobel? And keep your hands off my brother, you're not his type.'

Graham is on the stairs behind Dorothy, pumping up and down on top of a big-frocked girl, who presumably is his type, and I push my way past their intertwined bodies and run up the stairs to try and have one last attempt at finding Malcolm Lovat.

The first door I try appears to open into Mr and Mrs Walsh's bedroom, huge twin beds like barges dominate a room heavy with brocade. The next room reeks of Dorothy. It's frilly and girly and organized on lines of military precision – a shelf of science books, fiction in alphabetical order and toiletries laid out on the dressing-table with mathematical regularity. If a single Q-Tip moved in this room she would know about it.

I go up to the next floor and try another door. This bedroom is frilly and girly too but sporty as well – tennis rackets, sportswear and riding-hats everywhere – this must be Hilary's room. On the bedside table there's a photograph, head-and-shoulders, of a horse and on the bed a huge assortment of dolls – dolls with baby faces, dolls in full Highland regalia, dolls in flamenco dress, moppety rag dolls and antique dolls with yellowing ringlets and astonished expressions.

And there, incongruous amongst the dolls, lies the much bigger body of a supine Malcolm Lovat. He greets me cheerfully, and drunkenly, waving a half-empty bottle of gin in his hand. 'Hello, Izzie.'

'I didn't think you were here.' I take a swig of neat gin from the green bottle, slugging in a cavalier fashion, and I'm quite pleased with myself for not choking to death. 'Smell that,' Malcolm says, suddenly rolling over and plunging his face into the pillow, 'essence of horse!' How we laugh!

He pats the space next to him on Hilary's (almost certainly) virginal divan and I squash myself into the space. 'That's a big dress,' he says pleasantly and puts his arm round my shoulder and we lie there quite companionably, drinking gin and assigning imaginary personalities to Hilary's dolls, most of which are extensions of her own character.

We're approaching the bottom of the gin bottle now. The inside lining of my body feels as if someone's set a match to it, a not entirely unpleasant sensation, and the distracted globe of my brain has turned into porridge. Most of Hilary's poor dolls have been kicked to the floor by now. Or have jumped to safety.

I think I drift in and out of consciousness a few times. Time seems to have become slower, more viscous somehow, as if the molecules of time are indeed capable of changing state and are no longer an invisible gas but a flowing liquid (perhaps that's the Heraclitean flow). 'Kiss me,' I mumble suddenly, emboldened by gin and the strange fluidity of time. Malcolm opens his eyes, I think he's been asleep, and hauls himself up into a cobra position on his elbows and gazes at me. 'Please,' I add, in case he thinks I'm being impolite. He frowns deeply at one of the few remaining dolls – a baby-doll about the size of 'our' baby – and says, 'Isobel,' very seriously.

This must be it then – he's realized the cosmic links that bind us, he's about to kiss me and open the seals on our love – we will be transported to some transcendent place where the music is by the spheres and the lighting by Turner – I hope I don't turn into a tree before this can happen, or go flying through time again. I close my eyes hopefully. And pass out cold.

When I open my eyes again the room is dark and someone has covered me up with Hilary's eiderdown. Someone has also been busy gluing my brain onto the inside of my skull and when I try and sit up it does its best to wrench itself free in a way that's quite, quite horrible. For extra effect, the fibres of my brain have been soldered together. The bed-room door opens and I close my eyes against the shock of the light.

When I force them open a slit I can see a furious Hilary, mascara and lipstick smudged, hair a haystack, skin deathly pale (presumably because Paul Jackson has drained all the blood out of her body by now) staring at me in repulsion. 'What are you doing on my bed, Isobel?' I make an attempt at sitting up and break out in a cold, clammy sweat. Feebly, I try to wave a warning at Hilary with my hand because I know she isn't going to want to see what's about to happen.

But too late – I clutch my forehead in a vain attempt to staunch the throbbing and lean over the side of the bed and empty what remains in my stomach (bits of gin-soaked cocktail sausage mainly) all over Hilary's startled dolls.

Hilary starts screaming at me, a torrent of ladylike invective that pours from her mouth in a tumbling stream of toads and ashes.

'Drop dead,' I moan at her.

Mr and Mrs Walsh come home not long after ('What's happened to the *hoover*, Dotty?') and turf out the remnants of the party in disgust, including me, especially me. 'Get out,' Mr Walsh hisses nastily. 'God only knows what else you were doing in my daughter's bedroom. I can tell your sort, you're nothing but a whore.' How unkind. There's no sign of Malcolm Lovat, which isn't entirely a bad thing, because at least that means he isn't in Hilary's arms.

My foxes are waiting for me on the hall table and I pick them up and stagger out into the night – a night glazed with frost and freezing cold, so that I almost expect Mr Walsh to shout, 'And never darken my door again, young lady!'

'And I don't want to see your face in my house again, you little tart!' he shouts, in character. I get as far as the wrought-iron gates before being overtaken by the most overwhelming lethargy. I am indeed a fallen woman, or at any rate, a fallen girl – fallen by a huge laurel bush by the wrought-iron gates, fallen and crawled under and curled up and snoring as quietly as a hedgehog, determined to hibernate. Snow begins to dust my face like cold icing-sugar.

I'm rudely awoken by Malcolm Lovat trying to stuff me into the passenger seat of his car and muttering, less charitably this time, about 'what a bloody big dress' I'm wearing. 'That's how people die, you know,' he says crossly, starting up the engine and backing away from the Walshes' driveway. My brain is no longer glued to the inside of my skull, now it has shrunk to a hard, gin-pickled walnut and is rattling around, bouncing off bone, unanchored by membrane.

'Hypothermia,' Malcolm says, as if he's having a stab at naming our abandoned baby. We provide the perfect cautionary tale against alcohol as we weave a delicate drunken path along the icy road. 'Bloody hell,' Malcolm exclaims grimly as we occasionally skate across the road and pirouette and spin as if the car's turned into a tipsy Sonja Henie.

I have several attempts at lighting up a cigarette and on the fourth, successful, attempt drop a lighted match on my dress and a large pink patch of it instantly melts and I narrowly avoid turning into a human torch. How shall I die? Fire or ice?

Somehow or other we end up at the top of Lover's Leap once again but Loving and Leaping are the last things on our minds, wading through blood up to my knees would be easier and we both fall asleep the second the engine is turned off. When I wake up it's cold. A drizzle of saliva seems to have turned to ice on my chin and my eyes are crusted with sleep. I root around hopelessly in the glove compartment and am surprised to find half a packet of stale custard creams which I fall on like an animal. After a while I nudge Malcolm awake and offer him one. It's such a shame that I'm in no fit state (my head's about to fall off) to sit and appreciate his beautiful profile, the curve of his lip, the black kiss curl that loops around his ear. I open the car door and throw up on the ground.

We set off again on another seemingly endless journey. The streets of Glebelands are deserted, everyone is in bed waiting for the rising of the sun and the running of the deer. Our odyssey takes us once more past the street where the Walshes live, but here, unlike the rest of town, is the most extraordinary activity. I suppose if we hadn't been asleep on Lover's Leap we might have seen, from our vantage point, the fire engines racing across town, seen the flickering flames burning up the Walshes' house down in the little model town at our feet, heard perhaps the ringing bells of the desperate ambulances trying to save the occupants.

The street is choked with fire engines and ambulances and policemen. We stumble out of the car and hang around the wrought-iron gates like sight-seers. The red ribbons on the holly wreath hang limp in the still air. There is ash and soot in the air, the smell of charred frocks and canapés. I remember suddenly the net petticoat stuffed so carelessly behind the boiling water tank, imagine it catching and spreading to the neat stacks of sheets and towels, and eventually engulfing the entire house. Everyone has safely escaped the inferno it seems, except –

'Richard and Hilary,' Malcolm says, his voice blank with disbelief.

As we approach the streets of trees it begins to snow properly. At first the little fluttery flakes stick to the windscreen, crystallize and melt and are washed away by the windscreen wipers, but soon the flurry of snowflakes grows bigger and they begin to cling onto passing objects, aerials, chimney pots, rooftops, trees.

Instead of turning into Chestnut Avenue, Malcolm drives up Holly Tree Lane. We're both so numb with shock at the sudden demise of Hilary and Richard that I don't think we really know where we're going. (*Drop dead* – did I really say that to *both* of them?)

The snow is now swirling around in the darkness in a menacing kind of way. We are driving past Boscrambe Woods, the trees an inky black mass at the side of the road. Abruptly, Malcolm swings the car into one of the entrances to the woods and parks in front of a row of fire-beating brooms that poke up towards the stars. They're in the wrong place. There could be no fire in these woods tonight. The ground is hard as iron, the waters in the streams turned to stone. When Malcolm turns the engine off it's quieter than anything I've ever heard.

'Come on,' Malcolm says, opening the car door, even though the snow is now blowing a blizzard. Reluctantly I tramp into the wood behind him. In the wood there is no blizzard, everything is still. The snow must have been falling for hours longer in the wood than outside the wood (how could that be?), for snow is piled up everywhere – Christmas-card snow, winter-wonderland snow, crisp and virginal. The bare branches of the deciduous trees, rimmed with snow, spring and arc overhead like the vaulted roof of a great cathedral. It *is* like being in church, hushed and reverent, but more spiritual.

The wood is full of evergreens too, firs have gathered from all over the world – the Norway spruces (*abies picea*) and lodgepole pines (*pinus contorta*), alpine firs (*abies lasiocarpa*) and European silver firs (*abies alba*), the balsam fir (*abies balsamea*) and the beautiful noble firs (*abies procera*) crowd together under their snowcoats like an eternal Christmas waiting to happen.

We plod along, silent in the silence. It's like being the last two people in the world. Perhaps we are, perhaps we've entered a time warp that's propelled us forward to the last, cold days. Only in the wood can you truly lose track of time. A rabbit bounces across the snow in front of us.

Ahead of me, Malcolm stops suddenly and, turning to me, puts his fingers to his lips. A red deer, a female, is standing ahead of us on the path, sniffing the air for us, knowing we are here but not quite seeing us. Then, in one startled leap, she's gone, crashing through the frozen branches so that the sound of snapping twigs echoes noisily in the cold silence around us.

'That's lucky, I expect,' Malcolm whispers, and puts his arms round me. His breath is warm on my frozen cheek. This is it then. I close my eyes expectantly ... 'Time to go home,' he says suddenly, and ploughs back through the snow, dragging me by the hand. I expect if we weren't still full of Beefeater's anti-freeze we'd both be dead of the cold by now.

We find the car covered in a thick eiderdown of snow and have to brush it off with our poor ungloved hands. The tyres spin on the snow as the car reverses onto the pristine road. The snow has stopped falling now and we slip and slide down the twisting road. 'I think you're the only person I can be myself with,' Malcolm says, more articulate than he's been for hours. Why does everyone have so much trouble being themselves?

He glances across at me to check whether I understand what he's trying to say and from nowhere a deer suddenly appears ahead of us, caught in the headlights. Nightmarishly mute, I lift my hand and point at it. Malcolm carries on blithely about his true self and his problems finding it but then he follows the direction of my pointing finger and horrified stare and says, 'Oh shit—' It looks exactly like the deer we've just seen in the wood (although they all look alike really) but this is no time to be making comparisons. Not such a lucky deer, after all. Time starts to slow down. Malcolm slews the car to one side to try and avoid the deer. I can see it clearly – its eyes rolling, wild with terror, its muscles moving and rippling beneath its velvet skin as it gathers itself into one great desperate leap.

The deer jumps free. And so does the car – taking off, jumping clear of the road, flying slowly through the air, gliding down the steep bank at the side of the road as if it had wings, all in perfect silence, as if the soundtrack to the world has been turned off, but then it hits the ground for the first time and sound returns suddenly – the noise of metal rending and glass breaking, the sound of the world ending, as we bounce off the snowy ground, splintering a young tree, crashing through gorse in a mad flurry of snow, the car an unstoppable wild animal intent on self-destruction before finally being tamed by a big sycamore standing sentinel in the frozen field.

Everything's quiet once more. No-one will ever find us here. I feel very tired but also very peaceful. The words to "Silent Night" run through my mind. We could sing to keep our spirits up but it seems that neither of us is capable of opening our mouths, when I try to make the words come out they stick to my tongue. I can't move my head at all in fact. Perhaps time has changed state again, now it is a solid, a great block of ice that has us trapped, frozen inside like flies in amber.

By concentrating very hard on the muscles in my neck I manage to turn my head a few inches. I can just see Malcolm. His face is crazed with blood that glistens in the dark. He's trying to speak as well. After a long time I finally understand what he's trying to say. The words come out slowly, mis-shapen, grating in the silent night. 'Help me,' he says, 'help me.' But I know it's no good because he's already dead.

KILLING TIME

I WAKE UP. I'M IN MY OWN BED. IN MY OWN ROOM. IN ARDEN. GONE are the snows (of yesterday), the trees, the deer, the car, the dead Malcolm Lovat. I'm wearing my nightdress and my body shows no sign of having been in a car-crash, although my brain is a wreck.

My pink party dress is hanging on the outside of the wardrobe looking remarkably unsullied after everything it's been through. It even looks stiff, as if it still has its petticoat attached underneath. The view from my window indicates quite different weather from yesterday – a mizzling, drizzling rain instead of a sharp frost. Did I dream yesterday? Was it just some dreadful, vivid nightmare?

Out of the corner of my eye I catch a glimpse of something on my bedside table – the gift-wrapped box of Bronnley soaps. I sit up and release them from their wrapping-paper. From somewhere down below I can hear the sound of the radio playing carols and the baby crying. Thoughtfully I hold one of the soap lemons in my hand where it sits heavily like a sour little moon. Angels and ministers of grace defend us and help me Boab.

If yesterday was Christmas Eve then today should be Christmas Day – but of course I know that the laws of causality are as bent as time's arrow and I am not the person to be trying to make predictions about sequential events.

Perhaps there really is no permanent reality, only the reality of change. A disturbing kind of thought.

On cue, Charles comes bursting into my room and says, 'Have you got any wrapping-paper? I've only got one present left to wrap and I've run out.'

'What day do you think it is?' I ask, and he looks at me as if I'm mad (well, I am). 'It's Christmas Eve, of course. What day do *you* think it is?' (Can time be *this* relative?)

This is ridiculous. I put my head under the covers. Have I actually succeeded in calling back yesterday? Have I stepped in the same river twice? Is the whole dreadful day going to happen again? Isn't it enough to have had the nightmare once without repeating it? How many rhetorical questions can I ask myself without getting bored?

Maybe I've died and gone to hell and this is my punishment – to live the worst day of my life over and over again for eternity.

Perhaps I'm dreaming my life. Perhaps I'll wake up and find I'm a butterfly. Or a caterpillar. Or a mushroom, a mushroom dreaming it's a girl called Isobel Fairfax.

Do I still have free will – maybe if I just *stay in bed* – not go to the Walshes' party, certainly not go driving anywhere with Malcolm Lovat – then everyone will be safe. I close my eyes and try and force myself back to sleep (perhaps *this* is what cats are doing – sleeping to try and make things disappear. Dogs maybe), but I've murdered sleep as soundly as I've destroyed the laws of time.

But what if, I suddenly think, opening my eyes and staring at the pink dress, what if it isn't my malign influence that precipitated (or precipitates, or will precipitate – take your pick) events? What if they're going to happen anyway? And if they're going to happen anyway then maybe there's something I can do to stop them. And then, even if Malcolm and Hilary and Richard still die, at least it won't be my fault. Which is something.

But there again – for all I know they're dead already. I drag myself out of bed, like it or not, I'm going to have to find out what's going on. I lift up the skirt of the pink dress, yes, there is the petticoat, intact and in place. I give a weary sigh.

There's no-one about downstairs – Vinny, Debbie and Gordon are not at their previous stations, although the mince pies know their place in the plot, piled high ready on the kitchen table, nicely dusted with icing-sugar like snow. I eat one, then another, then a third – I'm ravenous. I haven't had anything to eat since last night's stale custard creams, although, of course, it's possible that I haven't actually eaten them yet. Reality's slipping away from me faster than I can think about it.

I phone the Lovats. Malcolm answers. 'Hello? Hello?' he keeps repeating until I put the phone down because I can't think of anything to say that won't sound insane. I try the Walshes next and Mrs Walsh's flutey tones penetrate my eardrum. I mumble something about Hilary and Mrs Walsh says she's gone into town with Dorothy.

I decide not to check on the Primrose household, I don't really care whether Richard's dead or not and two out of three isn't bad going. But how to keep them alive, that's the question. The kind of question that Charles could get his teeth into but there's no sign of him either. Arden's like the *Marie Celeste*, the only survivor of whatever invisible disaster has occurred is the baby (it's indestructible) which is in its pram in the hall wearing its lungs out.

I take it (I can't bring myself to call it Jodi) out of its pram and try and soothe it but it's in a terrible rage, screaming its head off (well, not *quite*), every so often its body going rigid and stiff as if it's having a fit. Its face is red with anger and its little fists are bunched up furiously as if it would like to punch somebody.

I try and wrap it in its shawl but it's too awkward so in the end I just kind of bundle it up like a cabbage and carry it round to Sithean. Maybe Mrs Baxter will be able to do something with it.

And anyway I'd like to talk to somebody about what's happening to me, and preferably someone I didn't help to kill yesterday.

There's an eerie feeling of abandonment in the Baxter household as well. Sithean seems as empty and deserted as Arden. There's no answer when I shout 'Hello!' to the empty air, the only sound the sobs and hiccups of the baby.

In the living-room a fire is blazing in the hearth and the Christmas tree lights blink on and off, but whether they're supposed to do that or it's due to my electrical interference I can't say.

In the dining-room, the table's been set with the best china and plates. Mrs Baxter makes almost as much fuss about Christmas Eve as she does about Christmas Day. If it was up to Mrs Baxter she would probably celebrate Christmas every day of the year.

In the middle of the table there are red candles and each place setting has a cracker and a Christmas paper napkin – red with green holly leaves – twirled into a fanciful shape. A prawn cocktail in a wineglass sits on each plate, ready to be eaten.

I sit down on one of the chairs and pull a lettuce leaf from the prawn cocktail and nibble at it while I try to figure out where everyone's gone. Perhaps the Baxters have taken to slipping down wormholes in time as well. Perhaps the Baxters are at this moment celebrating Christmas in the eighteenth century or the Dark Ages. I smear some of the pink-coloured salad cream from the prawn cocktail onto the baby's lips and it's shocked into silence.

Without meaning to, I find I've finished the prawn cocktail. Perhaps if I go round the table and eat the other two it would look better, then I could pretend there were never any to begin with. But too late – the back door slams and Mr Baxter marches down the hall, glimpses me through the open dining-room door, marches on and then doubles back and snaps at me, 'What are you doing here? Sitting in my place? Eating my meal?'

'Where's Audrey and Mrs Baxter?' I ask, jumping up from the table guiltily.

'What an interesting question,' he says in the voice he reserves for the pupils he considers to be the greatest idiots. His eyes are bulging with madness. 'I mean where are they?' he says, enunciating each word carefully. 'Hmm, let me see . . .' He makes a face of mock-puzzlement and looks down one end of a cracker. 'No,' he says, 'they're not in there.' (How tedious it must be to live with Mr Baxter.) This pantomime goes on for some time until the volume of noise from the baby (it has its uses) drives him from the room and he goes up to his study.

I carry the baby through to the living-room and sit on the sofa with it. The blinking lights on the Christmas tree make the baby quite peaceable. It's stuck its fist in its mouth as if to force itself to be quiet and my heart goes out to it. It's got all its life ahead of it to be unhappy in, it seems a shame it has to start so soon.

The back door opens and closes. I hope this is Mrs Baxter and Audrey and not Mr Baxter coming in the house for a second time without having gone out first (you become paranoid pretty quickly once time starts breaking down, or breaking up. Or whatever).

But thankfully it *is* Mrs Baxter and Audrey. They're wearing their outdoor clothes – coats and scarves and woollen hats – as if they've just been out for a walk. 'We've just been out for a wee walk,' Mrs Baxter says, 'to give Daddy a chance to calm down. He was in a bit of a stushie with himself,' she adds with a rueful little smile. She looks incredibly miserable.

At the sight of the baby Mrs Baxter goes into maternal meltdown and sends Audrey to look for its present under the tree. Audrey unwraps the baby's present – a rattle (as if it doesn't make enough noise already) – and gives it to the baby with a lovely smile. 'I'll put the kettle on,' Mrs Baxter says. 'You'll have a cuppie, won't you, Isobel?'

'Daddy,' Audrey says when Mrs Baxter's left the room, and then stops, apparently incapable of saying anything else. 'Is in a bit of a stushie?' I prompt helpfully. She takes the baby and cradles it protectively, resting her chin on the top of its red-gold floss. Her eyes fill up with tears and she makes a tremendous effort to stop them spilling over onto the baby. 'Boys,' she manages to say.

'Boys? He thinks you've . . .?'

'He's convinced I've been with a boy,' she whispers.

'And have you?' (She must have surely, how else can we account for the phenomenon of baby Jodi? Although if anyone's a candidate for immaculate conception then it's Audrey.)

She looks at me with her big pained eyes as if I've just asked the most ridiculous question and holds the baby closer. It's quietened down now, has fallen asleep in fact, its fist still jammed in its mouth, perhaps in case it's tempted to blurt out the truth in its sleep. They look like the perfect nativity scene, Audrey with her lovely Mother-of-God kind of smile and the baby sleeping happily in her arms. Cautiously, with one hand, Audrey unbuttons her coat, unwinds her scarf, puts her hand up to her head and takes off her woollen hat – but instead of shaking down her lovely Mother-of-God kind of hair there's nothing there. I gasp in horror at her shorn head, not the urchin cut of a hairdresser but the ragged shearing of a wartime collaborator. 'Daddy,' Audrey says.

Mrs Baxter returns with a tray piled high with Christmas baking and tries not to look at the results of 'Daddy's' stushie on Audrey's head. She's about to say something when we hear Mr Baxter pounding back down the stairs and we listen to his footfall as if we're in a horror film awaiting the entrance of some unknown monster and it's almost a relief to see he's still human when he comes barging in the room and scowls at me and says, 'Still here? You're a bad influence. I expect it's you who's been leading Audrey here astray, isn't it?'

'Daddy, don't,' Mrs Baxter says in her most cajoling voice.

'And you can shut your face,' he says in response. He puts his own face a few inches away from mine, a bully's stance, and says, 'Well, Isobel, who's Audrey been messing about with? Some boy's had her, who is it? Not that ugly little brother of yours, I hope.'

'Daddy, don't,' Audrey pleads.

'You shut up, you little whore,' Mr Baxter bellows, rounding on her, 'giving yourself to boys, letting them do God knows what to you! Who was it? Tell me!' Mrs Baxter's jigging on the spot, flapping her hands as if she's trying to learn how to fly. Mr Baxter takes something from the pocket of his tweed jacket and starts waving it around. Something dark and metallic and gun-shaped. A gun, in fact.

'Your old service revolver,' Mrs Baxter marvels. 'I thought you got rid of that years ago, Daddy.' Mr Baxter puts the gun down on the mantelpiece with all the Grand Guignol exaggeration of a pantomime villain – the same way, in fact, that he used to put his cane on his desk – so that his pupils' minds would all focus on it. (I suppose we were lucky he never brought the gun in as a classroom deterrent.)

Then he makes a move towards Audrey, grabbing her by the remains of her hair, pulling her in towards him and roaring at her, 'Who?' heedless of the baby which is screaming in terror. More to try and calm the baby down than to appease her father, Audrey finally answers his question and, in a very small voice, says, 'But, Daddy, it was *you*.'

I lunge at Mr Baxter to try and make him let go of Audrey without digesting what Audrey's just said to him. The next thing I know – WALLOP – Mr Baxter turns and punches me in the face. The blow lands square on my cheekbone, a prizefighter punch, the kind that splinters bones and causes brain damage.

I drop to my knees in agony, trying to cradle my entire head while fighting for air. I feel incredibly sick as if I've just been dropped from a great height.

Slowly, I grow aware of a strange silence in the room. We all appear to have been paralysed, as if time has actually stopped. I imagine us frozen in this tableau for ever, but just then, Mrs Baxter's cat, which has been disguising itself as a brindled antimacassar on the back of a Parker Knoll chair, suddenly rolls over and falls off, thudding heavily on its feet on the carpet, then the fire crackles noisily and a lump of coal falls out sizzling on the hearth and everybody wakes up.

Mrs Baxter murmurs, 'Daddy?' as if someone's just told her the improbable answer to a question she's long puzzled over. Then there's a little intake of breath from Mrs Baxter that makes me turn and look at her. She's staring, dumbfounded, at Audrey and the baby. It *is* obvious when you see them together, I suppose – they actually look quite alike, not just the hair and the small features, but the whey-faced expression of misery they both tend to wear. 'Audrey?' Mrs Baxter whispers as big teardrops roll down Audrey's cheeks. Audrey really should have put on her catskin coat and fled as far as she could from Mr Baxter before we got to this dreadful state of affairs.

Mr Baxter meanwhile walks calmly over to the fireplace, takes his pipe off the mantelpiece and knocks the ash out of it on the hearth as if nothing has happened. I watch as if in a trance as he re-lights his pipe, sucking hard on the stem so that the tiny volcanic glow in the bowl heats and cools, over and over again, until Mr Baxter's encircled in a faint blue haze. How can he be so calm in the face of so much domestic mayhem? But then I expect that Bluebeard probably locked up his secret butchery and went and made himself a cup of tea afterwards.

I grow suddenly aware of Mrs Baxter in the doorway, standing perfectly still, like a statue. She must have left the room and come back in again because in her hand she's holding a carving-knife.

I have actually managed to find a scenario worse than yesterday's! Christmas in Sithean is like being trapped in a nightmarish game of Cluedo – is it Mrs Baxter in the hallway with the carving-knife, or Mr Baxter in the living-room with a gun? Next it'll be Audrey in the kitchen with the candlestick.

Then Mrs Baxter starts to lumber towards Mr Baxter, in a kind of slow motion, a charging rhinoceros chugging resolutely towards its target. As she charges Mr Baxter, Mrs Baxter makes a dreadful noise, like the moaning wail of an animal in pain. 'What the hell are you doing, Moira?' Mr Baxter says irritably, but as Mrs Baxter continues to charge his expression changes to one of disbelief. He looks round, perhaps for his gun, but it's too late – Mrs Baxter has met her target, slamming into Mr Baxter (who makes a kind of *whumph* noise), sending him slumped to his knees on the hearthrug, so that for all the world he looks as if he's suddenly decided to worship Mrs Baxter.

His hands, clutching his stomach, are bright red. Not the red of holly berries. Not the red of poinsettias. Not the red of robins' breasts nor the red of tomato ketchup. The red of blood. The blood is oozing through Mr Baxter's fingers, the stain spreading across the front of his Fair Isle pullover, knitted by Mrs Baxter for his last birthday. Last in all senses of the word.

Mrs Baxter, standing over him, bloody knife in hand, is like some terrible figure from Greek tragedy, her face smeared with blood from her first kill. Mr Baxter looks up at Mrs Baxter in astonishment, then looks down at his stomach with equal astonishment. Experimentally, he takes one of his hands away and blood spurts in a thin red fountain, a little gusher so powerful that it sprays the wall.

I snatch a cushion from the sofa and push it up against the source of the blood fountain but almost as soon as I touch him he falls forward onto his face. I try to push him the right way up but he's too heavy. His eyes are nearly closed and his breathing harsh and shallow. And then suddenly there's no breathing at all. His eyes stare lifelessly at the carpet. Mrs Baxter has turned back into a statue. Audrey is sitting on the sofa smiling at the baby as if nothing has happened. Who is the maddest person in this room? Mr Baxter is certainly the deadest.

A low whistle from the doorway makes me jump out of my skin. Carmen is standing in the doorway. Eunice, a pile of presents in her arms, barges past her and kneels beside Mr Baxter, presents spilling everywhere, and feels the pulse in his neck professionally. 'Dead,' she pronounces, like a detective.

Eunice looks around the room, assessing the situation. 'What happened here?' she asks (staying in detective character). I explain as best I can (leaving out all references to time – this being my second disastrous Christmas Eve and so on – as that will only confuse the issue).

'But how can that possibly be?' Eunice puzzles, looking at Audrey and the baby. 'He's her father, he can't be the father of her baby *as well*.' There are some things it seems that Eunice doesn't know. Carmen explains incest and abuse to her in a way that's remarkably lucid for a girl whose head is full of cheese.

I suppose it must cross all our minds at some point that we could call the police but if it does we never voice the idea. Not even Eunice.

'Perhaps we should all stick the knife in,' I suggest miserably, 'then we'd all be guilty.'

'Then we'd all go down for murder,' Eunice points out sensibly.

The three of us sit for quite some time discussing what to do (Audrey and Mrs Baxter are good for nothing). Carmen proposes that we take Mr Baxter to the casualty department of Glebelands General and say that he fell on to the knife.

'While carving the turkey?' Eunice snorts with derision. If he'd been smaller we could have dragged him over to the hearth and immolated him on the fire. 'And say what?' Eunice says sarcastically. 'That he fell down the chimney when he was delivering the presents?'

I get up and switch the Christmas tree lights off, their winking and blinking is driving me crazy. Carmen shares cigarettes and in the extremity of the situation smokes two at once. 'I think we should bury him,' she suggests.

'Bury him?' I repeat in horror. Part of me is still waiting for Mr Baxter to get up off the floor and burial seems a bit of a final option.

Carmen passes round a packet of fruit gums. 'For God's sake, Carmen,' Eunice says crossly. 'But bury him where?'

Carmen continues, warming to the subject now. 'We could get Mr Baxter's car, and we could take him somewhere, tip him in the river or bury him in a wood or somewhere.'

'But none of us can drive,' I point out.

'We could have a go,' Carmen says, always game for anything, 'or we could just bury him in the garden, that would be easier.'

'Easier?' I query doubtfully. 'And what would we tell people? I mean, how would we explain where he'd gone? People don't just disappear.' (What am I saying?) Carmen eats her way through a mince pie with an appetite that does her credit.

By now the rain is lashing against the curtained windows of the living-room (now more of a dead-room really). 'Right then,' Eunice says suddenly and proceeds to come over all Girl Guidish, 'we're going to need gloves, a torch, some rope and –' She pauses her clicking brain momentarily overcome by the circumstances it finds itself in.

'A spade?' I offer.

'A spade, exactly!'

We find two spades in the garden shed and Eunice devises a two-on/one-off rota system for digging. Our attempts at excavation are feeble at first but eventually we begin to get the hang of it. Once you stop worrying about the circumstances (murder) and the weather (foul) and the mud (disgusting) it's surprising how you can get quite a rhythm going. We're soon sweating with exertion and at the same time shivering with cold. 'How far down do we have to go?' Carmen gasps, dragging deeply on a cigarette. 'Six feet,' Eunice says, leaning on her shovel like a professional gravedigger. 'Don't be ridiculous,' Carmen snaps back, 'this isn't a fucking cemetery, it's Mrs Baxter's vegetable patch. All we're trying to do is get him out of sight.' It would take us years to dig a six-foot hole. As it is we're quite pleased with the shallow pit that we manage.

We go back inside the house to get Mr Baxter. Nothing's changed. Audrey and the baby are both asleep now and Mrs Baxter's sitting on the sofa, the knife on her lap. 'It's nearly tea-time,' she says conversationally when she sees us, 'how time flies.'

Without replying, we set about dragging Mr Baxter out through the French windows. Carmen, who at some point in her life must have witnessed undertakers in action, smiles sympathetically at the newly created widow and says, 'It's time to take Mr Baxter away now, Mrs Baxter.' Eunice and I exchange uneasy glances, worried that Mrs Baxter might spring up from the sofa and suddenly understand what's going on, but all she does is smile and say, 'On you go then.' A real Mrs Eerie-Cheerie.

We drag Mr Baxter's lifeless shape out into the rain and along the garden path. Finally, with a lot of grunting and shoving and swearing, we tip him into his grave.

Eunice shines the torch on him. He looks less dead than he did two hours ago. 'We have to cover his face,' I say hastily as Carmen picks up her spade again. I run back into the house and snatch a handful of the festive paper napkins from the kitchen and then run back down the path with them and kneel at the side of the hole and put them on his face. 'Careful,' Carmen says, worried that I'm about to fall on top of Mr Baxter.

Covering him with soil is easy but disposing of the soil displaced by Mr Baxter is a grim job, trundling awkward wheelbarrows of the heavy wet stuff down to the bottom of the garden where we make a pile of it, like a dark sandcastle.

By the time we straggle back inside we look like we've just mined our way down under and back, filthy and soaked to the bone and speechless with shock. We take our shoes off outside the back door and stand under the porch light staring in horror at each other.

Meanwhile, in the kitchen, Mrs Baxter's making a pot of tea and laying out more Christmas cake and mince pies on plates with festive doilies and the paper napkins which are now doubling as grave-clothes.

Mrs Baxter shoos us into the living-room with the tea-tray, then, putting it down on the coffee table, she beams at us. 'Come on, come on, help yourselves.' My heart sinks. 'And you, Isobel, come on, eat up!' she urges, handing me a paper napkin, the sight of whose red and green makes me blench. The pain in my face where Mr Baxter hit me is growing more acute by the minute.

There's blood everywhere in the living-room, streaked on the walls, on the sofa, and the huge bloodstain that has become a macabre figure in the carpet. 'We'll have to do something about that,' Carmen says to me.

'Dearie me,' Mrs Baxter says, overhearing this conversation, 'we'll need to hire a Bex Bissell for that.' I'm sure the smell of blood – salt and rust – has seeped into the very air itself. 'Have a piece of shortie,' Mrs Baxter urges, 'I made it myself.'

Audrey stirs, opening her eyes sleepily and spying the baby in her arms smiles her lovely smile. It would take a crowbar to separate them now.

Eunice sighs and leaves the room, coming back with a bucket of hot water and a bottle of Stardrops and mutters, 'Come on,' rather viciously at me but I've reached a stage of weariness that's beyond anything. All my bones are sore and if there wasn't so much blood in the living-room I would curl up on the sofa with Mrs Baxter and fall asleep. 'It's nice to have so many young people in the house,' Mrs Baxter says gaily. 'Daddy will be so pleased when he gets back – he's a great one for the young people.'

A statement wrong on so many counts that I forget about the mud and the blood and the horror and sit heavily down on the sofa with my head in my hands.

'Don't be bothering yourself with that just now,' Mrs Baxter says to Eunice, who's on her knees scrubbing the carpet with an expression on her face that defies description. 'How about a game of something?' Mrs Baxter says brightly. 'How about Rhubarb Charades or Hot Potato? Get Home Safe, Mother – that's a nice quiet game. Human Croquet, that's a wonderful game – of course we need more people for that,' she adds wistfully. (How many people *do* you need for Human Croquet, for heaven's sake?)

I stand up suddenly and run to the kitchen and am sick in the sink. The kitchen door's still wide open, letting the rain in. Our muddy shoes are lined up neatly on the doorstep, like reminders of our lost innocence. I can't go back into that hellish living-room. I step over the shoes, into the dark unquiet garden and go home.

I have blood on my hands and no matter how much I scrub at my fingernails I can't get rid of it. I lie in the bath until the water turns cold and then wrap myself up in towels and pad damply out of the bathroom and into my bedroom. Then I lie down in my bed and sleep like the dead.

And dream about Mrs Baxter's garden in summer. Dream about scarlet runner-beans on a wigwam of canes, about marrows sheltering under their big leaves and the feathery fronds of carrots. A neat row of drumhead cabbages, like giant peas, and a row of cauliflowers, their big white curd heads bursting through their leaf-cowls. One of the cauliflowers seems different from the others. Slowly, as I watch, it turns into Mr Baxter's head, poking up through the brown soil and speaking angrily, shouting at me, telling me what a wicked person I am. Then Mr Baxter shoulders his way out of the brown soil, climbs over a row of lettuces and starts lumbering along the path. His flesh is putrid and he has the clumsy gait of a zombie. I turn to run but can only move on the spot as if I'm caught in a cartoon. I start screaming but my voice is as silent as if I was in the depths of space.

I come downstairs in my nightdress and make myself cocoa. Gordon is sitting in Vinny's armchair by the ashes of the fire, cradling the baby. How did the baby get home on its own?

'She's very fretful,' Gordon says, smiling at me. 'How did the baby get here?' I ask Gordon. 'Who knows?' he says, smiling vaguely. In the kitchen Debbie is making an inventory of the Welsh dresser, watching the willow pattern plates like a jailer. The carcass of a half-eaten turkey is on the kitchen table. Christmas dinner. I shake Debbie by the arm. 'What day is it?'

'It's Christmas Day, of course.'

'How long have I been asleep for?'

'What on earth are you talking about?' She moves a sauce-boat a fraction of an inch.

'Have I eaten Christmas dinner, for example?'

'For example?' Debbie frowns. 'Well, you've certainly eaten Christmas dinner. It wasn't much of an example.'

'Wish?' Gordon asks, coming into the kitchen and picking up the arc of wishbone and proffering it to me. I decline.

I have to go round to the Baxters', I have to find out if Mr Baxter's alive like Hilary and Richard (presumably) or whether he's at this moment turning into a vegetable. I run out of the back door and down the drive, the wind whipping through my hair and the rain soaking through my nightdress.

I'm running so fast that I can't stop at the end of the driveway and run straight into the normally deserted road. The oncoming car's on top of me before I even register that the dazzling light is coming from its headlights. Our paths are destined to cross exactly in the middle of the road, the driver must have a good view of my terrified face as I bounce on the bonnet before he swerves violently and goes crashing through the hawthorn hedge on the opposite side of the road and drives his car smack into a gnarled old hawthorn tree.

I have certainly seen *his* face, seen the horror on the features of Malcolm Lovat as he tries to avoid my unavoidable body.

I've landed half in the hedge and its thorns have torn at my face and hands. I crawl over to the car. The driver's door is hanging open and Malcolm is slumped in the seat. I kneel on the ground next to him and put my hand up to hold his. I know there's no escaping the dreadful words he's going to say to me. I wait patiently, almost peacefully, for them.

He half-opens his eyes. His hair's matted with blood, his face almost unrecognizable. 'Help me,' he whispers, 'help me,' and closes his eyes. I crawl away, back to my hedge, I really can't bear this.

I'm invisible. I'm like some dreadful mythical creature that turns up in other people's lives to wreak havoc and disaster. At the corner of my vision I can see people running from their houses to see what all the commotion is. I catch a glimpse of Mr Baxter, very much alive, running along his drive. I agree with Audrey – we know nothing. I watch the police and ambulancemen removing Malcolm from the wreckage of his car, hear one of them say softly, 'Is he gone?' and another one murmur, 'Poor bastard.'

Why must it always end this way? Why must it end with Malcolm Lovat dying? Again? 'That's Malcolm Lovat, old Doc Lovat's son,' someone says. 'That's a dreadful thing,' someone else says, 'a lad like that with such a great future . . .'

A policeman suddenly catches sight of me and an ambulanceman rushes over to me with a blanket but I am already gone, washed over by the wave of blackness that takes me down to the bottom of a Polar Ocean where everything is the colour of blue diamonds and only the seals and the mermaids swim.

PRESENT

MAYBE

THERE IS ANOTHER WORLD
BUT IT IS THIS ONE

THE SMELL OF FRYING BACON WAKES ME UP. MY BEDROOM'S WARM. It's never usually warm, except at the height of summer. The room's the same – but different. There are pretty flower-sprigged curtains at the window, a carpet on the floor I've never seen before and a pale striped wallpaper on the walls instead of the usual beige relief. What's wrong? Can you step in the same river *thrice*? The time is seriously out of joint in Arden, I fear.

There's no sign, I notice, of the box of soaps, nor of the pink party dress – absences only to be welcomed.

By the bed, a pair of fluffy pink mules are waiting for my feet, a lemon nylon négligé hanging on a hook on the door is similarly waiting for my body. Laid across my bed there's a stocking as heavy as if it still contained a leg. There's a gift-tag pinned on it and I reach down and turn the tag over so that I can read it. It says, *To Isobel from 'Father Christmas'*! What does this mean? Who is '*Father Christmas*'!?

271

Guiltily – for I may not be the 'Isobel' of the gift-tag – I investigate the contents of the stocking. Little gifts suitable for a girl – bath cubes and handbag vanity mirrors, hair bands and chocolate drops.

Half-reluctant, half-curious, I get out of bed and slip on the mules and the négligé. There's a large cheval-mirror in the corner, not a heavy one like Mrs Baxter's, but a pretty mock Louis-Quinze thing in gilded whitewood. I tread softly on my new carpet in case I'm treading on my dreams (you never know) and look in the mirror. I'm also the same and yet not the same. Some differences are obvious – my hair, for example, is much better tended than usual – but there are subtle changes that are more puzzling. Is it just my madness or do I look, well (how can I say it?), *happy*? What's wrong?

On my dressing-table there's an array of teenage cosmetics – pale pink lipsticks and pearly nail varnish. I open the whitewood wardrobe and find it's full of nice clothes – shirtwaisters and big dirndl skirts, soft Orlon sweaters in pastel colours, a little jersey suit. This is certainly an infinitely better version of Christmas than the previous three, but I hardly need remind myself that appearances can be deceptive – who knows what lurks beneath this pleasant surface? What kind of teenage Faustian pact have I entered into to bring about this change in my fortunes? Have I given up my eternal soul to Mephistopheles for nice clothes and a date every Saturday night?

From the wardrobe I choose a green linen sack-dress and a white Courtelle cardigan and exchange the fluffy mules for a pair of black kitten-heeled shoes and parade in front of the mirror, pleased with my transformation into a perfectly normal-looking person.

From the window I can see an outside world covered in a glittering white pantomime-frost. Out in the field beyond the garden the Lady Oak looks like a tree from an Arthur Rackham book, a fine-cut black silhouette against the winter sky. Four Christmases in a row and different weather each time. Pretty wondrous strange, if you ask me.

I go downstairs in this same-but-different house and follow the smell of bacon and coffee to the dining-room.

Charles is sitting at the table, tucking into a plate of bacon, scrambled eggs and fried mushrooms. Somebody says, 'Tea or coffee?' and Charles looks up and, smiling through a mouthful of fried bread, says, 'I think I'll have coffee, please.' Very gently, I push the door open a bit wider. Vinny is laminating toast with butter and marmalade. She looks more or less the same as usual, which is no surprise.

The table is covered in a thick white cloth and the Widow's silver is out, as well as her flower-sprigged china, all reconstituted from its broken pieces. The Widow's chrome teapot sits as usual in the middle of the table, clean and polished and wearing a newly knitted cosy in brown and yellow. The Widow herself ('Surprise!') is sitting next to Vinny, almost as spruce as her teapot, her grey hair in a tidy bun, her spectacles perched on the edge of her nose. She looks in remarkably good shape for one so old – certainly the Widow looks in very good shape for someone who's *dead* . . . this is, as usual, all very confusing. There's to be no more dying then?

A hand reaches over the table and takes a piece of toast. I open the door a fraction more to see who the hand belongs to. Gordon. Not the usual careworn Gordon, but a cheerful Gordon, grown slightly plump around the jowls and the waistline as might befit a prosperous grocer. He turns to Charles and says, 'Sure you don't want any more bacon, old chap?' and Charles mumbles through a mouthful of egg, 'No thanks.'

I could swear that Charles looks taller, but then he is sitting down so I can't really be sure. He certainly looked less spotty, less miserable, less idiotic. There's somebody else at the table, sitting next to Gordon, wreathed in cigarette smoke. Gordon turns to this invisible person and pours them another cup of coffee without asking, or being asked. I can see a hand belonging to this person – pale skin and long, thin fingers that end in scarlet nails.

I have to push the door open further to see who this person is – too far, for Gordon looks up and says, 'Hello, old thing, I thought you were never going to wake up. Come and have some breakfast.'

And the invisible person – who is now visible – says, *Darling, come in and sit down. What do you want for breakfast?*

I am a radiant being, I rise up and float for happiness, float round the dining-table, past my brother who has grown almost handsome now, past Vinny and the Widow, rest as lightly as a butterfly on the carpet and kiss Eliza on the cheek. *Merry Christmas, darling.* On her finger, a ring sparkles, emeralds and diamonds catching lights off the fire in the hearth. This is neither past nor future – this, surely, must be my parallel life, the one where everything goes right. The one where real, right justice prevails (the one with no pain). The one that should only exist in fiction.

And so the day goes on, every moment another gift unwrapped. 'What are you so cheerful about?' Vinny says and I laugh and plant a kiss on her withered-apple cheek and exclaim, 'Oh, Vinny – I love you!' and catch Charles' comic face, cross-eyed with horror.

The Christmas dinner is everything you would expect from such a day, the goose as fat and succulent as a goose raised by a genuine goosegirl, the roasted potatoes as crisp as crackling on the outside, as soft as clouds on the inside. 'This is nice apple sauce,' Gordon says and the Widow replies, 'From our own apples.'

Gordon brings in the pudding, flaming like a dragon, and the Widow picks up a silver sauce-boat and says, 'Now – who's for rum and butter sauce?'

When we're as stuffed as Christmas geese ourselves we play a quiet hand of rummy in the living-room, to the accompaniment of Christmas carols on a record the Widow brings out. Once we've begun to digest our dinner we play a noisy game of Racing Demon and then a hilarious game of Charades at which Eliza proves particularly talented. Someone should go and fetch Mrs Baxter, this is just the kind of Christmas she would love.

It's dark outside, but inside everything glows with its own inner light – the Widow's poinsettias, the polished mahogany of the table, the tinsel and Christmas cards, the holly with its red berries, the sprig of mistletoe hanging from the Widow's chandelier, beneath which Gordon is even at this moment kissing Eliza so fiercely that the Widow can't resist a little tutting.

Then it's time for more food, here is the Widow already with a big wooden tray piled high with mince pies and Christmas cake, turkey sandwiches and sticks of celery in the engraved celery glass. We eat sitting round the fire, then Gordon says, 'Let's have a sing-song, eh, Vin?' and we sing lustily, 'Early One Morning', 'Polly-Wolly-Doodle' and 'What Shall We Do With the Drunken Sailor?' to which (miraculously) I find I know all the words.

Then Gordon is prompted to sing 'Sweet Lass of Richmond Hill' which he does beautifully and follows it up with 'Scarlet Ribbons' which brings tears to Eliza's eyes. We finish up with 'One Fish Ball' and 'Some Folks Do' and even Vinny is inclined to cheer the merry, merry heart that laughs by night and day. This is pure wish fulfilment. We are an ideal family. We are a happy family. I am living the perfect plot, but what will the ending be like?

Is this real? Or am I imagining it? And what is the difference? If I imagine a Christmas table groaning under fatted goose and flaming pudding, why isn't it as real as one that really happened? How is an imagined Christmas different from a remembered one?

We've just embarked on another round of mince pies and pot of tea when a car horn hoots outside. Eliza pulls the curtain at the window aside and says (to me), *It's for you, darling, it's your boyfriend.*

My boyfriend – what a wonderful phrase. But who will my boyfriend be? 'Here's Malcolm,' Gordon says, striding towards him and shaking his hand as Vinny lets him in. 'Happy Christmas, Malcolm!'

'Happy Christmas, sir,' Malcolm Lovat says and goes around the room exchanging the season's greetings with everyone. He blushes when Eliza murmurs, *Happy Christmas, darling,* and kisses him full on the lips but Gordon laughs and says, 'You'll have to excuse my wife, Malcolm, she actually invented flirting, you know. We're trying to persuade her to take out the patent and make us lots of money!'

Oh, that's not fair, darling, Eliza says, *we were standing under the mistletoe − that's allowed.*

How long can this last? What if it could go on for ever?

We're going to visit Malcolm's parents apparently.

'Your mother too?' I ask cautiously, trying not to let the knowledge of the past cloud this wonderful present.

'Of course,' he grins, 'she's one of my parents, after all.'

'And she's quite well?'

'Perfectly.'

Perhaps nobody in the world is dead or dying? Perhaps everybody is alive and well − and happy, I muse, as I follow Malcolm out into the hallway. Perhaps there is no sickness or famine or war. A chorus of *Goodbyes!* echoes behind us and I pause abruptly on the front doorstep − of course! This is heaven. I have died and gone to heaven. I had died in the car crash − so has Malcolm and we're in heaven where our families have been waiting for us − but then they'd all be dead too. Has everyone died? Everyone in the whole world? Perhaps this is the Day of Judgement and the unnamed dead, those who the flood did and the fire shall − are risen up and reformed from the dust that they have been.

'Isobel?'

'Yes, yes, I'm coming,' I reply hastily and pull the front door shut behind me. As I climb into the car I glanced back uneasily at the door and its magnificent, ideal, holly wreath − what if I have just shut myself out of heaven? What a ghastly thought. But the engine is running, my handsome boyfriend is waiting for me and so away we go down the drive.

'I thought,' Malcolm grins (this is a more cheerful and carefree Malcolm than I've seen of late. Hardly the same person at all, in fact), 'that we might go for a little spin first? Get some time on our own.' Does he mean sex? At the very least he must mean kissing surely?

'Yes, why not? Sounds like a good idea to me.' This is a dream, a very good one, and I may as well make the best of it.

★

I catch a glimpse of Audrey at the front window of Sithean, her hair returned, a cloud of fire around her head. In every window we pass, a Christmas tree displays its cheerful lights. How strange to think that all the houses on the streets of trees are full of happy, not-dead people. Perhaps the turkeys and geese and ducks and chickens on the Christmas tables are also rising up and their bones are knitting together and their flesh is being regurgitated and reforming and their feathers are flying backwards and sticking into their bodies like arrows and any moment now they will fly out of the suburban windows and up into the night sky.

'Isobel?'

'Mm?'

'I was thinking, why don't we get engaged in the New Year? I mean I know I'm still at med school and everything, and I know you're only sixteen and you want to go to art college – and there's no way I would stand in your way, I think women should be more than housewives if they want to and would respect any decision you make . . .' (This is definitely, without any shadow of a doubt, a dream.)

It starts to snow, great flurries that hit the windscreen as if someone had thrown them from a bucket, like pantomime glitter. Hang on, something's wrong here. 'Hang on a minute . . .'

'What?' Malcolm laughs.

'Are we going to Boscrambe Woods?'

'I thought so, why not?'

'You're Malcolm Lovat!' I say to him accusingly. He laughs uproariously. 'Guilty,' he says, taking his hands off the wheel and holding them above his head.

'Don't!' I yell at him. 'Don't do that, we could have an accident. We're going to have an accident anyway. Don't you understand? Stop the car!'

'OK, OK, keep your shirt on.' He stops laughing and says softly, 'Izzie, what's the matter?' But it's too late – another car is careering down the hill from Boscrambe Woods, skidding helplessly on the ice. I'm dazzled by the headlights, a dozen suns in my eyes. 'Christ!'

Malcolm Lovat cries and pushes me over to the car door, trying to cover me with his body, trying to push me out, but it's too late and the other car hits us with an explosive bang, followed by an infernal shrieking and grinding of metal as it shoves us along, off the road and down an embankment.

An avalanche of white snow seems to envelop the car and we're plunged into a white world of silence, the silence of absolute deafness. I am doomed to relive this experience again and again, each time the details are different, but the ending is always the same.

Perhaps this is an ordeal I have been set – perhaps I am Janet to Malcolm Lovat's Tam Lin. Perhaps the Queen of Elfland – instead of turning him into a snake in my arms, or lion or a red hot bar of iron – is trying to wrest away her human tithe from me by constantly killing him. Again and again.

But it's no enchantment. Flights of invisible angels crowd the car-crash scene waiting impatiently. Malcolm Lovat's skin is as white as the snow, his lips as blue as ice. They open slowly, an ice hole from which emerges the only words possible. Tears are streaming down my cheeks, freezing as they leave my eyes, hanging on my cheeks like chandelier drops. 'Help me,' he says, refusing to be silent. 'Help me.' But I am helpless to help, this story must always, always, end badly.

A pair of warm lips cover my own icy ones. Someone begins to kiss me, but then I'm washed over by the cold, cold wave and dragged down, under the thick-ribbed ice and into the watery world below. Here is an iceberg as big as a cathedral, here are the long-dead bones of ships crushed by pack-ice. Shoals of silver fish shimmer and flicker and whales like great stately barques pass overhead as black shadows.

I pop up suddenly, like a cork through a hole in the ice. In the arctic world above it is snowing, the grey sky is full of snow. Mother Carey's chickens flock overhead, polar bears pad softly on the ice, but I don't stop, I carry on rising upwards, flying over the ice-cap on the top of the world, higher and higher, set free of gravity, set free of everything.

278

I am circling the globe of the world, I am visiting the round earth's imagined corners, the ice-locked northern wastes, the Lithuanian Forests, the great Tibetan Plateau, the cold deserts of Asia and the hot deserts of Arabia, lifted on thermals above the steaming jungles of Africa, skimming above the South China Seas like a flying fish, skating the endless Pacific blue that floods the southern hemisphere, racing the sunset to the Bermudas, down the spine of the Andes, down to the bottom of the world, and more ice, ice so clean and blue that it must have been frozen at the beginning of time when everything was new.

But I am leaving the earth, higher still, up into the inkiness of night, leaving the earth spinning down below, a blue and green ball. Now I am a new constellation in the night sky, spread across the northern hemisphere, Sagittarius on my left shoulder, Scorpio rising on my right – the metamorphosis of yet another hapless girl into something rich and strange. Blessed Isobel full of light, as bright as a million diamonds, soon I will turn into a supernova and explode in glittering fragments and spread to the edges of the universe. I am as full of ecstasy as an archangel – I am my true self. For a long time . . .

. . . then something dark and painful begins to pull me back to earth. I close my eyes.

When I open them I am in the fearful place, the heart of the heart of the forest. It isn't very good in the middle of the wood. Not very good at all. Twigs snap under the weight of unseen feet. Leaves rustle like predatory wings. Invisible claws flex, inches away from my skin. I can smell the mould of the forest floor and the blackness of night. I know I will never find my way out of the forest, never find the path that will take me back to the lit-up windows of the village; the friendly gossip of the Thursday market-place; the village virgins in their tablecloth-checked dresses, gathered around the well; the handsome rustic youths in their leather jerkins; the brave woodcutter dressed for best in green velvet and silver-buckles; the honking of the geese as the goosegirl harries them up the hill.

The only path I will find will be the one that leads deeper and deeper into the wilderness of fear. I lie down at the foot of a tree and close my eyes. Leaves drift down and cover my face. Small animals scrabble, digging up the soil and burying me, hiding me from the terror of the wood. I cannot open my eyes, my eyelids are the lead lids of coffins, soldered shut, I am buried in the deep in the cold ground, earth stops up my nostrils, gathers in my ears, my mouth is full of sour soil.

Something is pecking at my skin, someone is digging me up, pulling me up from my earth tomb, into the light. People loom in and out of focus, they seem to be aliens, white and fuzzy – spacemen without faces. They are experimenting on me, poking me with needles and sticking tubes in and out of me, probing me to discover my secrets. They are obsessed with my name, 'Isobel, Isobel,' they call out to me softly, urgently – stroking my cheek, pinching the skin on the back of my hand, 'Isobel, Isobel,' moving my toes and tapping my wrist, 'Isobel, Isobel.' They are trying to make me myself by naming me. But then I will disappear. I keep my eyes closed. Tightly.

One day, one of them acquires a face, a human face. Soon they all have faces and then they lose their alien nature and turn into nurses in blue-and-white stripes and frilled caps, serious doctors with coats and stethoscopes who swim in and out of focus.

My head hurts. My head feels as if someone's blown it up with a bicycle pump. It throbs dangerously, someone has cut the top off my skull and scooped out my brains and replaced them with a bag of tangled and frayed nerves, but I can't tell anyone because I have been robbed of the power of speech. I don't want to be in this metallic world of pain, I want to go back to the cold Antarctic and play with the mermaid seals.

And here is Gordon, leaning over me, whispering in my ear, holding my hand, 'Isobel, Isobel.' And Vinny, poker-backed on a hospital chair, saying, 'Better yet?' impatiently. 'Orite?' Debbie asks, worry creasing her eyes so that they almost disappear. And Eunice and Mrs Primrose with grapes and white chrysanthemums – the flowers of death, Mrs Primrose saying anxiously. 'Can she hear us, do you suppose?' and Eunice saying, 'Hearing's the last sense to go.' And Carmen munching her way through the box of Maltesers she's brought with her. Mrs Baxter and Audrey, Mrs Baxter dabbing her eyes with a tissue from my locker and Audrey saying, 'It's all right, everything's going to be all right, isn't it, Izzie?' and kissing my forehead, her breath smelling of the Parma violets she's been eating and her rope of hair falling on the sheets. I want to ask about Mr Baxter, is he dead or alive? But my tongue is like a roll of carpet in my mouth and all I can move is an eyelid that flutters and shakes.

'Izzie? Izzie?' Charles says, his face oddly solemn so that I feel like cracking a joke to make him put on his clown-face.

'There,' Mrs Baxter beams, 'you look so much better!'

'Where is Mr Baxter?' Mrs Baxter's face clouds over and she gathers herself to say, 'He's no longer with us, I'm afraid, Isobel.'

But where is he?

Slowly, slowly, everything begins to fall back into shape, like a kaleidoscope at rest, a jigsaw finished. The lips that came and kissed me, that felt like the kiss of death, were really the kiss of life. The first time I was ever kissed by a man must have been by the resuscitating lips of an ambulanceman, fighting to keep me alive. The cosmic journey I took was the world of the comatose.

The pain is better now that I'm in the soft poppy world of morphia. Everything is very white, the sheets, the walls, the starched nurses' aprons. There is another white bed in the white room, the sheets are fields of snow, the pillows crackling with ice. On the edge of my field of vision I can see that there is someone in the bed. Nurses come and go and talk to the other patient, their voices boom and fade. 'Just a minor wee op,' a nurse says smiling, as if the woman is being given a treat.

I know this other patient from somewhere. I hear her voice, strange and hypnotic, weaving its way through the white cotton wool that they've wrapped my glass body in. Her voice fills in the intervals between nurses and consultant's rounds, visitors and sleep. After days, possibly weeks, maybe years, I realize that she's telling me a story. She is my own Scheherazade, she knows everything, she must be the storyteller from the end of the world. But how does it begin? Why it begins, as it must, she says, with the arrival of the baby –

PAST

THE BONNY BONNY ROAD

THE LONDON HOUSE WAS A HIVE OF ACTIVITY AS THE STAFF GOT ready for the return of Sir Edward and Lady de Breville from abroad. Not alone, but with their new baby. Sir Edward de Breville had sent for his own nanny to come up from the family's country residence. Although Nanny had been enjoying her retirement in the heart of the country – all that gossip and rhubarb wine – she responded well to the call of duty and hauled herself up to town from Suffolk, tempted by a second-class railway ticket and the opportunity to shape another generation of de Brevilles. What's more, she had been promised a nursery staff of four – a dogsbody, two nursemaids and a second nanny – underneath her and was looking forward to throwing her weight around in her old age.

'All those people for one little baby,' the parlourmaid whispered to the footman, 'and to think, my mother brought up six of us single-handed.'

'Ah, but the rich are different,' the footman said, 'they take a lot more looking after.'

The de Brevilles had always been rich, ever since they came over with the Conquest and were handed lands left, right and centre by the Bastard (conqueror and king), for their zeal in subduing the stubborn English. Since then they had just got richer and richer, with their huge tracts of farmland in Wiltshire, their orchards in Kent, their fields of barley in Fife, their fields of coal in Yorkshire, a swathe of elegant buildings in Mayfair.

Edward de Breville, last of his line. Twenty-nine years old, tall and handsome, as was the birthright of all first-born de Breville sons. A responsible man, he didn't leave those orchards and coal-fields unvisited, or fail to keep an eye on his overseers. The rich do not get richer by neglecting their money. A war-hero, a captain of men, with a distinguished scar running the length of one handsome cheek where a German bayonet caught him. A man who believed in King and Country, despite everything he'd witnessed in the fields of Flanders. A man who believed in cricket on the village green and humility in the company of men of the cloth, even lowly vicars.

And the most eligible of bachelors – well-behaved girls swooned for him, society girls pretended innocence for him, fast young things slowed down and boasted about their domestic skills. 'Such a catch,' the society matrons whispered furiously over the lobster in aspic and the claret jellies.

In the first season after the Great War Edward de Breville was the most competed-for man in London. Which of the lovely, and not so lovely, well-bred English roses would he chose for a consort? He would not, surely, look across the Atlantic to all those upstart daughters of press barons and bankers and vulgar shipping millionaires, all of them dying to be duchesses?

No indeed, for Sir Edward's eye had roamed a little further south than New York or Boston – to somewhere more exotic, more outlandish – had been charmed by the lovely form of an Argentinian cattle heiress, Irene Otalora. 'Beef?' the society matrons gasped in horror.

Sir Edward didn't have to travel as far as the pampas to find his Argentinian bride, for she had a French mother and was quite the European, summering in Deauville, where Sir Edward discovered her, daintily sipping a *citron pressé*. They married abroad, quietly, to avoid interest in her problematic Catholic religion.

Sir Edward watched his wife on the night of their wedding, dropping her silken clothes around her ankles like Botticelli's Venus rising from the waves. She unwound the long black hair that curled to her waist and stepped out of her clothes and raised her arms above her head to display her body to her new husband and Sir Edward thought of Salome and Jezebel and the Queen of Sheba and thanked God for French mothers-in-law who educated their daughters so well.

For an untimely second, Sir Edward had a vision of a roomful of stone-cold English roses lying stiffly between the nuptial sheets like effigies, an entirely unwelcome vision immediately banished by the sight of his new wife gliding towards him. The grandee tilt of the head, the coquettish smile, the thrusting breasts with their dark-brown aureoles, the firm grasp of those brown fingers on his manhood . . . Sir Edward melted into his honeymoon bed and his honeymoon wife.

And now there was little Esme. 'A very pretty child,' was Nanny's pleased verdict. 'We'll make a real de Breville out of her.'

Lady de Breville visited the nursery every day and cooed prettily over her lace-clad baby and spoke high-class nonsense in French while Nanny smiled patiently and waited for her to go so she could get on with giving the child oatmeal and Scotch broth. Lady de Breville had the baby's ears pierced when she was only a few weeks old, so now she had tiny gold hoops in her little brown ears. Like a gypsy, Nanny thought, but managed to hold her disgust in. She was only a servant after all.

Every evening little Esme was brought down, long after Nanny would have had her in bed, and paraded in the drawing-room to be admired by Sir Edward and Lady Breville's dinner guests as they glittered and fluttered in their sequins and feathers drinking 'cocktails'. Being foreign, of course, Nanny thought, Lady Irene didn't know how to treat servants. Nanny didn't like the patrician line Lady Irene took with the nursery staff. Nanny didn't like it at all. Nanny began to mutter under her breath.

Lady Irene had cut off all that sensual hair and now had a sleek androgynous bob that didn't entirely go with her voluptuous Latin American figure. She showed more leg – and very good leg it was – than any other London hostess, and danced the Charleston as well as any chorus girl. Sir Edward had begun to notice the overbearing nature of his Buenos Airean brahmin, beginning to wonder if this marriage was such a good idea after all. He looked at girls like Lady Cecily Markham and Lady Diana de Vere with their pale well-fed skin and horse-riding hips and regretted rejecting them so peremptorily. They would have handled the servants so much better.

Nanny declared that she was very sorry but she was going to go back to Suffolk if Sir Edward didn't mind, it wasn't that she wanted to make trouble or anything but she didn't really see eye to eye with Lady Irene – foreign ways and so on – she had known Sir Edward as man and boy but really—

'Thank you, Nanny,' Sir Edward interrupted kindly, 'of course you may go.'

What a delight little Esme was, Sir Edward had started to visit the nursery almost every day. The second-in-command nanny – Margaret – was now in charge and doing a very good job. She was a very plain girl, very religious with lots of modern ideas about fresh air. The nursery dogsbody had broken an ankle, tripping in the muddy street, and was staying with her sister until she was better. There were two nursemaids, Mina and Agatha. Agatha was pretty in a very English way, blond curls, hazel eyes, snub nose. Edward's mother, the dowager Lady de Breville, had always had very strict rules about interplay with the servants, it simply wasn't done.

'This simply isn't done,' Sir Edward murmured through the blond curls as he caught Agatha on the back stairs and sank his hands into her ripe flesh. Sir Edward didn't mean to shout out quite so loudly as he shuddered to a climax somewhere inside the fustian petticoats of the nursemaid and Agatha certainly didn't mean to squeal quite so much when the aristocratic member penetrated her plebeian hymen – certainly neither of them intended to draw the attention of the mistress of the house. But in no time at all there was a terrible commotion on the back stairs and a dark avenging angel had whisked Sir Edward upstairs out of the servants' sight, but not their earshot, and was screaming in a polyglot language that pronounced Sir Edward a damned *cochon loco*.

The town house was in a certain disarray. Lady Irene retired to Paris for a few weeks to think things over. Not that she had the slightest intention of ending her marriage but Sir Edward needed to suffer a little, show a little repentance – an emerald necklace perhaps, or a racehorse. Agatha was dismissed without references. The nanny, Margaret, came down with a dreadful dose of flu. Mina was put out by the amount of work she had to do. 'When did I last have a day off?' she asked Esme, who gurgled and waved her tiny fists around in the air.

Mina was in love with one of the footmen, a callous, callow youth called Bradley. Mina had lately been rejected by Bradley. Mina's heart was breaking.

'I'll take you out for your walk then,' Mina sighed, carrying Esme down to the back hall where the huge baby carriage was parked. Mina, in her dull nursemaid's uniform, pushed the baby carriage along the leafy London streets, turned through the huge wrought-iron gates to the park, took bread from her pocket and threw it for the ducks, sat on a park bench and sang a little nursery rhyme, watched a drowsy Esme fall helplessly into sleep, ate a dry biscuit from her pocket, caught sight of Bradley across the other side of the pond — surely not? But it was his day off after all, she knew that — Mina knew what Bradley should be doing every second of the day. He had spurned her, used her and spurned her, taken her virtue and discarded her like an old rag (Mina read a lot of cheap fiction), but Mina still loved him, her heart would always belong to him.

Quackquackquackquaaak! went the ducks as Mina stood up suddenly, shedding biscuit crumbs and tears — there was *another woman* with him. Not just any other woman, but Agatha, the disgraced nursemaid — a scarlet woman. A fallen woman. Behaving in a very familiar way with Bradley. How long had she been behaving in this familiar way with Bradley? Mina strode off to question, to berate, to cling tearfully to Bradley and beg for the return of his affections, and if not the return of his affections then at least a little money to help bring up the disgrace he's seeded in her neat, round nursemaid belly. For Mina was also a fallen woman. Unbeknown to Mina and Bradley, Agatha is also a seed-pod, carrying Sir Edward's baby. So many fatherless babies concentrated in one London park. Baby Esme sleeps on peacefully.

Who was coming along the path now? A shabby woman, overweight and old for her years. A dingy brown coat that had never been in fashion, a big man's umbrella, a big Gladstone bag. Here was Maude Potter, wife of Herbert Potter, a clerk in a shipping company. The Potters had no family, only each other. Mrs Potter had lost four babies in the womb and had just come out of a charity hospital where she'd been delivered of the fifth, a dead little girl. Mr Potter's employers would not even give him the morning off work so he could come and accompany her home. In her big Gladstone bag she had her hospital nightdress and the baby clothes she'd hopefully taken in with her. Her breasts were leaking, her fat empty belly was wobbling, she was utterly distracted, thought she might throw herself in the boating pond.

Quackquackquack, went the ducks. Here was a turn up for the books, thought Maude Potter, a big posh baby carriage like you would see the royal family's babies in. Maude Potter looked inside the baby carriage. Lo and behold – a baby! Poor baby, surely it belonged to someone? She looked around, there on the other side of the pond a man and two women, one of them a nursemaid by the look of it, shouting and screaming and spouting language that no decent person would ever use. 'You whore!' Mina screamed at Agatha, 'You slut!' Agatha screamed back, while the footman tried to make himself invisible. Such people were clearly not fit to be in charge of a baby. Poor Baby.

The baby gave a little whimper in its sleep. Maude Potter thought she would just lift it out and give it a little cuddle. The baby opened its eyes and smiled at her. 'Oh,' said Maude Potter. Her breasts ached, her womb contracted. This baby didn't really belong to anyone, she thought, lifting it gently out of its covers, had maybe been abandoned? Had maybe been put in this park by God himself, to give Herbert and herself the child they deserved (Maude was very religious)? Yes, the baby had come down to earth like a fallen cherub. Or, now Maude becomes very fanciful, a gift child, like little Thumbelina, a present from the fairies . . . nightclothes tumbled from the Gladstone to make room, a little nest, a walnut shell . . .

Mina could hardly see for the tears in her eyes. Nearly fell in the pond as she marched away from Agatha and the footman, head held high trying to regain her dignity. She would not look back and see them arm in arm, walking away together, the seducer and his fallen woman. Mina stumbled back to the baby carriage, pulled the brake off, took it by its handle, felt its well-sprung rocking, pushed it off along the path – stopped. Brushed the tears out of her eyes in disbelief –

NO
BABY!

— Mina gasped, pulled all the blankets and covers out of the pram, the baby must be hiding somewhere in the depths of the baby carriage. Mina threw the pillows out, would have turned the carriage upside down and shaken it if it hadn't been so heavy. Mina's screams were so ghastly, so unearthly, that even Agatha and Bradley realized they must have been caused by something more than a jilted heart and came running across the park.

Herbert had seen the newspaper headline the day after the baby was first brought in the house, BABY HEIRESS KIDNAPPED. Maude told him she'd found the baby abandoned in the park and he'd wanted to believe her, he hadn't seen the lacy clothes or the aristocratic baby carriage, nor the earrings (taken out straight away by Maude, rather to the baby's distress), was willing to believe that poor Maude had done a good deed by rescuing the poor little thing, but then he'd seen that headline and he'd had a funny feeling in the pit of his stomach.

He bought a copy of the paper and read the description. 'Four months old, dark hair, dark eyes?' he said, waving the paper in front of Maude's face. 'Was this the baby?' She ignored him, rocking the baby on her knee, singing a little song to it. 'Was it?' he shouted, and the baby began to cry.

'Father,' Maude said in a gently reproving voice, 'don't upset Baby.'

Maude lay in her bed, propped up on her pillows, the baby feeding at her breast. Herbert averted his eyes. 'God has been very good to us,' Maude sighed happily. 'Now a name, Father — what shall we call her? Violet Angela, I think,' she said, without waiting for an answer. 'That would be a lovely pretty name, for a lovely pretty baby.'

Herbert sat at the table, his head sunk in his hands. Maude gurgled at the baby, whose cradle wasn't a nutshell at all, but the bottom drawer of a tallboy. Herbert wondered if he could just shut the drawer and forget about the damned baby. It wasn't going to go away – day after day, the newspapers screamed about the 'Breville Baby'. The same grainy photograph was reproduced of the baby's christening – a minor member of the royal family present as a godmother – the baby's parents, so rich, so beautiful.

It was too late to confess, they were too far in it now, they'd go to jail for life. Maude would be destroyed. It was too late to take the baby back, Maude would go mad if she was robbed of the little thing now. Herbert tried not to get fond of it, told himself it wasn't his, but it had his heart in its little plump hand already. 'Them Brevilles can have plenty more,' Maude said dismissively. Herbert sighed, 'The neighbours'll notice. You go into hospital nine months gone and come out two weeks later with a four-month-old baby—' The mathematics of it were a nightmare for him.

'We'll move then,' Maude said shortly. Herbert had never seen his wife so powerful. Maude gave him all the baby's expensive finery and he burnt it on a bonfire in the backyard.

'Pretty little kiddie, in't she?' Mrs Reagan said, looking at Violet Angela playing at 'house' in the corner of the room with Mrs Reagan's daughter, Beryl. Mrs Reagan had just moved into a bottom flat in the big ugly house that the Potters rented a part of now.

'How old d'you say she was?' Mrs Reagan asked as Maude handed her a cup of tea.

'Three – nearly four,' Maude answered proudly.

'Bossy little thing, in't she?' Mrs Reagan said, casting a doubtful eye on the way Violet Angela sat on a stool and got Beryl to do all the work in their pretend house. 'Oh, she knows what she wants, our little Vi,' Mrs Potter said. 'It'll be nice for her to have a little friend in the house.'

Violet Angela offered to sing Mrs Reagan a song, which she

lisped very prettily, Mrs Reagan agreed. 'Quite a little actress, in't she?' she said stiffly. Personally, Mrs Reagan didn't like children that were allowed to show off, but there you are, each to their own.

Mrs Reagan wondered to herself how two such dull, drab people as Maude and Herbert Potter managed to produce such an attractive child. She was like a little sprite, all quicksilver energy, with those big brown eyes and a head of jet-black curls that made Mrs Reagan very jealous when she saw it next to Beryl's dull brown bob. She was the kind of child who ought to come to no good, but probably wouldn't.

'Pretty little thing, in't she?' Mr Reagan said, taking his braces off after a hard day's work. Mrs Reagan joined him at the upstairs window, looked down on the scrubby garden where Beryl and Violet Angela and some of the neighbourhood boys were playing a wild, whooping game. 'How old is she?' Mr Reagan asked his wife, who pursed her lips and said, 'Too old for her age, a very forward little thing, eight years old, same age as Beryl, if you must know.'

'What are they playing at? Exactly?' Mr Reagan asked, a puzzled frown on his face.

'God knows,' Mrs Reagan said.

Violet Angela tied Beryl's hands behind the tree with the old bit of rope they'd found in a shed. 'Now you're going to be a human sacrifice,' Violet Angela told her. 'No!' Beryl wailed. Violet Angela despised little mousy Beryl, she was so weak and stupid, she wanted to make her *see* how stupid she was, make her sorry for it. She put her face an inch in front of Beryl's and said, 'Oh yes you are,' in a weird voice, rasping and high-pitch, 'because I'm a wicked brigand who's going to tear your heart out and eat it.'

'Steady on, Vi,' one of the boys said, growing worried by Beryl's breathless squeals. Violet Angela stamped her foot and made a fist at him. 'You are *such* a coward, Gilbert Boyd!' Gilbert steeled himself and said, 'All right then, tell you what, Vi – we'll burn her like a witch instead.' All the boys wanted to be liked by Violet Angela, none of them wanted to be thought a coward. 'Stop that silly nonsense, Beryl,' Violet Angela said crossly.

'Yeah,' the other boys chorused, growing excited. 'Who's got a match then?' a voice said. ''Ere,' another one said. They all crowded around the tree excitedly bringing bits of old wood and packing cases for the pyre. Violet Angela held the matchbox aloft so that Beryl could see it. 'This,' she hissed, 'is what people get for being stupid.' The boys were all chanting like savages, they started to do a war-dance round the tree, Beryl began to scream.

'Oswald!' Mrs Reagan shouted to her husband, 'I think you'd better get out there, sounds like our Beryl's being murdered.'

'Changeling,' Maude Potter said out loud to herself as she put the week's laundry through the wringer in the wash-house out back. That's what happened when you picked up a child without knowing anything about it. For all she knew that baby in its lace-clad finery had been placed in that pram, in that park, especially to fool them. As some kind of trap.

Violet Angela was twelve years old and a wicked little thing, she really was. 'She's getting beyond our control, Mother,' Herbert said, shaking his head in sorrow. 'That's what happens when you don't know anything about the history, about the parents – they might have been hob-nobs but who knows their character? They might have been liars, murderers, thieves – look at her, she's already been brought home once by the coppers for stealing, and that thing with Beryl Reagan . . . she could have been killed, and I don't know what she got up to with her fancy ways . . . she's a sinful little thing.'

Maude tried to beat the sin out of Violet Angela. 'This is for your own good,' she huffed and puffed up the stairs with 'Father's' leather belt. How could this be right, Violet Angela wondered? To be beaten half to death by your parents? Weren't they supposed to love and protect you?

Deep in the night, the walrus body of Herbert heaved itself between the darned sheets in her narrow little bed. 'Now, Violet Angela,' he said in a hoarse whisper, as his ink-stained fingers pushed and pulled, 'this is for your own good, and if you ever tell anyone then I swear God, who's watching over us right now, will kill you,' and, to demonstrate, his big hands encircled her thin little neck and when he felt how thin she was, how young she was, imagined her bird-bones snapping – then Herbert was suffused with shame at what he was doing. But it was too late now, he reasoned with himself, he'd already bought his ticket to hell, and hers with it. And, after all, it wasn't as if she was his daughter. He bought her bags of boiled sweets to make up to her.

Really, Violet Angela thought, I must have been stolen from my real parents, I wasn't meant to be with these ignorant, dreary people, I was meant to be a princess wearing expensive finery and beautiful dresses, and living in a castle on top of a hill with *hundreds* of servants. It wasn't fair.

It was Mrs Reagan who discovered fourteen-year-old Violet Angela with Mr Reagan. In the wash-house. Mr Reagan could fluster and bluster all he liked, but Mrs Reagan knew what she'd seen.

'Why, Vi? Why?' Mrs Potter whined poetically, 'Why have we been given such a wicked monster for a child?' overlooking the fact that Violet Angela was not given but taken.

'I'm not a monster,' Violet Angela sneered. 'Mr Reagan promised me things.'

'Things?'

'Pretty things,' Violet Angela said stoutly. 'He said he'd give me pretty things if I let him have his way.' Mrs Potter slapped Violet Angela's face and Violet Angela screamed, 'And he was only doing what he's been doing [she pointed dramatically at Mr Potter] for years!' Mr Potter slapped Violet Angela's other cheek. 'You little liar!'

'You little whore,' Mrs Potter yelled and Violet Angela ran from the room before she got slapped to death.

Violet Angela was locked in her room upstairs. 'What are we going to do?' Mr Potter asked, his head in his hands at the parlour table.

'Maybe we should give her back,' Maude offered.

'Give her back?' Herbert said, scratching his head.

'To where she come from – those Brevilles,' Maude said. 'Let's see *them* deal with her wicked ways.'

'We ain't got nothing to prove who she was,' Herbert says glumly.

'All I ever wanted was a nice little girl what I could dress up and show off,' said Maude sadly. 'This is all the thanks we get for bringing her up.'

'She'll come to a bad end, that one,' Herbert said, shaking his head.

They were all mad for it, her father, Mr Reagan, even Gilbert Boyd who'd stolen a diamante hair-clip of his mother's to give her, just so he could poke about inside her one wet Saturday afternoon. They'd give you anything to do it with them and then when you did they called you all the names under the sun.

She'd been locked in her room for days now, food shoved round the door at regular intervals as if she was in a condemned cell or something. If they could, they'd sell her into slavery rather than service. It was ridiculous. They kept telling her what a bad daughter she was, but had they *no idea* what bad parents they'd been? She couldn't forgive them. She could feel the wheals where Maude had hit her with the belt. Knew that all this had to stop. Now.

'I got her an interview, Mother – for a position,' Herbert said excitedly over a tea of kippers and bread and butter. 'Scullery maid – big house in Norfolk, what d'you think?'

'I think you're very clever, Herbert.'

'Where is she?'

'Locked in upstairs still,' Maude said proudly. 'I'll take her up her tea.'

Violet Angela picked up the plate of kippers and hit her mother in the face with them and ran full tilt down the stairs, slamming into Herbert, blocking her way at the bottom. 'Not so fast, milady!' he grunted as he grabbed hold of her, but she dodged and swerved and got past him and sprinted for the front door.

But she hadn't done yet. Later, much later, when the whole world was asleep, Violet Angela slipped in at the back gate, opened the outhouse door where the tools were kept and picked up the heavy woodchopping axe. She tiptoed up the stairs to Maude's and Herbert's bedroom. They lay sleeping on their backs. Ugly. Vulnerable. Maude snoring like a trooper. She had a hair-net on, like a bonnet, and her teeth were on the bedside table. A dribble of saliva trailed down Herbert's silver-stubbled chin. Violet Angela imagined lifting the axe and letting it fall down under its own heavy weight, cleaving Herbert's head in two on the pillow without him even waking up. His brains splattering the wall, splattering Maude's face. Maude waking up drowsily, opening her mouth to scream at the sight of her husband's brains spilt everywhere, Violet Angela stopping her scream with the axe.

She could do it, Violet Angela thought, feeling the weight of the axe in her thin arms, but she wasn't going to risk going down just for killing them. Instead she took the rent money out of its hiding-place in the tea-caddy and left the axe at the foot of the bed to give them a fright when they woke up.

Same man every Friday afternoon. He always got the table, table 2, by the window, even when it was really busy. 'How does he do that?' Mavis asked and gave a little screech as she scalded herself on the hot-water jug. 'Three teas, three teacakes, one fruit scone, table 16,' Deidre muttered to herself as she rushed past. 'He looks like an oily sea-lion to me.'

''E's a villain,' Mavis said, 'that's a well-known fact.' It was raining cats and dogs, 'and bloody great stair-rods,' said Deidre. It was grey and miserable outside, bright and steamy inside, but the rain brought melancholy with it wherever it went. 'I've had no tips today,' Violet said. 'Three teas, one coffee, two Eccles, one Jamaican finger, one coffee jap, table 8.' Deidre said, 'You wanna go to the flicks tonight, Vi?' The man at table 2 made a little gesture, almost imperceptible, to Violet.

'Nah, don't feel like it, let me get him.'

'Who?'

'The sea-lion.' Violet tripped over in her black and white, white broderie cap pulled low on her forehead, thick black stockings. Violet could see something in the sea-lion's eyes, knew it might be good for her. He *was* like a sea-lion, blubbery in an overcoat, old-fashioned really, 'Good afternoon, sir, what can I get for you today?'

'What's your name?'

'Violet.'

'What a pretty name. How old are you?'

'Eighteen, sir,' Violet lied sweetly. She was only sixteen.

'Imagine that,' he said with a smile and raised a small plump hand and touched her on the forearm. 'My name's Dickie Landers, sweetheart – have you heard of me?' and Violet said, 'Yes, of course,' although she hadn't. 'If you work very hard,' he said, half-closing his lazy eyes, more salamander than seal, 'I'll tip you very, very well, my dear,' and out of sight of the rest of the tea-shop, he reached out and stroked her thigh, just in case she was in any doubt about what he meant. She wasn't.

Dickie installed Violet in a flat in Bayswater, nothing fancy – a living-room, a bedroom, a scullery and her own WC, gas fires in the old-fashioned hearths and a gas water-heater over the sink. He called himself an 'entrepreneur', which, as far as Violet could see, meant that he had his fingers in lots of pies, and most of them very shady, if you could call a pie shady. He stayed at the Bayswater flat most of the time and bought her a lot of nice things. What did it matter? Violet thought. You did it for boiled sweets, you did it for a new dress, you did it for a roof over your head. And Dickie Landers was powerful, he even got her a new identity after she'd had a spot of bother with the law.

'Easy,' Dickie said, handing her a new birth certificate.

'Who am I then?' Violet asked. Eliza Jane Dennis.

'She was real,' Dickie Landers grinned, 'little girl, died before she was two.'

She made a mistake, falling pregnant and not managing to do anything about it, beyond gin and hot baths and jumping off the table. Dickie was furious and sent her to an 'acquaintance' of his, a struck-off surgeon, but he was so sleazy and his instruments so terrifying that, unusually, Eliza turned coward and left and had to pay the consequences four months later in the shape of a little boy. Dickie took him from the hospital and when she asked what he'd done with him, Dickie lit a cigar and laughed. 'Sold him back to the baby shop, sweetheart,' he said and when he saw the grimace on Eliza's face he patted her hand, rather awkwardly because Dickie wasn't too comfortable with emotion, and said reassuringly, 'Very respectable couple, a doctor and his wife, Dr Lovat.'

He took her out – to the theatre ('That's you,' he laughed when they saw *Pygmalion*), to night-clubs, to restaurants, even to the opera. There wasn't anybody that Dickie Landers didn't know, from high court judges to common criminals. Dickie himself was an aristocrat amongst criminals. He owned a West End club called the Hirondelle. The club was where he did 'business', reaching over the tables to murmur things in willing ears, rubbing his greasy fingers together to illustrate what he meant, leaning back and laughing expansively, stretching the stiff shirt of his evening suit. Eliza perched on a stool at the bar, drank gin, learned who was who. And what was what. She learnt to do all kinds of things, things that nice girls didn't know about, wouldn't have believed if they'd been told. 'But then I'm not a nice girl, am I?' Eliza said to her mirror.

Eliza wasn't just one of Dickie's girls any more, she was special. 'You're special, darlin',' he laughed and hired her out only to his best customers ('top whack'). Eliza learned to talk properly, learnt from films and from the aristocracy who slummed it at the Hirondelle, draping themselves on the arms of semi-criminals, wishing that Daddy could see how wicked they were being. 'I've made you into a lady,' Dickie Landers said to her and Eliza laughed and said, 'Darling, you've made me into a high-class tart, that's all.'

'If you say so,' Dickie said, running his hands up her back.

'I'm just like this bloody war,' Eliza sighed, 'a phoney.'

A nice town house in Knightsbridge ('top whack'), the owner in America for the duration. 'Got the lease, legal and proper,' Dickie said. 'God, I love this war, you know that?' Dickie smelt of money. Eliza went to the house two or three times a week. It was always someone high-ranking, an English general, a visiting American here in secret, a Free French officer, a Polish colonel. Dickie was working for the government, he thought it was a great joke. 'You're doing your bit for the war effort, really, that's how I look at it,' Dickie said to her.

Eliza was getting fed up with this life, she wasn't going to give up the money but she wasn't going to open her legs for it the rest of her life. Was she?

Sometimes, not often, faces became familiar. A little runt of a politician who couldn't manage it, a fat Belgian, an admiral who only wanted to dress up in her clothes. There was an English colonel, Sir Edward de Breville, very upper-crust, who was a big-wig in the War Cabinet ('top whack,' Dickie said, 'give him anything he wants'), he always brought her stockings and whisky and called her his gorgeous trollop. He said she reminded him of someone. 'That's what they all say, darling,' Eliza laughed. He kissed her ear and said, 'If my wife were dead, which unfortunately she isn't, I would marry you.' Sir Edward didn't have any children, except for 'some little by-blow by a nursemaid' that he paid the upkeep on. 'You'd give me a son and heir, I bet,' he said. Sometimes Eliza daydreamed about taking Dickie's gun and going down to the de Brevilles' house in Suffolk and shooting Lady Cecily in the head. Then Sir Edward − very handsome and very, very rich − might really marry her. But then gentlemen rarely married their whores and Dickie would never let her go, she was his golden egg-laying goose and he'd probably kill her before he'd let her go. Life wasn't fair, it really wasn't.

The shelter was cold and damp and smelt of wet earth. It was completely dark. At first Eliza thought she was the only person in there and when she heard a slight shuffling she wasn't sure whether it was a rat or a person. She flicked her cigarette lighter open, the gold monogrammed one that Dickie had given her, and in the yellow haloed flame saw a man in uniform shrinking into the corner of the shelter, his cap pulled down. Eliza said, 'Good evening,' and he mumbled something in reply. A distant thud of bombs outside. 'I don't bite you, know, darling,' she said and lit a cigarette, 'Want one?' 'Thanks,' he said hoarsely. 'Why are you so shy, darling?' Eliza asked as he came reluctantly closer to take the proffered cigarette. She expected there were government warnings about flirting in air-raid shelters, but she enjoyed it.

'Ever hear of Frankenstein's monster?' he asked, taking the cigarette.

'Why, is he in here with us?' she laughed.

'Yes,' the man said and pushed his cap back on his forehead. He flinched away from the lighter flame when she held it up to his face. One side of his face was livid and swollen, the skin stretched tight and shiny over the flesh. The shrunken eye had been dragged downwards by the scar tissue. 'Shot down on fire,' he said apologetically. In the flickering light she saw ginger hair, pale gold eyelashes and russet freckles that charted his unscarred skin. He was just a boy. A line of bombs thudded closer and the boy looked as though he was going to cry. Very gently, as if he was a wild animal, Eliza reached out and stroked the scarred skin. She extinguished the lighter and said, 'Well, all cats are grey in the night, darling.'

Afterwards, after he'd pushed her up against the brick wall of the shelter and moaned his gratitude to her, drowned out by the noise of the docks being blitzed, he kept apologizing because she was crying, and he 'felt an awful heel', and he was sorry because he'd 'never done it before with anyone', but Eliza sniffed back her tears and said, 'That's all right, neither have I.' Because really, she thought, it felt like the first time – tender and loving and, well – enjoyable, which wasn't how she usually thought about it at all. 'Top whack, darling,' she murmured sweetly into his hair when he was finished.

'Where've you been?' Dickie said when she came in. 'I thought that bloody raid had got you.'

'Don't be silly, darling, just doing my bit for the war effort.'

One of Dickie's sleep-dead arms was pinning Eliza to the bed. She moved it as she leant over to get her cigarette pack. She slid up the bed and rested on the pillows. The room was lit by moonlight, dull silver patterns moved around the walls as the net curtains billowed. Eliza searched for a match. She'd lost her lighter in the shelter. It was time to get out of this whole sordid business, become a normal person. She wanted a man who loved her, protected her, children she could dote on. An ordinary life. She dragged hard on her cigarette and thought about the ugly, scarred boy. She could still feel his cool hands on her, still smell the damp bricks of the shelter, still feel the liquid warmth of him inside her.

She was awake when the siren went off. She was dressed. She had on a suit, a coat, a hat and her best pair of shoes. But that was all she was taking with her. She needed a grand gesture, walking out in the clothes she stood up in. So she made sure they were expensive clothes.

She jumped at the siren but then thought that, on the whole, she couldn't really care less if she was blown up by a bomb. Dickie rolled over and said, 'Bloody hell,' but it was already too late.

The whole house shook and then again, even more violently. The noise was unbelievable, Eliza felt the house falling down round her ears, she couldn't breathe, she kept trying to take in lungfuls of air but all she could take in was dust. The shock-wave of the blast was still vibrating in her chest, she knew she was going to die –

– she wasn't dead. The front wall of the house had gone and she was on the ground floor, where a few minutes ago she'd been on the second. Far away, at the back of her head, Eliza could hear bells ringing and people shouting. She could smell burning. Someone was walking through the dust towards her. For a moment she imagined it was the ugly red-haired boy come to rescue her and she smiled. But it wasn't, it was someone else. He snatched her up and carried her out of the house, straight out where the front wall had been, and placed her on the pavement. 'Are you all right?' he asked, his voice full of concern. Eliza put out a hand and felt the cloth of his RAF greatcoat. He took it off and wrapped her up in it, very tenderly. 'My hero,' she said. She looked down at her feet, she'd lost a shoe. 'My shoe,' she said helplessly, 'I've lost my shoe.' She'd heard of things like this, escaping death by a cat's whisker and being obsessed with irrelevant things. It was shock, she was in shock. 'I'll get it,' he said, and moved as if he was in a dream. 'Would you?' she smiled. 'They were *so* expensive, darling.'

Her rescuer disappeared back into the building, came out with the shoe. Two firemen brought out Dickie Landers and no-one cheered. He was very dead. 'Did you know him?' her rescuer asked, taking off his RAF cap and wiping his brow. 'Never seen him before,' she said. He offered her his arm, 'Can I take you for a cup of tea? There's a café round the corner.' It was nearly dawn.

'The age of chivalry is alive and well,' she laughed, tears in her eyes, 'and is called?'

'Gordon, Gordon Fairfax.'

'Wonderful,' Eliza murmured.

And now there was a problem. *He* was the problem. She'd never meant to take him as a lover, never meant to be unfaithful to Gordon. The Widow and Vinny, of course, thought she was out committing adultery every night, but she wasn't, this was the first time. Really. But it was a big mistake, she had to stop it. She didn't even like him. He wasn't a nice person, he wasn't . . . kind.

It had just been a game really, she was bored and he was there, so nearby, so keen. And the sex with him was so . . . dark, there was a certain attraction in that. Gordon was so . . . wholesome. And that had been so wonderful at first, she had really loved him. Such a hero. But he couldn't keep on being a hero, more's the pity. She got restless. That was why she'd taken a lover, a little bit of fun, a little bit of power. Now it was a game she couldn't stop. She hadn't realized how inflamed he was by her, how obsessed. How mad.

He wouldn't let her go. She couldn't tell Gordon, couldn't tell anyone. She wanted to tell Gordon, wanted him to look after her, the way he always did. She was choking, she had to get some air. Maybe she could just leave, walk away and leave the whole sorry mess behind?

She loved Gordon, really she did, but he got on her nerves. He was so bloody good. And he made her feel so bloody bad. He followed her everywhere. Really, in her heart, she thought that the only person she'd ever truly loved – apart from Charles and Isobel, it went without saying – was that scarred red-headed boy in the air-raid shelter. She didn't even know his name, had only been with him for half an hour. Less. She'd half-expected Charles to be born with scar tissue on his face, was relieved when he wasn't. An invisible hand squeezed her heart when she thought about her children.

The old witch was driving her mad, a pair of witches, come to that. It was Gordon this and Gordon that, they had to get away from this house, live their own lives. Maybe she should kill the old witch, and Vinny too. This was ridiculous. She *was* going mad.

A picnic, it's half-term, after all, and we've done absolutely bloody nothing all week. We'll take the bus into town and meet Daddy at lunchtime and give him a surprise.

Gordon and Eliza were having this tremendous row. He just wouldn't leave her alone, would he, chasing after her in the wood, when she needed to be on her own. 'You're having an affair, aren't you?' he shouted, his words echoing in the silent autumn air. 'Be quiet,' she said sharply, 'the children will hear. Leave me alone.'

'I don't understand you, I don't bloody understand you.' Gordon was weeping. Eliza hated him when he was weak. He pushed her up against a tree.

'Stop it,' she hissed at him.

'Why should I bloody stop it? Admit it, you're having an affair.'

'You're hurting me. Gordon!' He *was* hurting her, he had his hands round her throat, pressing her windpipe, she began to struggle, he was frightening her. 'Admit it,' he growled, his voice unnatural. He let go of her throat. 'Admit it, you've been unfaithful, haven't you? And before me,' he said suddenly, 'were there a lot of men? There must have been a lot of men, weren't there?'

'Yes,' she spat at him, 'there were absolutely hundreds, I've no idea how many!'

He slapped her face, 'Liar!' and she kneed him hard in the groin so that he crouched down on the forest floor, gasping. Immediately Eliza felt sorry, gave him her hand, pulled him up, said, 'Oh, Gordon,' sadly, 'you're such a fool.' She wanted to tell him everything, sink onto his breast, feel the shelter of his arms around her, find redemption in this awful world. She leant her back against a tree and said blankly, without emotion, 'I was a whore, a common or garden whore who got paid for it. I fucked anyone who paid me, darling.' She could hear her voice, knew her tone was all wrong, couldn't do anything about it, she was so tired.

Gordon grabbed hold of her hair either side of her head and crashed her head backwards against the tree. She sank down onto her knees, onto the carpet of golden leaves and Gordon ran off through the trees, wildly, like a mad disciple of the great god Pan.

Eliza struggled to sit up. Her head hurt horribly. The back of her skull was bruised and sore. She didn't have a watch on, didn't know what time it was. She was cold. It would soon be dark. They shouldn't have fought like that. Gordon would come back soon and find her, look after her again like he always did, gather up his family and take them home. She would explain to him properly, he would forgive her. She'd tell him about Herbert Potter and Mr Reagan, and Dickie Landers, tell him about her ghastly adulterous lover who wouldn't let her go.

Eliza started to cry. She felt tremendously sorry for herself. It was growing darker and she was suddenly frightened. She shouted Gordon's name. Someone was approaching through the trees, 'Gordon, oh thank God,' she struggled to her feet. But it wasn't Gordon.

'Oh it's you,' she said coldly, trying to pretend she wasn't frightened. But she was. 'What are *you* doing here? You've followed me, haven't you? This has to stop—' Eliza's voice grew more high-pitched, terror crept over her, she broke out into a cold sweat, he was mad, unhinged.

She tried to pull herself together, to placate him. 'Come on, let's go back and find the path, let's be sensible, Peter, darling – please. . .' Eliza wasn't very good at pleading, she knew it was no good. He had one of her shoes in his hand. She looked down at her feet in surprise, she only had one shoe on. He lifted the shoe up, it had a very thin heel, her heart was fluttering, it was trying to escape from the cage of her ribs, she was clammy all over, her body felt as if it was going to shut down with fear.

Her feet wouldn't move, she had to move, she turned and started to run but he was on top of her, hitting her with the shoe on the back of the head. 'If I can't have you,' he said breathlessly, 'then nobody will, you bloody whore.' She cried out and dropped to her knees and started to crawl away. She looked back. He was lighting his pipe, very calmly, as if he was in his living-room at home. Eliza thought maybe that was the end of it, maybe he'd got rid of his anger now and would leave her alone. She crawled further away, further into the forest.

She was beneath a tree, kneeling on a carpet of leaves and acorns. A golden leaf drifted down past her eyes and brushed her cheek. Eliza struggled into a sitting position, her back against the stout trunk of the tree. For a moment she couldn't see him, but just when she thought he must have gone, he stepped out from behind a tree. The aura of madness around him was a sulphurous yellow and he was grinning like a skeleton. 'I am older than you, you know,' he laughed, 'and I do know more.'

'Please,' Eliza whispered. She was shivering uncontrollably. She was so very cold. 'Please don't,' but he grabbed hold of a handful of hair and yanked her head forward and began to hit her skull again with the heel of the brown shoe, grunting with the effort. Again and again he hit her, long after the trees around grew dim and Eliza had slipped into blackness. Then he walked away, discarding the shoe like an old piece of paper.

And that was the end of Eliza. Or Violet, or Violet Angela, or little Lady Esme. Or whoever she was.

Of course, she wasn't really the de Brevilles' daughter. After the wedding a doctor in Paris told Lady Irene that she would never be able to have children. Although she didn't know it at the time she was already suffering from the disease that killed her. Sir Edward was so besotted by his new wife and his new wife was so distressed at the idea of being childless that he went out and got her a baby. He would probably have lived to regret corrupting the de Breville bloodline, but then he didn't have to, it was taken out of his hands, Esme was taken out of his hands.

He bought her in Paris. You can always buy children. Gypsies probably—

PRESENT

THIS GREEN AND LAUGHING WORLD

I FEEL THE TOUCH OF SOMEONE'S LIPS ON MY FOREHEAD AND THE sound of someone whispering in my ear, so quietly that I can hardly hear the words – *You go to sleep now, darling.*

Another hallucination.

I drift out of a heavy drug-induced sleep. 'Where's the woman in the other bed gone?'

'Who?' the brown-haired nurse says absently, preoccupied by a syringe she's about to jab me with.

'The woman in the other bed.' The bed is neatly made and empty.

The nurse furrows her brow. 'There hasn't been anybody in that bed.'

'I've seen you taking her temperature and talking to her.'

'Me?' the nurse laughs.

From my bed I can see the top branches of a tree waving around in the breeze. The branches are covered in new leaves. Can

313

it be spring already? How long have I spent in the under-world?

'What's the date?' I ask the red-haired nurse.

She frowns. 'April twenty-third, I think.'

'April twenty-third?' Can I really have lost that much time? 'Really?'

'I know,' she says with a smile, 'we lost you for a couple of weeks there, didn't we?' She fills up the water jug on my bedside locker, smoothes the sheets and looks at my chart and says, 'That's right – you came on the first of April, that's over three weeks you've been here now.'

'The first of April?' I repeat, puzzled, but she's gone and I'm soon asleep again. I think I must be catching up on all the sleep I've been deprived of over the years. Or maybe I'm turning into a cat.

When I wake up there's a student doctor investigating my chart and trying to look as if he knows what he's doing. He smiles encouragingly when he sees I'm awake. 'What year is it?' – a familiar question somehow – I mumble at him. He looks disconcerted, '1960.'

'April twenty-third, 1960?'

'Yes.'

It's still happening then. Or is it? I fall asleep, I just cannot keep my eyes open.

'How did I get here?' I ask a staff nurse when she brings me my lunch.

'In an ambulance.'

Eunice and Carmen come. 'You look a lot better,' Eunice says and studies my chart as if it means something to her.

'How did I get here, Eunice? What happened?'

'A tree fell on you.'

'*A tree fell on me?*'

'That old elder by your back door, it was rotten and your dad was chopping it down. It fell the wrong way or something. It was really windy.'

'It was your birthday too,' Carmen adds sympathetically, trying to inhale a sweet cigarette.

'They thought you were going to die,' Eunice carries on, 'they had to give you the kiss of life.'

'Better than the kiss of death,' Carmen says, nodding her head sagely.

'An ambulanceman?'

'No, Debbie.'

'Debbie?'

'Debbie.'

Audrey is sitting by the side of my bed and greets me with her lovely crescent moon smile. 'Mr Baxter?' I say to her and the smile vanishes behind a cloud.

Mr Baxter has not been killed by Mrs Baxter, he has killed himself, shooting the top of his head off with his old army revolver. Depression, according to the inquest, over his impending retirement. Audrey and Mrs Baxter discovered his body in his study and are, as you might expect, subdued in their narrative of events.

Mr Rice, on the other hand, in this alternative version of events, is still with us, as is the Dog ('He appeared on the doorstep one day,' Charles says, so that much is the same). The baby, however, is non-existent. Where has it gone to? (Where did it come from?)

Hilary and Richard are as alive as they ever were, thank goodness, as is Malcolm Lovat. But, alas, he is not here – he's driven his car off into the future. Left university and home and gone. 'Where?'

Eunice shrugs, 'Who knows? The police say it happens all the time. People just walking out of their lives.' And so it does.

It's as if reality is the same, and yet . . . not the same. So, it was my comatose brain that played tricks on me, not time? Yes, says the neurologist. Although, actually – as Vinny kindly informs me – I have many of the symptoms of fly agaric poisoning, especially the hallucinations and the death-like sleep. Gey queer, as Mrs Baxter would say.

I suppose reality is a relative kind of thing, like time. Maybe there can be more than one version of reality – what you see depends on where you're standing. Take Mr Baxter's death, for example, perhaps there are other versions. Imagine—

It wasn't her time of the month. Audrey hadn't had it for, let me see, thinks Mrs Baxter, three months now. Mrs Baxter thought it was because Audrey was so thin and peely-wally, still a little girl really. That's what the doctor said. Late maturing. Makes for irregularity.

And then finding her all curled up in pain in a corner of her room, like a poor wee animal trying to get as far away from the pain as possible. You couldn't tell it was a baby, it was just a bloody mess of a three months' miscarriage. Mrs Baxter knew that one well. She'd lost more than one baby at that stage. Audrey was the only one she'd ever managed to keep and now Daddy had done this to her.

At first Mrs Baxter couldn't take it in, how could Daddy do such a thing? But then something in her, a little voice, a tiny whisper, said – yes, this is just what Daddy would do.

Mrs Baxter would like to cut her throat in the middle of Glebelands' market square so that everyone can see how she's failed to protect poor wee Audrey, see what a bad mother she's been. But not as bad a mother as he's been a father.

Audrey is all tucked up in bed now, like a small child, with blankets and hot-water bottles and aspirin and Mrs Baxter's in the kitchen making Daddy's tea. His favourite – mushroom soup. She makes Daddy's soup with a lot of care, slicing the onions into moons and stirring them round and round in the frothing yellow butter. The fragrance of onions and butter filling the kitchen, drifting out of the open door into the April garden. From the cooker she can see the lilac outside the window, its purple heads still hanging wet and heavy from this morning's shower of rain.

When the new-moon onions are soft and yellow Mrs Baxter adds the mushrooms, little cultivated buttons that she's wiped and chopped in quarters. When they're all nicely coated in butter she adds the big flat horse-field mushrooms that grow in the corner of the Lady Oak field, like huge gilled plates, their dark brown the colour of the earth. She stirs the fleshy slices around until they begin to wilt a little and then she adds the olive-coloured fungi that also grow in the field but are not nearly so common – a treat for Daddy, for this is Mrs Baxter's special recipe for mushroom soup.

As she stirs and stirs Mrs Baxter thinks about Audrey upstairs in her child's bed and thinks of Daddy creeping into that bed. Then she puts some water in the pan, not too much, and salts it with tears and sprinkles in pepper. Then she puts the lid on and leaves it to simmer.

When the soup is cooked, Mrs Baxter whirrs it around in the liquidizer attachment on her Kenwood, taking each puréed batch of soup and placing it in a nice clean pot. And then when all the soup is smooth she adds some sherry ('just a wee drappy') and half a pint of cream, then leaves it to keep warm on the stove. This is such a special soup that Mrs Baxter makes *croûtons*, crisp golden cubes that she scatters on top of the bowl of soup, along with a handful of parsley.

'Mm,' says Mr Baxter, coming into the kitchen and taking off his bicycle clips, 'that smells good.' Mrs Baxter is so unused to getting compliments from Mr Baxter that she blushes.

Mr Baxter enjoys his soup. He eats alone at the dining-room table, listening to the six o'clock news on the radio. After his soup Mrs Baxter serves him lamb chops and mashed potatoes and minted peas and for his pudding a golden, steaming, syrup sponge-pudding in a sea of yellow Bird's custard.

'Why aren't you eating?' he asks her and she says that she'll get a bite to eat later because she's had one of her headaches all day and is 'fair-scunnered'. Daddy doesn't express any sympathy, or even interest.

Mrs Baxter takes some sponge-pudding and custard up to Audrey in her bedroom and feeds it to her like she did when Audrey was a baby. Then she gives her a mug of hot milk and two of her sleeping tablets.

It is growing dark by this time and Mr Baxter has gone upstairs to his study to do some marking.

Mrs Baxter washes up all the pots and pans, scouring them with bleach and wire-wool and then cleans the kitchen, wiping everything down with hot water and Flash. Then she gives the cat a saucer of milk and sits at the kitchen table and has a wee cuppie.

By this time she can hear Mr Baxter groaning in agony, vomiting ('boaking') in the upstairs toilet. She thinks she might just have another cup of tea before she goes upstairs to see how he's doing. He's not doing very well – writhing in agony on the floor of his study, his face a dreadful colour, his muscles in spasm. He splutters something unintelligible and Mrs Baxter kneels down on the carpet to hear him better. 'What's that, Daddy?' He seems to be querying what has happened to him and Mrs Baxter explains, very gently, that it must be the Death Caps having an effect.

Mr Baxter isn't going to get better, there is no antidote to Mrs Baxter's special soup, so she takes his well-oiled service revolver from the secret drawer of his desk and puts him out of his misery. The same happened to their old cat, the vet had to put him down after he'd eaten rat poison. Mrs Baxter always suspected that it was Daddy who put the rat poison down.

The noise from the gun is tremendous, a crack that echoes around the streets of trees. Mrs Baxter wipes the gun clean and puts Daddy's fingers round it and then lets it drop to the floor. Poor Audrey is woken from her drugged sleep by the report of the gun and comes in the room and sees Daddy lying in a pool of his own blood. She doesn't flinch.

Trevor Randall, the young policeman who is first on the scene, used to go to Mr Baxter's school. Mr Baxter used to beat Trevor a great deal with his strap and Trevor has no kind feelings about him. 'Suicide then,' he says.

'Suicide', says the coroner. It was so obvious that Mr Baxter had died because he'd lost his head that no-one ever looked at the contents of his stomach. Real right justice. Done.

'The shoe?' I ask Charles. The lock of hair? The handkerchief? He shakes his head sadly, 'If only, Iz.' Wishful thinking. I've been cheated by my own imagination. The imagination unbound, unconfined by cause and effect. But then how else can we make things work out right? Or find redemption? Or real right justice? But then Charles reaches into his breast pocket and with a smile hands over –

'The powder-compact?' I handle it reverently, press open the blue and gold oyster-shell of memory and find the pearl-pink powder. Charles snatches it back when my tears begin to moisten the powder. I expect there is little chance that we can reconstitute our mother from such meagre remains.

It's like Alice waking up and finding she dreamt the looking-glass world. It is difficult to believe that all those things that seemed so real have not happened. They felt real then, they feel real now. Appearances can be very deceptive.

I am home for May. By June I feel almost normal. Whatever that is. Although still a little confused by the different versions of reality. The Dog, for example, is delighted to see me and is virtually the same Dog as before, but not quite (doG, perhaps). Its brown eyes have turned blue and its tail is shorter. And The Lythe Players' production of *A Midsummer Night's Dream* is due to take place as before, but Debbie for some reason is now playing Hermia rather than Helena, only a few letters different and much the same plot function, but none the less mystifying. It's these little differences that are the most puzzling to me, like having permanent *déjà vu*.

Debbie's standing at the cooker, waiting for milk to boil for her bedtime cocoa. She's not long in the house from a rehearsal. (Will she have another nightmarish experience in the forest of Arden, I wonder?) In this current version of history, Debbie betrays no great signs of madness, certainly her problems with the identity of close relatives now extends no further than scowling at Vinny's back and asking, 'Who does she think she is?'

She's wearing a little frown on her face. I feel differently towards her since she saved my life, as if somehow by giving me life a second time I could permit her to have a maternal role now. The frown deepens. 'What's wrong, Debbie?'

She turns to look at me and the milk boils over. I snatch the pan off the cooker and turn off the gas. Debbie clutches her stomach and gasps. 'What's wrong?' I ask her more urgently. 'Have you got a pain?' She nods her head and grimaces. I coax her through to the living-room and she sits heavily on the sofa.

'God, that was horrible,' she says.

'But you're all right now? Shall I fetch Gordon?'

'Oh no, don't be silly,' she says, 'I'm fine, I just −' She breaks off and gives a little scream, clutching herself round the middle. 'I'll call the doctor,' I say hastily. Her eyes open so wide that they look almost big, she takes a huge breath of air and chokes on the word 'No!'

'No?'

'No,' she grunts, 's'too late.'

'Too late for what?' But she's kneeling on the carpet making strange gestures at me and I shout for Vinny to come. 'Something's wrong with Debbie,' I tell her, 'get the doctor!' Debbie screams again, not a high-pitched noise but a kind of groan that comes from some primitive place she didn't know existed inside her.

She's right, it's too late, the baby's head has already appeared. 'Bloody hell,' Vinny says succinctly. 'Where did that come from?'

Vinny, more the midwife from hell than Queen Mab, gets down on the floor with Debbie while I rush and put the kettle on because we all know that's what you're supposed to do.

Debbie grunts and huffs and puffs and nearly blows Vinny down in her effort to give birth to this sudden child. The Dog stands by, head cocked to express interest, ears pricked to show it's ready to help if necessary.

Vinny has a skirmish trying to get her to lie on her back but Debbie screams, 'Not bloody likely!' between two particularly violent contractions and then suddenly the baby shoots out and is caught – to her everlasting surprise – by Vinny. Vinny gets the first yell in, ahead of the baby and Debbie asks, quite calmly, for her dressmaking shears and with one confident *ssslicing* of blades sets the baby free of her. 'Has that kettle boiled?' she asks me impatiently. 'I'm dying for a cup of tea.'

'Your sister,' Vinny says, quite tenderized by so much emotional trauma and hands me the scrap of baby, wrapped now in a towel.

'Your sister,' I say to Charles who comes home from work at that moment and takes the baby from me automatically but then nearly drops it. 'Sister?' he says, utterly baffled. Debbie chuckles and Vinny lights up a cigarette and I have to explain to him. Gordon comes home from work and Charles passes on the parcel, saying, 'Your daughter.' Gordon's mouth drops open, 'My what?' and I jump up and explain to him that it's not me, shrunk and gone backward in time but a whole new surprise Fairfax. 'Just like that?' he murmurs in amazement.

The baby already sprouts a crest of soft red-gold hair from its 'Fontanelle', I tell Charles knowledgeably.

'Fancy that,' Debbie says, 'she's got Charles' hair. Someone in your family must have been red-headed, I wonder who?'

'It must be a recessive gene,' Gordon says quietly, as if this idea makes him sad somehow.

Apart from the red hair there are few similarities between this baby and the prototype doorstep baby. We call the baby Renee.

Midsummer's Eve comes round for a second time for me this year. It's a lovely hot day and I take a book into the Lady Oak field and sit in the dappled green shade of the tree while the Dog runs marathons around the field, stopping only to investigate the steaming piles of fresh horse manure left by Hilary. (Or rather, her horse.)

I soon fall into a pleasant summery doze in the green shade. I wake up slowly and watch the pattern of green leaves above my head, the occasional flash of sunlight, listen to the hum of bees and insects. This moment is timeless – I could be at any point in the last five hundred years, I have no way of knowing until I sit up and see the aerials, chimney pots, rooftops, trees, until I hear the sound of lawnmowers and car engines and see sheets flapping on clothes lines. It's so nice to be myself again, free of the madness of the imagination.

I stand up. If I look very closely at the trunk of the tree I can make out the famous faint initials of 'WS'. I embrace the Lady Oak like a lover, feel its bark, its age, its electricity. I close my eyes and kiss the faded initials. What if it really was Shakespeare himself who carved his name here? What if we had both touched, embraced, admired, this same tree.

I call the Dog, we must be away – before the fairy king and queen make their appearance in the field. 'Ah, Isobel,' Mr Primrose says, striding towards me, his ass's head under his arm, 'come to watch the performance?' What fools these mortals be.

I watch *A Midsummer Night's Dream* from the safety of my open bedroom window. From this distance, in the gently dimming midsummer light, you could almost imagine it was a different production. The reborn Audrey has been persuaded to take the role of Titania and she looks every inch the Faerie Queen with her beautiful hair set free of elastic bands and Mr Baxter. You could almost imagine yourself back in the past.

The costumes look authentic, the dialogue is just a murmur on the air.

There are enough people in the field for a game of Human Croquet, and I think they're all in the right spirit too. At last.

The sun setting behind the Lady Oak bathes the green in gold. This is an ideal thing. Not a real thing. I sigh and turn away.

He's there. He's lying on my bed, one cynical, quizzical eyebrow raised at me, a lopsided smile as he watches me. I know him. I've always known him. Spaniel eyes and chestnut hair. Not yet bald, slightly greasy. Leather boots. Doublet and hose and rather grubby linen. I walk over to the bed and sit on the edge, next to where he is sprawled. It's very warm in this room, under the eaves. There is a strange quality to the air . . . like magic, only less real.

I have only one question for him. 'It *is* all about death, isn't it?' I say to him. He's chewing a stalk of grass. A wood-pigeon on the dragon-scale slates above our heads gives a soft trill. He throws his head back and laughs. His breath smells of liquorice and he doesn't answer, only extends an arm towards me. 'And the end of the world, and time's thievish progress?' I persist, but he just shrugs.

If I take his hand will I go beyond time for ever? His forearm is curved and manly, a dusting of dark auburn hair. His fingernails are dirty.

The only sound is that of opalescent fairy wings, beating in the dark air and the sweeping of the tiny fairy brooms, cleansing our house. I take his hand. I let him pull me down next to him. I let him kiss me. He tastes of cloves. We melt into one and time collapses.

Only the imagination can embrace the impossible – the golden mountain, the fire-breathing dragon, the happy ending.

PAST

THE ORIGINAL SIN

THE FIRST TIME I EVER SAW ROBERT KAVANAGH HE WAS DANCING at my wedding. He was wearing a green velvet doublet and a silver-buckled belt. He danced well for an Irishman and had a very pleasing curve to his calf. 'My forester thinks himself a gentleman,' my new husband said.

The torches burned bright in the hall of my husband's new house and the scent of fresh-cut pine still lingered beneath the smell of grease and roasted oxen. Sir Francis spared no expense on his wedding – roasted swan and breast of lapwing, jewel-like jellies and custards as smooth and pale as my Lady Margaret's cheek. My new husband ate near on a whole suckling-pig to himself and claimed that it tasted exactly like fresh-cooked baby. That is the kind of man he is.

Everyone was made to admire the jewel he gave me for my wedding present – but for all its gold and emeralds it was still a picture of the dance of death which, if you ask me, is not such a pretty jewel to give your bride on her wedding day. I, of course was as much to be viewed by his fawning retinue as were his trinkets and baubles. He displayed me to his assembled company, lifting a strand of my hair and observing me with his thin-lipped smile. 'Scotch,' he said, as if I was a prized savage creature, and I corrected him, for that is a kind of mist.

On our wedding-night I began to understand what kind of a man it was that I had married. But I will not speak of it, only to say that he knew more tricks than the de'el himself. And then a few more. And now, also, I understood what manner of man it was he gathered around himself in his little court, the more corrupt and depraved, the more my master liked him. They pandered to his whims and inflated him like a puffed toad.

And as for my Lady Margaret ... Sir Francis claimed Lady Margaret was his ward, but there was no document to this effect, no record, no provenance for her at all. He claimed she was the bastard of his dead brother Thomas, but rumour had it that she was his own ill-gotten child. Rumour would also have had it (there was much rumour in that God-forsaken country) that his relationship to her was far from that of protector.

Nothing there was as I thought it would be.

I came upon my lord and his so-called ward in a position which did not suggest consanguinity, unless it was customary practice in that country for an 'uncle' to be so familiar with his 'niece'. I thought Lady Margaret a sly thing, she would never meet my eye, only bob her demure little curtseys, yes m'ladying and no m'ladying to me. Yet I was a harsh judge of her for she was barely sixteen, nothing but a child, and was as much prisoner as I myself was.

She had a tutor still, as if she was a royal bairn and spoke three languages and sang very prettily. My Lady Margaret's tutor, a Master Shakespeare, wrote Sir Francis an epithalamion, full of flattery of my lord, which was this tutor's character. These folk were not fit company for any woman.

★

The first time we met was as I walked in the wood one spring morning. He was on his black pony and stepped off the path and dismounted for me to pass and bowed his head almost to his knee and I remembered that he thought himself a gentleman. He said nothing, but as I passed I saw that my good hound Finn, a very discerning animal, could not stop his tail from wagging at Master Kavanagh, which was the stamp of his approval.

I came unannounced into my Lady Margaret's bedchamber – suspicious, thinking I would catch my husband in her embrace – and instead saw my Lady Margaret's naked back – thin and supple as a deer, a young girl's back of arcing blades and knuckled spine – and covered over all, as a map of the world, with a vast expanse of black continent – here and there shaded in yellow or purple. She covered herself hastily but not before I voiced my distress.

Who had made these vile marks? But I did not need to ask, my heart could tell me the answer. 'My lord has a most foul and unnatural temper,' she whispered. I told my husband, who was in his cups as ever, that she was not his dog to be whipped. In answer, he threw me across the room.

The first time we spoke was in the wood. I knew him well by then, our paths had crossed many times in the great forest, each time he bowed low and did not speak so that I began to wonder if he was dumb. But he was a man of few words, unlike our Master Shakespeare who gabbled like a goose. Master Kavanagh had that look about him, as if he felt himself to be no man's servant. I could tell.

I was often in the forest, it was the only place in my lord's domain where peace still reigned, for there was no peace to be had in the sty that was my lord's house. I was not mistress there, the lord of misrule had sway. In the forest, I could imagine myself to be mistress of all the trees, they bowed their branches in obeisance, rustled their leaves in a murmur of fealty.

'My lady will catch cold,' he said, startling me half to death, for I had not seen his soft approach and my dog Finn was sleeping on the watch. But Master Kavanagh was no enemy. He wore a puzzled frown as if he could not understand why the mistress of so much should be making do with so little – and it is true I was not a happy sight, sitting on the ground in the cold and the drizzle under the shelter of a great oak tree. Wrapped in a thick wool cloak and with only my wet hound for company I was truly no better off than one of the serving-girls. And the first time I touched him was when he held out one of his brown, old-callused and new-blistered hands and said, 'My lady, please, get up off the cold ground.'

I would my lord had looked at me with his eyes.

My Lady Margaret was with child. This was obvious to all. We need not ask the father. How came Lady Margaret into this den of vice? She could not remember, she was but a little child, she said. She had had no mother, no sister, no friend or comforter all those years. Her childhood had been stolen from her. 'My lord has had me since a child,' she said. She meant in every way.

Her cheek was pale. Her tutor feigned indifference for he was my husband's pet, but he was not bereft of Christian feeling. 'My lady is dreadful pale,' he said to me, stopping me in the dark corridor and I replied, 'Aye, as pale as any glass.' I knew he had a fondness for her himself, I had seen the tender looks he gave her when he thought himself not overlooked.

There were no torches lit in the hallway, all was darkness, a single tallow candle waved wildly in the draughts. The wind had residence in this wicked house. Poor Shakespeare's face was all craters and hollows in the feeble light, like the moon. I could see his skull. I could see the tear in his eye glitter and reminded him that he had behaved as badly as any man in my lord's retinue. But he had me by the sleeve and would not let me go and I had to comfort him and tell him I would look after her.

The first time I saw him naked was in the heat of that summer when my Lady Margaret swelled and my lord grew blacker

330

and the house that was so cold in winter became a sweltering stew.

I was sitting under a great tree, flapping away the forest flies with my hand, in a doze of heat, when the noise of chopping raised me from my slumbers and, treading quietly on the mossy path, I was able to view Master Kavanagh at work, chopping down a tree half-felled in the great winter storms. He was stripped of leather jerkin, and of his sark also, so that I was able to admire the fine brown skin of his back with its coat of sweat, like dew and the black curls of his hair lying damply on his neck. And much more. For a moment I could think of nothing but what he would feel like if I reached my hand out and ran it over his skin.

Lacking all shame, I followed Master Kavanagh deeper into the forest and when he left the path I left the path also and when he divested himself of his nether garments it would have taken a deal more than self-will to turn my head and not watch him dip himself in the cool black pool where the flag irises waved and the frogs were startled.

He knew I was there, he was a man who could hear the tread of the deer and the rabbit, who could hear the leaves unfurl and the cuckoo sleep, but he did not turn around – for he was a gentleman, remember – but continued with his exhibition of himself. And I was most pleased with what I saw. Sir Francis was no picture, he had nor flesh on his bones nor hairs on his head and his breath was rank and his farting more so. Naked, we are equal before God, they say, but I think Master Kavanagh would have seemed more noble than my husband.

I watched my son, who was a sickly thing, tainted with my lord Francis's thin, bad blood, playing hoopla on the lawn. Maybe my husband had fathered something more robust on the Lady Margaret. She sat weeping by the fish pond, the great mound of her belly shaking with her grief. My lord had ordered her to a nunnery.

★

I saw him in the kitchens when I went to speak to the cook, for I had some say in my kitchens still, if nowhere else. He was sitting at the big scrubbed table eating bread and cheese. He was hardly ever seen in the great house, he had his own rough cot in the forest where, I had heard said, the deer would come to his door and feed from his hand. But that was probably rumour too.

I blushed. He blushed. We blushed. We were caught in the cook's disapproval. 'Manners,' she said to him and hit him on the back of the head with a clout and he stumbled to his feet and laughed, then bowed and said, 'Lady?'

I had never been this deep in the wood, never trod on this path before. Though I knew where it led. It led to great danger. It led to the little house in the heart of the forest. The forest paths were deep in leaves, like gold.

The fire was dead and the ashes were cold. Half a stale loaf was on the table, a rotten apple, a burnt-down candle. It was like a still life of what must come to us all, when we will dance with death and have our foot finally stilled. I shivered in the cold air.

But then his little dog came bounding over the threshold and he himself filled the doorway, silhouetted against blue October sky.

He did not bow. I thought he would say that I should not be there but he said nothing, only entered his own house as if it were a stranger's, delicately, with trepidation, like a half-tamed deer. So that I had to encourage him and hold out my hand. And so he moved closer and stood before me, closer than he had ever been before, so close I could see the new-shaved bristle on his chin, the greenness of his eyes, the fleck of hazel that seemed gold. 'Well, Master Kavanagh,' I said, rather sternly, for my nerves were somewhat frayed, 'here we are.'

'Here we are indeed, my lady,' he said, which was a very long sentence for him. And he took a step closer, which brought him very close indeed, so I took a step back and so we jigged prettily for a while until I had nowhere to go, for I was pushed up against the table. I could feel the heat coming from his body, see the sharpness of his eye-tooth and the fine shape of his top lip.

First the burnt-out candle went flying with a great clatter and then the rotten apple went rolling to the far corner of the room. And heaven only knows what happened to the loaf of bread. Then there was no more speaking, only the exquisite moans and dreadful sighs that must accompany such violent delights.

Lady Margaret was with us no longer, hanged herself from a tree in my lord's apple orchard with rope from the stables. A gardener found her, dangling like a common felon, in the early light of morning, the babe already still in her womb. I locked myself in my room and wept fierce tears all morning and would answer to no-one, until Master Shakespeare wore me down, knocking at my door to tell me he was going and I replied that he may go to hell for all I care, but eventually I opened the door to him. He kissed my hand and said there was nothing to keep him at Fairfax Manor now and I told him he was right for there was no future for any of us in that accursed house.

He was leaving with the actors who had been with us and at whose words our poor Lady Margaret had both laughed and cried such a little time ago. These players were acquainted with our Master Shakespeare from his previous life and it was 'Our Will' this and 'Our Will' that and he was more than happy to join their baggage carts. I wished him well, though he was something of a weasel. He had already left wife and children and now he was leaving us. 'You must do likewise, madam,' he whispered, as he brushed my hand with his lips and I nodded my head and smiled for my husband had entered the room.

I had to walk through the forest at night to reach his little cottage the night that we left and there were many times I was feart to death, not by those things that I could see, but by those I could not.

We went on his black pony for the grooms would have been disturbed if I had saddled my fine dappled mare. It pained me more to leave my dappled grey than it did to leave my son, for he was a boy in his father's image, only weaker. I was already carrying

Robert Kavanagh's child in my belly and I cared to take nothing of my husband's with me. But I would take my dog. For he was a very good dog.

We left under the cover of the cloak of darkness but my husband was canny and had us followed and would have killed us with his arrows but he was not the great shot that he always liked to think himself. He would have to make do with a fine plump deer instead.

I ripped his not-so-pretty jewel from my neck and flung it through the trees and I felt Master Kavanagh flinch a little for that jewel would have paid our way into the unknown, but no matter. And the last time I saw my lord Francis, he was scrabbling in the leaves for his precious trinket. I would have taken all my fine silks off as well and gone from him as naked as Eve, but the leaves were already dropping from the trees and I would not freeze of the cold.

Robert Kavanagh put his arms around me and we trotted quickly on our way, our dogs bounding on ahead. He was my shelter and my safety, he was as strong as a great oak and as gentle as my hound. If you had known the full troubled history of my life, you would have sped me on my journey with many a blessing. A great happiness seized me at that moment, as if I had been given a vision of paradise.

'And where will we go, Master Kavanagh?' I asked him, when we reached the northern edge of the forest. And he turned in the saddle and smiled at me, showing his good teeth and replied, 'The future, my lady, we shall ride into the future.'

FUTURE

STREETS OF TREES

THE WHIRLIGIG OF TIME SPINS ON. THE WORLD GROWS OLDER. PEOPLE live their lives, each life filling all the time available and yet – on the grand, cosmic scale – taking up less time than the tick of the clock.

Audrey became one of the first women to be ordained in the Church of England. She married a teacher with a beard and had three children. Her parish was a run-down area of Liverpool where she occasionally did a small amount of good (which is probably the best we can hope for). All three of her children, when they were babies, looked like variations on Arden's imaginary doorstep baby. Perhaps that baby was a kind of ideal baby.

Audrey grew into being a mystic and a universalist, believing that every man, woman and child, every animal and plant, was a revered example of the unity of creation. And in this, we must presume, she was correct.

Six months pregnant, Carmen died, along with Bash, in a car crash in 1962.

Eunice married an engineer but never had her two children. She worked as a geologist for an oil company, digging down into the history of the earth, but then her life took a quite different turn and eventually she became an MP for the Liberal Democrats. She died of lung cancer when she was fifty-two and her funeral was surprisingly warm-hearted and generous. I missed her.

Hilary became a solicitor, married a doctor, had two children, divorced the doctor, married a journalist, had another child (born with a slight mental handicap), became a barrister, divorced the journalist, became human. Became my friend.

To the gods, looking down on earth, our lives might seem this simple.

Charles went to America and ended up on the West Coast working in the movies as a director of cheap science-fiction films, reviled by the critics and hopelessly unsuccessful at the box office but, as time went by, he came to have a cult following and by the time he was in his sixties he was in constant demand for retrospectives and chat shows and lecture tours and even had a television mini-series made about his life. Charles had a succession of beautiful blond wives and beautiful blond children and enjoyed his life enormously.

Debbie and Gordon were middling happy for the rest of their lives. Their baby, Renee, my sister, grew up to be a perfectly normal, cheerful person and ended up working as the senior secretary in Hilary's practice.

I can tell you something about Malcolm Lovat. When he drove off into his own future he went all the way across Europe and then back again. He worked in Paris as a hospital porter, stayed in Hamburg, lived with a woman in West Berlin and then moved to Corfu where he lived for a year in a commune of artists.

Eventually he came back to England, to London, and got involved in the music scene, becoming the manager of a group of teenagers from Hull with good teeth and hair and hardly any musical skill who went all the way to the top. By then Malcolm had got into wild excesses of drink and drugs.

I last saw him in a pub in Fulham, in 1967, when he was very drunk and morbid but none the less, when he suggested I stay the night at his place I did, because that was 1967 and in 1967 I slept with anyone.

He was completely different, of course – I suppose he'd become the person he used to have to hide inside himself.

In bed, in his staggeringly untidy garden flat in Chelsea, his limbs were marble, his flesh was ice. Sex with Malcolm Lovat was like the dance of death. 'I always wanted you,' he whispered, 'I just never knew how to tell you.' Of course, it was too late then. 'We're so alike,' he sighed. But I don't think we were, not really.

He died six months later in circumstances so squalid that the inquest became a *cause célèbre*. Afterwards, I carried him around with me in a small secret place inside me (the heart, which was the same place I kept my mother). Just because you can't see someone doesn't mean they're not there.

Vinny lasted the whole century, outliving both Gordon and Debbie, lingering on in Arden with the support of a succession of home helps. She celebrated the millennium and a hundred years of Vinnyhood by turning into a cat – small, tortoiseshell and disappearing into the night. Probably. I came back to nurse her at the end and somehow stayed on. It was my house after all.

I was successful by then – I wrote historical romances, (under my own name – an appropriate kind of name) – and Arden was a good place to work in. I turned the dining-room into a study and hired a man to clear the garden and trim the hedges so that I had a view of the Lady Oak. The tree didn't last long into the twenty-first century, succumbing to some kind of terminal rot. I watched them chop it down, although they didn't chop – but lopped all its arms off and then sliced through its trunk with huge whining chainsaws. I watched its death and wept.

My daughter, Imogen, came up to stay with me and then joined a self-styled tribe of tree people who were camped out in Boscrambe Woods preparing to fight the road contractors who were building the Glebelands Outer Ring Road. I drove out there sometimes, taking food parcels, video cameras, e-mail, anything else they wanted. When the time for the final battle drew nearer I lay in bed at night fretting over my aerial child hanging high up in the trees, climbing on webs and suspended by harnesses like some grubby Peter Pan. She was arrested several times and was finally bound over to keep the peace and when she refused was sent to prison for a while.

By that time, the contractors had moved in and trees that had stood for hundreds of years were felled in an afternoon. Not long after they'd started clearing the first trees someone spotted a long bone poking through the soil in the shovel of a JCB. The forensic pathologists eventually recovered nearly a whole skeleton from the spot that must have once been in the heart of the heart of the forest. A woman who died a long time ago, they said, too long for them to be able to say how she died, everything but the bones had decomposed and foxes had disturbed the body. Imagine – small animals eating the flesh, pulling at the bones, the eyelids closed by drifting leaves.

Hilary, who was having an affair with one of the forensic pathologists, told me that they had found a gold ring still circling one of the fingers. She said the ring was set with diamonds and emeralds and inscribed with the words '*To EF with all my love, G*' and that that made her feel very sad somehow.

I believe my mother had such a ring but I knew she couldn't be the forgotten body in the wood for I never thought of her as dead, and anyway she had made herself manifest to me not long before. I was standing in the queue in Tesco's and the woman in front of me – in her late twenties, immaculately dressed in a tweed suit, narrow belted at the waist, high-heeled shoes and seamed stockings, black hair in a French pleat and make-up like an actress. She was just paying as I lifted out a plastic bag of fruit to put on the conveyer belt when the bag burst suddenly and the fruit went tumbling everywhere. We both bent down and scrabbled around picking up the apples –

Red Delicious, waxed and polished so that they didn't look at all real. I was so near to the woman that I could smell her grown-up scent – *Arpege* and tobacco. My own perfume by then. She stood up, teetering slightly on her heels, and handed me the last apple and she said, *There you are, darling.*

And then she was gone and I knew there was no point in saying anything to the check-out girl about her because some things are known only to ourselves.

Other lost things were also found – the Fairfax jewel, so long sought after, was discovered not far from the unknown woman's body and took pride of place in the Glebelands Museum.

When I was clearing out after Vinny had gone I found a whole box of photographs – photographs not just of the Widow and her family and her ancestors, but of Charles and Gordon and me – and Eliza, a treasure trove of Eliza. An Eliza forever young, forever beautiful, squinting against the sun or laughing in the back garden. I wept for days over my newly found mother. Although in some ways the photographs made her even more unreachable and mysterious, it was, none the less, a relief to have tangible proof of her existence in this world.

Time carried on its thievish progress towards eternity. Imogen became a mother, and so I became a grandmother. Mrs Baxter met a mysterious end, the only person who truly disappeared – walking, they say, into the side of a green hill one day. Some say that at the moment she vanished she was transformed into the Queen of Elfland and wore a dress of finest green and a crown of glittering gold. But that was just rumour.

The world carried on spinning. So many stories to be told, so little time.

How does the world end? In fire? With a great star falling from heaven? Imagine – the comet Wormwood ploughing through the night sky at 40,000 miles an hour on its apocalyptic journey to Earth, burning like a billion suns as it falls. Nearer and nearer. The mayhem that must follow – the hail and fire mixed with blood, the massive earthquake at the impact site, the crater a hundred miles wide, the rocks vaporized, the thunderings and lightnings, the molten rocks flung into the atmosphere and raining down on earth, a third part of the trees burnt up, and all the green grass, the great mountain that falls, burning with fire, into the sea, the sea turning into blood while the debris from the impact spreads across the skies, so that the sun and the air are darkened, extinguishing the moon and putting out all the stars. Imagine.

Or in ice? With no cataclysm, only slow decay, the stars burning out, the black holes sucking in everything around them and the slow gravitational dance of death stretching the elastic universe further and further apart. A slush of sub-atomic particles. Pea-soup.

Or in green? Imagine the wood at the end of time. A great green ocean of peace. A riot of trees, birch, Scotch pine and aspen, English elm and wych elm, hazel, oak and holly, bird cherry, crab apple and hornbeam, the ash and the beech and the field maple. The blackthorn, the Guelder rose and twined all about – ivy, mistletoe and the pale honeysuckle where the dormouse nests.

The forest will be full of flowers, snowdrops and primroses, bluebells and cowslips with pearls hanging in their ears. Woodruff and herb Robert will grow, columbine, lords and ladies, Solomon's seal and the heart-leaved valerian, enchanter's nightshade and oxslip, love-in-idleness and the common dog violet.

On the forest floor the insects work hard – click beetles and the robber flies, weevils and hornets, slugs and snails, the spiders and the patient earthworms. And the invisible life, the amoeba and bacteria cleaning up and recycling.

The sound in the world now is birdsong – the joyful treble of the mistle thrush announcing spring, the chaffinch singing for joy, the beautiful trilling of the wood warblers. Blackbirds and robins, soft wood pigeons and pied flycatchers, the long-eared owl and the greater spotted woodpecker, the world belongs to them now.

And also to the voles and the badgers, the squirrels and the bats, the hedgehogs and the deer and the little foxes that play untroubled by hound or man.

And, finally, the wolves come back.

Here and there in the green and gold of the sunlit wood flicker the fragile purple emperor, the white admiral, and the Duke of Burgundy fritillary. Soft moss and ferny green and the splash of toad and frog in the dark ponds in the cool glades. The song thrush in the trees spins his threads of song three times. Lilies of the valley and heart's tongue fern crowd the shade. The tiny wren bird hops from branch to branch and the pearl-bordered fritillary kisses the strawberry and the wild thyme. The smell of sweet musk roses and eglantine.

Autumn must come. *Et in arcadia ego*. The surreal, sprouting landscape of the fungi takes over – the pennybun caps, King Alfred's cakes and Jew's ears, stinkhorns and witches butter. Everything is mould. Angels' wings sprout from the rotten conifers and elf caps run riot on the oak stumps. The last powdered Quakers and Kentish glories visit the night. The soft *hoo-hooo* of the owl fades. The leaves fall, drifting down like feathers. The nights draw in.

Colder and colder. One day, the last bird sings its feeble farewell and drops like a stone. On another day the final leaf falls and no more buds come. In the beginning was the word, but at the end there is only silence.

I am the storyteller at the end of time. I know how it ends. It ends like this.

'Ah see ye not that broad broad road
    That lies by the lily leven?
  O that is the way of wickedness,
Tho some call it the road to Heaven.

  'And see ye not that narrow road,
    All beset with thorns and briers?
  O that is the way of righteousness,
    Tho after it but few enquires.

'And see ye not that bonny bonny road,
    Which winds about the ferny brae?
  O that is the road to fair Elfland,
Where you and I this night maun gae.

From 'Thomas the Rhymer', Anon

A GOOD GAME FOR A PARTY

A GAME WHICH PROVIDES LITTLE EXERCISE, BUT PLENTY OF LAUGHTER, is **Human Croquet**. A large number can take part, and no previous experience at all is required.

First the 'hoops' must be placed in position – scattered about the field, in approximately the same fashion as for real croquet. Each hoop consists of two people who stand facing each other, with hands clasped and arms raised so as to make an arch under which another person can walk. It will not be necessary for the hoop to remain in this position all through the game; it is quite enough if the two people assume it whenever a player is wanting to pass.

Each 'ball' is a person who is blindfolded, and who does not move except when ordered to.

Finally, there are the 'players', each in charge of a 'ball'.

As far as possible the game follows the style of ordinary croquet. Each player has one stroke in turn, and is allowed an additional one when his ball passes through a hoop or hits another ball.

To begin the play the first player gets his ball on to the starting line, standing behind him gripping his arms, and aims him at the first hoop – which of course the ball cannot see. Then the player says 'Go,' and the ball trots forward, until his owner calls 'Stop.' If the ball has passed through the hoop another 'stroke' is allowed; if not, the second player makes his attempt.

Every ball must run in a straight line, and must promptly stop when ordered. When two balls collide the one that is struck stays where it is, but the other is given another 'stroke', and ordered off afresh. No player may speak to his ball while it is in motion, except to stop it, nor touch or re-direct it in any way.

That player wins who first gets his ball through all the hoops, in their proper order, and back to the starting line, or to a post at the middle of the 'court'.

Interest and fun is added to the game if each player and his or her ball are made to wear some distinguishing colour – either ribbon or hat or rosette, so that couples are more obviously linked.

Hoops must never move from their stations, and must give no indication of their whereabouts to oncoming balls. When one game has been played the players and balls exchange roles.

Playing Human Croquet, showing how two players link hands to form hoops. Other players, blindfolded, are balls.